# A Dead Man Walking

JD Kirk is the author of the multi-million bestselling DCI Logan series, set in the Highlands of Scotland. He also does not exist. Instead, JD is the pen name of former children's author and screenwriter, Barry Hutchison, who was born and raised in Fort William. He still lives in the Highlands with his wife and children. He has no idea what the JD stands for.

## Also by JD Kirk

### DCI Logan Crime Thrillers

*A Litter of Bones*
*Thicker than Water*
*The Killing Code*
*Blood and Treachery*
*The Last Bloody Straw*
*A Whisper of Sorrows*
*The Big Man Upstairs*
*A Death Most Monumental*
*A Snowball's Chance in Hell*
*Ahead of the Game*
*An Isolated Incident*
*Colder than the Grave*
*Come Hell or High Water*
*City of Scars*
*Here Lie the Dead*
*One For the Ages*
*In Service of Death*
*A Dead Man Walking*
*Where the Pieces Lie*
*A Killer of Influence*

# JD KIRK

# A DEAD MAN WALKING

CANELOCRIME

First published in the United Kingdom in 2023 by Zertex Crime

This edition published in the United Kingdom in 2025 by

Canelo, an imprint of
Canelo Digital Publishing Limited,
20 Vauxhall Bridge Road,
London SW1V 2SA
United Kingdom

A Penguin Random House Company

The authorised representative in the EEA is Dorling Kindersley Verlag GmbH.
Arnulfstr. 124, 80636 Munich, Germany



A CIP catalogue record for this book is available from the British Library.

Paperback ISBN 978 1 80436 833 6



Printed and bound in Great Britain by Clays Ltd, Elcograf S.p.A.

Look for more great books at
www.canelo.co
www.dk.com

1

# *Chapter 1*

For sixty-seven of his seventy-nine years on earth, Montgomery Wilhelm McQuarrie had been a cantankerous, sadistic, ill-tempered bastard, and he was damned if he was going to change now.

And why should he? Being a cantankerous, sadistic, ill-tempered bastard had stood him in pretty good stead so far.

He'd come from nothing—the son of a farm girl and a simpleton—born in Soviet-occupied East Germany in the late 1940s, with the spectre of Adolf Hitler still hanging around like an embarrassing and unfortunate smell that nobody wanted to accept responsibility for.

His earliest memories were of hunger, first literal, then metaphorical. He soon outgrew those around him—not literally in this case, as he peaked at five foot seven, but his raw ambition and ruthlessness brought him success after success, appeasing one of his hungers, while further fuelling the other.

Eventually, decades later, it had brought him here.

He ran a hand across the rough stone wall of the corridor beside him, his gnarled fingers tenderly stroking the castle he called home. The castle he'd had shipped, brick-by-brick, from Austria back in the late 70s, and had rebuilt here on the West Coast of Scotland.

It had cost millions.

No. It was meant to cost millions, but in truth had cost ten times as much. This was largely due to the ineptitude of the various teams of contractors who had been employed to carry out the work, and who had consistently and repeatedly proven their complete lack of skill and worth.

Upon completion of the job, he had bought all the companies involved, manipulated them almost immediately into bankruptcy, and taken immense pleasure in personally breaking the bad news to the hapless employees.

He'd lost a lot of money in doing so, of course. But then, what was the point of being rich if you couldn't enjoy it?

You couldn't take it with you, after all.

There was something of a skip in his step as he rounded the corner of the corridor, and approached the curved staircase that led to the floor above. He contemplated jogging up it. He hadn't done so in years, decades of fine dining and heavy drinking having turned even light exercise into something of an extreme sport.

Tonight, though, he took the first half of the staircase two at a time, then let out a breathless little laugh just shy of the midway point and slowed to his usual pace.

It was wrong, of course, to feel this way. It was wrong to have such a sense of elation after what he'd just said to the boy.

The lad had tried not to show his emotion, of course. Montgomery had instilled that much in him, if nothing else. Emotion was weakness. Emotion was for other people. It had been his first and most important lesson to his children.

But they'd failed at that, like they failed at everything, and so he'd witnessed every ounce of hurt in his son's eyes as he'd twisted the knife again and again.

And he'd enjoyed it. God help him, he'd delighted in it.

That probably wasn't normal, he had to admit. Rejoicing in the suffering of one's own offspring—suffering that oneself was the root cause of—probably bordered on the demented.

And yet, he couldn't quite bring himself to care. It was just how he was. It was just *who* he was.

Montgomery Wilhelm McQuarrie had come from nothing to become one of the richest men in Europe. And he certainly hadn't got there by being *normal*.

He stopped at the top of the staircase and took a moment to get his breath back. There was a tightness in his chest that sent a tingling tickling down his left arm. Rather than worry him, though, it only served to remind him that he was alive.

In fact, he felt more alive than he'd felt in a long time. Ruining the lives of one's ungrateful, parasitic offspring clearly had a rejuvenating effect.

Besides, there were a lot of younger, fitter, desperate men out there in the world. He could always buy a new heart.

Again.

The door to his study was further along the narrow stone passageway that lay straight ahead. The mouth of the corridor was flanked by towering portraits of his parents that he'd commissioned thirty or so years previously.

He looked up at them both in turn, taking in their vacant eyes and goofy expressions. He had gone through several artists until he'd found one who could really do his vision of his parents justice. There had been no photographs to work from, just Monty's own recollection of them.

He liked to think he'd nailed it.

'*Mutter. Vater,*' he said, acknowledging them both with a nod. He very rarely spoke any of his native tongue these days, and decades of international travel meant that his accent had long ago been replaced by the brogue of nowhere in particular.

Like most things he did, including changing his surname, the choice of accent had been deliberate. He enjoyed cultivating an air of mystery around himself—Montgomery McQuarrie, the eccentric and reclusive billionaire business mogul and titan of industry that, despite thousands of op-ed pieces in broadsheets and tabloids all over the globe, no one could really get a handle on.

He was a man who harboured a host of secrets.

Just like his castle.

The door to his study was set into a recessed alcove near the end of the passageway.

Although, 'passageway' probably wasn't correct. That implied there was a way in which to pass to, whereas this particular corridor ended abruptly at a wall of solid stone. The last thing he had wanted when the children had been younger was to hear them running past the door, squealing out their ear-splitting peals of laughter.

Blocking off the end of the corridor had been one of the changes he'd made to the castle's original layout. One of the many.

And it had worked. Up here, tucked away in his study, he'd been able to work undisturbed. Many a deal had been brokered in that little room. Many a secretary buggered over the desk.

He fished the big iron key from his pocket, clunked it anti-clockwise in the lock, and savoured the rush of the smell and the memories as he eased the door open.

'For God's sake!' he barked, his mood doing a complete about-turn before he'd even stepped inside the room.

She'd done it again. That useless bitch of a maid had been shifting his bloody furniture.

Nobody else would've noticed, but he could see the little round dunkles on the rug where the feet of the coffee table should've been. Instead, it was at least a foot from where it was meant to be, and not even lined up straight.

He turned back in the direction of the stairs, the wispy grey caterpillars of his eyebrows butting heads above his nose.

'Fire that fucking imbecile girl! She's been pissing around with the furniture again!' he bellowed. He wasn't bellowing to anyone in particular, but over the years he'd discovered that, for a man of his means, bellowing generally brought results, regardless of the direction in which it was aimed.

Muttering his annoyance, he pressed on into the windowless room, slammed the heavy wooden door, then locked it behind him.

He took a moment to give the key an extra half turn so that it couldn't be pushed out from the other side. There was no particular reason for this—nobody in their right mind was going to attempt to enter while he was there—but it had become something of a habit.

A spare key inserted from the other side would dislodge his own, knocking it onto the study floor and allowing the door to be unlocked. He had learned this the hard way, when his third—fourth?—wife had come in unexpectedly one day to find him being ridden like a bucking bronco by a journalist twenty-eight years his junior.

She had filed for divorce two days later.

She'd then thrown herself from her bedroom window three days after that, after she'd knocked herself about a bit, and failed to strangle herself with her own bare hands.

At least, that was how his lawyers had successfully argued it.

With the door secured, Monty crossed to his drinks cabinet, poured himself a glass of port, then took up residence in the battered leather chair by the desk and sighed as he relaxed into its well-worn grooves.

Most of the room was in darkness, the only light coming from the flickering lamp that sat on the side table by the door. It was a solid tangle of metal and glass, and the flame within it danced all day and night thanks to the gas feed from the kitchen two floors below.

It gave the place a cosy, snug sort of atmosphere, though it was an absolute bastard to try reading in, even before his eyesight had gone to hell.

Montgomery sipped his drink, then flipped open a cigar case and reached for a particularly chunky Cuban. As he ran it back and forth below his nose, inhaling the scent, his fingers traced across a few of the many notches he'd carved into the mahogany desk. One for every conquest, both commercial and carnal.

On a good day, he could remember maybe ten per cent of them, though even those tended to blur together into a heaving orgy of bodily fluids and hostile takeovers.

He cut the end off the cigar and reached for the lighter he kept on his desk. It had once belonged to his grandfather, who had scavenged it from the home of a Jewish neighbour after the trucks had come, then used it to help burn their house to the ground.

Even as a child, a full decade after the war had ended, Montgomery had always loved that story.

Metal sparked against flint as he rasped the mechanism around and around. Finally, after the fifth or sixth attempt, the wick caught, and a single flame sputtered into life, forcing the shadows behind Montgomery back just an inch or two, revealing the spines of some of the books on his shelves.

And the glint of a blade.

The cigar was lit.

The flame snapped off.

And as the light from it faded, fabric rustled in the darkness.

# *Chapter 2*

DCI Jack Logan shuffled through the kitchen, scratching his head, yawning, and simultaneously acknowledging the waggly tailed bundle of excitement at his feet with a quick bend-and-pat movement.

'Aye, aye, all right,' he mumbled, his dry mouth making a series of unpleasant *clacking* sounds as he spoke.

The night before had been a late one. It had been a whole week of late ones, in fact, thanks to Shona's insistence on them bingeing their way through all her favourite horror movies.

It turned out she had a lot of favourite horror movies.

He'd endured three last night—two *Friday the 13th*s and one of the many *Evil Dead*s—and though he'd nodded off at least half a dozen times, her near-constant breathless narration of the events happening on-screen had meant that the respite was always cruelly short-lived.

*'Don't go in there, for Christ's sake!'*

*'Watch out, he's got a dirty great knife!'*

*'Run, you silly bitch, run!'*

She'd watched them all half-hidden behind a cushion, eyes like saucers, screaming in terror at the scary parts as if she hadn't already lived through them a dozen times before.

It had been charming for the first couple of nights. By the time he had survived five different—yet broadly similar—*Nightmares on Elm Street*, the shine had well and truly worn off.

Still, it all ended tonight. Tonight was the main event.

Tonight, in every sense, was *Halloween*.

Down on the floor, Taggart continued to run in circles. He seemed particularly excited this morning. Maybe he could sense that the horror movie countdown was almost complete. Certainly, he hadn't seemed to approve of Shona's high-pitched squeals of fright when he was trying to get forty winks on the couch between them.

Although, he was always quick to hoover up the spilled popcorn.

Or maybe it was the weather that was making the dog more highly strung than usual. The wind had whistled and creaked its way around the house all night, while rain had assaulted the windows with a level of determination that was unusual even for the Highlands.

Still, if the experts were to be believed, this was only the warm-up act.

A storm was coming. A storm so epic that reports of it had leaked over from the weather forecasts into all the main news programmes and the front pages of all the tabloids.

The first named storm of the year was going to be the worst one to hit the country in living memory.

Storm Agatha was coming, and she was going to be a belter.

Whatever the cause of the dog's edginess, Logan wasn't awake enough to deal with it.

'Aye, right, piss off. I'll let you out in a minute,' he said, gently brushing Taggart away with the side of a foot. 'Not that you'll bloody go out in that, anyway.'

He would go out in it eventually, of course, but only if Logan went and stood out there with him, getting soaked to the bloody skin while the dog took its time finding the *exact* right spot to have a shite—a process which could take anything from one minute to fifteen.

No, Logan couldn't quite face that yet. Not without a cup of coffee in him first.

He yawned again, clicked on the kettle, then headed for the big American-style fridge freezer that had appeared in the kitchen a couple of months previously. Shona had found it for sale on one of the local Facebook groups and had snapped it up.

It had been too big for the previous owner's kitchen. And, if Jack was being honest, it was too big for this one, too.

But the crushed ice dispenser on the front was quite handy, and though the brushed metal front now bore the word 'BOLLOCKS' spelled out by Shona in colourful plastic fridge magnets, he couldn't help but appreciate the sleekness of it.

Yawning for a third time, he opened the door, reached for the milk, and was instead confronted by a small, quite uncomfortable-looking werewolf.

'*Raar*!' it cried, and its Irish accent was somehow detectable even in that short outburst.

Still holding the door, Logan gazed impassively into the empty eye sockets of the rubber mask. Behind him, Taggart let out a volley of confused barks.

'Relax. You're fine. It's not actually a werewolf. It's just me,' Shona assured the stock-still Logan, her voice echoing slightly inside the headpiece.

'Aye,' Logan said. 'Aye, I guessed that, right enough.'

'I thought I'd hide in the fridge.'

Even with all the shelves removed, she'd had to contort herself to fit inside it, and one forearm was buckling the mask against the side of her head, somewhat spoiling the effect.

'So I see,' Logan said. He looked her up and down. 'Why?'

'Just, you know, to scare you,' Shona replied. 'Did it work?'

Logan considered this for a moment, then smacked his lips together and nodded. 'Aye,' he confirmed.

'Right. Good. Because you didn't seem like you were scared.'

'I mean, maybe not in a jumpy, *ooyah fucker*, sort of way,' Logan admitted. 'But in a long-term concern for your mental health sort of way? Very much so. You know you could've died in there, aye?'

'Oh, God, yeah!' Shona said, and she almost sounded excited by the prospect. 'Can you imagine? What a way to go!'

She untangled herself enough to thrust a hand out. He took it and half-led, half-dragged her out of the fridge. She fell against him, and the hair of the mask tickled his nose, almost making him sneeze.

Once out, Shona looked back at the cramped, refrigerated space she'd left. 'Always wondered what that must be like,' she remarked, before pulling off the mask to reveal a face that, despite the cold of the fridge, had turned bright red. Sweat had plastered her hair to her forehead, too.

Logan really hoped it was worth it.

'I was going to make breakfast. Where did you put all the food?' he asked.

Shona jerked her head in the direction of the back door. 'I stuck it outside.'

'Outside? You put all the food outside? In this weather?'

'Just for a few minutes. And it's under the back canopy, it'll be fine,' she said.

She opened the door, gazed out through the rain at the back step for a moment, then closed it again.

'Nope, it's all blown away,' she announced, turning away from the door. 'I mean, there's still a tub of cottage cheese, but I'm not going to insult you with that.' Shona smiled weakly. 'You can probably grab something on the way to work, can't you?'

A fourth yawn almost split Logan's head in two. He ran a hand through his hair, then down over his face, wiping some of the sleep from his eyes.

'I suppose I'll have to.'

'That's the spirit! I'll get shopping today. Assuming ASDA hasn't been swept out to sea, or whatever.'

She was still holding the werewolf mask, and now plucked at some of the stray hairs. Clearly, she was building up to something, and Logan knew full well what it was.

'So, um, you given any more thought to the whole... you know? The situation?'

'What situation?' Logan asked, stalling for time.

'The whole Olivia situation,' Shona said. 'About her living here. About the whole, like, fostering thing.'

Logan shifted his weight from one bare foot to the other. 'I've been a bit preoccupied with teenagers being butchered.'

Shona frowned. 'What? When did— Oh! The films. Gotcha. For a second there, I thought you'd been holding out on me on the old work front.' She smiled, but it looked as forced as it no doubt felt. 'It's just, they sort of need to know. Social Services, I mean. They sort of need to know what's happening.'

'She's nearly sixteen,' Logan said.

'She's barely fifteen,' Shona corrected. 'And she's got no one, Jack.'

'She's the daughter of a drug dealing murderer that I put in the jail.' He tapped himself on the side of the head, like a thought had just popped in there. 'Oh, and she's also a psychopath.'

Shona tutted and rolled her eyes. 'But, like, only in the colloquial sense. It's not like she's got a diagnosis or anything.'

'Oh, well, that's all right, then.'

'She's just a kid. Just a troubled kid, who's had a rough time of it. She just needs someone.'

'I'm not disputing any of that. But why us?' Logan asked, not for the first time.

And, not for the first time, he got the same answer.

'Because there isn't anyone else. Because nobody else will have her.'

Logan grunted. Outside, the wind and rain sent what should've been his breakfast swirling around the back garden.

'We can talk about it later,' he said.

'There isn't much later left, Jack,' Shona said, taking one of his hands in both of hers. 'We can help her. You could, you know, help guide her. Be a better father figure than her dad ever was.'

Logan looked down into Shona's wide eyes. It would be the easiest thing in the world to surrender.

But the easiest thing wasn't always the right one.

'I've not exactly won any World's Greatest Dad awards myself,' he reminded her.

Before he could say any more—and to his relief—a chime from Shona's work mobile rang out.

'Shit, hang on,' she muttered, releasing her grip on his hand and fumbling around in her pockets until she found the phone. She checked the screen, muttered below her breath, then tapped out a response.

'Got a shout?'

Shona nodded. 'RTA. A82, just south of Drum. Near the castle.'

'Fatalities?'

'Not confirmed yet, but it's a mess, apparently. Geoff and his team are going to meet me there.'

Logan winced. Dealing with the aftermath of a car crash was never a good time. In this weather, and with Geoff Palmer to contend with, it would be gold standard awful.

'Right, well, good luck with that,' Logan told her. 'And be careful on the road, eh?'

'Course, yeah,' Shona said. She prodded him in the centre of the chest with a finger. 'To be continued, Mr Logan.'

'Aye,' Logan said. He may have dodged the Olivia Maximuke conversation for now, but there was no way she was letting him off the hook indefinitely. 'To be continued.'

–

The drive to the house had been an uncomfortable and unpleasant one. The weather had played its part, of course, the car's windscreen wipers fighting a losing battle against the rain's full frontal assault.

But the atmosphere inside the vehicle had been even worse.

'You sure you're all right?' asked Detective Constable Tyler Neish, after he'd brought the car to a stop as close to the house's front door as possible.

Beside him, in the passenger seat, his wife and fellow DC, Sinead, unfastened her seatbelt with a single violent prod of the button.

'I told you, I'm fine.'

'Right. Good. That's good.' Tyler drummed his fingers on the steering wheel, in time with the *thunking* of the wipers. 'It's just, you don't really *seem* fine. You seem—'

She shot him a look that made '*DANGER!*' signs flash up before his eyes.

'Stressed,' he concluded, sticking to the safer end of the spectrum of descriptors he'd been considering. 'Crabbit as fuck', had been up the other end, but he'd wisely chosen to steer clear of that one.

'Stressed?' Sinead said, the inflection of her voice rising all the way through the word. In the back seat, the twins, Cal and Lauren, rumbled in their sleep. 'Me? Stressed? What would I have to be stressed about, Tyler?'

Tyler shrugged. He flicked his tongue across his dry lips. 'Is it the money thing again?' he asked.

The way she turned to look out of the side window was answer enough.

'It's the money thing,' he concluded. 'I told you, don't worry about it. I'm working on it.'

'How are you working on it, Tyler?' she asked, her head snapping back around again. 'Hmm? What's your plan?'

Tyler let his mouth fall open, hoping that a fully worked-out and carefully costed scheme would come tumbling out of it.

The truth was, he had no idea how he was going to deal with their current financial predicament. A decade of overtime, maybe? A cheeky lottery win? A magic lamp? None of them felt particularly reliable, and given the current Police Scotland funding issues, the first one was probably the most fantastical of the lot.

'I'm working on it,' he assured her.

'Great. So, next time a pair of pissed-off Sheriff's officers rock up at half-seven in the morning, I'll just tell them that, will I? I'll tell them you're working on it.'

'You should've shouted,' Tyler said. 'I didn't hear them at the door because of the shower. You should've shouted me. I'd have handled it.'

'I'd already told them you weren't in,' she replied. 'But you can't dodge them forever. They said they'd be back later.'

Tyler smiled. It was a little too cheerful and frazzled-looking to be in any way convincing.

'Well, tough luck for them. I'm not going to be in. Neither of us will be.'

Sinead sighed. It wasn't a heavy one done for his benefit. In fact, Tyler wouldn't even have been aware of it had it not been for the way her breath fogged her window.

'We need to tell them,' she said, after a long pause. 'The boss, I mean. Or Mitchell, or whoever. We need to tell them.'

'What? No. We can't do that. We can't tell them,' Tyler insisted.

'Well, we can't keep hiding it. That's a sackable offence, Tyler. They need to know.'

Tyler winced and shook his head. 'No. I don't want them knowing. I can't.'

She turned back to him, and though her expression was still stern, there was a suggestion of softness in the look she gave him.

'If we hide it, they could think we're compromised. Or at risk of it, anyway. That's what the policy's for. We need to be open about it.'

'It's not you, though. It's just me,' Tyler said. 'It's all in my name. I'm the one who ran it all up. They can't do anything to you. You're not in debt.'

She hesitated for a moment, before sliding her hand across the gulf between their seats and placing it on his leg. 'We're married. We're in it together. If you're in the shit, I'm in the shit. All right? And I wouldn't want it any other way.'

Tyler felt a prickling way at the back of his eyeballs. He cleared his throat a couple of times, then nodded.

'You're right. No. You're right. I'll tell them.'

'Today?'

'Today.'

They leaned over, met in the middle, and kissed.

When they broke it off a moment later, a woman was scowling in at them through the passenger side window, her face practically pressed against the glass.

'Jesus Christ!' Tyler yelped, jumping so violently his seatbelt almost throttled him.

Outside, her tight bun of silver hair soaking up the rain, Berta Hoon, the older sister of their disgraced former detective superintendent, Robert, rapped a bony knuckle against the glass.

'Can you two dirty bastards maybe stop molesting each other for two minutes?' she asked, in a voice that rang out through the worsening storm. She pointed to the sleeping babies buckled into the back seat, her eyes blazing with excitement. 'And hand over those two delicious wee bastards right now.'

# *Chapter 3*

Detective Constable Tammi-Jo Swanney was talking when a dripping-wet Sinead and Tyler entered the office. This was not unusual. Talking was Tammi-Jo's whole thing, and she spent most of her day spitting out an endless stream of words like they were bullets from a belt-fed machine gun.

Today, it seemed, was no exception. Her voice had met Tyler and Sinead halfway along the corridor, though they hadn't been able to decipher the excited babble of it.

The husband and wife team were the last to arrive, and while they weren't surprised to hear Tammi-Jo talking, it was unusual to find her holding court the way she was. Most days, people tried to quickly make their excuses and leave.

DCI Logan sat perched on a desk, while DI Ben Forde and DS Hamza Khaled flanked him in their office chairs, the three of them facing the detective constable. Taggart lay on his back under one of the desks, his legs all splayed. He was either asleep, or had been the victim of some particularly dramatic doggy murder.

There was no sign of PC Dave Davidson, but then they hadn't expected to see him there. He'd taken some time off after the last case he'd been involved with, and while there were rumours of his imminent return, nothing official had been announced.

All four of the detectives had damp hair, suggesting they'd not long arrived. Long enough to have made tea and coffee, though, which Logan, Ben and Hamza were all slurping away at, while Tammi-Jo swirled a small glass of milk around like it was a glass of Scotch or fine wine she was encouraging to breathe.

Her eyes lit up when her two fellow detective constables entered and shrugged off their wet jackets.

'Aha! There they are! Here they come! The gang's all here!' Tammi-Jo announced. 'We've been waiting for you. I've just been sort of filling time until you got here before I make my big announcement.'

'Wait, there's a big announcement?' asked Hamza, looking up from his mug.

'Yes! I told you that already.'

'Did you?'

'Yes! I told you, like, five times.'

'When?'

'Over the last few minutes!' Tammi-Jo told him. 'I kept saying, "Big announcement! Big announcement!"'

Hamza stared blankly at her, slowly shaking his head.

'I kept ringing this little bell!' Tammi-Jo said, raising a tiny handbell and *ding-dinging* it back and forth. 'I brought it specially.'

'I must've missed that,' Hamza said, shrugging.

Tammi-Jo's eyes narrowed. 'Wait. Are you winding me up?'

A smirk broke through the detective sergeant's defences. 'You know, now that I think about it, I might be, aye.'

Logan looked back over his shoulder at the two new arrivals. 'DC Swanney's just been filling us in on how storms happen,' he said. 'She's been doing some reading on it.'

'A lot of reading,' Ben added. He wore a slightly pained expression. 'A phenomenal amount of reading.'

Tammi-Jo nodded enthusiastically. 'It's all to do with pressure. And… Other stuff. Mostly pressure. Anyway, doesn't matter, forget all that.'

'Already done,' Logan remarked.

'Now we're all here, I can make my big announcement.'

'Are you pregnant?' Ben guessed.

'What? No!'

'Are you dying?' Tyler asked.

'Jesus! No!' Tammi-Jo cried. She bit her lip, her certainty evaporating. 'Although, there's this weird blotchy thing on my knee. Red mark. Looks a bit like a face. You think that's anything?'

'Probably not,' Sinead assured her.

'No. No, it's probably nothing.. You're right. Although, I'm pretty sure it winked at me yesterday,' Tammi-Jo said, before dismissing her growing concerns with a shake of her head. 'Anyway, that's not the big announcement. I'm not pregnant, and I'm not dying.'

She took a deep breath. There was a shake to it. A rawness that was at odds with her big beaming smile.

'I'm leaving.'

Logan rose to his feet. 'You're what?'

'I'm leaving,' Tammi-Jo said again, a little louder this time, as if the DCI had simply failed to hear her. 'We knew I was going to be transferring now that Sinead's back. And, well, Detective Superintendent Mitchell called me in last night and said it's happening. The transfer. My transfer. It's happening.'

'She didn't tell me. She should've bloody told me,' Logan said.

'I, uh, I asked her not to. I said I'd quite like to do it, sir,' Tammi-Jo told him. 'She wasn't happy, but she said that as long as I did it first thing today, that it was fine. So, here we are. First thing today, and I'm doing it.'

'She should've told me first. Before she said anything to you,' Logan complained, but Ben waved him into silence.

'We're going to miss you,' the DI said. 'It's no' going to be the same without you.'

'It'll be quieter,' Tammi-Jo said, getting to the obvious punchline before anyone else could.

She looked down at her hands. Her fingers on each one were flailing about, hammering against their opposite number like two spiders having a drunken slapping match outside a nightclub.

'I'll miss you, too,' she said. 'All of you. You've all been so nice to me. Even when I've been annoying. Because I know that I can be. Annoying, I mean. A lot of people have made it very clear that I can be a bit full-on. And I know I can really grate on some people and get on their nerves, but…' She raised her eyes and glanced around at them all. 'You never made me feel that way. You never made me feel like I wasn't welcome. And, well, that was nice. Different, but nice. You just… You accepted me, and that meant a lot.'

'Look around this room,' Logan urged. He gestured at the others. 'There's nobody here who hasn't been a royal pain in the arse at some point, even me.'

'Especially you, boss!' Tyler said, earning himself a glare from the DCI. He cleared his throat. 'Sorry, boss. That just slipped out.'

Logan turned his attention back to Tammi-Jo.

'Anyway, the point I was trying to make before he opened his mouth is that we didn't accept you, Detective Constable,' Logan told her. 'We didn't need to. You fit right in.'

Tammi-Jo's immaculate eyebrows crept up her forehead. 'Oh,' she said, after a pause. 'Permission to cry a bit, sir?'

'Oh, God, no. Permission denied,' Logan told her, and the DC laughed as she wiped an eye with the end of her sleeve.

'Too late!'

'When do you go?' Hamza asked.

Tammi-Jo sniffed, dabbed at her nose, then mumbled a morose-sounding, 'Tomorrow.'

'Tomorrow?!' Logan cried. He'd sat down briefly, but was back on his feet again now. 'This is the first I'm hearing about it, and you're leaving *tomorrow*?'

'Technically, I'm leaving today, sir,' Tammi-Jo said. 'This is my last day here. I'm meant to be on the train tonight, reporting for duty first thing in the morning.' She took in all their faces again, then added, 'They're short-staffed,' by way of explanation.

'Where are you going?' Ben asked. 'Not back across to Aberdeen?'

'Glasgow,' Tammi-Jo replied. She patted her pockets. 'I'm going to be working under a…'

Several seconds of searching eventually resulted in her producing a neatly folded sheet of paper from her blazer.

'A DI Heather Filson.'

'Fuck!' Logan ejected. He clamped his hand over his mouth in an attempt to stop the word getting out, but that horse had well and truly already bolted.

Tammi-Jo smiled, but it was laced with concern. 'You know her?'

Logan realised that his hand was still covering his mouth. He moved it away, and tried to disguise his shock with a nonchalant sort of chin scratch.

'Eh, aye. Aye, I know her,' Logan confirmed. 'We've all had the pleasure, in fact.'

'Some of us more so than others,' Ben remarked, with a slightly salacious raising of an eyebrow. 'Eh, Jack?'

'Is she good?' Tammi-Jo asked, with a directness that robbed Logan of a response. 'Oh! Not like that. I didn't mean… A copper, I mean. Is she a good copper?'

'Define "good",' Logan said. 'Is she good as in well-behaved, toeing the official line, head down, following orders? No. Is she good in the sense of being a generally nice person with other people's best interests at heart?'

He shook his head.

'Also no. But is she effective? Aye. She is,' he continued. 'You'll learn a lot from Heather. My advice is that you try and forget most of it as quickly as humanly possible.'

Tammi-Jo waited for a big laugh from the others that would reveal all this as just another wind-up, but it didn't come.

'OK, now I'm scared,' she said.

'Don't be,' Sinead told her. She smiled supportively. 'Heather's all right. There's nothing to worry about.'

'She knows potential when she sees it,' Logan added. 'Give it a month, and the two of you will be getting on like a house on fire.'

Assuming, of course, that Tammi-Jo survived that first thirty days.

'Fingers crossed!' DC Swanney said, then she made a show of crossing as many of her fingers as possible, so it looked like the drunken spiders from earlier had been involved in some terrible industrial accident. 'I guess I'll find out tomorrow.'

'I wouldn't count on that,' Ben told her.

He nodded over to the row of windows that looked out onto the Longman Estate. It was nine thirty, but the thick covering of black clouds meant the city was still largely in darkness. The rain rattled against the glass like ball bearings on a tin roof, the wind egging it on.

A long traffic jam had formed on the dual carriageway after the ampersand had blown off the sign on the front of B&Q and landed in the middle of the road.

'Can't see the trains going anywhere tonight,' the DI continued.

'They're not,' Hamza confirmed, tapping at the screen of his phone. 'Buses are off, too.'

'How the hell did you check that so fast?' Ben demanded, a note of outrage in his voice. 'It takes me half an hour just to find the website for Google.'

'It's just Google,' Logan told him.

Ben frowned. 'What?'

'It's Google. You just type Google-dot-com, or whatever.'

'Oh, no. No, too bloody complicated for me, that,' Ben said. 'I just search for it.'

A few looks of confusion were shared by the other occupants of the room.

'But how?' Hamza eventually asked.

Before he could get an answer, though, there was a knock at the door. A uniformed sergeant waited to be invited, then entered. He held a printout in one hand, and before he'd even opened his mouth, they all knew what was coming.

'That's Control been in touch, sir,' the Uniform announced. He handed the printout to Sinead, who glanced at it, then passed it along the line to Logan. 'There's been a shout.'

'Great,' Logan said. He cast his gaze across the page, then thanked the sergeant and sent him on his way. 'What do you say, Detective Constable?' the DCI asked, turning to Tammi-Jo. 'You fancy doing one more for the road?'

DC Swanney straightened herself up and stuck out her chest. 'Yes, sir,' she said, snapping off a salute. 'It would be an honour, sir.'

'Aye, well, let's no' get carried away,' Logan told her. He clapped his hands together, then turned to the others. 'Right, let's minimise risk here. We'll take my car and Hamza's. No point everyone driving in this weather. Tyler, Sinead, you're with me. Tammi-Jo, you're with DS Khaled. Hamza drove you around on your first day with us, only fitting he does the same on your last.'

'That's very kind of you, sir,' Hamza deadpanned.

'And I suppose I'll just sit here on my todd, drinking tea and eating biscuits, will I?' asked Ben. To his credit, he at least tried not to sound too delighted by the idea.

'We can swap, if you like,' Logan told him.

'Not on your bloody Nelly! Away you all go and gie's peace.'

'Aye. Thought so.'

Logan whistled through his teeth, and Taggart performed a full flip-up onto all four feet. Before dog or detectives could go anywhere, though, the office door opened again. This time, there was no knock or waiting for an invitation.

Detective Superintendent Mitchell glanced around the room before Logan's sheer size drew her eye. She pointed to him without a word, then made a beckoning motion with the same finger.

‘We’ve had a shout, ma’am,’ he told her. ‘We were just heading out the door.’

‘Yes, well, this won’t take long,’ Mitchell told him. Her usual curtness was tempered by something, but Logan couldn’t quite tell what. Something less abrasive, certainly.

‘Can’t it wait?’ he asked.

‘No, Jack. It can’t.’

Logan tutted quietly, then looked around at the others. ‘Two minutes.’ He tossed the keys to his BMW to Sinead. ‘You all head down. Take the dog. I’ll meet you at the cars. I’ll lead, Hamza, you’ll follow.’

‘Jack,’ Mitchell urged, and something about the way she said his name made the knot of dread that was a constant fixture in his gut tighten itself a little further.

‘Aye. Coming,’ he told her, then he picked up his coat, instructed Taggart to stay with the others, and followed the detective superintendent out of the room.

# *Chapter 4*

'A phone call?' Logan looked at the telephone receiver sitting on Mitchell's desk, the time on the display steadily ticking up. 'That's it? A phone call?'

Mitchell nodded and gestured towards the phone, but Logan didn't yet move to pick up the handset.

'Who's phoning me on your number?' he wondered aloud. He shuffled his feet. He didn't know why, but something about the phone and the ticking up of its digital display was making him uneasy. 'Why would anyone be calling me on your line?'

'It went round the houses a bit,' Mitchell explained. She indicated the receiver with an open hand. 'Please. You should take it.'

He watched, nonplussed, as she backed out of her office and into the corridor. She smiled at him—a small, sad sort of smile that was probably meant to be comforting, but had precisely the opposite effect.

And then she closed the door, leaving him alone with whoever was on the other end of the line.

He smoothed down the front of his coat, fiddled with a button for a moment, then tutted and grabbed for the handset. Whatever it was—*whoever* it was—he didn't have time to waste.

'Detective Chief Inspector Jack Logan,' he began.

He listened to the voice that came back to him.

Listened, but didn't quite take it in.

'Wait, wait. Sorry, what?' he said, scowling so hard that the muscles at the corner of each eyebrow formed two solid knuckles. He ran a hand across his forehead, smoothing it back down. 'Start again.'

Once more, he listened. This time, he was ready for the words. This time, they'd lost some of their power.

'How bad?' he asked.

It wasn't the question he wanted to ask. Close, but not quite. That one felt a little too brutal to voice out loud.

He nodded his way through the reply, like the person on the other end was a cashier reading his fast food order back to him.

'Right. Aye. I see,' he said, once the line had gone silent again. 'And he said that, did he? Oh. Well, then how—' He listened again. Nodded again. 'Right. Aye. Well, I can't make it. Not today.'

There was a note of surprise in the reply. Of mild outrage, maybe.

'Aye, well, this is important, too. And, let's be honest here, seeing me's no' exactly been a priority for the past God knows how many years, has it?'

He zoned out a little when the voice came again, distracted by the rattling rain against the window. Maybe it was the size or the shape of it, but Mitchell's office seemed to amplify the sound. Magnify it.

If he focused on it, he was sure he could completely tune out the voice of the woman on the phone.

He could probably tune out the whole world, in fact.

Instead, he cut the woman on the other end short and asked the question he should've asked back at the start. The one he hadn't dared to.

'How long?' he demanded. 'How long does he have left?'

–

The wind tried its damnedest to wrench the door from Logan's hand as he threw himself into the driver's seat of his BMW and blew a dangling raindrop from the end of his nose.

'Jesus Christ. It's getting worse,' he announced.

'It's not going to hit properly until later this afternoon, boss,' Tyler informed him from the back seat.

He spoke with all the authority of a trained meteorologist, rather than of a man who had caught part of a weather forecast in the car on the way to work, and who even then had only been half-listening.

'Reckon it's going to be a bad one. Storm Agatha.' Tyler watched the rain rolling down the window beside him. 'My mum had a mate called Agatha. Cow. Total cow. If it's anything like her, we're in trouble.'

Logan blew out his cheeks, shrugged, then began searching his pockets for his keys. He had just started to get annoyed when Sinead realised what he was looking for and passed the keys across from the front passenger seat.

'Sorry, sir. You looking for these?'

Logan took them without a word, searched for the keyhole into which to insert them, then remembered the car didn't work like that.

With a tut, he tossed the key into one of the dookits in the dash and pressed the button that started the engine.

'Everything all right, sir?' Sinead asked.

'Fine. Aye.'

'Was the, uh… The call. Important?'

Logan shook his head. 'No. Not important. You fit?'

'Uh, yeah,' Sinead said. She glanced at her husband sitting in the back, Taggart partly sprawled across his lap. 'But, um, while we're driving, Tyler has something he wanted to talk to you about.'

'What, now?' Tyler all but squealed.

Sinead gave him a nod of encouragement. Logan angled his rearview mirror and locked eyes with the detective constable. The glow of headlights filled the cabin as Hamza's car pulled up behind them.

'Well, Tyler?' Logan urged. 'What did you want to say?'

A vein pulsed at the side of Tyler's forehead. He swallowed three times in rapid succession, like he was trying to dislodge something stuck in his throat.

'It's just, eh… It's just…' The DC ran the back of his hand across his lips and found them desert dry. 'I was just going to say…'

He smiled. The expression was nine-tenths desperation to one-part fear.

'Happy Halloween, boss,' Tyler concluded.

He held Logan's gaze in the mirror. It was that or meet the eye of his wife, who had turned in her seat to glare at him.

'Was that it?' Logan asked.

Tyler's smile broadened, becoming even less convincing in the process. 'That was it, boss.'

'Right,' Logan said after a lengthy silence. 'Good. Well, if there's nothing else…'

A gale rushed in as Sinead's door opened. She unclipped her seatbelt, and it whipped across her like it was beating a hasty retreat.

'Actually, sir, if it's all the same with you, I'll travel with DS Khaled.'

She got out of the car without waiting for a response, lowered her head against the rain, then made a bolt for the vehicle directly behind Logan's.

'What the hell was that about?' asked the DCI, finally turning to look directly at the younger officer in the back.

Tyler pressed himself into the seat, like he might be able to convince it to swallow him whole. 'Beats me, boss,' he said.

Logan narrowed his eyes, not buying a word that was coming out of the detective constable's mouth.

On balance, though, he decided it could wait.

'Right, well,' he said, turning to face front again. 'Looks like it's just me and—'

Another hurricane swirled in, sending old car park tickets and sweetie wrappers spiralling around the inside of the car.

‘Hootcha mamma!’ Tammi-Jo declared, smoothing down the windswept nest of her fine blonde hair as she planted herself in the spot Sinead had only just vacated. She flashed one of her more enthusiastic smiles at both men and the dog. ‘Sinead said that, since it’s my last day, I should ride up front with you.’

‘Did she?’ Logan said. He readjusted his rearview mirror until Hamza’s reflected headlights dazzled him. ‘Well, wasn’t that incredibly thoughtful of her?’

## *Chapter 5*

Two hours later, and sixty-ish miles north-west, it was becoming apparent that they were almost certainly lost.

Logan couldn't even blame the weather. Not fully, at least. Aye, it was a shitshow out there, but the wipers and headlights were coping for the most part, and the surface water wasn't troubling the BMW too much.

No, the weather wasn't the problem. The problem, by and large, was Tyler.

'It's not on the map, boss,' the DC insisted from the back seat. 'It's definitely not on the map.'

'McQuarrie Hall,' Logan said. 'It's called McQuarrie Hall!'

'I know what it's called, boss. You've told me what it's called. You can tell me all you want, but it isn't there!'

He held up his phone and waved it at the driver and passenger up front, his frustration very much obvious. The screen showed a map of an area just along the coast from Ullapool, with a big red error message overlaid on top.

'"No results found. Please adjust your search." That's all it says. Every bloody time!'

'Are you spelling it right?' Tammi-Jo asked. 'You might need to spell it right.'

'I've spelled it every way I can possibly spell it. M-C. M-A-C. M-C-C. A-R-R-I-E. A-R-R-Y. There's only so many ways you can spell "McQuarrie".'

'What about "Hall?"' Tammi-Jo asked, with what seemed to be genuine sincerity. 'Are you spelling that right?'

'Of course I'm spelling that right!' Tyler snapped.

'All right, all right, steady. Just checking!' Tammi-Jo replied, holding her hands up as if to fend off an attack. 'We all make mistakes.' She tried, but failed to stop herself asking the question that was niggling at her. 'Double L, right?'

'Yes! Of course double L!'

'It's a fucking huge castle!' Logan cried. 'How the hell do we keep missing the bloody— Wait!'

Tyler and Tammi-Jo both grabbed for handholds as Logan swung the wheel hard to the left. There was a roar of water being churned up beneath the wheels, and the thud of a scraggy wee dug hitting the plastic interior door trim.

A horn blared behind them. Hamza's headlights once again filled the inside of the cabin.

'Shite!' Tyler cried, ducking his head and covering it with his hands to protect himself from an impact that somehow didn't come.

Logan was already reaching for the 'Answer' button on the car's display when the phone rang and Hamza's name flashed up.

'Sorry, my fault,' the DCI said before Hamza had a chance to speak. 'Just spotted the turnoff and reacted.'

'We nearly smashed right into you,' the DS said. There was reproach in his tone. Well deserved, too.

'Aye, well, good reactions, Sergeant.' Logan eased a foot down on the accelerator and steered the BMW onto a narrow, single-track road, past a sign informing him that McQuarrie Hall lay half a mile ahead. 'Either of you been able to find the place on the map? Tyler's having no luck.'

'He's probably got it upside down,' Hamza said.

'Very funny,' Tyler said, leaning forward and projecting his voice. 'It's on my phone. You can't turn phones upside down.'

'Wow. What kind of phone have you got?' Tammi-Jo wondered.

'The map, I meant!' Tyler shot back. 'You can't turn the map upside down. Obviously, you can turn the phone upside down.'

He did just that, turning the handset over to prove his point. Although, exactly what that point was, nobody—him included—really knew.

'We couldn't find it either,' Hamza admitted.

'Ha! See?' Tyler cried from the back. 'Told you.'

Logan gripped the wheel as the car rumbled along the uneven track. Water had pooled in hundreds of potholes, and it was impossible to tell how deep any of them were. Hit the wrong one too fast, or at a bad angle, and he could kiss his front coil springs goodbye.

Assuming cars still had front coil springs. It had been a few years since he'd last had cause to check. There was definitely a suspension, though, and the last thing he wanted way out here was for a wayward ditch to knacker that.

'Is that a bridge?' Tammi-Jo asked, peering ahead through the rain.

Logan squinted through the streaky glass. It was officially daytime, but an impregnable layer of black cloud meant it may as well have been midnight.

'Where?' he asked.

'There. Up ahead. The big wooden thing giving off a real bridgey sort of vibe.' Tammi-Jo shot him a slightly worried sideways look. 'You can see it, yeah?'

'I see it,' Logan confirmed after a moment or two. He pressed a thumb first into one eye, then the other, then blinked to clear away the film that had formed there. 'Definitely a bridge.'

'Is it safe?' Tyler asked, sitting forward.

'Aye. Should be,' Logan said.

'That's good to know, boss,' Tyler said. 'What are you basing that on, though?'

'It's a road bridge, Tyler. It's designed to take the weight of cars.'

'Are you sure this is even technically a road, though, boss?' the DC asked. 'I mean, it's still not on the map. According to Google, we're just driving across a big green square.'

'It's fine,' Logan assured him. He flexed his fingers on the wheel as the car trundled closer to what now looked to be quite a flimsy wooden structure. 'It'll be fine. Although… Maybe best we do it one at a time.'

'What, on foot?' asked Tammi-Jo.

'I've not brought my wellies, boss.'

'No. Not on foot. Of course not on bloody foot. One car at a time, I mean,' Logan said.

He instructed Hamza to hang back, and the headlights of the following vehicle fell away as the DS brought his car to a stop in the middle of the track.

Logan inched the BMW up to where the pockmarked road gave way to the smooth, slick wood of the bridge. There was a raised tarmac tread all the way across it, and the markings of a thousand sets of tyres.

'See? It's definitely meant for cars,' Logan said. He nudged down on the accelerator, and the bridge gave a solid yet ever-so-slightly worrying *kaklunk* as it took the Beamer's weight.

Tyler and Tammi-Jo both looked out in opposite directions, staring down into the surging waters below. The river was perhaps only thirty feet wide, but it raged against the underside of the bridge, firing flecks of foam up through the gaps in the wooden boards.

'Aye, very good, boss. Can we get off it now?' Tyler urged.

Water crashed against the side of the bridge like a wave. From beneath the car came the slow, lazy groan of wood being put under pressure.

'Eh, aye. Good idea, son.'

Logan's foot pressed down further. The BMW crept onwards, gradually picking up speed.

From the sound it made, the bridge was not impressed.

'Eh, sir. Slow down.' Hamza's voice was an urgent bark over the car's speaker system. 'The bridge is wobbling.'

'I know it's wobbling, Sergeant,' Logan said through gritted teeth.

'We can feel it wobbling!' Tyler yelped.

'What do we do?' Tammi-Jo asked, her voice lowered to a whisper like she daren't risk the weight of a few extra decibels.

'We should go back, boss. Reverse.'

'No!' Sinead's voice was so loud and urgent that they almost heard it in stereo—once from the speakers, and once from behind them. 'Go. Go! Get off!'

Logan took her word for it. He jammed a foot to the floor just as the car gave a sudden sickening sideways lurch.

Tyler screamed. Tammi-Jo clutched at her head. Taggart barked furiously.

And Logan hissed through his teeth and held tight to the wheel, as the bridge was rocked by the weight of the car, and the thundering might of the river below.

'You're not going to make it!' Hamza cried.

'Yes, we bloody are!' Logan bellowed back at him. He rocked in his chair, like the shifting of his weight might spur the car onwards.

The track on the other side was barely ten feet away now. Eight. Six.

'Come on, ya bastard!' Logan boomed.

Wood splintered. Water crashed.

'Sinead, I love you and I'm sorry!' Tyler howled.

Then, the front tyres found purchase on the unfinished surface of the road, and the car powered onto solid ground.

The front left wheel found a puddle that turned out to be mostly hole. There was a sudden bang, a drawn-out screeching of metal on metal, and then the BMW's back end was thrown out, skidding the car around in a tight one-eighty so it was facing back the way it came.

From there, the occupants of the vehicle watched in a shaky, breathless silence as what was left of the bridge toppled sideways to be torn apart in the foam of the rushing river.

Logan's gaze went from the empty space where the bridge had just been to the headlights on the river's far bank, then down to his own hands, which were clutching the wheel so tightly his knuckles were practically transparent.

One by one, he willed his fingers to release their grip. They were understandably reluctant, given what they'd just experienced, but they eventually gave in.

'See?' the DCI mumbled. 'Told you we were going to make it.'

'Jesus Christ! I thought we were dead, boss!' Tyler cried. 'I thought we were dead. I really thought we were dead!' He leaned forward again. 'Sinead! I thought we were dead!'

'Maybe we are dead,' Tammi-Jo reasoned. Her eyes performed a full loop as her gaze swept around the inside of the car. 'We're probably not, though,' she eventually concluded.

'Sinead?' Tyler said, when no reply came. 'Hello? Sinead, you there?'

There were a series of bleeps from the car's speakers, then Hamza's name vanished from the display.

'No signal,' Logan said, indicating the greyed-out icon at the top right of the screen. 'Bollocks.'

'How's that happened, boss? There was a signal a second ago. Where's it gone?'

'I don't know, Tyler! Do I look like a bloody… telephone scientist?'

'I don't think that's a real job, sir,' Tammi-Jo remarked.

'There's no signal. That's all we need to know,' Logan snapped.

'Aye, but there was, boss.'

'Well, there's not now.'

He flashed his headlights a few times, braced himself, then wrestled opened the door and immediately stepped into a puddle that went up over his ankle.

'Bastard,' he hissed, but the word was immediately stolen by the wind.

'Careful, boss!' Tyler warned, after winding his window down a fraction. 'Ground's wet.'

Logan ignored the comment, and squelched towards the few remaining fixings that marked where the bridge had been. The river was coursing past, a churning carpet of angry white foam.

Across on the other side, the front doors of Hamza's car were opened, then almost immediately torn off their hinges by a driving gale. DS Khaled and DC Bell quickly climbed out, forced the doors closed, then were shoved onwards down the slope towards the river.

They stopped half a dozen feet from the edge, where the ground fell away sharply into the frothing water below. Logan waved both hands above his head to make sure he had their attention, and Hamza acknowledged him by repeating the action.

'You two head back to HQ!' bellowed the DCI, cupping his hands around his mouth.

The wind howled around him, drowning him out. It was blowing directly towards him, and he got the feeling it was trying to blow the words right back down his throat.

Hamza's reply, on the other hand, was wind assisted. It was carried across the river, but arrived as a bit of a distorted jumble. Logan got the gist of it, though.

'Can't hear you, sir!'

'GO! BACK TO BASE!' Logan boomed, simplifying the message a bit.

When it was clear it still hadn't got through, he simplified it even further.

'FUCK. OFF!'

He added a big dismissive hand gesture, like he was ushering them away, then pointed back down the track behind them.

He watched, dazzled by the headlights and half-blinded by the rain, as Sinead and Hamza had a hurried conversation, then Hamza made a funnel with his hands and shouted, 'We're turning around!'

There was more to it than that, but whatever detail followed was lost to the storm, and Logan didn't care to stand out in the rain long enough to go over it all fully.

Instead, he raised both hands above his head, thumbs extended, then turned and hurried back to the warmth and comfort of the car.

By the time he was back inside, Hamza's headlights were on the move, retreating back along the track, the uneven road making them bounce up and down as they faded into the distance.

'They're going back to base,' Logan said, running a hand down his face, then flicking away the water that had accumulated in the lines and crags.

'Is Sinead all right?' Tyler asked. 'How did she seem?'

'She seemed soaking wet and far away, son. I don't know what more I can tell you than that.'

Tyler grimaced. 'Aye, she has been a bit distant.'

'I meant literally far away. On the other side of the river.'

'Oh! Aye. Haha, boss! Aye. That's what I meant,' Tyler said, before sitting back and looking away.

Logan decided not to delve any deeper into the detective constables' marriage problems. Instead, he put the car into reverse, whispered a silent prayer to any gods that might be listening, and then groaned when the front end of the vehicle let out a low grinding noise as soon as he touched the accelerator.

The BMW jerked violently to a stop, then rolled forwards again into the pothole.

'Bollocks.'

Logan tapped and swiped aimlessly at the screen for a few moments until he found one that was positively brimming with warning lights and discouraging messages.

'I think your car's broken,' Tammi-Jo said.

'Oh, you think so?' Logan snapped. It had been a long enough trip even before the whole bridge incident, and the stress of it was getting to him. 'And what makes you say that?'

'Well, that big noise,' Tammi-Jo reasoned. She pointed to the screen. 'And all them.'

'It was a rhetorical question, Detective Constable,' Logan replied, his nostrils flaring just a little. He lowered his head until his chin touched his chest, sighed heavily, then straightened again. 'Right, I hope you were kidding about not having brought your wellies, Tyler, because it looks like we're walking from here.'

–

They reached their final destination in just under ten minutes and three arguments. Both these metrics were better than Logan had been bracing himself for.

He'd been forced to carry Taggart the whole way, the daft dug too scared by the storm to walk so much as the length of himself. He had cooried away inside Logan's coat, shivering in fear, and occasionally expressing his gratitude by giving Logan a little lick on the underside of the chin.

Tyler spotted the house first, through a gap in the twisting trees that had lined the track for the previous few hundred yards or so.

Although, 'house' wasn't remotely the right word for the mountain of old stone and twisting spires that appeared through the sheets of rain at the far end of the track.

Lights burned in a dozen or more windows dotted across the castle's frontage, no two panes of glass the same shape or size. The movement of the rain made the lights appear to flicker and dance, so for the first minute or so of their final approach, it looked like the place was on fire.

At the sight of it, they'd picked up the pace, hurrying on through the downpour towards the sanctuary the building offered. Tyler led the way, breaking into a run at first, then slowing as the building loomed larger.

At first, Logan couldn't understand why the DC had stopped running, but as Taggart shivered inside his coat, Logan began to realise why.

There was something off about the place. Something… not wrong, exactly, but far from right. Maybe it was the weather making it look that way, but there was a touch of the old *Hammer House of Horror* about the castle.

It had a real presence. No, more than that—worse than that—it had a real *malevolence*. Logan half-expected to turn around and find a crowd of villagers with flaming torches and pitchforks racing up the path behind them.

A solitary police car was parked out front, along with two other vehicles—a big white van with a satellite dish on the roof, and a small red car that must've looked quite sporty when it was built in the mid- to late 80s.

Trees surrounded the building. They clustered around it and yet, with their bare spindly branches stretching away from the house like long, trailing fingers, they seemed to be trying to flee from whatever lurked inside.

'I don't like this place, boss,' Tyler remarked, having slowed almost completely to a stop. 'It's creepy as hell.'

'Grow up, Detective Constable,' Logan said, putting aside his own reservations. 'It's just an old castle. There's hundreds of the bastarding things dotted around the country.'

Although, Logan had to admit, he'd never seen one quite like this.

'I quite like it,' Tammi-Jo remarked. The rain had played havoc with her makeup, and watery lines of black mascara were running down both cheeks, giving her a real Alice Cooper vibe.

'Well, no bloody wonder. You look like the secret sister the Addams Family keeps locked up in the loft. You'll fit right in,' Tyler said, his voice heading towards the hysterical. 'But I mean it. I've got a bad feeling about this place, boss.'

'What, besides the fact that someone's been murdered in it, you mean?'

Tyler gasped. 'God, I hadn't even thought about that! That's even worse!'

He ran a hand through his hair. Whatever product he'd used to sculpt it seemed to be impervious to anything Mother Nature could throw at it, as not a single strand was out of place.

‘Creepy castle, storm of the century, dead guy… on Halloween. *Halloween*, boss!’

‘Oh, shut up and get a grip of yourself, son,’ Logan said. ‘It’s a big house, that’s all. There’s nothing bloody supernatural about it!’

Just then, the track and the trees around them were lit up in electric blue, as a jagged fork of lightning tore across the sky behind the castle, casting its ramparts and spires into a dark, brooding silhouette.

‘Aye, boss,’ Tyler said, in the brooding silence that followed. ‘You were saying?’

# *Chapter 6*

'Look at the door knocker, boss,' Tyler whispered. He pointed to the black iron gargoyle-like head with a heavy ring gripped in its mouth, but kept his distance from it. 'You can't tell me that's normal.'

'Of course it's not normal. This is a rich bastard's place. None of them are normal.'

He gripped the metal ring and rattled it a few times against the plate that was fastened to one of the two wooden front doors. Oak, Logan thought, though it had been given so many coats of varnish over the years that the grain was hard to make out.

Over the whistling of the wind, he thought he could just about make out the sound of bickering from somewhere inside, then a mechanism rattled, and the door swung open with a creak.

'Fuck!' Tyler ejected when he saw the woman standing inside.

She was painfully, agonisingly, alarmingly thin, with cheekbones so sharp they looked in danger of taking someone's eyes out, and most probably her own. She wore a long silver dress that sparkled all over like a disco mirror ball. It hung from her shoulders like she was a clothes hanger, falling almost straight down over the bony ridges of her flat chest.

Though she was somewhere in her late thirties, her hair was completely white. A choice, most probably, though an odd one. It was piled on top of her head like a Mr Whippy soft serve ice cream, with two strands hanging down either side of her face.

They looked a bit like little legs, as if the hair was getting ready to climb off her head and run away.

Logan wouldn't blame it if it did.

She smoked a stubby cigarette through one of those long, thin holders usually only seen in old black and white movies, clutching it between two long, pale fingers with chipped black polish on the nails.

Her features were fine and delicate, with the exception of her right eye, which was a good twenty per cent larger than the left. None of the features seemed to have been assembled correctly though, and the overall effect of her face was oddly disconcerting.

While Logan was sure that someone somewhere would consider the woman to be beautiful, he didn't think he'd like to meet them.

'Yes. What? Who are you? Are you the police? What on earth has taken you so long? Is that a dog? What on earth is it doing in there? Well, don't just stand there, come in!'

Logan wasn't sure which question to answer first, so he ignored them all and just led the way inside. The woman's accent was all over the shop, and while there was a definite suggestion of 'upper-class English toff' in there, the rest was a mystery he had no desire to unravel.

The castle's front doors opened into a grand hall, which could have comfortably accommodated Logan's entire house twice over, and still have room left over for a wee outdoor seating area and shed.

The scale of the place was the first thing they noticed. The second thing they noticed was the army of dead things.

They stood in the corners. They hung from the walls. Stags, and rabbits, and otters, and birds, their eyes glassy, their fur and feathers faded by the passing of time, and a lacking of care.

Heads jutted out from wooden plaques. A full-sized red deer and a smaller fawn stood frozen, dead eyes fixed on the main entrance, so it looked like they'd just been disturbed by the opening of the door.

A flightless bird—an ostrich or an emu, it was too badly neglected for Logan to be sure—slouched in the far corner, its long neck sagging, its feathers half-missing.

Up on another wall, two large, stuffed carp were affixed to the same display plate, so they appeared to be swimming past each other—just two long-dead, awful-looking fish passing in the night.

Logan heard Tammi-Jo let out a low whistle below her breath. 'That's all a bit creepy,' she muttered, and the DCI couldn't really disagree.

Doing his best to ignore all the stuffed and mounted dead things, Logan cast his eye around the rest of the place. While the assorted animal parts took pride of place, they weren't the only decoration in the entrance hall. Far from it.

Paintings and tapestries adorned the rough stone walls, all of them depicting great battles, men on horseback, and the offspring of people who'd clearly married their relatives.

A staircase, wider than a main road, curved up to a mezzanine level above, then onwards to a second storey far overhead.

A chandelier—or possibly some sort of light sculpture—stretched twenty feet down from the ceiling, all gnarled metal and droplets of frosted glass.

An ancient patterned rug the size of a five-a-side football pitch covered the centre of the scuffed flagstone floor. Several leather chairs and a few antique tables were assembled there. Empty decanters and crystal glasses suggested a gathering had recently taken place, though only the woman who'd answered the door and a man who, based on appearance alone, was unmistakably her younger brother remained.

'Bloody hell,' Tyler muttered, echoing many of Logan's thoughts on the place.

'Nice room. Not keen on the stuffed animals, but good otherwise. Funny shape,' Tammi-Jo remarked, looking around with her hands on her hips. 'It's sort of a bit round with a sticky out bit and little dunkles at the edges, isn't it?' She looked directly at the woman with the Mr Whippy hair. 'What shape would you call that?'

The other woman regarded her through hollow, sunken eyes.

'I have no idea,' she eventually said, then she flicked her attention over to Logan. 'You are the police, yes? The detectives? You're here about Daddy?'

Logan produced his warrant card, then introduced himself and the team.

'Helen. Helen Bach,' the woman replied. 'Charmed.'

She held a hand out to him like he was supposed to kiss it. Instead, he gripped the ends of her trailing fingers, shook them once, then let them go.

'Funny,' Tammi-Jo said.

Helen turned to her and raised one eyebrow. It was the one above the larger of her two eyes, and it only served to emphasise the size difference. 'I'm sorry?'

'Your name. Helen Bach. Hell and back. It's good. It's funny. Did you choose it yourself?'

'What's that got to do with anything?' Helen demanded. 'Of course I did. So? What of it?'

Tammi-Jo shook her head, like she was worried she'd caused offence. 'No, nothing. I wasn't saying anything. I just liked it. Well done, you!'

She gave the other woman a light, playful punch on one of her bare shoulders. For a moment, Logan worried that she'd shatter like glass. Instead, she just stared at where the detective constable had touched her with an expression that made clear she was going to slather the spot in disinfectant at the earliest available opportunity.

'Daddy?' Logan said, circling back to Helen's earlier remark. 'Your father's the deceased?'

Helen nodded. 'He is, yes. Montgomery McQuarrie. I'm sure you've heard of him.'

Logan shook his head. 'Don't think so.'

'Oh.' Something about that seemed to please the woman. 'Well, lucky for you he's not around to hear you say that. He'd lose his mind.'

'What the hell kept you?!'

Helen's brother had the same mismatched eye size going on as his sister, and while he didn't share the colour or sheer volume of her hair—his was a nutty brown and receding just a little above the temples—they were otherwise very similar. Not twins, Logan thought—he was younger than she was—but eerily alike, all the same.

The man stormed over to meet them, his expensive shoes slapping on the stone floor. The water dripping from the detectives had begun to pool into puddles, which made him keep his distance.

While he was heavier than his sister, there was still very little of the man in terms of bulk. He was tall—a whisper over six feet, Logan estimated—but he had the build of a pencil. And all the presence of one, too, despite his scowl and raised voice.

'We've been waiting hours! Hours, I say!'

His accent was far easier to place than Helen's. Everything about it—everything about him, in fact—spoke of a private education somewhere south of the border. Somewhere expensive, where they served pheasant nuggets in the school tuck shop, and you lined up for PE alongside future kings and prime ministers.

Still, Logan would try and not hold any of that against him. It wouldn't be easy.

'Papa's been up there. Like *that*. Just up there. All this time!'

'And you are?' Logan asked.

Despite his obvious distress, the younger man responded immediately, as if blind obedience to authority had been drilled into him at some point. That could be handy.

'Montgomery McQuarrie,' he said, pushing his shoulders back.

'Aren't you supposed to be dead?' Tammi-Jo asked.

'The second,' the man added.

'Junior,' Helen corrected. 'Montgomery McQuarrie *Junior*. Don't try and big yourself up, Monty, dear. It doesn't suit you. You know Daddy didn't approve of "the second". You're Monty *Junior*. Little Baby Monty Junior.'

'Just shut up, Helen! You're such a child!' Monty hissed, turning on his sister, anger blazing in his eyes. One more so than the other.

'Oh, that's rich, *Junior*! Need I remind you that I'm older than you, brother dearest?'

'No, you don't need to remind me, *sister dearest*. It's blindingly obvious! One just has to look at you to see you're an old hag!'

Helen gasped so sharply that Taggart, who had been poking his head out of Logan's coat and watching events with interest, buried himself back in.

'How *dare* you? How actual dare you? I look half my age!'

'Oh, really? Do you? I'm sorry, I didn't realise you were *a hundred and twenty*! Congratulations on being the oldest person in the world! Have we called the *Guinness Book of World Records* yet? I'm sure they'd love a tip-off.'

'I'll tip *you* off in a minute, you toadying little shit!'

'What does that even mean?' Monty Jr shrieked. He followed the question with a shrill, braying sort of laugh. 'You can't even form basic sentences. Have all those drugs you take over in New York finally addled your brain?'

Logan cleared his throat, interrupting them before things could deteriorate into pulling hair and dead legs.

He waited until they were both looking his way before pointing a finger up towards the stone ceiling overhead. 'You said he was up there, aye?'

Helen smoothed down her sparkly dress, patted her hair like it needed emotional support, then nodded. 'Yes. Daddy is in his study. Top of the stairs, take a left, then up the second set of steps. Your'—she waved vaguely with her cigarette holder—'*police friend* is already up there.'

Logan looked back over his shoulder at Tyler and Tammi-Jo. 'You hear that? Our police friend is already here.'

'Aw, nice one. Haven't seen him in ages,' Tyler remarked.

'I hope Mrs Police Friend's been keeping well,' Tammi-Jo said, getting in on the act.

'OK. Well, we'll go and get to it, then,' Logan said, turning back to the brother and sister. He fixed Monty with a lightly taunting look. 'You. Junior. Can you do me a favour?'

Without waiting for a response, Logan opened his coat, grasped the squirming Taggart in both hands, then held him out to Monty. The dog hung limply in his grip, looking a little self-conscious about the whole situation.

'Hang onto that for me, will you?'

'Ugh! What? No! I don't like animals!'

Logan looked very deliberately at all the various dead things assembled around the hall. 'You could've fooled me,' he said. Then, ignoring Montgomery's protests, he deposited the dog in his arms and led the two other detectives towards the grand staircase.

Stopping by the bottom step, he turned back.

'Oh, one quick question, Mrs Bach.'

'Mx.'

Logan sucked in his bottom lip and spat it back out again, already sensing some new frustration looming in his immediate future. 'Sorry?'

'It's Mx Bach, not Mrs. Bach is a name I've adopted, not a married name. I'm not married. Marriage is a sham. It's Mx Bach. Not "Miss" or "Ms". *Mx*.'

'Mucks?' Logan said, having a bash at it.

'Close. But don't drag it out. Mx.'

'Mucks,' Logan said again.

'Mx.'

'Mux.'

'Close. *Mx*.'

‘You’re saying the exact same word as I’m saying!’ Logan insisted. ‘We’re saying it the same way!’

He rubbed a hand across his eyes, like he was suddenly weary, not just of this conversation, but of life in general.

‘Forget it, I’ll call you Helen,’ he decided, though he said it more to himself than to anyone else. ‘Helen. One quick question. That bridge out there. Is there another way to get here? Another road, I mean?’

Helen shook her head. ‘No. It’s that track, or miles of bogs and trees in every direction. Why do you ask?’

Logan caught the looks from Tyler and Tammi-Jo, but ignored them both.

‘No reason,’ he said.

And with that, he turned and led the way up the stairs.

## *Chapter 7*

The detectives found their 'police friend' standing guard outside Montgomery Senior's study door. Logan introduced them all, and the constable identified himself as PC Rab Rowan. He was one of two PCs working out of the nearby Ullapool, and had been the first—and until now, the only—officer to attend the scene.

'Where's the other constable?' Logan asked.

'Tenerife,' Rab told him. 'Having a lovely time, too, if her Facebook's anything to go by. Not that I'm jealous with this weather.'

The DCI nodded past the PC to the study door. It had been badly damaged around the area where the handle met the frame, but someone, possibly Rab, had managed to get it to close.

'He in there?'

'The dead fella? Yeah,' the PC confirmed. 'The family says they last saw him around ten fifteen last night when he headed up here. When they realised something was wrong this morning, they took an axe to the door. One of them big battle axes. From the old days.'

'The door was locked?' Tyler asked.

'Well… aye. I mean, presumably,' Rab confirmed. 'Pretty sure they'd have tried the handle before wellying shit out of it with medieval weaponry.'

'You'd hope, aye,' Logan agreed. 'Mind you, have you met them?'

The constable smiled. 'Fair point, sir. They're a bit eccentric, right enough. The TV folk seem to have their heads screwed on, though.'

Logan frowned. 'TV folk?'

'Aye. Off some satellite channel. *Ghost Spotters* or something.'

'No way! I've seen that,' Tyler exclaimed. 'It's one of them real-life haunted house documentary shows where a psychic guy wanders about trying to find ghosts.' He glanced around, like he might find a spectre lingering somewhere nearby. 'Great, that's all we need!'

Logan tutted. 'Aye, well, but it's no' a documentary show, is it? If it's some fella fannying about, pretending he can talk to dead folk.'

'Be handy if he can, sir,' Tammi-Jo said. 'He could chat to...' She jerked her head in the direction of the door a few times. '*You know who.* That'd help us out no end.'

'Aye, well, let's not put all our eggs in that basket,' Logan said. He turned his attention back to the constable. 'Who's been in?'

'Oh, everyone, I think,' Rab replied. 'Think they all swarmed the room when they broke the door down. Your telly woman, Yvonne something, she reckoned there was seven or eight of them in there at one point. Some of them took turns trying to get the knife out. Uh, because there's a knife. I probably should've said that. Sorry, sir. This is all new to me.'

'Don't worry about it, son. You're doing fine,' Logan told him. 'Right, then.'

He reached into his coat pocket, pulled out a set of rubber gloves and shoe coverings, then shrugged the coat off to minimise the amount of water he'd otherwise be dripping all over the place.

There were a few elasticated *snaps* as Tyler and Tammi-Jo followed suit with their own PPE.

'Let's go see what we're dealing with.'

Logan, Tyler and Tammi-Jo stood just inside the doorway of the study, staring at the body sitting in the high-backed leather chair.

'Any thoughts on cause of death, boss?' Tyler asked. 'Because if not, I've got a theory I'd be happy to run by you.'

Montgomery McQuarrie senior slouched with his head back so he was facing the ceiling. The hilt of what looked to be a kitchen knife stuck out from his forehead like a unicorn's horn. Two trickles of blood had taken different routes down his face, parting ways at the bridge of his nose before getting temporarily lost in the grooves and pockmarks of his wrinkled cheeks.

Finally, they'd reunited in his big handlebar moustache, turning patches of the white hair a deep, brooding shade of pink.

The dead body sitting at the desk was obviously the room's big headline news, but Logan turned away from it for a moment, taking in the rest of the study.

It would've been a good-sized room in most houses, but compared to the grandeur of the entrance hall downstairs, it felt oppressively compact.

The walls were the same stone as all the others they'd seen so far. While the others had been adorned with artwork of various sizes and skill levels, these were decked out with cork boards, calendars and a row of analogue clocks showing the current time in various capital cities.

A gas lamp burned on a table just inside the door, but a ceiling-mounted fluorescent strip light had been switched on, casting a sickly white glow across the whole room.

The back wall, a few feet behind the victim, was lined with bookshelves, with the books ranging from hefty leather-bound volumes that could choke a hippo to slim paperbacks that may well have been run off on someone's home printer.

The arrangement of the volumes looked to be completely haphazard at first, but the more Logan looked at it, the more impressed he was. Whoever had organised the shelves had achieved 'peak book'—not a single inch of space had been wasted, to the extent that slipping so much as a solitary sheet of A5 paper onto the shelves would likely prove an impossible task.

There was something not entirely unlike a bed tucked away in the corner of the room. There was a duvet and pillows, at least, although quite what sort of structure was supporting them, Logan couldn't immediately say. The whole thing had the feel of a big dog's bed about it, or perhaps some sort of giant nest.

Clearly, Montgomery had slept there at times, although he had been fully dressed when he'd been killed.

The rest of the room looked expensive, yet largely nondescript. There was a rug not unlike the one downstairs, but a fraction of the size. A wingback armchair was positioned next to a low coffee table, facing the door.

Never mind some daft ghost-hunting programme, both pieces of furniture would likely go down a storm on *The Antiques Roadshow*.

There was a rustic wooden bowl on the table beside the lamp. Tyler was poking around in the contents, his eyes wide with wonder.

'Anything?' Logan asked.

DC Neish continued to study the bowl's contents, transfixed.

'Tyler!'

The sharpness of Logan's tone made the detective constable look up.

'Boss?'

'Anything?' Logan asked again.

'Um, no. Well, aye. Just, like, gold rings. Fancy cufflinks. Diamonds, maybe.'

Tammi-Jo whistled. It was the sort of *woot-woo* that was usually reserved for a catcall. 'Must be worth a fortune, that stuff.'

Tyler's gaze fell back down to the contents of the bowl. 'Aye,' he quietly agreed. 'Must be.'

Trinkets and knick-knacks weren't Logan's current concern. Turning, he cast a glance at the items on the dead man's desk. An empty glass. An open box of cigars with three or four missing. An ashtray with just a smear of black across the bottom.

No computer, paperwork, or anything else to suggest the victim had been hard at work when his killer came calling.

Then again, from what Logan knew of the man, Montgomery McQuarrie hadn't needed to do a stroke of work for the past several decades. Money was not exactly a problem.

Despite what he'd told the man's daughter, of course he'd heard of the man. There were probably only a handful of people in the country who hadn't heard stories about the reclusive and eccentric multi-billionaire, even if very few—Logan included—would be able to say where he'd got all his money from.

He had been variously described over the years as a business magnate, an industrial tycoon and a titan of industry. Such titles covered quite a wide spectrum, Logan thought, and he wasn't aware of anyone having drilled down too deeply into the specifics.

Suffice to say, the man had reached the point of being richer than God, and he was damned if he was going to share the secrets of how he'd got there.

'We're all agreed it's definitely murder, yeah?' Tammi-Jo asked.

'I think that's a pretty safe bet,' Logan conceded.

Tammi-Jo nodded and took a couple of half steps closer to the body. 'Does it make anyone else think about *The Sword and the Stone*, or is it just me?' she asked. 'Like, if you pull it out, are you the new rightful king?'

'Good luck pulling that out,' Logan said. 'The bodily fluid suction effect will make it a right bastard to shift.'

Across the room, Tyler dropped a gold sovereign ring back into the bowl and shuddered. 'That's not a phrase I was particularly desperate to hear, boss.'

'You've got worse ahead of you than that, son,' Logan said.

'How do you mean?'

The DCI shook his head. 'Doesn't matter. All in good time. Thoughts, you two?'

Tyler shot a look at the body. 'What? Besides, "Ooyah bastard"?'

'Apart from that,' Logan confirmed. 'Look around. Anything jumping out at you?'

'There's no window, boss,' Tyler said, seizing on the most obvious thing before Tammi-Jo had a chance to beat him to it.

'Correct.'

'And the door was locked,' DC Swanney added.

'So…?'

'So the murderer probably locked the door behind them on the way out, sir.'

Logan raised an eyebrow, but said nothing. Both detective constables exchanged glances. Then, in unison, they looked at the door.

'Key's in the lock!' Tyler said, getting there a fraction of a second before Tammi-Jo. 'It was locked from the inside.'

'Unless someone put the key in there afterwards,' DC Swanney reasoned. 'Maybe when the family came in, they picked it up and put it there out of the way?'

'If someone dropped the key after locking the door, it'd be in the corridor outside,' Logan pointed out.

Tammi-Jo tapped at her chin. 'Oh, yeah. So why take an axe to the door, if they had the key?'

'What's your thinking then, boss?' Tyler asked.

Logan ran a hand down his face, then scratched at his chin. 'Not sure yet,' he admitted. 'Go out and talk to that Uniform again. See if he can tell us anything else, either based on what the family told him, or local knowledge.'

Tyler stole a glance back at the bowl of jewellery, then nodded. 'Will do, boss. Anything else?'

'Aye,' Logan said, stepping aside to let the younger officer pass. 'See if you can find someone to rustle up a cuppa, will you? I'm bloody gasping here.'

–

PC Rowan was nowhere to be found when Tyler stepped out of the study. The spot where he'd stood was now empty, the constable having apparently vanished into thin air.

Or, more likely, simply gone somewhere else.

'Hello?' Tyler called. He took a moment to dredge the man's name up from his short-term memory. 'Rab? You there?'

His voice echoed off along the darkened passageway. When it bounced back to him, it sounded thin and anxious.

'Eh… Constable? You down there?' Tyler asked, peering into the gloom.

The only response was his own trembling echo.

He backed up towards the staircase they'd climbed a few minutes previously. It led to a long curved mezzanine below, which branched off into a spider's web of corridors and passages, and onwards to the castle's many wings and rooms.

Much of the mezzanine level was tucked away in deep, dark shadow. Tyler tried very hard not to imagine something coming lunging from the darkness, taking the stairs two at a time, then devouring him whole.

He tried, but for the most part, he failed.

'Hello?' he said, and his voice was a whisper soon absorbed by the cold stone walls. 'Anyone down there?'

If there was, they weren't saying anything.

He headed back in the direction of the study, then stopped and gazed up at two bloody awful portraits that hung on either side of the corridor's mouth. They were of a man and a woman, or some misshapen variation on the theme, at least.

The woman's features were sharp and elongated, her nose like a dagger, her ears like a bad cosplay of Mr Spock. Her fingers ended in tiny knives and forks, and her two blonde pigtails were upturned into big letter U's on either side of her head.

As Tyler looked at her, he got a sense that this exact woman had probably popped up in his nightmares once. Or, if she hadn't, she sure as hell would start making appearances from now on.

The painting of the man wasn't much better. Whereas his counterpart's face was all jagged lines and pointy bits, his features were rounded and blunt, as if every part of him had been sculpted out of lumpy mashed potato.

His eyes were crossed and his tongue was hanging out, like a cartoon boxer who'd taken one too many punches to the head. He was dressed in a hessian sack that had been split open down the front. What Tyler had initially thought were intestines spilling out of him were, in fact, strings of sausages and cuts of beef. His pudgy hands were desperately trying to force the meat back inside his torso, even while mice and birds nibbled and pecked at it all.

Tyler regarded each portrait in silence for a while, like an art critic might.

'Well,' he eventually concluded. 'They're fucking weird.'

He had just set off in search of PC Rowan again, when he heard it—a faint musical lilt from along an adjoining passageway on his left.

Someone was humming, or perhaps singing below their breath.

Someone was up there with him.

Someone who hadn't answered when he'd called.

He held his breath and listened. Despite the din of the blood whooshing through his ears, the melodic humming became clearer and more distinct.

Female, he thought.

Young, he thought.

A child, he thought.

'Aw… Jesus.'

Though he whispered, the words sounded alarmingly loud, and he ducked like they might echo back and hit him between the eyes.

He was worried whoever was up there might hear him, but the music continued.

A young girl humming.

In a spooky old castle.

On Halloween.

Despite every fibre of his body urging him not to, Tyler swallowed down a breath, clenched his fists to his sides, and crept onwards through the corridor in search of the source of the sound.

## *Chapter 8*

'There. There's one!'

Sinead tapped on the passenger side window of the car, drawing Hamza's attention to the sign they were about to pass. It hung on two short chains from the post above and was jerking around wildly on the wind, so it had taken her a moment to work out what it said.

'VACANCIES.'

Hamza nodded and applied the brakes, bringing the already slow-moving car to a near stop. The wipers were battering back and forth, but the rain was a ceaseless torrent that smeared the world beyond the windscreen.

There was no way they were getting back to Inverness in this. Not until the storm had passed. Neither of them fancied the idea of staying in the car for the next ten-to-eighteen hours, depending on which forecast you believed, so they'd backtracked towards Ullapool, hoping to find a hotel or B&B along the way.

A pair of wrought-iron gates stood open at the bottom of the house's short driveway. Hamza eased the car through what turned out to be quite a tight gap, then pulled up behind an old Ford Mondeo estate.

A sticker in the car's back window read, 'My other vehicle is THE LORD,' which neither made sense nor bode particularly well for what they might find waiting for them inside.

Still, needs must. They'd almost gone off the road twice already. Venturing any further in this weather would be inviting disaster.

Hamza looked across to Sinead and took hold of his door handle. 'Ready?'

Sinead reached for the handle on her side. She nodded. 'Ready.'

That was all the cue they needed. They threw open the doors, being careful to hang onto them this time in case they were ripped away by the wind. Thankfully, the bulk of the red brick house beside them offered some protection, and they were able to race all the way to the front door without too much trouble.

'You ring the bell,' Hamza urged, stepping aside for the DC.

'Why?'

Hamza glanced back at the Mondeo's bumper sticker. 'Just think it'll be better,' he said, wrinkling up his nose.

A gust of wind pushed Sinead forward a step, like the world itself was urging her on. She rang the bell, and a cheerful but largely tuneless jangle of notes rang out from somewhere inside the house.

A moment later, a light came on beyond the frosted glass. Sinead wrapped her arms around herself, pinning her jacket to her sides to try and trap in some body heat.

Over the roar of the wind, she heard voices. A lock was turned. Then another. Then a third.

The door opened, and Sinead found herself staring into empty space, before she recalibrated and looked down to find two wrinkled, white-eyebrowed faces gazing up at her from around the five-foot-three sort of area. One of them was male, the other female, Sinead reckoned, though their advanced years and the fact that only their heads were visible made it hard to be sure.

Their gazes fell on DS Khaled, who was trying to make himself inconspicuous behind Sinead.

'Oh! Goodness! No, no, no. We can't have this!' cried one of the white-haired pair. A woman, definitely. The voice was a dead giveaway.

'No, no! Lord, no! We won't stand for this!' agreed the other… what? Octogenarian? Nonagenarian?

Thinking they were protesting the detectives' arrival, Sinead prepared to launch into a grovelling apology and a request for shelter.

Instead, the door was pulled wide open, revealing the couple in their full stooped and hunched glory.

'We can't have you out there on a day like this,' the woman said. 'In. Come in, come in. Christian, don't just stand there, go and get the kettle on!'

'Yes, dear! On my way, dear! Won't be a mo!'

He set off at a slow shuffle, his slippered feet sliding one at a time across the carpet so he looked like he was trying to ski uphill. A cup of tea would be amazing, Sinead thought, but she wasn't pinning her hopes on it arriving anytime soon.

'Thank you,' Sinead said.

She stepped inside, then coughed, almost choking on a thick floral scent that seemed to be crocheted into every molecule of the air. Jars, bowls, glasses and general scatterings of potpourri covered almost every flat surface in the hallway, from the telephone table near the door, to the foot of the stairs leading up to the rooms above.

Instinctively, Sinead's hand moved to cover her mouth and nose. Thankfully, the old woman didn't seem to notice, much less take offence.

'In you come, in you come,' the lady of the house urged, beckoning Hamza in. She smiled at him, though there was a touch of uncertainty to it, and she shot a slightly puzzled look from him to Sinead and back again. 'Don't be shy. In you get before the rain gets us.'

'Eh, cheers,' Hamza said, stepping into the hall.

The woman pushed the door closed with a bang that rattled all the dried flowers and sticks of cinnamon in their various jars. The detectives watched as she secured all the locks again, before turning to face them.

'Now, let's get a look at you!' she said. There were a pair of glasses hanging from a string around her neck. She placed them on the end of her nose, but then peered at them over the top of the thick plastic rims.

She stood there for what felt like quite a long time, her hands on the hips of her elastic-waisted slacks, studying them both and chirping a series of *uh-huh*s and *mm-hm*s as she looked them up and down.

'Lost, are we?' she finally asked. 'Not a good day for it!'

'Uh, no. It isn't,' Sinead agreed. 'And no, actually, not lost. Not exactly. We're with the police,' she said, hoping this might stand them in good stead with the couple. 'I'm Detective Constable Sinead Bell, this is Detective Sergeant Hamza Khaled.'

'Hello,' Hamza said, fixing on a friendly smile despite a lingering sense of unease.

The look she'd given him hadn't been hostile, but it had been… something. Add in the fact that he could see three different depictions of Christ on the cross just from where he was standing—two paintings and a 3D Plaster of Paris-style sculpture—and he got the feeling he might not be wholly welcome here.

'Oh! Police!' the woman said, and the twinkle in her eye told Sinead she'd made the right call. 'So you're not…? You two aren't…?' She lowered her voice to a whisper, as if discussing some embarrassing medical plight. 'Together?'

Ah. So that was it. Of course, the one B&B they'd found, and it was going to turn out to be run by a couple of old racists.

'No, we're not together. Just work colleagues,' Sinead said. She glanced across at Hamza, and something about his expression made her continue. 'Why? Would it have been a problem, if we were?'

'Sinead, don't,' the DS urged.

'What? I'm just asking.'

'A problem? Would the two of you'—she gestured at them both—'being a couple be a problem?'

'Would it?'

'Sinead?'

'Lord, no!' The woman laughed. It was a light, trilling sort of laugh that belonged to someone a quarter of her age. 'It'd be easier. I was hoping you were married. We've only got the one room, see? The others are being decorated. Still, I'm sure we'll figure something out. Oh, I'm Chrissie, by the way. Lovely to meet you both. *Christian!*'

The suddenness and sheer volume of the shout made the detectives jump.

'Yes, dear?' came the cheerful reply from the kitchen.

'That tea ready, yet?'

'Almost at the kettle, dear!'

Chrissie smiled up at Sinead and Hamza, then removed her glasses from the end of her nose, despite not once having looked through them.

'Well, then. Come on with me through to the dining room. I'll bet you two could get on famously with a nice wee spot of lunch.'

–

Logan turned towards the study door just as a pale-faced Tyler came in and closed it behind him. The DC pressed himself against the wood, his eyes wide, his palms flat against the door like he was barricading it.

'All right?' Tammi-Jo asked. She had her phone out and was taking photos of the body that still sat slumped in the chair.

Logan looked very deliberately at Tyler's empty hands. 'Kettle on, is it?'

'There's a spooky wee girl, boss,' Tyler replied breathlessly.

Logan, who had been dictating his thoughts into the voice recorder on his phone, lowered the mobile to his side.

'Eh?'

'Out there, boss. Along the corridor. There's a spooky wee girl.'

'What the hell do you mean, "there's a spooky wee girl"?'

'I mean there's a girl, boss!' Tyler cried. 'And she's spooky.'

'And wee,' Tammi-Jo added. 'You said she was wee.'

'She *is* wee!' Tyler snapped.

Tammi-Jo shifted her shoulders a little indignantly. 'I know. That's what I'm saying.'

Logan turned to look at her. 'What, have you seen her, too?'

'No. God, no. I'm just repeating what he said, sir. Sort of, you know, summarising. I've not seen any wee girls, spooky or otherwise.'

'Aye, well, all right for some!' Tyler cheeped. 'I have. She was out there singing. And Rab's gone. The constable? He's fucked off somewhere. Or disappeared.'

'Or turned into a spooky wee girl,' Tammi-Jo suggested. 'Which would be a fun twist.' She put her hands on her hips as she thought this through. 'Maybe not for his wife. I don't know if he's married. Is he married? We should find that out. Someone should break the news.'

'What news?' Logan demanded.

Tammi-Jo side-eyed him like he was the one rambling nonsense. 'About the spooky wee girl thing.'

Logan stared at both DCs in disbelief. 'Jesus Christ. What's got into you two? I mean, you're always a bit… weird,' he said, gesturing to Tammi-Jo. 'But Tyler, you're acting like you've just seen a bloody ghost.'

'What if I have, boss? What if that was a ghost? How do you know it wasn't?'

Logan buried his face in one hand, his finger and thumb massaging his temples.

'Because there's no such thing as ghosts, son. It's just your imagination.'

'My imagination, boss? You think I imagined a spooky wee girl skipping along the corridor, singing to herself? You think I can just conjure an actual child out of thin air?'

'Be handy if you could,' Tammi-Jo said.

Tyler blinked. 'Why? Why would that be handy?'

The other DC narrowed her eyes and chewed on her bottom lip, thinking hard.

'Schools?' she eventually said, which felt like a bit of a wild stab in the dark.

Logan shot her a confused look. 'Schools? What the fuck would…? You know what? Forget it.' He shook his head quite sharply, like he might be able to erase the whole conversation from the Etch-a-Sketch of his memory. 'There's nobody there, Tyler. All right? Trust me, son. There's nothing out there.'

There was a knock on the door. The solid rapping of knuckles on wood.

Tyler launched himself into the room, spun on the spot, and flailed both hands in a series of frantic karate chops.

When nothing else happened, he froze like a statue, only one side of his mouth daring to move.

'You were saying, boss?' he whispered.

'Oh, for God's sake.'

Logan crossed to the door, turned the handle, and opened it wide. Constable Rowan stood out in the corridor, his cap tucked under one arm.

'Just letting you know I'm back, sir. Sorry, had to run for a pee. Been holding it for hours and was about to burst.'

Logan looked back over his shoulder, shot Tyler a scathing look, then returned his attention to the PC. 'No bother, son.'

'Did you see her?' Tyler asked, rushing to join the other men at the door.

'See who?' asked Rab.

'The spooky wee girl,' Tyler said, his eyes darting back along the passageway. 'Skipping along and singing to herself. Did you see her?'

Rab frowned. 'Who, Claire?'

Tyler hesitated. 'Claire?'

'Aye. Girl. Yon high.' He held a hand out to just above waist height. 'She's the daughter of the telly man. The psychic fella. Seems like a nice lassie. Why do you ask?'

A long moment passed.

Tyler swallowed and forced a smile. 'No reason,' he said. 'Just wondering.'

He pulled a sharp about-turn, took out his phone, and joined Tammi-Jo in photographing the scene while doing his best to pretend that the last few minutes hadn't happened.

'Right, well, I'll just be out here, sir,' Rab told Logan. 'Shout if you need me for anything.'

'Will do, son. Cheers,' Logan said. He started to shut the door, then opened it again when a thought struck him. 'Actually, there is one thing.'

Rab straightened up. 'Sir?'

'I don't suppose you know if this place has WiFi?'

# *Chapter 9*

It took a good ten minutes for Christian to come through with the tea, carrying it carefully on a patterned tray, the cups rattling noisily in their saucers. Hamza got to his feet to help, but the look of alarm on the old man's face stopped him.

'Whoa there! Best leave me to it, son. I've mastered the takeoff and landing, but I'm not so sure about a mid-air handover.'

Hamza stood back, clearing the way for Christian to bring the tray in for a touchdown on the floral design tablecloth. The old man leaned there for a moment, his shoulders sagging as he let out a sigh of relief.

'Another successful mission flown!' he said, straightening as much as he was able to and saluting the detectives.

'Oh, you silly old fool!' Chrissie giggled, jostling her husband aside so she could deposit two big plates of sandwiches and sausage rolls down next to the tea tray. The sausage rolls were short, pudgy and rustic-looking in a way that suggested they'd been lovingly, if not particularly skilfully, homemade.

The sandwiches were smaller and daintier, with a rainbow of different fillings.

'I cut them into fingers,' Chrissie said with a note of pride. 'It's *fancy*.'

'Looks lovely,' Sinead said.

Chrissie beamed at that. She pointed to a small bunch of grapes garnishing the side of one of the plates and nodded to draw their attention to it.

'Really nice. Thank you,' Hamza said, taking his seat again.

Chrissie shot her husband a wary look, then cleared her throat, being careful to keep her smile in place.

'We, um, we weren't sure about the'—her eyes went to the meatier end of the sandwich spectrum—'ham, and what have you. You know, with you being… If you are, I mean. We don't know. We didn't like to ask. If you were. Are, I mean.'

'Muslim?' Hamza asked.

'Yes. Exactly. We didn't know if you were a… You know, a…'

'Muslim,' Hamza said again. 'And yes, I am.'

The couple shared a look, and Hamza got the impression a whispered debate in the kitchen had just been settled.

'Practising?' Christian asked.

'No. I think I've got the hang of it by this point,' Hamza said.

It wasn't a great joke. It was a literal dad joke, in fact—he'd heard his father using it many times before.

Still, it landed well. Christian let out a great peal of laughter that, like his wife's, seemed meant for someone much younger.

'You've got the hang of it! Brilliant!'

Chrissie joined in with the laughter, and patted the seated DS on the shoulder. 'He's a sharp one, this!' she said to Sinead. 'You sure you don't want to get your hooks into him? It really would make the room situation a whole lot easier!'

Sinead smiled and flashed her wedding ring. 'Not sure my husband or his wife would approve.'

'Ah! No. Well, in that case, we'd best see what we can work out. We're not putting you out in this weather!'

The detectives thanked the couple, then tucked into the tea and sandwiches while they waited for them to shuffle their way out of the room.

'I feel like I owe them an apology,' Hamza mumbled through a half-chewed mouthful of egg, mayonnaise and wholemeal bread. 'I assumed they were going to be mad old racists.'

'In your defence, I think you're probably right on the first two,' Sinead said. 'They seem lovely, though.'

'They do,' the DS confirmed. He took out his phone, checked the screen.

'You got a signal?'

'Yeah. Three bars, not too bad, given where we are, and the weather.'

'Nothing from the boss or Tyler, though?'

Hamza shook his head. He looked across the table at her as he used his tongue to clear a clump of egg from the roof of his mouth.

'Everything all right with you two?'

'What, me and the boss? Fine, aye.'

'You know what I mean. Just, you know, riding with me. Much as I appreciate the save, and much as I enjoy your company, it seemed a bit… out of the blue.'

Sinead plucked a grape from the bunch, turned it over in her hands like it was some rare treasure she was seeing for the first time, then shrugged.

'It's nothing. Just home stuff. Shouldn't be bringing it to work.' She tossed the grape in her mouth, then bit down until it popped. 'We should call HQ. Let the DI know what's happening.'

'Right. But we don't actually know what's happening,' Hamza pointed out, though he unlocked his phone and swiped to the contacts.

'True. But I'd imagine the boss will have been in touch by now,' Sinead reasoned. 'So, maybe base can let us know what's going on.'

'Worth a try,' Hamza agreed. He nudged one of the plates towards her. 'And here, try one of these egg pieces. They're bloody lovely.'

'I'd better not. I wouldn't do that to you,' Sinead said, pushing the plate back. 'Egg plays havoc with my stomach, and the way things are going, we might yet end up sharing a room…'

–

It had been a couple of weeks now since they'd changed the phone system at the Burnett Road Police Station, and it was safe to say that Ben was still having difficulty adapting.

There had been no reason for the change, as far as he'd been able to tell, other than for change's sake itself. The other phones had worked fine. Aye, they'd been a bit past their best, but they'd functioned. All the buttons made sense.

Not like these new contraptions they'd been saddled with. These were all touch screens, and you had to tap and swipe your way through a dozen different menu options just to find the numbers.

It wouldn't have been so bad, had there been a bit of logic applied to the menus. Or, for that matter, had the screen been responsive enough that you didn't have to tap it three or four times before it would so much as acknowledge your existence.

Now, the bloody thing was bleeping at him, a red number one flashing on and off at the top right of the display.

'Christ, what now?' Ben muttered, then he picked up the receiver and said, 'DI Forde,' in his best phone voice.

The bulky box on his desk continued to bleep, the number still flashing away.

'Oh, for…'

He returned the handset to the cradle, waited a moment, then picked it up again.

'Hello? DI—'

The bleeping stopped him going any further. The digit continued to flash. Ben sighed. Where was Hamza when you needed him?

Cradling the handset to his ear, he gave the screen a few experimental pokes.

'Hello? Hello? *Hello*?' he tried after each jab, but all to no avail.

Elsewhere on his desk, his mobile let out a *cha-ching*. Lowering his glasses down from his head, he checked the screen and found a text message from Sinead.

*Press the green button, sir.*

Ben tilted his head back and peered at the message, then at the landline phone's base unit. After a few back and forths, he spotted a little green circle and gave it a reprimanding prod.

'Hello?'

'All right, sir?' Hamza said, and Ben could actually hear the grin on the detective sergeant's face. 'Sinead reckoned you might need a wee hand.'

'Stupid bloody contraption,' Ben said, firing the bulky base unit a dirty look. 'Anyway, I wondered where you'd been. I was getting worried. That you there?'

'Eh, not exactly, sir,' Hamza began. 'Not all of us, anyway.'

Ben leaned back in his chair and listened while Hamza filled him in on what had happened with the bridge, his face paling at the thought of what might have been.

'Sounds like a close call,' he remarked, once the DS had finished.

'Aye, you can say that again, sir. There's been a few close calls up here, to be honest, hence us stopping at this B&B for a bit.'

'Just you be careful,' Ben warned. 'The storm's meant to get worse yet. You bed down until it's safe.'

'Think that's best, sir, aye,' Hamza agreed. 'Roads up here are pretty shocking at the best of times.'

'Lovely part of the world, though,' Ben replied. 'Near the coast. All that fresh air. I'd actually thought about retiring up that way. Moira and I were chatting about it just last week.'

There was near silence from the other end of the line, broken only by a faint electronic echo.

'Retiring, sir?' Hamza finally said.

'Aye. I mean, not yet, obviously. No' right away. But none of us can keep going forever, son. We all have to stop at some point. And maybe that time's approaching. I mean, at my age, it's a wonder they didn't force me out years ago.'

'They know when they're onto a good thing, sir,' Hamza said. 'They wouldn't dare.'

'Oh! Hang on!' Ben said, sitting forward. He squinted down at his mobile, the screen of which had just lit up. 'Jack's calling. Well, it says it's Jack, but I can see my own face. Oh. I'm moving. Why's my face moving?'

'Sounds like it's a video call, sir,' Hamza told him. 'Tap the camera icon.'

Ben regarded the screen, his lips moving as he silently recited the instruction.

'What one's the camera icon?'

'The wee icon that looks like a camera.'

'Got it!'

After a couple of misfires, Ben's finger found the target. The image of himself zoomed up to the top right corner, while the main screen was filled by the face of DCI Logan.

But something wasn't right.

'You're sideways, Jack,' Ben said, raising his voice. 'You're no' the right way. You're sideways.' He brought the receiver back to his ear. 'There's something up with him. He's sideways.'

'Just turn your phone, sir,' Hamza suggested.

'What way?' Ben asked.

Logan responded before the DS had a chance to. 'So I'm the right bloody way up!' he said gruffly.

Ben picked up his mobile, turned it a couple of times, then let out a little cheer of triumph when Logan's picture righted itself on the screen.

'Christ, maybe I'm getting the hang of this stuff, after all!' he declared.

'Was that Hamza you were talking to?' Logan asked. His eyes shifted left and right. 'Is he there?'

'No. He's still up near Ullapool. Weather's too bad. They're stopping in a B&B.'

'You could stick me on speakerphone, sir,' the voice in the DI's ear suggested.

'Let's not get ahead of ourselves, son,' Ben countered. 'I think I've exhausted my technical expertise for one day.'

'Just press the big icon that looks like a speaker. That's all there is to it, sir,' Hamza urged.

Ben looked doubtful, but checked the screen of the desk phone. After a moment, he poked at something he thought looked promising.

'Speak,' he urged.

'Eh, hello,' said Hamza, and his voice rang out from the base unit with impressive clarity.

'Two out of two!' Ben cried. 'Look at me, am I on a bloody roll, or what?'

'Aye, very good,' Logan said. 'You all right, Hamza?'

'We're fine, sir,' the DS confirmed. 'We're holed up in a guest house about halfway between you guys and Ullapool. You made it to the castle all right?'

'Aye. Had to walk it, though. Car's knackered.'

Sinead's voice faltered from the speaker. 'Is Tyler all right?'

'Well, he's in a near-constant state of terror because he's convinced the place is haunted, but other than that, aye. He's ticketyboo. I've left him and DC Swanney photographing the scene. Any word on what's happening with Shona and Palmer?'

Ben winced. 'Eh, aye. Bit of a hold up there. They're still dealing with the RTA. Shona's expecting to be back at the hospital within the next hour or so, not sure how much longer Palmer's going to be.'

'They'll have to be choppered in,' Logan said. 'The road's out here. No way to get to us by land.'

'Aye, I heard about your bridge incident. Hairy stuff,' Ben told him. 'But even with the best will in the world, nobody's going to be flying a helicopter in this.'

Logan sighed, but his face didn't change. Clearly, he'd come to the same conclusion, but had been hoping he was wrong.

'I hate to be the one to break it to you, Jack,' Ben said. 'But, until this storm has buggered off, it looks to me like you three are on your own.'

# *Chapter 10*

A few minutes later, when the call had ended, Logan sat on one of the wide wooden stairs that led down to the mezzanine and further on to the hallway below.

He had sworn a bit at the news that backup wasn't coming anytime soon. Not excessively or anything, just enough to get it out of his system.

Then, they'd all said their goodbyes, and he'd slumped down on the uppermost step, allowing himself just a moment to wallow in his misery.

'Bollocks,' he eventually declared, then he pulled himself back to his feet with the help of the staircase's ancient polished bannister.

'That doesn't sound promising.'

Helen Bach blinked into existence at the bottom of the stairs like some sort of apparition, though Logan soon reasoned that she'd simply walked around the curve of the steps and up onto the mezzanine.

He hadn't heard her approaching, although given that she probably weighed about half a stone, her stealth was hardly surprising.

'Nothing you need to worry about,' Logan assured her. 'I hear there are a few people here in the hotel?'

'Castle,' Helen corrected. 'Daddy had it operating as a hotel a few times, but not lately.'

'Fine. Well, whatever it is, I'm told there's a few people staying at the moment. That right?'

Helen nodded. The movement made the swirl of ice cream that was her hair teeter unsteadily atop her head.

'There are. My brother, who you've had the misfortune of meeting already, the people from that ghastly television show—there are three of them, plus a girl. One of their daughters, I think. There's Francois in the kitchen, of course, Daddy's chef, and I think that's… Oh! And my partner, of course. He's here, too.'

She shrugged, and Logan would've sworn that he heard her bones rattling around below her skin.

Logan caught the look of surprise before it had a chance to spread all the way across his face. Helen had looked peculiar enough downstairs, but here in the dim half-light, looking down on her from above, there was something almost monstrous about her.

'Your partner?'

'Yes. He's here. Somewhere. Donatello Liberace. Not that you asked, but that's his name.'

Logan fought the urge to sigh. 'Of course it is.'

'Have you heard of him?'

'No,' Logan said, and this time he was being completely truthful. 'I can't say that I have.'

'You've clearly lived quite a sheltered life, Detective Chief Inspector,' Helen teased. 'First my father, and now Donatello. I'm starting to wonder if you've got your finger on the pulse.'

Logan was starting to wonder if the woman at the foot of the stairs even had one. He chose not to pass comment.

'Right, well, it'd be good to get everyone together to introduce myself. Can you round them all up?'

'They're not cattle,' Helen replied. There was a pause while she sparked up another cigarette. 'But I'm sure I can track them all down. Shall we say the reading room? Ten minutes?'

'Reading room? What's that, like a library?' Logan asked.

Helen's laughter taunted him from below. 'No. The library is where we keep the books. The reading room is where we read them. The clue's in the name.'

'Right. Aye. Fair enough, my mistake,' the DCI replied. 'The library in my house doubles as both. I should probably get my finger out and build another wing to get that sorted.'

He turned his back on her, stepped up onto the landing of the floor above, then spoke over his shoulder.

'Reading room, then. Ten minutes. Bring everyone.'

–

If anyone asked, Tyler wouldn't be able to tell them why he was holding his breath. He had no idea, and so had no answer to give.

He also wouldn't have been able to tell them what he was thinking, even though he did know the answer to that one. He just daren't voice it out loud.

The stuff in the bowl had to be worth thousands. Tens of thousands. Hundreds, maybe. The cufflinks alone would likely fetch a few grand. Just one of the rings would probably clear off all his debts, and leave a bit of spending money left over to treat Sinead.

He could take her somewhere nice, maybe. A wee package holiday to Spain, or something. Nothing too elaborate.

Or even just a shopping trip, or the like. Since she'd found out about the debts he'd run up, she'd taken complete charge of their finances and forced them both to tighten their belts. There had been no meals out, no takeaways, and he'd even had to cancel his subscription to PlayStation Plus. That had been a kick in the teeth, though mostly because Harris had been using it, and so was being forced to miss out, too.

Yet more suffering that Tyler had caused.

But one of those rings? A pair of those cufflinks? That gaudy big earring lying buried beneath it all? That could fix everything. That could put things right.

Tammi-Jo had left the room. Rab was showing her where the toilet was. Aside from the dead guy with the knife through his skull, Tyler was alone in the study.

'Nah,' he said out loud.

He turned his head, looking away from the bowl, and the jewellery, and the temptation. His body, though, didn't shift, his feet remaining planted to the spot.

Slowly, inch by inch, his head turned back.

The guy was dead. And even if he hadn't been, this stuff had just been dumped in this dish. Practically cast aside. Had he even known it was here? Even in a world where someone hadn't embedded a chef's knife through the middle of his forehead, would he have actually missed any of it?

Tyler shook his head. No. This wasn't him. He wasn't actually going to take any of this stuff. He wouldn't. He couldn't. He didn't have it in him.

He'd just pick one of them up. See how it felt. Get the weight of it.

That was all.

He plucked out a ring. It wasn't as bling or as gaudy as some of the others. Compared to the rest, in fact, it was positively understated. A yellow gold band with three clear sparkling stones set in a rose gold fixing, a big one in the middle, and smaller ones on each side.

It was definitely the quiet man of the bunch. Even someone familiar with the contents of the bowl could look through it for hours and not realise that this one was missing.

'What you doing?'

Tyler dropped the ring like the metal was molten hot and took a hopping step back from the bowl.

'All right, boss?' he replied. 'I was just having a poke about. Looking for stuff. Clues and that.'

Logan stared at him for what felt like an eternity.

'Something you want to tell me, Detective Constable?'

Tyler's heart pounded against the inside of his chest. Each thumping beat felt so violent that he was sure Logan would be able to see the movement through his shirt.

'What do you mean, boss?'

'I mean, like why you're not wearing gloves while you're poking about in there,' Logan snapped. 'This is a crime scene, son, no' a bloody jumble sale.'

Tyler looked down at his bare hands. 'Aw. Shite. Sorry, boss. Took them off so I could use the phone camera. The touchscreen doesn't work well with…'

The rest of the sentence dried into dust at the back of his throat. He dipped his head in apology, and quickly wriggled the rubber gloves back on.

'Sorry, boss. Won't happen again.'

'See that it doesn't,' Logan warned. 'Now, where's Tammi-Jo?'

'Toilet, boss,' Tyler said. 'She'll be back any minute.'

'Good.' Logan glanced around the room, letting his gaze linger on the dead man for a moment. 'Because I've called everyone together downstairs.'

He turned towards the door and beckoned for the DC to follow him.

'I think it's high time we met our suspects.'

–

Sinead picked at the pastry of a sausage roll, and contemplated the phone in her hand.

'I'm going to have to call Berta,' she said, not sounding particularly enthusiastic about it.

Hamza swallowed the sandwich he'd been munching on. It was his fourth egg in a row. They were completely addictive. So much so, in fact, that he'd probably have forgiven Christian and Chrissie even if they had turned out to be bigots.

'Berta? What, Hoon?'

Sinead nodded. 'She's been doing some babysitting. Can't ask my auntie to do it all the time, and have you seen how much childcare costs?'

Hamza blew out his cheeks. 'You don't have to tell me about that. Mental.'

'She's good with them. Great. She seems to really love having them.'

'Aye, but is Hoon not around?' Hamza asked. 'Is that not a bit, you know, risky? With him being a total headcase, I mean.'

'We did worry about that to start with,' Sinead admitted. 'But I think a lot of that's an act. I think he's a big softy, really.'

'Hoon?' Hamza spluttered, almost choking on the final few crumbs of his sarnie. 'Robert Hoon? Our old Super? You think *that man* is a big softy?'

Sinead chuckled. 'Aye. I mean, he hides it well, obviously, and I wouldn't like to get on the wrong side of him.'

'Because he'd put his thumbs through your eyes and rip the rest of you out through your own arse,' Hamza said.

'He's not that bad,' Sinead insisted. 'He's not usually around when we come to pick them up, but Berta says he fusses all over them when we're not there. He's building them a wee playpen thing.' A flicker of doubt crossed her face. 'Although, he does keep calling it a baby jail.'

'Well, good luck with that,' Hamza said. 'When they both get expelled on their first day of school for telling their teacher to ram her homework up her fishy hoop, don't say I didn't warn you.'

'Fair play to them if they do,' Sinead said, laughing along. 'What sort of evil cow gives a kid homework on their first day in Primary One?'

Hamza smiled, conceding the point. He watched as Sinead toyed with her phone, not yet picking it up.

'So, what's the problem?' he asked.

'Nothing. I'm just working up to it. I'm going to have to ask her to hold on to the twins for longer.' She looked over at the dining room window, and at the waterfall cascading down the outside of the pane. 'We're not getting home today, are we?'

'Doubt it,' Hamza conceded.

'I'm going to have to ask her to keep them overnight. And they're proper wee arseholes at night. Like *proper* wee arseholes. I feel bad.'

Hamza's smile grew. 'And obviously you'll miss them both dearly.'

'Oh, aye, obviously that, too,' Sinead said with a smirk. 'Someone's going to have to get more stuff from the house for them, though. I'm not sure I want Hoon rooting around in my fridge for bottles of breast milk.'

'I'm sure he's rooted around in far worse places,' Hamza said. 'It'll be fine. They'll understand. Give them a ring. I need to phone home, anyway, then we can figure out our next steps.'

Before either of them had a chance to call anyone, the door to the dining room opened and Christian and Chrissie set out on the long shuffle across the floor.

'Good news! We've been able to make up another room,' announced Chrissie, in a booming voice that felt like it should've had a, 'Hear ye! Hear ye!' in front of it.

'We were able to clean up one of the rooms the boys have been working on. There's no paint on one of the walls, but if you don't look that direction, you'll be fine,' the old woman continued. 'There's nothing on that side worth looking at, anyway, so you'll no' be missing much. It's up to yourselves who takes it. Either one of you can have it.'

Sinead raised her hand a little, like she was bidding in an auction. 'I'll take it.'

'No, you will not,' Chrissie replied. She shot Hamza a scathing look. 'You're not letting her take a half-finished room, are you?'

'You won't be standing for that, I wouldn't have thought,' Christian agreed.

'Uh, aye. Fine. Don't mind,' Hamza said.

Chrissie's and Christian's faces both lit up with delight. 'I *knew* it,' Chrissie said.

'He's a good lad! He's a fine lad,' Christian chimed in.

'I bet he even foots the bill!' Chrissie concluded.

At that, she produced a small white plastic card reader, and placed it on the table before the detective sergeant.

She stepped back, smiling encouragingly, her wrinkled hands clasping together.

'It's fifty-five each for the night, but we've rounded it down to a hundred,' she said. 'Lunch is on us, and we'll hear no word of argument about it.'

'Oh. We pay up front?' Hamza asked.

'Yes, dear. We've had a few runners over the years, I'm afraid, so we've no choice, have we, Christian?'

'None, dear,' her husband confirmed. 'No choice at all.'

'No bother,' Hamza said. He patted his pockets, then his face fell.

Across the table, a tingle of uneasiness crept up the back of Sinead's neck.

'Argh. My wallet's in the car,' Hamza announced. He met the DC's eye and raised his eyebrows. 'You fancy paying? You can claim it back when we're back at base.'

Chrissie wasn't hanging around for an answer. She stepped in, slid the card reader across the tablecloth so it was in front of Sinead, then stepped back again.

'Eh, aye. Sure. No problem.'

Sinead felt the weight of their looks as she reached into her pocket and took out the slim wallet where she kept her bank card. She inserted it into the machine, checked the total on the little rectangular screen then, after a moment's pause, typed in her PIN.

Chrissie pounced on the device like a selfless soldier on a hand grenade. Her old eyes puckered into narrow slits as she stared at the display, then her face fell when the device let out a disappointed-sounding bleep.

'Declined, dear,' Chrissie announced.

'Oh.' Sinead swallowed. 'Maybe I put in the wrong number.'

'Oh, no, dear. The number was fine. It tells you if the number's wrong. It's just saying "declined".'

Sinead frowned. She couldn't see her own expression, but it felt far too exaggerated and over the top. She blushed at the thought of how pathetic she must look, and studiously avoided Hamza's eye.

'Huh. Weird. Don't know why that's happened. There's definitely money in the account.'

Was there, though? There was definitely *some*. She was sure of that. But was there enough?

They'd been paying down some of the debts. Their finances were all a bit skin-of-the-teeth. She hadn't factored in a surprise hundred quid bill.

'Try again,' Christian urged. 'Give it another go. Sometimes it's a bit funny.'

Sinead could actually feel her ears turning red as the card reader was placed in front of her again. On Chrissie's instruction, she pulled the card out, waited a moment, then slid it back in.

Her finger hovered over the first digit of her PIN, a prickling of shame and embarrassment pinkening her skin.

'Actually, wait,' Hamza said, rising from his chair. He tapped himself on the forehead like he'd just remembered something. 'It'll be better if I do it. For claiming back, I mean. It'll be easier.'

Sinead didn't look at him. She couldn't. It made no difference to the reimbursement process whether a DS or a DC was the one making the claim.

He knew, or at least suspected, the truth.

'That's more like it! That's a proper gentleman!' Chrissie said, whipping Sinead's card out of the reader and handing it back. 'But you stick your jacket on before you go out to that car. I'm not having you catching your death!'

# *Chapter 11*

Logan left Constable Rowan guarding the door to the study, and led Tammi-Jo and Tyler down to the hallway through which they'd originally entered. Despite their weight, the front doors rattled in their frame, Storm Agatha continuing her frenzied assault on the castle and the country at large.

All around the hall, the glassy eyes of dead animals stared stoically ahead.

'Right, they're in the reading room, apparently,' Logan said. 'Which, by the sounds of it, is literally a room just for reading in.'

'That's too many rooms, boss,' Tyler said. 'If you've got a room just for reading in, you've got too many rooms.'

'There's sixty-six bedrooms,' Tammi-Jo said. 'I read it on a leaflet in the bathroom, from when they used to do tours. *Ghost tours*,' she added, then she waggled her fingers in Tyler's direction and added a, 'Woo!' for dramatic effect.

'Sixty-six?' Tyler gasped. 'That's nearly six-six-six. That's nearly the number of the beast.'

'Och, my arse it is,' Logan shot back. 'It's six hundred numbers away from it.'

'Aye, but it could be on the same street, boss.'

'The neighbour of the beast,' Tammi-Jo said.

'It'd have to be a hell of a long street. It wouldn't even be the same bloody postcode.' The DCI waved a hand, signalling the argument was over just as they reached the bottom of the staircase. 'Anyway. Question. Either of you two heard of some guy called Donatello?'

'Aye, boss. Why?'

'Who is he?'

Tyler frowned, like he was sensing a trick question. 'He's one of the ninja turtles, boss. The purple one.'

'I thought they were all green?' Tammi-Jo said.

'The one with the purple mask, I mean.'

'Ah. Gotcha.'

'For fu…' Logan pinched the bridge of his nose, sighed, then tried again. 'No. He's no' a turtle. He's an artist. Not the actual proper one, though, obviously. He's dead. He's a modern artist, or in a band, or… I don't know. He's here, anyway. He's the daughter's other half. Thought you might have a bit of background for me, but forget it, I shouldn't have asked. We'll wing it and see what happens.'

'You all right, boss?' Tyler asked, eyeing the DCI warily.

'Fine, why?'

'You just seem a bit on edge. More so than usual, I mean. There something wrong?'

Logan thought back to the call he'd received that morning, but then quickly jumped back to the present.

'It's just the council estate boy coming out in me,' he said. 'Rich bastards like this lot make me uneasy.'

'Um, aye. But you've seemed a bit out of sorts all morning, boss.'

Logan tutted. 'Well, maybe it was driving through a bloody hurricane, having a bridge collapse out from under me, then having to trudge half a mile in the rain.'

This still didn't appear enough to convince Tyler, but the DC had the good sense not to push it further.

Logan turned away and looked around the hallway. There were at least half a dozen doors leading off from it in various directions. Holes drilled in the stone beside some of them suggested there had once been signs directing people where to go, but they'd all been removed.

'Now, do either of you two have any idea where people usually keep their reading rooms?'

The castle's reading room was bloody nonsense.

That was how Logan described it below his breath when he opened the door to reveal a roughly forty-by-thirty-foot room that contained nothing but two leather couches, a couple of antique armchairs, an imposing fireplace, and a towering portrait of some mad-looking auld fella on what was presumably meant to be a horse.

Logan had heard that horses were notoriously difficult to draw, but he hadn't realised they were quite *that* difficult.

He could only assume that the artist responsible had never actually set eyes on a horse before, and had only heard rumour of them in passing. With its long neck and rounded head, the thing looked less like a mighty stallion than it did a worm with legs.

If he ever saw a horse like that in real life, Logan wouldn't hesitate to put it down. Preferably with napalm.

'Jesus Christ, what is that?' Tyler whispered.

At first, Logan thought he was referring to the horse, then he followed the DC's gaze and caught sight of one of the people waiting in the centre of the room. All thoughts of the stallion's wormishness were immediately forgotten.

'Oh, for Christ's sake,' he muttered below his breath.

The detectives' footsteps echoed on the polished wooden floor as they made their way over to the knot of people gathered in the seating area. They were a motley-looking crew, and the fact that the room was practically ringing with silence suggested that none of them were particularly on speaking terms.

They all sat or stood around, saying nothing while Logan led Tyler and Tammi-Jo across all the wasted floor space. The only exception was the child attempting to do a handstand up in the far corner, who muttered words of encouragement to herself as she tried and tried again. Tyler's 'spooky wee girl', presumably.

Taggart stood beside her, watching on, his whole back end wagging with delight. He glanced over at the sound of Logan's approach, but the handstand action was clearly too good to miss.

That suited Logan just fine. Maintaining authority at a time like this was important, and it would be made all the more difficult by an excitable mongrel trying to climb its way up him to lick his face.

Although he reckoned he had the measure of most of them—one in particular—even before he'd joined them on yet another of the castle's ludicrously large rugs, Logan tried to remain open-minded as he introduced himself and the two detective constables, and invited all those assembled to do the same.

He looked to Helen and Monty Jr, fully expecting one of them to do the honours. Instead, the first person to speak was a slightly dishevelled man in his early fifties, who had laid claim to one of the armchairs and was currently puffing away on a large cigar.

'I'm sure I don't need to introduce myself,' the man crowed. There was a wee waft of Belfast to his accent, but he'd rounded it off and filed down the serial numbers, presumably for the sake of his TV career.

Logan had seen him a couple of times while Shona had been channel-surfing on the couch beside him. The name escaped him, though.

'Oh, you'd be surprised, darling,' Helen drawled. 'The detective chief inspector here doesn't appear to know *anyone* of relevance. Do you, Mr Logan?'

'Depends how you define relevance,' Logan replied, barely glancing at her. 'You're the ghost man, aren't you? The mind reader.'

The man in the armchair snorted. 'I don't read minds.'

'Probably just as well,' Logan muttered.

'I'm a spiritualist medium. I commune with those beyond the veil.'

Logan fought the urge to sigh. It was becoming a bit of a habit on this case, despite the fact the investigation had barely started. Something about these people brought it out in him, and a glance around the group told him there was worse to come than a TV ghost hunter.

'Do you?' the DCI asked.

'No, course I bloody don't! There's no such thing as ghosts. It's all woo-woo and nonsense for the idiots watching at home.'

'Eh, I'd rather you didn't say that out loud, Marcus,' a smaller man standing a few feet behind him objected. 'There's a certain illusion we want to maintain.'

'Oh, fuck off, Gavin. None of this lot gives a shit. And if they believed any of that bollocks, where would I be then, eh? They'd be wanting me to give the dead man upstairs a quick knock to see if he could shed any light on the whole sorry mess.'

'We wouldn't want that,' Logan assured him.

'Yes, you say that now, but in a few hours, when you're at your wits' end, you'd come calling.'

Logan shook his head. 'I really wouldn't.'

'You say that, but we both know the truth. Anyway...' He swapped the cigar to his left hand, heaved himself forward a few inches, and extended the now freed-up right hand. 'Marcus Doyle, star, creator and executive producer of *Ghost Spotters*.'

Logan regarded the hand in silence for a while, then begrudgingly gave it a shake. 'Pleasure,' he lied.

'I'm Gavin. Gavin Hall,' the man lurking behind the chair said. His movements were jerky and rabbit-like, and gave the impression that he was someone who lived on his nerves. 'I'm the show's producer and cameraman.'

'Isn't that normally two jobs?' Tammi-Jo asked.

Gavin smiled at her. It looked like an apology. 'It's a very cheap show.'

'It's a very *cost-effective* show, is what he means,' Marcus corrected.

Gavin's smile remained defiant. 'Marcus forgets that I do all the budgeting, so...'

The man in the chair turned and shot the producer a dead-eyed glare. 'And Gavin forgets that producers are ten a penny, and that I have full control over the hiring and firing on the show, so maybe he should consider his words a bit more carefully before biting the hand that feeds him.'

'And Marcus forgets that I handle all the social media accounts and online advertising for the show, and I could drop him right in the shit if I left unexpectedly.'

'Are you threatening me? Was that a threat?' Marcus demanded.

'No. Not threatening. Just reminding you,' Gavin said.

The awkwardness of the moment was diffused by a perky twenty-something with a bob of red hair, a pair of baggy jeans and a T-shirt bearing the logo of a heavy metal band that had broken up a good decade or more before she was born.

'Uh, hi. Hello! Hi!'

She had been sitting at the corner of one of the couches, as far from Marcus as it was possible to be, but jumped up and inserted herself between Logan and the two TV men.

'Yvonne Meadows. From *Ghost Spotters*.' She brushed a strand of hair back over her ear, and pulled a face like she was embarrassed to even mention the next part. 'And *Sasha's Happy House* on CBBC. Which, you know, ugh, embarrassing'—she rolled her eyes—'I won a few awards for. You probably haven't heard of it.'

'No,' Logan confirmed.

The word was like a pinprick to the ego that had been rapidly inflating before everyone's eyes.

'No. Well, you probably don't have young kids in the house,' she reasoned. 'At your age, I mean. But it was very successful and well-known within its demographic. Three series, fifty-two episodes each. You sure you haven't...?'

'No,' Logan said again.

'I've seen it,' Tyler said. 'It had that hippo thing in it, didn't it?'

'Yes! That's it!'

'Was she Sasha?' Tyler asked.

'What? No. I'm Sasha.'

Tammi-Jo cut in. 'I thought you said you were Yvonne?'

The woman in the 90s jeans blinked. 'No, I am. Sasha was just—'

'The character. Got it,' Tammi-Jo said. She had her notebook open, her pen hovering over the page. 'So… what was the hippo called?'

Logan didn't turn to look at her, and instead just raised a hand. 'Don't write any of that down,' he urged, then he nodded to Yvonne, and she scurried back to her seat.

The man beside her was going to be hard work. Logan skipped over him, and settled on the woman sitting on his right.

'Helen Bach. We've already had the pleasure,' Logan said.

'Such a fun name,' Tammi-Jo remarked.

'You're Montgomery's daughter. Correct?' the DCI asked.

'The one and only.'

Logan glanced from her to her brother on the opposite couch. 'I must say, neither of you two strikes me as being particularly upset.'

'Ha! Shows what you know!' Monty Jr snapped.

Helen waved her cigarette holder around in a vaguely dismissive sort of motion. 'Daddy didn't encourage displays of emotion. He found them crass and vulgar. If he thought we were down here openly shedding tears, he'd be turning in his grave.'

'Or making plans to, anyway!' The man on her left sniggered and looked around at the rest of the group like he was expecting a round of applause, or at the very least a congratulatory high-five. 'You know, since he's not in the grave yet?'

The comment was completely ignored. Logan took some satisfaction from that. It was clear the man was going to be utterly insufferable, but at least everyone else had already worked that out for themselves.

'Of course, even if it were not for that,' Helen continued, 'I can't imagine there'd be any great wailing or gnashing of teeth over the old bastard's demise. Not all fathers are quite so *free* when it comes to letting their children do what they like as Mr Doyle here.'

'What's that supposed to mean?' Marcus demanded.

At the back of the hall, Taggart spun in an excited circle as the girl finally achieved a full handstand against the wall.

'Oh, don't get me wrong, I think it's wonderful. It's so refreshing,' Helen trilled with a wave of her cigarette holder. 'God forbid, if I ever have children, I'll let them run riot and make annoying little shits of themselves, too.' She beamed with a calculated innocence, and looked up at the towering Logan. 'Daddy, on the other hand, was an absolute tyrant. Dreadfully cold and distant. Cruel, even, if you can imagine such a father as that.'

Logan could. He didn't even have to try.

'Papa was a good man!' Monty Jr insisted.

'Oh, please! You don't need to suck up to him now. He's gone. He's out of the picture! He is no more!'

Saying that she didn't seem particularly upset was a massive understatement, Logan now realised. She was practically basking in her father's death, savouring the freedom of no longer having him around, even while he slowly decomposed two floors above.

There were just two other people in the room, and neither one struck Logan as the chef, Francois, that Helen had mentioned earlier.

He still couldn't bring himself to address the man sitting between Helen and Yvonne, so he turned instead to the woman sitting in the other armchair, dabbing at her eyes with a crumpled-up bundle of tear-soaked tissue.

After quickly running back over the list of names Helen had given him on the stairs, he concluded that either this one had been left off, or 'Francois' was more gender-neutral than he thought.

She didn't look like a chef, though. In fact, she didn't even look like someone who particularly enjoyed a good meal. The woman wasn't as skeletal as Helen—Logan suspected there were very few people on earth, or on this side of it, at least, who would be—but she clearly watched her weight closely. The velour jogging outfit and matching wristbands suggested she'd either recently been working out, or had been on her way too.

Bit odd for a woman whose husband had just been murdered.

At a guess, Logan put her somewhere in her mid-forties. She must've been beautiful once, he thought, though her attempts to hang onto her youth through repeated rounds of cosmetic surgery had left her looking like a living caricature.

Aside from the lack of meat on her bones, there was no physical similarity between her and Helen, and she bore even less of a resemblance to Monty Jr. Even if the age gap—or relative lack of one—hadn't been a giveaway, it was clear that this wasn't the children's mother.

Whoever she was, she seemed to be the only one even remotely put out by the death of Montgomery McQuarrie senior.

'Sorry for your loss…' Logan said, leaving the sentence hanging and giving the woman an encouraging nod.

'Thank you, kindly,' she said through a volley of snivelling sobs. 'That's very sweet of you to say.'

She sounded American. Somewhere in the south, Logan thought, though his knowledge of US accents pretty much ended there. Hers was a strong one, though, without a lot of subtlety of nuance.

'Sorry, I didn't catch your name,' Logan said.

'Oh, where are my manners? I'm Krystal. Krystal McQuarrie.' She brought her tissue to her mouth, then squeaked out the next few words. 'I'm Monty's late wife.'

The tut and the rolling of eyes from Helen did not go unnoticed by Logan.

'He was your late husband, you mean,' the DCI corrected.

Krystal sniffed a few times, her razor-thin eyebrows lowering in the middle. 'Beg your pardon?'

'You're not his late wife. He's your late husband,' Logan explained.

The look he got back was largely blank.

'Oh, for the love of… You're not dead, Krystal. He is,' Helen said.

'I know that!' Krystal cried, staring daggers at the other woman. 'Don't you think I know that? I know he's dead! I saw him with my own eyes. I held him with my own hands!'

'I'd rather you hadn't done that,' Logan said. 'You may have compromised the scene.'

'They all did!' Krystal said, suddenly on the defensive. 'Not just me, everyone. They were all in there! Trampling around the place, tugging and pulling on that knife like it was the pump of a milk wagon! I was the only one to even think to check for a pulse.'

'He had a knife through his skull, sweetheart,' Marcus pointed out. 'We felt the lack of pulse was pretty much a given at that point.'

Even Tyler appeared taken aback by the level of sheer stupidity on display.

'So, what?' he began. 'You *all* went into the room and messed with the body?'

'I wouldn't say any of us "messed with it",' Monty Jr protested. 'It isn't as if we molested him or anything, if that's what you're getting at.'

That definitely wasn't what Tyler had been getting at, though he was relieved to hear it all the same.

'But you all went into the room? You all touched the body?'

From behind Marcus's chair, the producer, Gavin, raised his eyebrows and nodded solemnly. 'They did. Everyone. I tried to stop them.'

Marcus harrumphed in his chair. 'You should've gone back for the camera and started bloody filming, like I told you.'

Gavin ignored him. 'By the time we heard the screaming and figured out where it was coming from, everyone else was in the room. I told them they were making things worse, but, well…' He swept an accusing look across the rest of the group. 'They didn't really listen.'

'Our father had just died!' Monty protested.

'Oh, like you even gave two hoots about that, Montgomery McQuarrie Junior!' Krystal cried. She aimed the next part at the room in general. 'Most of y'all couldn't wait to get rid of him. Weren't one of you who loved him like I did!'

'What, for his money?' Helen drawled. 'No, I'm pretty sure we all loved him like that.'

'How *dare* you?' Krystal shrieked. Despite all her surgeon's hard work, her face crumpled up like her tissue. She wiped frantically at her disconcertingly symmetrical nose. 'I loved that man with all my heart, and now he's gone. Taken from me by someone right here in this room!'

Logan picked up on the comment immediately. 'What makes you say that?' he asked. 'Why do you think it was someone in this room?'

'Why, because there's nobody else here,' Krystal said. 'Ain't nobody come or gone since last night, sugar.'

'How do you know?'

'Well, we know nobody has left,' Helen said, indicating the others with a wave of a bony hand. 'And the doors were all locked, so nobody could get in.'

'And the camera,' added Yvonne. 'On the van.'

'Camera?' Logan asked, and Yvonne deferred to Gavin with a shrug and a tilt of her head.

The producer cleared his throat. 'The gear in the van, it's expensive, so we've got a sentry cam watching to make sure nobody breaks in. It has quite a wide field of view that takes in the front of the castle, and around one side. Yvonne and I went out and checked it earlier.'

'And? See anything?' Logan asked.

'Just a lot of rain,' Gavin said. 'I've downloaded it to my phone, if you want to go through it yourself.'

Logan nodded. 'Aye. That'd be useful. Thanks.' He looked around the room again, then settled on Helen. 'You said there was a chef. Francois?'

'Oh! Yes!' Helen's neck seemed to stretch a little as she turned and took the place in. 'He's not here.' She shot an accusing look at her stepmother. 'Krystal, you were supposed to get him.'

'I told him. I did,' the American insisted. 'He said he had to prepare vegetables.'

'And that's more important, is it?' Helen demanded. 'Preparing vegetables. That's more important than this?'

'What do you want me to say? I told him. I told him to come!'

'It's fine. I'll go find him shortly,' Logan said.

He groaned then. There was no putting it off any longer.

With a reluctance that was clear for all to see, Logan turned his attention at last to the man sitting between Helen and Yvonne.

'And you must be Donatello,' the DCI intoned.

The man on the couch perked up at the mention of his name, his eyes widening to better reveal his shining silver irises.

His face was a gallery of tribal tattoos and Chinese symbols that spread from one cheek to the other, covering his mouth like a grin. A pair of eyes had been tattooed onto his cheeks, right below the real ones, though these didn't share the same artificial colour of his actual irises, and were a natural looking brown rather than an alien silver.

Across the bridge of his nose and up onto his forehead he'd somehow affixed a series of stubby golden spikes that reminded Logan of a dinosaur he couldn't recall the name of. He was fairly sure, though, that it wasn't one of the more impressive ones.

What the DCI had initially thought was a necklace of padlocks around the man's neck turned out, upon closer inspection, to be a series of hoops embedded into the flesh of his throat and the underside of his chin, from which the locks were hanging. They dragged down on the skin, pulling his mouth into a perpetual petulant frown.

The top of his head, for reasons Logan wouldn't like to contemplate, let alone attempt to explain, was covered in plastic bees. They were stuck on like hair, all swarming together in untidy rows, their transparent wings pointing in all different directions.

Throw in the baggy blue parachute pants, the frilly cream shirt, the Wonder Woman-style gold wristbands, and the pink high heels and he was, Logan reckoned, the most tiresome, attention-seeking bastard he'd ever had the misfortune of sharing the same air with.

'Guilty,' Donatello said. 'Donatello Liberace. *The* Donatello Liberace.' He put an arm around Helen's neck and tried to pull her in for a hug. She did not look particularly impressed by it. 'Because there's only one of me, right, babes?'

Christ. He was from Essex. And here Logan had been thinking the man couldn't get any worse.

'Well. That's some small mercy,' Logan remarked, but the chaos of the man's face made it hard to tell if he'd picked up on the dig.

'He hasn't heard of you,' Helen said, smirking up at the DCI.

'You what? You're joking? Biffin's Bridge?'

Logan raised an eyebrow. 'Sorry?'

'My band. You must've heard of that, right? "Deaf Girl Drum Dream"? "A Hundred Down on the Down Duck Down"?'

'What are you…? You're just saying words,' Logan said. 'None of that means anything.'

'They're songs, mate! They're songs, ain't they? They're hits.'

Monty Jr responded with all the venom that Logan would've very much liked to. 'No. They're not hits. Hits are successful. They *hit* the top of the charts. That's why they're called hits,' he hissed, jerking forward on the couch.

'Yeah. Yours sound more like *shits*, son,' Marcus chimed in, and he looked quite pleased by the gag. 'I mean, don't get me wrong, I've never heard them, and I hope to Christ I never do, but yes. Agreed with your man there. They sound bloody awful.'

'Well, shows what you fucking know, granddad,' Donatello shot back.

'I know not to stand behind you at an airport metal detector,' Marcus replied. 'I'd be there all week.'

'No need to worry about that. You won't find me at no airport. Flying kills the planet. That's why I don't go on planes.'

'Well, that and your lifetime ban from EasyJet,' Helen said. She smiled sweetly at him, like she'd just done him a favour. 'It's mostly that, actually. Right?'

Donatello shifted awkwardly in his seat, his eyes flitting from face to face, his downturned mouth dragging itself upwards at the edges. Though he was trying to portray himself as the big man in the room, his and Helen's relationship dynamic was starting to paint a very different picture.

'Yeah, babes,' he conceded. 'And that, too, yeah, yeah. I just don't do planes.'

'Like B. A.,' Tammi-Jo said.

All the little spikes on Donatello's forehead knitted together in confusion. 'British Airways?'

DC Swanney shook her head. 'No. B. A. Baracus. From *The A-Team*. He didn't go on no planes, either, *sucka*!'

She glanced around at all the blank looks, then conceded that it probably wasn't a particularly relevant point, before urging Logan to continue.

'We're in a bit of an unusual situation here,' the DCI said, addressing the room at large. 'Normally, in a situation like this, we'd already have a forensics team working at the scene, and a pathologist confirming the time and cause of death.'

'Cause is pretty self-explanatory,' Marcus said.

'Maybe. Aye. But maybe not. We'll be keeping an open mind,' Logan continued. 'We're going to want to talk to all of you, find out what you know, what you heard, and what you saw.'

Everyone around the seating area looked at one another, then they all started talking at once, rushing to be the one to get their side of the story out first.

'Not yet!' Logan bellowed, raising his hands for silence. 'Not out here. We'll talk to you one at a time in private. Is there a room we can use?'

'Take your pick,' Helen said, gesturing at the castle around them.

'Thank you. We'll need a place to do interviews, and somewhere we can set up as a hub.'

'Like I said, Detective Chief Inspector,' the woman with the Mr Whippy hair replied, 'you have the run of the place. Take your pick. Far be it from me to stand in the way of justice being done.'

On the opposite couch, her brother had looked like he was about to object to not being consulted, but the last sentence shut him up. Arguing with that point would only make him look suspicious.

Logan nodded. 'I appreciate that. Before we get started, let me just say this. If Mrs McQuarrie is right and the killer is here, we'll find them. I give you my word on that. So, if anyone would like to save us all a bit of bother and own up now…?'

All three detectives waited in silence. Nobody raised a hand.

'Bugger it. It was worth a try.' Logan clapped his hands together. The sound echoed all the way to the far end of the needlessly large room. 'Right, nobody leaves this building until I say so,' he instructed, then he turned and set off towards the door. 'Detective Constables, you two are with me.'

## *Chapter 12*

Logan's phone began to buzz almost the second the detectives stepped back into the hallway. The display looked different, and it took him a moment to realise the call coming through was a *FaceTime* from Shona.

'Eh, you two see if you can find somewhere for us to set up, then put a call into base. Give them the details of that lot in there, and get them to start digging,' he told the DCs as he headed for the stairs. 'I'm going to take this.'

He waited until he was past the mezzanine level and safely out of earshot, then tapped the icon to answer the call.

'All right, gorgeous?' he said, keeping his voice low for fear that anyone might hear him. Public displays of affection were not generally his thing, but something about being trapped in this castle, stranded miles away from home in a storm, made him break the habit of a lifetime.

He'd picked the wrong day for it.

On-screen, the ruddy red face of the SOCO, Geoff Palmer, lit up with glee.

'Not bad, sweetheart!' Palmer blew a kiss to the camera. 'How about you?'

Shona ducked into view from behind the phone, so part of her face appeared upside down at the top of the screen.

'Jack! Hello! There you are! I've got Geoff here.'

'So I see,' Logan said, his heart sinking into his stomach.

Palmer was still grinning. It wasn't even a particularly funny incident, but Geoff would be spinning the anecdote for months to come, milking every last drop of humour from it. Hopefully, he'd save it to use as material for his stand-up gigs, since no bugger ever went to them.

'Detective Superintendent Mitchell's been filling us in,' Shona said. She walked around from behind the camera and Palmer shuffled aside just a fraction so that she had no choice but to sit shoulder-to-shoulder with him. 'The helicopters are grounded. They reckon they'll be down for another eight to ten hours at least, maybe well into tomorrow, depending on what Agatha decides to get up to.'

'Bollocks,' Logan muttered. It wasn't unexpected, but still not what he'd hoped to hear.

'Maybe if someone hadn't collapsed a bridge…' Palmer said. He was still grinning like a madman, as if this whole thing was some victory he'd won over the DCI.

'I didn't collapse a bridge, Geoff. A bridge collapsed.'

'I've been thinking you've been putting on the weight, but I didn't like to say,' the Scene of Crime man continued. 'Maybe I should've mentioned something.'

Logan reached the second floor, and set off along the corridor towards Montgomery McQuarrie's study. Shona said something, but her image jerked around and her voice came as a sputtering of stuttered syllables.

'Hello?' Logan said, raising the phone a little in search of a stronger signal. 'You hearing me.'

'Aye, we've got you,' Shona said.

'You broke up for a bit,' Logan told her.

He proceeded more carefully along the corridor, keeping the phone held up. Up ahead, Constable Rowan tapped his cap and stepped aside, getting out of the DCI's way.

'The image quality's not exactly top-notch,' Shona said. 'You've gone a bit sort of pixelly.'

'Is that not just his normal face?' Palmer asked, and he looked delighted by what he clearly considered another absolute zinger.

'I'm on the WiFi,' Logan explained. 'But the signal's not great.'

'No real surprise. The walls'll be too thick for full, proper penetration,' Palmer reasoned.

On-screen, Shona visibly recoiled, then shuffled a couple of inches away from the man beside her.

'Jesus, Geoff,' she muttered.

'What? Oh! Not like that! God Almighty!' Palmer laughed, shook his head, then jerked a thumb in the pathologist's direction. 'Dirty mind this one, eh, Jack? Haha! You're a lucky man!'

His laughter continued for a few more moments, sounding increasingly hollow until it fell away into silence.

'You're a lucky man,' he said again, a little more subdued this time.

The uncomfortable silence that followed was eventually broken by Shona slapping her hands on her knees and declaring, 'Aaanyway! Are we able to get a look inside?'

'Aye. Hang on.'

Logan searched the screen for the button that would switch to one of the phone's rear-facing cameras. The close-up of his face was replaced by a view of the study door.

'That better?'

'Much,' Palmer said. 'We don't have to look at your ugly mug! Eh? Eh?'

The SOCO elbowed Shona, encouraging her to join in with his laughter. When she didn't, he shook his head and let out an exaggerated sigh.

'I'm wasted on you lot.'

Logan watched as, on-screen, both Shona and Palmer looked up at someone off-camera. Shona beamed and tucked a strand of hair behind her ear, while Palmer bit his lip, quietly seething.

A moment later, a strikingly handsome young man entered the shot, placed a cup of tea in front of each of them, then slipped the pathologist a foil-wrapped biscuit and winked.

He turned just long enough to flash a wave and a Hollywood smile at the camera, then he retreated out of frame again.

It had to be Neville, Shona's new assistant, Logan realised. She'd said he was a good-looking lad, but she hadn't gone into detail. Or rather, she had gone into detail, but Logan had swiftly changed the subject.

Jesus Christ, though, the guy was in a whole other league. He could be a model. He *should* be a model.

Logan would have to have a word with him and suggest he should at least go and try. Shona hadn't even wanted an assistant, anyway. She'd be glad to be rid of him.

Although, she hadn't been complaining nearly as much of late…

'Here, how come you got a Kit-Kat?' Palmer demanded, spying the biscuit in Shona's hand. 'Why didn't I get one?'

'This is the last one,' the pathologist explained. 'Sorry.'

'It's got two fingers. You can break me one off!'

'I can't,' Shona said, her face scrunching up apologetically.

'Why not?'

She looked down at the Kit-Kat, then back at Palmer. 'I don't want to.'

Logan cleared his throat, drawing their attention. 'Right, no saying how long this signal's going to last. We all paying attention?'

'Yes! Absolutely!' Shona said. She sat her biscuit down on her right, out of Palmer's reach, then took a big slurp of her tea. 'Crack on.'

Logan took a moment to show them the door first. The wood was splintered where the handle area met the frame, and part of the frame itself had been sheared away into long, dagger-like spikes.

'What happened there?' Palmer asked, leaning in so his pudgy red face took up most of Logan's screen. 'Axe?'

'Aye. Medieval battleaxe, apparently,' Logan confirmed.

'Have you seen it?'

Logan shot the constable an enquiring look. Rab shook his head.

'No, actually. That's a point. We haven't clocked it yet.'

Palmer's eyes darted around in a full roll. 'Well, you'll probably want to track that down. Once you do, send me photos of the door and the blade, and we'll see if it matches. Can you manage that, aye?'

Logan swallowed back the first four or five responses that came to mind. How they'd opened the door wasn't particularly relevant, since the victim was already dead by then.

Still, better to build as complete a picture as possible.

'I'll get my best man on it, Geoff,' he said, then he opened the door to reveal the study beyond, and the dead man still sitting in his chair.

'Ah, that's more like it!' Shona said. She side-eyed the man beside her. 'Sorry, that came out sounding a bit more enthusiastic than it was meant to. That'll be our victim, then.'

Logan stepped into the room, keeping the phone camera fixed on the dead man in the chair.

'Aye, this is him. Montgomery McQuarrie. Self-made billionaire, apparently,' Logan said, in a tone that suggested he didn't believe there was really any such thing.

'OK, well, cause of death, big old knife through the forehead,' Shona declared. She slapped a hand on her knee again. Just the one this time, as she was still holding her mug of tea. 'Boom! Done. Next?'

'You think?' Logan said. 'I mean, aye, it's the obvious one, but there isn't much blood, so I wasn't sure if he was already dead before it happened.'

Shona took a sip of her tea. 'Nah. Not a lot of arterial action going on up that neck of the woods, and the hilt's going to act like a plug. It'll be a tricky auld fella to get out.'

'Aye. Suction.'

Palmer practically elbowed the pathologist aside so he could lean into the camera. 'Now who's got the dirty mind? Eh?'

Logan and Shona sighed in stereo.

'Jesus, Geoff, can you try being professional for two bloody minutes?' the DCI asked. 'Is that really too much to expect?'

Palmer opened his mouth to make some other comment, then thought better of it and sat back. 'I mean it,' he mumbled. 'Absolutely wasted.'

'As I was saying,' Shona continued, speaking over him. 'Barring any other injuries I'm not seeing, I'd say the cause of death was the obvious one.'

'I'm reckoning from the angle of entry that he was sitting down,' Logan said, advancing further into the room.

'Yeah, but looking up,' Shona agreed. 'Maybe talking to someone. Looking at the attacker, anyway.'

Palmer crossed his legs, rested an elbow on his knee, and placed a finger on his mouth, like a philosopher about to impart some great words of wisdom.

'The desk would be in the way,' he said. 'Unless the killer's nine feet tall, he wouldn't be able to reach.'

Logan lowered the camera so it revealed the victim's feet. They had rolled onto their sides, so the bottom of his legs were angled out to his left.

'It's a swivel chair,' Logan said. 'I reckon he was facing the other way, then either the momentum from the blow, or maybe the killer themselves, turned him around.'

Palmer shifted around on the bench, like his underwear was suddenly full of wee biting insects. 'Maybe,' he conceded. 'Could be that.'

'Might even have been the family that moved him,' Logan continued, bringing the phone back up again so the dead man's face filled the screen. His eyes were open, and he'd been dead long enough now that closing them wasn't going to be an option.

Palmer's groan was a tinny-sounding thing over the phone's speakers. 'God. Have they messed with the scene?'

'Trampled all over it,' Logan confirmed. 'A whole crowd of them. They took turns trying to pull out the bloody knife, too, would you believe?'

'Why?' Shona wondered. 'Did they think it'd magically bring him back to life or something?'

Logan shrugged. 'Not sure. I get the impression most of them wouldn't want to bring him back, even if they could.'

'Do we have a time of death for him?' Shona asked.

'We have a time he was last seen alive,' Logan replied. 'Last night. Roughly quarter past ten. I was hoping you could help place the actual time he was killed.'

'From a hundred miles away, on a toty wee screen, with a dodgy internet connection?' Shona asked.

She took another slurp of her tea, then unwrapped her Kit-Kat and took a big bite out of both fingers, largely just to spite the Scene of Crime man sitting beside her.

'Sure, I always did like a challenge!'

# *Chapter 13*

Tyler sidled along yet another corridor, his eyes scanning the shadows that filled the occasional recessed doorways and alcoves.

They'd passed two different suits of armour in the last few minutes, and he'd been convinced both times that they were going to make a grab for him as he'd hurried by.

He was pretty sure that he'd hidden his suspicions, though, and that the way he'd given each suit as wide a berth as possible had appeared perfectly natural and nonchalant.

He knew, deep down, that nothing was going to happen. The place wasn't *actually* haunted. The logical part of his brain understood that full well.

Unfortunately, the logical part of his brain had always been something of a minority stakeholder, and the rest of it was currently a heaving morass of paranoia and dread, made all the worse by the moth-eaten, stuffed animal carcasses that lurked in some of the shadowy alcoves, just waiting to scare the bejesus out of him.

McQuarrie Hall would've been spooky enough on a normal day. With a storm raging outside, a dead guy upstairs, and a murderer still stalking the corridors, Tyler was starting to feel like a character in a horror movie.

He didn't particularly like horror movies. Nor did he understand any of their rules. But he was pretty sure that the plucky wee white guy with the nice hair didn't usually survive to see the end credits.

Tammi-Jo didn't seem to share his reservations about the place. She walked a few paces ahead, pointing at all the tapestries and antiques with a sense of wonder, and providing voices for the people in the paintings they passed.

Tyler really wished she'd stop doing some of the creepier ones. Her sinister croaking was doing his nerves no favours at all.

'I think these are all just bedrooms. Are these all just bedrooms? I'm not sure,' Tammi-Jo wondered aloud, apparently debating herself.

She had an impressive ability to hold entire conversations all on her own, taking on both sides, which meant that Tyler had been able to concentrate on not wetting himself with fear whenever another round of driving rain rattled against a window just as he was passing it.

A portrait of a rotund, red-bearded man with a feather in his helmet came into view along the wall, and DC Swanney immediately launched into character.

'Ee by gum, lass, I'm afraid I can't help you there,' she said, taking a stab at a Yorkshire accent. 'Nobody tells me nowt! Do they 'eck, as like.'

She switched back to her own voice to eject a sudden, 'Wait!' then raced along the corridor, leaving Tyler to scurry frantically to try and keep up.

'Hold up. What is it?' he called after her, shooting a wary look at the life-sized portrait of what, in fairness, did look quite like a Yorkshireman. 'What's the rush?'

The other detective constable stopped in front of a large arched doorway. Unlike the others, which mostly had numbers attached to the wall beside them, this one had a large brass plaque screwed into the wood itself.

'Library.'

Tammi-Jo pointed enthusiastically to the sign, ran her finger along the bottom a couple of times like she was giving Tyler plenty of time to read it, then she turned the big metal doorknob, and eased the door inward.

The hinges creaked loudly, because of course they did. A waft of stale-smelling air hit Tyler in the face like the breath of some great and terrible creature.

Tammi-Jo poked her head inside. When she took it out again, her smile had doubled in size.

'Oh, yeah,' she declared. 'I reckon this will do nicely!'

## *Chapter 14*

After a bit of back and forth, and a closer look at various parts of the deceased than Logan was entirely comfortable with, Shona had speculated that Montgomery had been killed soon after he'd last been seen alive.

'I'd say we're looking at about half-ten. Midnight at the latest,' she reckoned. 'Based on the way rigor seems to be setting in, and the colour of his lower extremities. But that's just guesswork, really. I won't know more until I've got my hands on him.'

Still, it was a start. Logan could work with that. Even though it was a vague one, it was good to get some sort of answer on something, because there were still plenty of things here that the DCI didn't understand.

The key in the door had them all stumped. Assuming that nobody in the family had placed it there after the door had been opened, then it very much suggested that the door had been locked from the inside.

There was no window, and Logan had checked the bookcases for any sign of a hidden passageway. He'd felt slightly ridiculous doing it, but in a place like this, a secret entrance was not beyond the realm of possibility.

They'd all been firmly secured to the wall, though. The big rug underfoot seemed fixed in place and weighted down by furniture. If there was some other way in or out of the room, Logan was yet to uncover it.

Late at night, with only the gas lamp burning, much of the room would've been in darkness. The killer could've already been in there when Montgomery entered, hiding in the shadows, waiting to strike.

But what then? Once he'd skewered the poor bastard with the kitchen knife, how did he get out and lock the door behind him?

The kitchen knife.

The chef. He was still to meet the chef, he remembered.

'The family must've moved the key. They must've,' Shona reasoned. 'Either that, or your killer can walk through walls.'

'Or it was an elaborate suicide,' Palmer added. He reached up, formed his hand into a tight circle like it was clutching the handle of a knife, and mimed stabbing himself in the forehead. 'Like that. Is that possible?'

Logan bit back a smirk. It was childish, he knew, but he couldn't resist.

'I'm not sure. Can you maybe do that again, Geoff?'

'What, that?'

Palmer pulled his hand away from his forehead and repeated the motion a few times.

It was midway through the third time that he realised he was doing the universal sign for 'dickhead'.

'Very mature,' he seethed. 'Now who's being unprofessional?'

'No. That's not possible,' Shona said, fighting the same urge to smile as Logan was. 'His arms would have to be twice as long, and his skull half as thick.'

That point hadn't been lost on Logan.

'I was going to say, it'd have to be someone pretty strong, right? To put that amount of welly behind it.'

'Not necessarily,' Shona said, after a moment's consideration. 'If the blade's sharp enough, and you've got enough of a swing, it wouldn't be too much of a problem. I could probably do it, although my aim's not great, so I'd probably end up stabbing myself in the thigh or something. But I'd have the strength, as long as I'm swinging down. The fact that he was seated would help.'

That wasn't what Logan had been hoping to hear. If the fatal blow had required some Herculean feat of strength, he could probably rule out at least half of the people in the house.

Even though she couldn't see his face, Shona somehow sensed his disappointment. 'I mean, it'd help, obviously. The more force behind it, the easier it would go through. But it's bone, not rock. A sharp knife and a bit of welly's all you'd really need.'

'A look at the blade would be useful,' Palmer said. 'We could see what sort of state it's in.'

'Aye, well, that'll have to wait,' Logan said. 'Because I'm sure as hell not yanking it out.'

'No. God, no, don't try that,' Shona said. 'Leave him to me. But we're going to have to stick him somewhere if we're going to get anything useful out of him. You can't just leave him sitting there.'

'No. No, suppose not,' Logan conceded, though he didn't sound particularly happy about it. 'Any suggestions?'

'That place used to be a hotel, right?' Shona said. 'Have they got a big walk-in chiller?'

'I don't know. Maybe.'

'I bet they do. Place like that. If they do, you're going to double-bag him. Four big black bags, two each, top and bottom. Tape them up in the middle, if you can. He might be a bit stiff, so I'd imagine you'll need help.'

'Fine. I've got Tweedledum and Tweedledumber here with me. Tyler and Tammi-Jo. Or Tammi-Jo and Tyler. I'm not sure which is which in that scenario. They can give me a hand.'

'Oh! Is that the really fit detective constable?' Palmer asked eagerly.

Logan pulled a surprised face. 'I mean, I suppose he's all right, if that's your sort of thing. Bit heavy on the hair products, though, and I'm pretty sure he's spoken for.'

'I meant—'

'We all know what you meant, Geoff,' Shona said, shutting him down and getting back to business. 'He'll be heavy, too. Your dead fella. And awkward. You might need more than just those two. Ideally not family, though. You don't really want to have them bending him back into shape on the carpet.'

'I think his daughter might jump at the chance,' Logan said. 'But understood.'

'Then get him into the fridge. Two to five degrees, preferably. Keep him cool, but don't go mad and freeze him,' she added. 'Oh, and wash your hands before and after, but that's just good advice anytime.'

'Right. Double bagged, two to five degrees, got it.'

'And wash your hands.'

'And wash my hands. Anything else?' Logan asked.

Shona gave the question some thought. 'Oh, yes,' she said, at last. 'Try and get him on some sort of trolley, if you can. But, whatever you do, no matter how great the temptation, don't go using that big knife sticking out of his head as a handle to steer him with.'

She squirmed around on the bench and took a quick sip of her tea.

'That sort of thing rarely ends well…'

# *Chapter 15*

Roberta Hoon stood in the centre of her brother's kitchen, a sleeping baby nestled in the crook of one arm. She was a large, heavy-set woman, though her size alone didn't explain how she seemed to fill the entirety of the room.

Her hair was dragged back into a tight grey bun, and her clothes were made of sturdy materials in sensible shades of brown.

Everything about her, from her outfit to the look on her face, seemed to come from another time. Quite when that time was, it was hard to tell, but it definitely wasn't this one, and it was entirely possible that there were dinosaurs in it.

The smell of homemade scones wafted around the kitchen. A batch of fresh Scotch pancakes sizzled away in a large pan, tiny bubbles just starting to form on the batter's top.

It had taken her a while to get used to her brother's oven. It was a basic electric thing, and not a patch on the AGA she'd had back at her own place. That house was gone now, of course. The AGA, for all she knew, could well still be standing. Those buggers were built to last.

The handset of the landline phone was jammed between her shoulder and her ear. She rocked her weight from foot to foot, gently jiggling the infant in her arms as she listened to the string of apologies coming from the other end.

'Right. I get it. Enough,' she said, once the self-flagellation became too much to bear. She picked up a spatula and flipped the pancakes one by one. 'It's an unfortunate situation, but there's no point in fucking crying about it.'

‘Well, no,’ Sinead replied down the line. ‘I mean, I wasn’t actually crying, but…’

‘I’ll be the judge of that,’ Berta told her. The pancake batter sizzled, stirring the baby in her arms. She shushed softly, went back to rocking, then backed away from the hot pan. ‘Anyway, you won’t hear me complaining. I could gobble the wee buggers right up.’

Sinead laughed. ‘Ha. Yeah!’ she said. ‘You do say that a lot. About eating them, I mean.’

‘Well, they’re a couple of delicious-looking little fuckers, aren’t they?’ Berta replied.

Sinead laughed again. She wasn’t quite sure how else to respond. ‘Ha. Yeah. How have they been?’

‘Lauren’s fast asleep. Callum’s been a bit of an arsehole, but he’s settling now.’

Sinead felt she should probably challenge that description of her only son, but she’d used it often enough herself, so couldn’t really argue.

‘It’s just “Cal”,’ she pointed out. ‘It’s not Callum.’

Berta flared her nostrils and took the frying pan off the heat. ‘That’s not a real name. That’s part of a name,’ she countered. ‘You can call him what the fuck you like at home, but here, he’s Callum. All right?’

Sinead didn’t dare argue. Since coming back to work, she’d relied more and more on Berta looking after the twins, and she didn’t want to jeopardise that set-up.

Also, and perhaps more importantly, the woman was bloody terrifying.

‘We’re probably going to be away overnight, is the only thing,’ Sinead said, changing the subject. ‘Which means they’re going to need some stuff from the house.’

‘Aye, aye, I figured that out already,’ Berta said. ‘Already taken care of.’

There was a momentary silence from the other end of the line.

'How do you mean?' Sinead asked.

'Bobby's already off to your place to get everything. Should be back in half an hour.'

'But… he doesn't have a key, and Harris is staying at our aunt's.'

'A key?' Berta let out a short, sharp laugh that made Cal jump in his sleep. 'Oh, I wouldn't worry your bony arse about that, lass,' she said, dropping her voice into a soothing whisper. 'Bobby might be a hopeless bastard with few, if any, redeeming qualities to speak of, but I shouldn't imagine he'll let a little thing like a locked fucking door stop him!'

## *Chapter 16*

The castle's library was going to work well as their makeshift Incident Room. It was more than large enough to accommodate them, it had a few desks and chairs scattered around, and a blank patch of wall that could serve as a Big Board, provided they could track down a packet of Post-its, or some paper and Blu-Tack.

It would be a bit inconsiderate to go sticking their notes to the wall with pins. And, because the wall was made up of solid stone blocks larger than the detectives' heads, it would also be impossible.

Importantly, the library only had a couple of small non-opening windows, and no obvious other way in and out. They could lock it up so that nobody could poke their noses into the evidence they were gathering.

Unless, of course, one of the many bookcases served as the door to a secret passageway. Both DCs had posited that theory, although with thousands of books on the shelves, finding one that activated a hidden mechanism would be like looking for a needle in a haystack.

Or, more accurately, a needle in a needlestack.

'Thousands' was probably selling the place short, Tyler reckoned. There must be tens of thousands of titles lining the shelves, mostly big old leather-bound works, with titles like *Russo-Japanese War Cartography*, or *Set Theory and the Continuum Hypothesis*, in faded embossing on the spine.

There wasn't, as far as Tyler could tell, a single James Patterson or any of the *Fifty Shades of Grey* books in sight.

‘It’s a lot of books,’ Tammi-Jo said, looking around with her hands on her hips. ‘So many books.’

‘Too many, maybe,’ Tyler ventured. ‘There’s no way anyone could get through all these even if they wanted to. And, I mean’—he tilted his head to read the title on a spine—‘does anyone really want to read, *Letters to Mr. Volney, Occasioned by a Work of His Entitled Ruins, and by His Letter to the Author*?’

‘Oh, I’ve read that one. It’s an absolute banger,’ Tammi-Jo said. She crossed her fingers hopefully. ‘Still holding out for a sequel.’

Tyler smiled. ‘Aye, well, it looks about two hundred years old, so I wouldn’t hold your breath.’

DC Swanney beckoned him over and he helped her lug a table closer to the bare patch of wall. There was more than enough furniture to accommodate the smaller-than-usual team, but it was scattered around the room, and far too heavy for either of them to move on their own.

‘Oof. Jesus!’ Tyler grunted, once he’d lifted his end off the floor. ‘Has someone filled the drawers of this thing with concrete?’

‘Go, go, go,’ Tammi-Jo urged.

They waddled along with the table’s feet skimming a few inches above the wooden floor. The weight was immense, and Tammi-Jo did what she usually did to take her mind off anything. She talked.

‘Some people probably like reading that stuff. I mean, they must, surely? Or they did. Once. What about you?’ she asked.

Tyler shook his head, red-faced from the effort of shifting the furniture. ‘I’ll wait for the film.’

‘I meant, are you a reader?’

‘Oh. Right. I mean, I *can* read,’ Tyler said. It came out sounding a bit more like a boast than he’d intended.

‘Good for you!’ Tammi-Jo said. ‘Down.’

Tyler let out a gasp of relief. They set the table on the floor for a moment and shook out their arms, both wondering what the bloody hell the thing was made of.

'But some people are too into books, aren't they?' Tyler continued. 'I mean, being into books is fine, and everything, but some people are *too* into them.'

Tammi-Jo flexed her fingers, working the feeling back into them. 'How do you mean?'

'Like, they know everything. All the books, all the authors. They're always reading meaning into them that's probably not even there.' He adopted the voice and facial expression of some imagined intellectual type. '"Oh, she was using a blue pen. Yah. Yah. Oh, that represents her inner turmoil and childhood melancholy."'

He switched back to his normal voice and shrugged.

'Or, you know, maybe she couldn't find a black one. Maybe blue's just her favourite colour. Maybe the writer just wanted to hit their word count for the day so they could go and, I don't know, build Lego.' He shook his head. 'Some people are just way too into it all.'

Tammi-Jo laughed, and nodded to the table again. They both hooked their fingers under the edges of the polished top and resumed their uncomfortable waddling across the room.

'And what gets me,' Tyler continued, in full flow now, 'is that we treat them like they're amazing for it. Like, the more into books you are, the more impressed we're all meant to be, like they're this big genius, or whatever. Down.'

They set the table on the floor with a *clunk* and a slightly concerning scraping sound that they both pretended they hadn't heard, then immediately went back to shaking the pain out of their hands.

'But if someone was that into, like, *Coronation Street*, say, we'd just think they were weird, or a bit of a div,' Tyler reasoned. He shrugged. 'I've only willingly read about ten books in my whole life,' he confessed. 'And three of them were *Beano* annuals. Is that bad?'

'Well, it's not good,' Tammi-Jo replied, but before Tyler could offer any further response, a sound from out in the corridor made them both turn to look at the door.

At first, the sound was impossible to identify. The detectives held their breath, listening, and eventually it became clear that what they'd thought was one sound was actually two taking place simultaneously.

The creaking of footsteps.

The *shush-shush-shush* of something heavy being dragged along the floor.

Or… not dragged, perhaps. There was a third sound mixed in there, too—a low-volume but high-pitched squeaking that made Tyler think of a rusty old wheel slowly turning, turning, turning.

The resulting combination filled him with a sense of sudden, spontaneous dread. It was an odd, unsettling sort of noise.

And, he realised, his skin prickling into goosebumps, it was getting closer.

'What the hell's that?' he whispered, hoping Tammi-Jo would be able to give an answer that would explain it all away.

She just shook her head, though, apparently as disturbed by the sound as Tyler was.

Damn it. If she was as creeped out as him, then he'd have to be the one to go and investigate. DC Swanney had been very impressed by him when they'd first met, and had been able to rattle off a big list of his achievements on the force.

Well, *a list*, at least.

He felt he'd managed to remain reasonably impressive during her tenure with the team so far, and it would be a shame to throw that all away at the last minute by shiteing himself and legging it from what might well turn out to be a cleaning lady.

The sound continued.

*Creak.*

*Shush.*

*Squeak.*

It was definitely getting louder. Definitely getting closer. Whoever was out there—whatever was out there—would be at the door any second.

Tyler looked around for something to defend himself with, but the best he could find was *Siris: A Chain of Philosophical Reflexions and Inquiries Concerning the Virtues of Tar Water*, by George Berkeley.

As weapons went, it wasn't ideal, but it was heavy enough that a well-timed swing would do some serious damage to an unsuspecting assailant.

*Creak.*

*Shush.*

*Squeak.*

The sound was closer still. It was almost right outside the door now.

Tyler suddenly didn't want to be trapped in here. He didn't want to see the door creaking inward, and some hideous, ghostly face peek in through the opening.

Because, in the few seconds since the noise had begun, and despite all reason and some quite vocal protests from the logical minority of his brain, the source of the sound had become something supernatural.

Clutching the book with both hands, he crept towards the door. Better to face whatever it was out there in the corridor than in here. At least out there, they could make a run for it. In here, they were cornered. In here, they were trapped.

As he reached the door, the sound stopped, save for a single, final squeak that was a little more drawn out than the others had been. It had come from just on the other side of the wood.

Whatever was out there, it was right outside the room.

He glanced back over his shoulder. He'd expected Tammi-Jo to still be standing by the table, so almost jumped out of his skin when he found her standing just inches behind him.

'Fuck!' he cheeped, then he brought a finger urgently to his lips, as if the other detective constable was the one who needed to be silenced.

Then, his heart fluttering in his chest, Tyler slowly—ever so slowly—reached for the doorknob. A spark of static electricity crackled at him, making him draw back.

When he finally grasped the knob, the metal was icy cold to the touch, the chill biting at the tips of his fingers.

The metal mechanism groaned as he eased it around until it slid free of the housing in the frame. At once, the door was pushed inwards, forcing him back a step, and sending the big, heavy book slipping from his grasp.

He grabbed for it and held it up, bracing himself from some demonic spirit or—if he was lucky—some demented murderer to come crashing into the library, flailing at him with its ghostly tendrils or a dirty great knife.

Instead, the door bumped back against the frame, the sudden inrush of wind from outside squeezing the equivalent amount of air back out of the room, and nudging the door closed once more.

A breeze. That was all. Just a breeze.

But the wind hadn't caused the sounds they'd heard. Something was still out there.

'Ready?' Tyler whispered back over his shoulder.

'Ready,' Tammi-Jo confirmed. Then, doubt struck. 'Wait. For what?'

'I'm going to open the door.'

'OK, yes. Right.' She nodded. 'I'm ready for that.'

Tyler hesitated. 'Why, what else did you think I was going to do?' he whispered.

'I don't know. I wasn't sure,' the other DC whispered back. 'That's why I asked. I didn't want to say "ready", and then find out I was meant to be, you know, conversing with someone in German, or something.'

Tyler lowered the book a little, his brow furrowing. 'Conversing in…? Why would you be…?'

Tammi-Jo waved insistently at the door. 'Forget it. Just see what's happening.'

Tyler turned away from her again, *Siris: A Chain of Philosophical Reflexions and Inquiries Concerning the Virtues of Tar Water*, now clutched in his left hand, ready to swing.

With his right hand, he took hold of the doorknob and then, with a sudden jerk and a shaky, '*Weurgh!*' he pulled the door wide and launched himself into the corridor.

No killer lunged at him from the shadows. No evil spirit rushed to take possession of his immortal soul. Besides the fraying edges of a tapestry wafting on the wind, nothing moved in the passageway.

And yet, someone had clearly been there.

'Where did that come from?' Tammi-Jo asked.

Tyler looked both ways along the corridor, but there wasn't anyone to be seen.

Outside the library, someone had left what looked like some kind of workshop trolley. It was five or so feet long, made of scuffed and dented metal, and supported on six shopping trolley-style wheels.

A few of the legs, and the recessed top, were blackened, as if they'd been subjected to tremendous heat at some point. A spaghetti of shiny scratches suggested someone had gone at the marks with wire wool, but had given up before making any real progress.

'I don't know,' Tyler admitted.

He stretched out a leg and gave the trolley a quick experimental nudge with the toe of his shoe. It rocked back an inch, then settled again with the same metal-on-metal squeak that they'd heard from the other side of the door.

'But someone obviously brought it.'

A sudden shout from along the corridor made both detectives recoil in fright, Tyler swinging his antique book out in front of him like it was a shield.

'There you are. I've been looking bloody everywhere for you two!' Logan barked. He beckoned them both with the crooking of a finger. 'With me. I need your help with something.'

He started to turn away, then stopped, turned back, and pointed with the same finger he'd summoned them with.

'And bring that thing. We're going to need it.'

## *Chapter 17*

Bob Hoon stood by the sink in Sinead and Tyler's kitchen, two-thirds of the way through what had, until his arrival, been a full jar of pickled onions.

He'd already scoffed half a packet of ham from the fridge, and washed it down with a can of some wanky craft lager that he'd found in amongst the soft drinks and baby bottles, and which had been so insipid that he'd been forced to attack the pickled onions just to get the taste out of his mouth.

There was a packet of Farley's Rusks open on the worktop, the folded foil wrapper visible within the open box.

'Don't mind if I fucking do,' Hoon said, helping himself to one. He nibbled the end, grimaced at the way it became a mush of nothing in his mouth, then took a bigger bite.

It was, despite all the odds, significantly less unpleasant than the lager.

Still, he wasn't here to drink piss and eat baby biscuits. He had a job to do.

He set to work, and had just found an extra pack of nappies and grabbed six of the filled baby bottles from the fridge when someone knocked on the front door. Considering that the wind was blowing a hoolie, and the rain was absolutely chucking it down, Hoon was surprised that anyone would be out and about, let alone chapping on doors.

Then again, there was no force on earth that would dissuade a determined Jehovah's Witness.

He stuffed the bottles back in the bag, picked up the Farley's box, and headed for the front door. The knocking came again.

Out in the hall, it sounded louder. Determined. A polis knock, maybe.

He turned the knob that unlocked the door, then pushed down the handle to reveal two surly-looking bastards clad in black, hunching together on the front step, the canopy above offering them only a partial suggestion of shelter.

Hoon looked them up and down, getting the measure of them, then leaned against the door frame and crossed one foot over the other, making it very clear he had no intentions of inviting them in.

'All right?' he said.

'Are you Tyler Neish?' asked the larger of the two men. He wore a thick gold chain around his neck, though it was partly hidden by an impressive beard. His slightly smaller mate was clean-shaven and favoured a single dangling earring and blow-dried mullet look.

'Who the fuck are you pair meant to be?' Hoon asked, still looking them up and down. 'The ghosts of the dead Bee Gees? I mean, I know it's Halloween, but are you no' a bit fucking old to go guising?'

'Are you Tyler Neish?' the bigger man asked again.

'What do you think?'

'I think you're in his house.'

'Well fucking spotted, pal. No fucking flies on you. I *am* in his house,' Hoon agreed. He unrolled the foil packet he was holding, and extended it to the men. 'Rusk?'

Neither man took him up on the offer.

'Suit yourself,' Hoon said with a shrug.

'Do you mind if we come in, Mr Neish?' the shorter of the men asked.

'Aye. Very fucking much so,' Hoon told him.

'Well, tough,' the bigger man barked. 'We were only asking out of courtesy. We're well within our rights to force our way inside.'

Hoon took a bite of his rusk and nodded slowly as he chewed it into a paste. 'You're well within your rights to fucking try.'

He swallowed the mouthful of tasteless nothingness, picked a mushy lump from between his teeth with a pinkie nail, then flicked it past the men and out into the storm.

'But, before anyone does anything they might rapidly come to regret, maybe one of you two 'Staying Alive' singing bawbags should tell me what the fuck this is all about…'

# *Chapter 18*

'You can't be bloody serious! I can't be dealing with this!' Marcus Doyle cried, making a *shoo* motion in the direction of Montgomery McQuarrie's corpse. 'I'm BAFTA nominated!'

'The Welsh BAFTAs,' corrected his producer, Gavin. 'And the nomination wasn't for you, it was for the show.'

'I am the show!' Marcus fired back. 'You think people tune in for the shaky camera footage and night vision lenses, *Gav?* No. They tune in for me. For this guy right here. Anyone else is expendable. You more than most. I could replace you in a heartbeat. I could replace you like *that*.'

He clicked his fingers quite violently just inches from the other man's face, making him flinch.

'Same with Twinkletoes downstairs. You know how many perky-titted twenty-somethings would give their eyeteeth to be on telly?'

'No,' Gavin admitted.

'A lot. That's how many, Gavin. A lot.' He waved a finger at the producer, but there was an uncertainty to it, like he couldn't quite remember the point he was trying to make. 'So, you know, keep that in mind.'

With a sniff, he turned, then recoiled when his gaze fell on the body again.

'Christ! I keep forgetting he's there,' he muttered, averting his gaze again. 'I am not touching it. No way. You can piss right off. I was voted "Star of the Week" by TV Quick. Twice! I make entertainment, I don't lug corpses around.'

Logan counted slowly down from five, fighting the urge he'd had all day to just start shouting randomly at people. The fact of it was, he needed their help. And, to be fair, straightening out a body in the grip of rigor mortis, wrapping it in bin bags, and lugging it down two flights of stairs was a pretty big ask.

'I know it's not pleasant,' the DCI said. 'But it's important we preserve the body as best we can.'

'Why? It was obviously the kids that did it!' Marcus said.

'He doesn't mean that,' Gavin said, quickly stepping in. 'Marcus, you can't say that.'

'Why not? It's blindingly clear.'

'What makes you say that?' Logan asked.

'Because kids hate their dads, don't they? Especially if they're successful,' Marcus said, with a grunt of something that might have been resignation. 'You do everything you can to keep them happy, you try your best for them, but all they'll do is mump and moan, and then horse a big knife through your forehead, first chance they get.'

'Mine don't,' Tyler interjected. 'My kids don't hate me.'

'Are they over seven?' Marcus asked.

'Not yet,' Tyler conceded.

Marcus laughed bitterly. 'Well, give it time, son. Give it time.' He pointed to the body of Montgomery McQuarrie. 'That'll be you before you know it. You mark my bloody words.'

Gavin hurried in to smooth things over. Logan got the impression that this was a key element of his job.

'He's generalising, of course. Not all kids hate their parents. Most don't!' the producer said. 'I didn't. My own mother passed recently, Marcus, as you very well know, and I was devastated.'

Marcus rolled his eyes. 'Yes. Tell me about it. Three weeks off *and* I had to chip in for the bloody funeral. Never even met the woman,' he told the detectives. 'Can you believe that?'

Gavin's cheeks burned with embarrassment. 'You didn't *have* to, Marcus. I just asked if… And that wasn't meant for…' He glanced at the detectives, his shame apparent. 'Anyway, the point is, there's no evidence to suggest that Helen or Monty Two was involved.'

'Except they're weird, aren't they?' Marcus pointed out. 'And they were hardly grief-stricken when they found the body. The boy put on a show, but take it from a man who knows someone faking it when he sees it, it was bollocks. And the daughter, she didn't even bother to pretend. She just lit up a fag, then took her turn trying to tug out the knife like it was an attraction at a bloody fairground.'

Logan beckoned Tyler and Gavin over to join him by the body while Marcus hung back, still ranting.

'Mind you, if the son was faking it, then Christ on a bike, the wife was something else. Wailing, throwing her arms around, gnashing her teeth. Hugging and kissing him, despite the bloody dagger sticking out of his face.'

'Was it just the three of them in the room?' Logan asked. 'When you got there?'

'Four. Yvonne got there ahead of us,' Gavin said.

'The chef—French fella, forget his name—he rocked up about four or five minutes after we arrived,' Marcus added. 'And then old *bees-for-hair* arrived behind him.'

'What the hell is all that about?' Tyler asked, taking up his position on the opposite side of the dead man's chair from Logan. He tugged at the wrist of his gloves to make sure they were on tight. 'I mean, I thought the padlocks on his neck and the extra eyes on his cheeks were weird, but the bee hair is something else.'

'Christ knows,' Marcus said. 'They're an odd bunch. And he's a *performance artist*, apparently, which, from what I can tell, is just a further excuse to make an absolute twat of yourself.'

He stepped back and turned away, not wishing to watch as Logan and Tyler carefully hoisted the body out of the chair, with Gavin assisting from the periphery. Gavin wasn't a particularly large man, and Marcus's much broader frame would've been more useful when it came to the heavy lifting.

'Oh, God!' Marcus heard the producer cry. 'That stinks! He's shat himself! Has he shat himself?'

'They usually do, aye,' Logan replied. 'You get used to it.'

Marcus grimaced, keeping his eyes fixed firmly on the door. When he spoke again, his voice sounded slightly different, due to the fact that he had moved quickly to stop any air entering or leaving through his nose.

'But if you ask me, my money's still on the kids. The daughter, if I had to choose, but I wouldn't be one bit surprised if they were both in on it. Bastards.'

He risked a glance back over his shoulder, then dry heaved at the sight of the staining on the back of the old man's trousers as the body was guided carefully down onto the floor.

'Christ. Picked the wrong time to look,' he remarked, whipping his head to the front again. 'You could've bloody warned me!'

'I literally just said, "He's shat himself", Marcus!' Gavin cried. His voice was muffled now, too, his mouth and nose buried in the crook of an arm. 'Seriously, how do you get used to that?' he asked, eyes flitting from one detective to the other.

'You don't,' Logan replied. 'You just learn to stop whinging about it. Here, pass me them bags.'

'Hold on, boss,' Tyler said. He pointed to the dead man's right hand. 'Check it out.'

'What am I meant to be looking for?' Logan asked. Aside from Marcus, who was keeping well out of it, he was the farthest away from the hand, and had to squint to examine it.

'Oh! I see it!' Gavin ejected a little cry of triumph. 'The ring finger. There's a mark! I see it! I see it!'

'All right, calm down, Gavin,' Marcus spat, still facing the other way. 'What do you want, a pat on the head? A box of bloody Bonio?' He stole a half-second glance, his curiosity getting the better of him. 'What is it? What do you see?'

'Looks like he usually wears a ring, boss,' Tyler told Logan.

The DCI nodded his agreement, having now had a chance to look more closely at the hand. There was a faint break in the mottled purple colouring of the finger—just enough to suggest a ring had been there until recently.

Upon closer inspection, a slight distortion to the finger itself implied a break in one of the bones.

'Looks like someone took it off him, either during or after the attack,' Logan posited.

'So… what? It was a thief?' Gavin asked. 'Someone broke in, killed him, and took his ring?'

'There's loads of jewellery over there, boss,' Tyler said. He nodded a little self-consciously at the bowl he'd been poking around in earlier. 'If they'd come to rob the place, why would they take just one ring?'

'Maybe it was the most valuable one?' suggested Gavin. Clearly, despite his initial reaction to the bodily fluids of the deceased, he was starting to enjoy himself. 'Guy like this, it could've been worth millions!'

Logan considered the mark on the dead man's finger for a moment. Whatever his thoughts on the matter were, he was keeping them to himself.

'Right, let's get these bags around him,' the DCI said. He shot a look at Marcus's back, and raised his voice so there would be no doubt as to who he was addressing. 'And if you think you're getting out of helping us lug him down the stairs, you can bloody well think again.'

-

Down at the bottom of the stairs, watched by the eyes of a hundred dead animals, Tammi-Jo and *Ghost Spotters* co-host, Yvonne, stood guarding the workshop trolley.

DCI Logan had doubted the need for it to be guarded, but as it had appeared out of nowhere, Tammi-Jo had argued that it had just as much chance of vanishing back into the ether if nobody stuck around to keep an eye on it.

She had invited Yvonne to come stand with her, and when the presenter had expressed her reservations, had used a convoluted 'two heads are better than one' argument that wouldn't have stood up to the flimsiest of scrutiny. By that point, though, Yvonne had just wanted her to stop talking, and so had agreed to come along.

A decision she was now very much coming to regret.

'What about when the lights go out? Is that real?' the detective constable asked.

'As in, do they really go out?'

'No, I mean, is it really random, or is it planned?'

Yvonne delayed replying for a few seconds, like she was hoping Tammi-Jo might figure out the answer for herself.

'It's planned,' she admitted, when the DC just continued to smile expectantly at her.

'Wow! Seriously? You always look so surprised. You have me fooled every time. You should be an actress!'

Yvonne sniffed. 'I am an actress.'

'Well, no. Yeah. I mean, you should be a *proper* actress, though. A proper actress doing proper stuff. Like *Hollyoaks*. Or, no! That *Inspector Morse* one. The prequel. You could be the killer. Nobody would ever suspect you. They'd think you were too nice to do that sort of thing, because you were in kids' telly.'

Yvonne shot her a sideways look across the top of the trolley. 'Me as a person, or my character?'

This gave the DC cause to stop and think. 'Both,' she said. 'You know what they say. "Act what you know."'

'They don't say that,' Yvonne countered.

'Well… I've heard people say it, so…' Tammi-Jo pulled a face and shrugged in a way that said she was *definitely* correct, but was prepared to let the argument go for the sake of keeping the peace.

Yvonne, too, decided it was best not to pursue the matter any further. She checked her watch and looked up the wide steps to the mezzanine level above. There was no sign yet of movement or sound from the stairs higher up.

'How much longer are they going to be?'

'Shouldn't be too much longer,' the DC promised. 'Why, you in a rush? I don't think we're going anywhere, anytime soon. Have you seen the rain? It's mad. Well, not mad. If it was mad, it'd be going up. But heavy. It's really heavy.'

'I noticed. And no, not going anywhere. But we're meant to be doing talking heads,' Yvonne said, before quickly adding, 'Not the band.'

'What band?' Tammi-Jo asked.

On the other side of the trolley, the presenter looked relieved. 'God, I don't know. It's a joke Marcus makes. He's made it over and over. Everyone laughs, even me, and I've got no idea what he's on about.'

'Oh. Right. Why's that?'

'He just thinks he's funny.'

'No, I mean why do you laugh if you don't find it funny?'

Yvonne's eyebrows dipped, but a little smile turned up the corners of her mouth, like the other woman's naïveté was endearing.

'Uh, well, maybe because I like my job?'

Tammi-Jo cocked her head a little, looking the other woman up and down. 'Do you?'

'Yes! Of course I like it.'

'It's just, whenever I've seen it, you've always looked pretty unhappy about it all. Bit embarrassed, sort of thing. Especially when Marcus gets possessed by evil spirits who threaten to sexually assault you.'

'Wow. You really do watch the show.'

Tammi-Jo wrinkled up her nose. 'I've seen bits of the latest one. While flicking,' she said. 'Plus all of series one to six.'

Yvonne smiled. 'Aha! So, you're a fan!'

'Oh, no. I don't enjoy it,' Tammi-Jo said, and the sincerity of her reply took the wind right out of the other woman's sails.

Spotting this, Tammi-Jo quickly moved to change the subject.

'What brought you here?' she asked, pointing to the floor by their feet.

'You told me to come with you,' Yvonne reminded her.

'No, for filming, I mean. I've often wondered how you choose places. I mean, there can only be so many haunted houses.'

'Gavin chooses,' Yvonne explained. 'Well, whoever's the current producer chooses. Marcus usually scares them off after a series or two. Marcus has picked the last few.'

She stared up the stairs in silence for a few moments, then turned back to the detective constable.

'And no, OK. You're right.'

Tammi-Jo hesitated. 'About what?'

'I don't like *all* of it, obviously. There are definitely bits of it I could do without. But it's the exact same situation with all jobs, isn't it?'

'What, the ghosts that take control of your boss's body keep threatening to rape you?' Tammi-Jo shook her head. 'No, I'm pretty sure that's just yours.'

'Not that specifically. I just mean, everyone's got bits about their job they don't like.'

Tammi-Jo gazed at the other woman, her blue eyes dulled by the furrowing of her brow. 'No,' the detective constable said finally. 'Nothing so far.'

'Nothing?' Yvonne almost choked on the word. 'There's nothing about your job you don't like?'

'Well, maybe the hat,' Tammi-Jo said. 'But I don't have to wear that anymore, so… No. No, don't think so.'

At the sound of muttering from somewhere above, she turned and looked up the stairs.

'Aha!' she announced. 'Sounds to me like we're in business!'

# *Chapter 19*

DI Forde dunked half of his chocolate digestive in his tea, held it there absent-mindedly, then muttered darkly when over-exposure to the hot liquid turned the biscuit to mush.

He tried fishing it out with a finger, but it had already sunk down and settled at the bottom of his mug, meaning the situation was now officially beyond salvaging.

'Ach, it'll give it texture,' he remarked to the empty room, then he dunked the remaining half of the digestive just once, and popped it in his mouth.

Meanwhile, his computer continued to defy him.

It had been on a go-slow for most of the day. Ben blamed the weather, although he had no idea if the wind and rain could have any bearing whatsoever on what the machine on his desk did or didn't do.

The whole thing was a mystery to him. He understood the basics—the keys were for typing, the mouse moved the pointy thing—and he could navigate his way to at least half the information he generally needed without having to dig around too much, or shout for someone to come help.

Granted, that was partly due to the extensive notes Hamza had left him on the little whiteboard by his monitor, but he liked to think that, even without those, he'd muddle through somehow.

Today, though, nothing was doing what it was supposed to. Every click of a link made the pointy thing turn into a little spinning doohickey that then rendered the whole bloody machine unresponsive for a good five to ten minutes.

Right now, the spinny thing was whirling away, and the computer itself was making a series of low crunching sounds like it was munching through its own bits, or bytes, or whatever the hell it was filled with.

He took a sip of his slightly grainy tea and checked the names on his list while he waited. So far, of the eight Tyler had phoned through with, Ben had only been able to check up on one. Even then, all he could say for sure was that Montgomery McQuarrie Jr had no criminal record beyond two minor driving offences, dating back three and four years respectively, for which he'd received a statutory fine and a combined three points on his licence.

Other than that, Ben had been able to dig up no more information on the man. Or, thanks to the computer issues, on any of the other names on the list.

It was a pity DS Khaled wasn't here. Hamza would've rattled through the lot of them by now. If there was dirt to be found on any of them, he'd have dug it up. If there was anything out of the ordinary about them, he'd have pinned it down.

When it came to computers and technology—which seemed to be the key to ninety per cent of police work these days—the detective sergeant was a wizard.

Ben considered himself to be at the other end of that spectrum. Whatever the opposite of a wizard was, that was him. A tech witch? Was that a thing?

Whatever. To the DI, computer jargon might as well be a foreign language, and he never felt older or more redundant than when faced with an unfamiliar screen or nonsensical error message.

That said, he'd be quite happy with an error message now. An error message would at least be something to try and work out. It would be a pointer in the right direction. Right now, all he could do was wait, and waiting was getting him nowhere.

He looked at the list.

He thought of DS Khaled.

'Ah, bugger it,' he said. He reached for the handset of his desk phone, then thought better of it and took out his mobile. 'It's not like he's doing anything else.'

–

Tyler stopped at the sight of the knife. The man held it expertly, swiping it back and forth against a sharpening rod he clutched in his other hand. His impassive gaze was fixed on the trolley being pushed by Logan and Tammi-Jo, and steered at the front by DC Neish.

'Whoa,' Tyler warned, then he hissed and jumped clear as the bottom shelf of the trolley walloped the back of his ankle.

'Sorry! We didn't *whoa* quick enough,' Tammi-Jo said from the other end. She tilted her head towards Logan, who had been doing most of the pushing. 'I'll be honest. He did. He *whoaed* in time, but I…'

She spotted the reason for their sudden stop, and let out a little *ooh* of surprise.

'That's a big knife,' she pointed out. 'That's too big a knife, surely?'

Logan released his grip on the trolley and straightened up. The trolley's handles were quite low, and the double-wrapped body on top made reaching them awkward. He grimaced at the stiffness in his lower back, but powered on through it.

'Are you Francois?' he asked, sizing up the man with the knife. 'The chef.'

'*Oui.* I am Francois.' His accent, predictably, was French. Strong, too. Thankfully, his English was pretty much perfect. 'You are the police inspector investigating this 'orrible business?'

'Aye. Detective Chief Inspector Jack Logan.' He presented his warrant card. The chef gave it a few seconds of scrutiny, then waved his sharpening rod to say he was satisfied. 'We're led to believe you've got a walk-in refrigerator we can use.'

Francois barely glanced at the bagged-up remains of his former employer before jerking the blade of his knife towards a metal door at the back of what was a surprisingly modern kitchen for such an old building.

The work surfaces were all brushed stainless steel, and everything—from the ovens and fryers to the pots and pans hanging from a rack overhead—were immaculately clean. Clearly, someone took real pride in the place, and judging by his pristine chef's whites, it was almost certainly the Frenchman.

The kitchen was on the ground floor of the castle, somewhere near the centre of the building. This meant that, like Montgomery's study, there were no windows looking out into the world beyond the castle's walls.

Back here, tucked away from everything, you could almost forget Storm Agatha raging furiously outside.

'Go ahead and put Monsieur McQuarrie in there,' he said, jerking the sharpening rod in the direction of the fridge door. There was a small, porthole-like window in the metal, but the space beyond it was dark. 'Just keep 'im away from the pheasant, *s'il vous plait*. I will be serving that for dinner this evening.'

'Wait, what?' Tyler said. 'We're not leaving the food in there with him, are we?'

'What else do you suggest?' the chef asked. 'I 'ave one refrigerator. Inside, you will find meats, caviar, handmade delicacies and the finest cheeses from all corners of the world. Do you suggest I cast these aside? Will you compensate me for such a loss?'

Tyler shifted uncomfortably. 'I mean, no. I suppose not.'

At the mention of all that food, Logan's stomach let out a growl.

It had been a long time since he'd last eaten. Breakfast hadn't happened thanks to the werewolf-in-the-fridge incident, and the weather had dissuaded him from picking up anything on the way to work.

Other than a biscuit at the office and a stale-tasting Sherbet Lemon he'd found lurking in the door pocket of the car, he hadn't had a bite to eat since a few handfuls of popcorn the evening before.

Despite standing several feet away from the detective, the chef picked up on the sound.

'Hungry, Inspector?' he asked. 'Would you like me to rustle you up a little something for lunch?'

Logan's stomach answered for him, but he was quick to back it up. 'I wouldn't say no.'

'Seriously, boss? You can seriously be thinking about eating right now?'

Tammi-Jo motioned down at the inexpertly bagged-up corpse. 'Even after all that?'

'Especially after all that,' Logan replied. 'If you two aren't hungry, you can help me get this wheeled into the fridge, then go back and finish getting our Incident Room set up. Have you found us somewhere to do the interviews yet?'

'Not yet, sir,' Tammi-Jo told him. 'Still working on it.'

'Right, well then, we all know what we're doing.'

His stomach rumbled again. The wheels of the trolley squeaked as he gave it a shove.

'Let's get cracking.'

# *Chapter 20*

Francois hadn't asked Logan what he wanted to eat, but by the time the detectives emerged from the fridge, the smell of piping hot bacon and melting cheese was already filling the kitchen.

Tyler and Tammi-Jo had once again declined the offered lunch, so Logan had sat down at a rustic wooden table with the chef, and they'd both got stuck into salty, greasy towers of bacon, bread, toasted cheese and the single best bowl of homemade tomato soup that Logan had ever tasted.

His plan had been to question the chef while they ate, but the meal was so distractingly delicious that he could do nothing but let out the occasional groan of pleasure, and the odd whispered, 'Sweet Jesus!'

Once he was done, he nudged the empty bowl and plate into the middle of the table, then leaned back and gave his stomach a pat.

'That was something else,' he said. 'Cheers for that.'

'You are welcome,' Francois said. 'It is a pleasure to see my food being appreciated for once.'

Logan's eyebrows shot halfway up his forehead. 'What? Who doesn't appreciate it? The family? Jesus. Don't tell me they don't enjoy a feed like that?'

Francois shrugged. He was eating the same meal as Logan, but taking much longer over it. He peeled away a strip of his toasted triple-decker sandwich and dunked it in his soup with a flourish.

'They would not eat this,' the Frenchman said. 'Though it would do them good to do so. But they have… How you say? An image to protect. Even from themselves. Only from themselves, perhaps. No good, honest food for them. Instead, they insist on eating that which they often do not even like, but which they believe is fitting for their status.'

He popped the now soup-coated chunk of sandwich in his mouth and chewed it thoughtfully.

'I am asked to prepare oysters twenty, thirty times each year. Not one of them likes oysters. Monty Junior is even mildly allergic, I think. But still, they insist.'

He gestured enthusiastically to Logan's empty plates and smiled. 'So this? This, for me, is joyous. To see a man who clearly enjoys his meals'—he gestured to Logan's stomach—'take such pleasure from something I 'ave prepared?'

He brought finger and thumb to his mouth and kissed them, fully embracing the French chef stereotype. '*C'est bon.*'

'The pleasure was all mine, believe me.'

Logan sat forward again, subtly shifting attention away from his gut.

'While we're here, Francois, you mind if I ask you a few questions?'

'Like how did one of my knives come to be used to murder my employer?'

Logan smiled grimly. 'Seems like as good a place to start as any.'

'I do not know, Inspector. That is my honest answer. I was as shocked as anyone to discover that it was a knife of mine that had been used to murder Monsieur McQuarrie.'

Logan nodded slowly, picking over the slightly odd phrasing of the response.

'But you weren't shocked that he'd been murdered?'

Across the table, Francois frowned. 'Pardon?'

'You said you were shocked it was one of your knives that had been used to kill him. Not that you were shocked he'd been killed.'

There was a lengthy silence while the chef replayed the last few moments of conversation in his head. 'Apologies, Inspector.

It may be the language, but I do not see your point. Did I expect to find Monsieur McQuarrie dead? *Non*. Of course not. But the real shock for me, for me personally, was seeing that one of my own knives was the murder weapon. A knife I had believed to be safely under lock and key.'

'They were locked up?'

'Of course. In that drawer.'

Logan followed the direction of the Frenchman's nod. 'Mind if I have a look?'

Francois nodded, then slipped his fingers into the pocket on the front of his whites and produced a small silver key.

Both men got to their feet, and Logan watched as the chef unlocked the drawer, then slid it open.

There were a dozen knives of various shapes and sizes stored neatly in a custom-built tray inside the drawer, plus two empty spaces where a long, thin blade and a shorter, wider one should be.

A glance around the worktops revealed the second knife sitting on a chopping board. It had been the one the chef had been sharpening when the detectives had entered.

The other knife, though—the longer one—was nowhere to be seen.

'Is that the one that's missing?' Logan asked, indicating the indent in the tray.

'Missing? *Non*, Inspector. I know precisely where it is,' Francois said, throwing a meaningful look in the direction of the big walk-in fridge. 'Was that the murder weapon? *Oui*. When I came downstairs to check, that knife was missing.'

'Right. I see. And when you were opening the drawer and handling the other knives, I don't suppose you were wearing gloves, were you?'

Francois frowned. 'Gloves? *Non*. But I had washed my hands thoroughly, I can assure you.'

'I'm sure you did, but it wasn't hygiene I was worried about. If someone had got into the drawer and taken the knife—'

'Ah! Of course! *Je suis un idiot!*' Francois cried. 'Fingerprints, yes? That is your concern?'

Logan admitted that, aye, it had crossed his mind.

'My apologies, Inspector. I was so disturbed by what I had seen that I did not think. It did not occur to me. I had to know if my knife was indeed the weapon. And, as you can see...'

'Who else has access to the drawer?'

'Only Monsieur McQuarrie himself. He has a key in his desk drawer, but when I go back upstairs and check, there it is. Still there.'

'And it's still there now?'

'I believe so, *oui*. And that one, I did not touch! Perhaps you can obtain evidence from that?'

'Maybe,' Logan conceded, though he didn't sound particularly hopeful. 'And that's it, though? Just the two keys?'

'*Oui*. Monsieur McQuarrie was very particular about who had access to different parts of his home. *Regardez*.'

He scurried across to the wall by the door, where an old wooden box had been firmly fastened to the grey stone. Pinching his fingers into another pocket, Francois produced an even smaller key than the one he'd used on the drawer.

In a moment, he had unlocked the box, and stepped back as he pulled the door open to reveal seventy or more other keys all hanging from labelled hooks.

'*Voilà*. The keys to the castle, Inspector. Monsieur McQuarrie did not trust his family with their safeguarding, and instead bestowed the responsibility upon *moi*.'

Logan's gaze flitted over the old-style iron keys, then scanned the labels above them. Most of them were numbered, but a few had words written above them in neat block handwriting that the passage of time had rendered almost indecipherable.

'Is there a key to the old man's study in here?' he asked.

'*Oui*.'

The chef's hand stretched past him, indicating a key hanging one row up from the bottom, second on the left. The freshness of the label had already caught the DCI's eye, but the words on it had meant nothing.

'The Nest,' he said, reading the recently written tag. He turned to Francois. 'What's that?'

'It was a joke by his children. One. Both. I do not recall. That is what they called his study, after he started sleeping up there. "He's gone to his nest", they would say. "He has flown up to his nest once more."'

'And what? The old man got in on the joke and changed it?'

Francois seemed amused by the comment. 'Monsieur McQuarrie? Amused? I would not say so, Inspector. I do not believe this was ever the case.'

Logan turned his attention back to the key. 'So, if he didn't write it, and I'm assuming you didn't, someone else must've had access.'

'Not that I am aware of, Inspector. I assumed one of the children must have taken their father's key in order to make the change.'

Logan scratched thoughtfully at his chin. 'And how long ago was this?'

'Eight years, perhaps? Nine? I would not like to say ten, but it is not out of the question.'

'Right. And, maybe a daft question, but if you knew there was a spare key, why didn't you come get it this morning when the study door was locked?'

Francois shrugged. 'I was down here when I heard the scream. By the time I got to the room, it was no longer locked. And the rest of them—the family, the television crew, Helen's 'orrible boyfriend—they were all inside the room, feasting on the drama of it like pigs feasting on swill.'

'You're sure they were all there?'

'Ah, *oui*, Inspector. They are not a group of people you readily forget.'

'Aye, you can say that again.'

Logan stuck a mental flag in the man's remark. According to Marcus and Gavin, Donatello Liberace had been the last to arrive on the scene, but if Francois was to be believed, he was already there when the chef arrived.

Something to think about later.

'Why didn't any of them come and get the key?' Logan wondered aloud. 'If they knew the spare existed? Why not come get it before setting about the door with an axe?'

The chef held his hands up like he was surrendering. 'This, I think, is not a question for me, but for them, Inspector. I would not like to give reasons for things I, myself, do not understand. Although, I can tell you that they all have a taste for the dramatic, I think.'

'Did you happen to notice if the spare key was still here when you got back?'

*'Oui*. I opened the box when I came down to check for the knife. Nothing was out of place. It was exactly as you see it now.'

'And that's definitely the only spare key to the study?'

'That is what I have been led to believe,' the chef confirmed. 'I have no reason to think otherwise.'

Logan mulled this over for a while, then thanked the Frenchman for both his time and the free lunch.

'You will be staying for dinner, I assume?' Francois asked.

It was impossible to hear Storm Agatha from the kitchen, but there was little chance of her having abated her assault.

'I'd imagine so, aye.' He indicated his empty plates. 'Feel free to serve up the same again, if that's easier. You'll no' hear me complaining.'

Francois smiled, then bowed his head gratefully. '*Merci*, Inspector. I shall see what I can do.'

Logan was about to head for the door when a thought struck him. 'Oh, one more quick question, if you don't mind?'

The chef's smile faltered a little, but he gave the DCI the go-ahead with a brief nod.

'Earlier, I asked everyone to meet me in the reading room. You didn't show up. Why was that?'

'Oh. That!' The Frenchman relaxed a little. 'It is an old building. There are faults in parts of the structure where the rain is getting through. I had to fix some leaks.'

'Right. I see,' Logan said. 'But that's strange, because that's not what Montgomery's wife said. She said you couldn't come because you were preparing vegetables.'

Francois appeared taken aback. '*Non*. That is not true. There is no urgency to preparing vegetables, but the water… The damage… I felt I needed to attend to it right away.'

While the chef had been talking, Logan had let out just a suggestion of a groan. He thought of Krystal, and her deep-south American accent.

'I take it you used those words to her? You told her you "had to fix some leaks"?'

'Uh, perhaps. *Oui*. Why? Does it matter what words I used?'

Logan sighed. 'I think she's mistaken leaks'—he pointed upwards at the ceiling—'with *leeks*. The vegetable. I reckon she thought you said you were *fixing leeks* as in preparing them.'

'Water leaks?' Francois said, still not quite catching on.

'No. The ones you eat. No' an easy mistake to make, I'd have thought, but she doesn't strike me as the brightest.'

'*Au contraire*, Inspector,' Francois replied. His expression had hardened a little, so his emotions weren't easy to read. 'I do not believe the latest Madame McQuarrie is quite as much of an imbecile as she likes to portray. I think she is… How do you say? *A manipulative bitch*.'

'Oh? What makes you say that?'

'Have you spoken with her, Inspector?'

'Just in passing,' Logan said.

Francois nodded. 'Then, for fear of prejudicing your mind on the matter, I shall say no more. I have my view. Perhaps yours may differ.'

'Aye. Maybe,' Logan confirmed. He opened the door. 'Guess there's only one way to find out.'

## *Chapter 21*

Hamza sat on the end of a single bed in a partially decorated room, shivering inside his jacket with his shoulders hunched and his laptop balanced on his knees.

The smell of the still-drying paint had almost choked him when he'd been led up to his room at the guest house, and despite the raging storm outside, he'd been left with no choice but to open the window.

He'd only raised it a few inches, but Agatha had come *whooshing* inside so quickly it had felt like the whole house might start inflating and float away. Fortunately, the walls had held firm, though the door was rattling in its frame, making a constant *tap-tap-tapping* that, along with the paint fumes, was helping to rustle up a stinker of a headache.

Occasionally, like now, the door would give a few proper thumps against the frame, making it sound like someone was outside, knocking to be allowed in.

Unlike the last couple of times this had happened, when he'd got up to check and found nobody out there, Hamza kept his attention fixed on the screen of his laptop, willing the bloody thing to start working properly.

It was only when the knocking came again, and was followed by a questioning, 'Hello?' that the DS realised this wasn't another false alarm.

Discarding the laptop on his bed, he hurried to the door, unfastened the lock, then opened it to reveal Sinead standing out in the hallway.

Her hair had dried off while they'd been downstairs, but it was damp again, suggesting she'd taken a shower. Hamza would've liked a shower, but the amenities in his room extended to a hook on the back of the door, and a notice explaining where to evacuate in the event of a fire.

'Outside' was the short answer. By any means necessary.

'Oh! You are in,' Sinead remarked, and Hamza realised she'd been in the process of turning away. 'When you didn't answer, I wasn't sure if maybe you'd popped out, or…' She shook her head. 'Well, not out, obviously. That would be crazy. But downstairs. Or whatever.'

'Sorry, yeah, no. I was here. Door's been rattling with the wind. Didn't realise you were a real person knocking.' He stepped aside and gestured into the room. 'You want to come in?'

Sinead stepped closer and leaned inside, her feet not crossing the threshold. She tried to keep a neutral expression as she took in the narrow bed, the mostly bare floor, and the stacks of paint cans and rollers that had been pushed into the far corner.

There was an arm fixed to the wall that was presumably meant to hold a TV, but didn't. Which was probably just as well, because the fronts of all the sockets had been removed while the decorating was being done, so there was no place to plug a television in.

Or anything else, for that matter.

The wind billowed the curtains, then whistled as it whipped a big gust of moist, chilled air around the room.

'Not really,' she said, wrinkling her nose up. 'Lovely offer, though it is.'

'You slagging off my new gaff?' Hamza teased.

'God, no. I wouldn't dream of it,' Sinead said, then she bit her lip to fend off a smile.

'You should, because it's shite.'

Sinead let out the laugh she'd been holding back, then indicated the door across the hallway with a jerk of a thumb. 'You want to come to my room, instead? It's got a desk. And a carpet. And it doesn't smell like a migraine waiting to happen.'

'I thought you were never going to bloody ask,' Hamza said, snatching up his laptop. 'Don't suppose it has a heater, does it? A heater would be nice.'

'Already up and running,' Sinead assured him.

'Brilliant!'

After shutting and locking the door to his room, Hamza crossed the hall into Sinead's, and let out an appreciative whistle.

'You weren't joking, were you? You really do have a carpet.'

'And fully painted woodwork,' Sinead said. 'And, I don't mean to boast, but I even have electrical sockets, not just taped-up wires sticking out of a wall.'

'Hey, only one of the sockets is like that, I'll have you know,' Hamza shot back.

'Oh, do the rest work?'

Hamza shook his head. 'Nah. They just didn't get around to taping the other wires up. So, you know, bit of a death trap.'

'Sorry, I shouldn't laugh,' Sinead said, though the apology came much too late.

'And yet, you are, so…'

This only made her laugh all the more. She was still chuckling when she gestured to the chair by the desk, then picked up the kettle.

'You can get set up there. WiFi code is on a bit of paper, I think,' she said, heading through to the en suite with the kettle in hand.

'I got on the WiFi already. That's the only thing I managed to do,' Hamza said, raising his voice so she'd hear him while she filled the kettle in the bathroom sink. 'It's either really slow, though, or there's a problem with the VPN I use to connect to HOLMES.'

Even as he was speaking, Hamza flicked over to a new browser tab on the laptop, pulled up a broadband speed test, and let it crunch the numbers.

'Speeds seem to be fine,' he announced, when Sinead emerged from the bathroom again. 'Think it might be HOLMES itself that's playing up. DI Forde couldn't get anywhere with it, but I assumed that was just him being, you know, him.'

'Could it be to do with the weather?' Sinead asked, plonking the kettle back on its base. A blue light illuminated when she flicked the switch to turn it on. 'Could that be causing outages somewhere?'

'Maybe. Probably. Aye,' Hamza said. 'Definitely possible. Storm like this, phone lines will be down all over the country. It's lucky we've got a connection to anything at all.'

His gaze remained steadfastly fixed on the screen.

'That's probably what happened with the card reader earlier. A glitch in the connection.'

Sinead hesitated, then reached for the little jar that contained a big handful of teabags. 'Aye. That was probably it,' she said.

Hamza tapped a few keys, then watched as his mouse cursor became a spinning wheel.

'Because you'd tell me if it was anything else, wouldn't you?' he said, and the note of concern in his voice was unmistakable.

He still hadn't turned towards her. Sinead studied the back of his head.

Her sergeant.

Her friend.

'Of course,' she said. 'Everything's fine. If there was anything else, Ham, you'd be the first to know.'

## *Chapter 22*

As luck would have it, Krystal McQuarrie was not difficult to find. She came rushing in through the front doors just as Logan returned to the main hall, the wind and rain driving against her back like the outside world was rejecting her, forcing her back inside.

The storm had taken its toll on her carefully coiffured hair, which now had a distinctive *through a hedge backwards* look to it. She'd donned a dark green Barbour jacket to go outside in, zipped right up to the neck. Despite the protection it offered, she was shivering as she forced the doors closed.

She leaned her back against the wood, let out a sigh, then jumped to attention when she spotted the DCI standing at the foot of the stairs.

All around them, the glassy eyes of a dozen dead things watched on in solemn silence.

'Why, Detective Chief Inspector Logan! I almost didn't see you there!' Krystal cried. She took several big steps away from the door, like she was trying to distance herself from it metaphorically as well as physically.

'Aye, I'm easily missed, right enough,' Logan replied. He nodded past her to the doors, making it clear she wasn't getting away that easily. 'Rain still on, then?'

There was a pause, just a beat, like she was having to rethink her conversational strategy on the hoof.

'Oh, my, yes!' she said. 'I thought I'd just pop out there and see for myself.'

'The windows give a pretty accurate insight, I'd have thought,' he said, looking very deliberately at the hallway's many glass panes.

'But ain't nothing like experiencing the real thing up close and personal!' she replied, then she flashed him a smile and moved to walk past.

'You got a minute?' Logan asked.

She faltered to a stop a few feet from him.

'Uh, well, I really should go get myself dried off and warmed up. Maybe we could talk later…?'

Logan paid no attention to the request and pressed right on with his questioning.

'You said the chef wasn't around because he was preparing vegetables. Is that right?'

Krystal's eyes seemed to shimmer in their sockets, like they were moving around quickly, unable to settle on anything.

'That's right.'

'What did he say, *exactly*?'

'Exactly? Well, I don't know about exactly, but I believe he said something like he was fixing us up some vegetables. Or, I don't know, carrots, maybe. Why?'

Logan almost laughed at the absurdity of it, but at least his suspicions—and the Frenchman's story—had been confirmed.

'Did he was he had to go and fix leaks?'

'You know, that sounds right. I think maybe he did say he…' Krystal's words tumbled away into silence. Her head seemed to shrink into her shoulders, and she slapped a hand against her soaking-wet forehead. 'Oh, my. He meant…'

'Aye,' Logan confirmed. 'He did.'

'He meant water problems. Dripping. Not vegetables.'

'Not vegetables, no.'

Krystal laughed. 'Easy mistake to make, I guess!'

Logan gave a noncommittal tilt of his head, but said nothing.

'Was that all you wanted, Detective Chief Inspector?'

Water was dripping off her jacket and pooling on the floor around her feet. Logan had no idea who had made the delicate cream leather boots she wore, but he assumed they'd charged a bloody fortune for them.

'You were there in your husband's study this morning.'

'I was. I already told you so. We all were,' Krystal said, sounding just a touch defensive. 'Ain't none of us hid that fact.'

'Who got there first?' Logan asked. 'Do you remember?'

Her eyes darted left and right. Either she was searching her memory for the information, or hurriedly making it up.

'I'm not sure. Monty's children were both there before me. I heard them trying to break down the door with an axe of some kind. They'd just about got it open when I arrived, and when they did… When they got the door open…'

Her hand went out, searching for something to lean on. All it found was the arse of a stuffed deer, and the dead animal wobbled unsteadily as its spindly legs took some of her weight.

'When I saw him there, sitting there like that, I screamed. I didn't intend to. Didn't plan on it. It just happened, without me even realising I was doing it,' she said. 'I heard it before I even knew it was my mouth the noise was coming from. I even remember thinking to myself, "Who the hell is making that damned racket?" Isn't that the craziest thing you've ever heard?'

Logan assured her that it wasn't, and that the mind did strange things when confronted with situations like the one she'd found herself in.

'Why the need to break down the door?' he asked, returning to his questioning.

She seemed to realise all of a sudden that she was leaning on the stuffed carcass of a dead animal and jerked her hand away. A moment later, she gave the spot she'd been touching a quick pat, as if in apology.

'My Monty was always an early riser. When he hadn't appeared and didn't answer, Monty Junior, well, I guess he and Helen got concerned.'

Logan shook his head. 'No. I get that. I meant, why not just get the spare key from the kitchen?'

'I believe they tried. Helen ran down there, but the kitchen was locked up, and Francois was nowhere to be found,' Krystal said.

'I see.' Logan put a mental flag in that, too, reminding himself to come back to it. 'One other question for now, Mrs McQuarrie. It's a big one, I'm afraid, and there's no easy way of asking it but'—he watched her carefully, ready to note what she didn't say as much as what she did—'do you have any idea who'd want to murder your husband?'

She put her hand on her chest, her eyes and mouth forming three perfect circles of surprise. It was as if the thought that someone might want to kill Montgomery had never occurred to her, despite the fact that his corpse had now taken up residence in the castle's fridge.

'No! Of course not! Nobody would've even thought such a thing, let alone done it,' she cried. The exaggerated movements of her surprise became smaller and more nuanced. 'And yet...'

'Someone did,' Logan finished for her. 'You said you thought it was someone in the house. In the reading room, in fact.'

She shook her head. 'I don't know. It's probably just me talking crazy. What do I know about who did what to whom?' She touched two fingers to her artificially enlarged lips, like she was trying to hold back the next sentence. 'And yet...' she said again.

Logan nodded encouragingly. 'Go on.'

'This isn't an accusation. I don't for one second think he killed his father. Not for one second.' She took a breath and went back to leaning on the stuffed deer. 'Montgomery—my Montgomery—had been having... *problems* with Monty Junior.'

'Problems?'

'Heated discussions. Arguments. I didn't know why, and I didn't ask. That was their business. Man's business, not for me to worry about.'

'You've got no idea?'

'No. But Monty Junior wasn't happy about something. I heard them arguing one night. Really going at it. Junior sounded real ornery, like. Some things got thrown around. I think there was a scuffle.'

'A scuffle? When was this?'

'Three or four nights ago, I reckon.'

She suddenly looked worried, like she'd said too much.

'But that's out of character. For both of them, I mean. Junior is not a violent man. Not remotely. Not at all. There's no way he could be a killer! No way on this earth!'

Her voice cracked with emotion. She turned to the side, looked down at the floor, then up at the ceiling—directing her gaze anywhere but at the detective.

Finally, she met his eye once more.

'Could he?'

Logan smiled grimly. 'We're going to do our best to find out, Mrs McQuarrie,' Logan promised. 'We'll sit down and talk to Monty shortly.'

Krystal dabbed at the corners of her eyes with the sleeve of her still-soaking jacket. 'I'm sure you'll get to the bottom of this whole terrible situation, Detective Chief Inspector,' she said. 'But, word of advice, if I may?'

'Please.'

'When you're interviewing Monty Junior, should you wish to try to sweeten him up or, uh, you know, *appeal to his base instincts*?'

She glanced around the hallway, then put the back of her hand to the side of her mouth as if sharing a secret.

'You might want to bring along that handsome young gentleman detective, because I don't think that pretty female colleague of yours is going to have quite the same effect.'

# *Chapter 23*

Twenty-five minutes after winding up the conversation with Krystal, Logan stood before the blank patch of wall that was supposed to serve as a makeshift Big Board. Tammi-Jo had managed to source some Post-it notes from elsewhere in the castle, but though this mission had been a success, failure had swiftly followed.

The curved, porous, uneven stone walls of the library did not, it turned out, lend themselves well to the sticky strip of a Post-it. The notes would adhere to the wall for anywhere between three and fifteen seconds, before fluttering off and falling to the floor.

Taggart, who Logan had stumbled upon while searching for the library, had woofed excitedly the first few times the notes had fallen, then had grown bored enough to wander into a corner and fall asleep.

When yet another Post-it had fallen like the leaves of the trees on the castle grounds, a frustrated Logan had picked up one of the library's big antique tables, tipped it onto one of its narrow ends so that it stood almost as tall as he did, and slapped all their notes to that, instead.

'That's probably worth millions, boss,' Tyler had remarked, as he watched the DCI hoist the table upright.

'Probably, aye,' Logan conceded, before continuing undeterred.

It hadn't taken long to stick all the information they'd gathered so far onto the tabletop, since they didn't yet have all that much to be going on with. The victim's details, the murder method, and the names of all the potential suspects had been laid out for all to see.

Logan had clustered them together in two groups—victim and murder details in one, suspects in the other—and had laid out the names of the potential killers in a way that loosely indicated their connections and relationships.

Tammi-Jo had offered to take care of arranging the 'board' but the day had already been difficult and frustrating enough, so the DCI had insisted on doing it himself.

Once it was all set up, Tyler placed a video call to Hamza, and then—after some trial, error, and quite a lot of impatient muttering on Logan's part—Ben was successfully added in.

Tyler's phone was now balanced on top of a stack of books, angled so the screen and front camera were facing Logan and the upended table.

Once they were all connected, they got the admin business out of the way first. The force's main computer information system, HOLMES, was currently down, and access to several other police systems was spotty at best. Lightning strikes down south had fried a number of key network components, and the ongoing storm was making repairs a challenge, if not completely impossible.

'So, it wasn't just me, then?' Ben said. He raised his mug of tea as if in toast to himself. 'And here was me thinking it must have been something I'd done.'

'Not unless you've suddenly developed god-like powers, sir,' Hamza said.

Ben winked. 'Here, who says I haven't had them the whole time?'

'Looks like you'll be doing things the old-fashioned way,' Logan said, shutting down the banter before it could really hit its stride. 'Get on the phones. Dig up everything you can on the names on that list Tyler gave you. I want to know who these people are beyond what they've told me.'

'You think they've been lying to us, boss?' Tyler asked.

He and Tammi-Jo had dragged chairs over, and were sitting either side of the stack of books with the phone balanced on top. The stack was set back a little, so the DCs were just visible at each side of the screen to those on the call.

'I know they've been lying to me, son. We're polis. Everyone lies to us.' Logan's voice was a gruff bark, his nostrils flaring with anger. 'If you've no' learned that yet, then for God's sake, what are you even doing here?'

Ben's voice came quietly over the phone's speaker. 'Oh-ho. Someone got out of the wrong side of bed this morning?'

'What was that?' Logan demanded, and there was an intensity to it that made Tyler and Tammi-Jo both lean back in their seats.

DI Forde, however, remained undaunted. 'I'm just saying you're coming across as a bit of a crabbit bastard, Jack, that's all.'

For a second, it looked like Logan might bite back at him, but instead he just shook his head and turned his attention to the upturned table with the stickers on it.

'Right, then,' he announced. 'The story so far…'

First, he told them what they knew of the night Montgomery McQuarrie senior had died. He'd retired to his study around ten fifteen and, based on what little Shona could see via the video link, had been murdered soon after.

There had been no other injuries found while moving the body, so the cause of death was almost certainly the dirty great knife that had been rammed through the front of the man's skull.

'Aye, that'll do it,' Ben chimed in.

Before Logan had left Krystal, he'd asked her about the key to the study. As far as she'd been able to tell him, it had been in the keyhole when they'd forced entry, which meant the door had definitely been locked from the inside.

And, with no windows, that meant that the death was either suicide—almost certainly physically impossible—or there was another way in and out of the room.

'The bookcases, boss. Got to be,' Tyler said. 'I should just go up there and start pulling books out.'

Logan shuddered at the memory of an escape room game he'd been forced to take part in with the DC a year or so earlier. It had ended in chaos and with a lot of books scattered across the floor while Tyler had searched for a secret exit.

'Let's no' rush into tearing the place apart quite yet, son,' the DCI replied. 'Maybe someone in the family can tell us something.'

Since he'd now landed on the subject, Logan talked a bit more about the family. He told the others what Krystal had said about the McQuarrie siblings being the first on the scene, about the alleged recent arguments between father and son, and the 'scuffle' that Krystal had overheard.

'So one of them got violent?' asked Sinead over the speaker of Tyler's phone.

'Again, she just said she thought it was "a scuffle", but she couldn't tell me any more than that,' Logan replied. 'Could've been nothing, but I'm going to pull him in for questioning after this meeting and see what he has to say for himself. Krystal suggested I might want to take Tyler into the interview with me.'

'Knows talent when she sees it, eh, boss?'

'Something like that, aye,' Logan said.

'Well, far be it from me to deprive you of my help, boss. Count me in.'

'Oh, thanks. But I wasn't really giving you an option.'

'What about the sister?' Hamza asked. 'Any gen on her?'

'Helen Bach,' Tammi-Jo clarified, mostly because she just enjoyed saying the name out loud.

'She's a weird one,' Tyler said.

'They're all bloody weird ones,' Logan countered. 'The whole lot of them.'

'The chef seemed like a nice enough guy,' Tammi-Jo said.

Logan raised his fingertips across the stubble on his chin. 'Aye. Maybe. But his story on who arrived at the scene and when doesn't quite line up with Krystal's, so one of them's full of shite.'

'Or one of them's just mixed up,' Ben suggested. 'Stressful situation, lot of people around, possible someone just lost track.'

'You're a more generous man than me, Benjamin,' Logan said. 'But maybe. The chef's the only one with access to the spare key to the study, though.'

'And it was a kitchen knife used in the attack, boss,' Tyler pointed out.

'Aye. And he confirmed it was one of his,' Logan said. 'And, interestingly enough, he said he was in the kitchen when he heard the scream from upstairs, but Krystal said the kitchen was locked when Helen went down to get the study key.'

'So he's definitely lying, then?' Tyler asked.

'Or Krystal is. Or Helen was.' Logan sighed. 'And the man with the only key to the room using his own knife as a murder weapon all feels a bit too convenient, meaning he probably had hee-haw to do with it. But we'll talk to him, too. Formally, this time.'

He rattled quickly through what little else they currently knew: the fact that Montgomery and his wife didn't share a room, much less a bed; the missing ring on the dead man's finger; and the hints that Krystal had dropped regarding Monty's sexuality.

'What's that got to do with anything?' asked Sinead.

'That depends on how his old man felt on the matter,' Logan replied. 'And how he reacted if and when he found out.'

'Sounds like you're going to have your hands full for a while yet, Jack,' Ben said.

'Aye. Tell me about it. No word on backup getting through?'

'Mitchell won't even entertain the idea yet,' the DI replied. 'Still far too dangerous for the choppers, and there's no way by road now that the bridge is out.'

'Looking at the forecast, nothing's getting through until much later tonight, sir,' Hamza said. 'I reckon you're stuck there.'

'Wait, what?' Tyler leaned forward in his chair and shot a worried look at his carefully balanced mobile phone. 'Stuck? Here? Like, *spending the night* stuck?'

'Based on the forecast, maybe,' Hamza confirmed. 'Why? Is there a problem?'

Tyler glanced around the room, his gaze sweeping across the rows of books, the old stone walls, and the dark, shadowy ceiling far overhead.

'Problem?' he said, his voice artificially bright and cheerful sounding. 'Spending Halloween night in a creepy old haunted castle with a murderer on the loose?' He swallowed. 'What could possibly be the problem with that…?'

## *Chapter 24*

Once the recap was finished, and the part of the team not currently in the castle had confirmed they understood what was expected of them, Tammi-Jo led Logan to the interview room they'd sourced.

Judging by the layout, it had been some sort of guest lounge at some point. A couple of couches, an armchair and an old CRT television had been covered by white dust sheets, and this—coupled with the faint smell of damp—suggested the room hadn't been used in a while.

A table and four chairs had been uncovered at the back of the room, next to a window that ran almost all the way from floor to ceiling. A pair of thick red drapes hung on either side of the glass, framing the dark, rain-slicked panes. A few of the panes were cracked. All of them were partially covered by cobwebs, as were the light fittings, and much of the cornicing up by the ceiling.

It was not a room anyone would choose to spend any longer in than absolutely necessary.

For his purposes, it was perfect.

Logan's phone sprang to life in his pocket. He sent DC Swanney off to help Tyler locate Montgomery McQuarrie Jr, while he answered the video call.

'Hey! How's it going?'

Shona Maguire's face filled the screen. The angle wasn't the most flattering, and afforded him a clearer view of the inside of her nose than he'd necessarily have chosen for himself.

'You get your man put away in the fridge?'

'Aye, he's in. Took a bit of doing, but he's in there now on a trolley Tyler and Tammi-Jo reckon appeared from nowhere.'

'That's handy,' Shona said. Her face contorted, then she quickly moved to adjust the angle of her phone until she found a less nasally invasive one. 'How is it going otherwise?'

'Well, not brilliantly,' Logan admitted. 'We're completely cut off here. Looking like we'll be staying the night.'

'Ah, bollocks! We're meant to be watching *Halloween*,' the pathologist reminded him. 'I painted a William Shatner mask white and everything. I was going to scare the living shite out of you with it.'

'Like the werewolf?'

'Exactly like the werewolf! Though not in the fridge, obviously. I'm not drinking from that well twice. I was going to hide behind the panel on the side of the bath and jump out when you went to the toilet.'

Logan stared at her face on the screen of his phone for what felt like an eternity.

'You've got a problem. You know that?' he finally asked.

'It's *Halloween*, Jack!' she said. 'I can't believe you're going to miss it.'

'Aye. I mean, obviously I'm devastated…'

Shona smirked. 'Oh, well, in that case, we'll wait until you get back.'

'No, no. You fire on. Don't let me spoil your plans,' Logan insisted.

'It's not a bother. We'll do another mini-marathon the moment you're back home!'

'Oh, great,' said the DCI, making no effort whatsoever to hide his disappointment.

Shona grinned, enjoying the look on his face. 'How's Taggart doing?'

'Aye, fine. He's standing guard outside the crime scene with one of the local bobbies. Mostly because the lad's got a bag of treats with him. I think word of Tyler's various canine encounters has spread.'

'Good idea to be prepared,' Shona said. 'You won't get Taggart away from him now.'

'That's the plan,' Logan said. 'Looks like you were right, by the way. About the cause of death.'

'No other injuries?'

'Nothing I saw, no. I mean, it's possible he was poisoned, I suppose, but my money's still on the big knife through the forehead.'

'Mine, too. There'd usually be signs of poisoning,' Shona agreed. She was still in her office at the hospital, and at the sound of a creaking door she turned and looked off-camera. 'Can you give me a minute, Neville?'

The reply was too low for Logan to hear, but a second creak told him Shona's assistant had left again.

'That George Clooney, was it?'

Shona laughed. 'Come on, he's nothing like George Clooney!' she said. 'He's *way* younger, for starters.'

That didn't make Logan feel much better, but he decided not to comment any further on the matter. It wouldn't do for him to look jealous of a twenty-something mortuary assistant.

Not that he was jealous, of course. But it wouldn't be good if it looked like he was.

Which he wasn't.

Before the DCI could fall much further down that particular rabbit hole, a question from Shona stopped him.

'Detective Superintendent Mitchell told me you had a call this morning.'

On the surface, it didn't appear to be a question at all. At first glance, it was a harmless statement of fact.

But there was an implied question there. He could hear it jostling for space between the lines.

A question that he wasn't yet ready to answer.

'How did that come up in conversation?' he asked. 'In fact, why were you and Mitchell even having a conversation at all?'

'She was asking about the RTA,' Shona told him. 'She called me up to check some details.'

'What sort of details?' Logan asked.

Shona shrugged. 'Just name and age of the deceased. That kind of thing. Why, does it matter?'

Yes, it bloody well mattered. Checking the basic details of an RTA, even one with fatalities, was so far below the Det Supt's rank that she'd need an abseil rope and a strong stomach just to see the top of it.

That hadn't been the real reason for Mitchell's call, regardless of what she'd said to the pathologist.

'What else did she have to say for herself?'

Shona's hesitation was hard to read. Maybe she was making up an answer. Maybe she was trying to decide how much of the truth to reveal. Maybe the internet connection had simply stuttered again, momentarily freezing her in place.

Whatever the reason, when she finally spoke, Logan couldn't shake the feeling that she was lying.

'She didn't say a lot. Not really. Just that the call seemed... personal.'

'That's right,' Logan confirmed. There was a harshness to his tone, like the edges of all the words had been clipped short.

'What bit?'

'It's personal,' he told her.

On the screen, Shona tried to arrange her face into a smile, but her shock shone through it.

'Jack, if there's something wrong, you know you can talk to me.'

'There's nothing wrong. And if there was, it'd be nothing I'd want to discuss,' he told her. He checked his watch, being sure to make a bit of a show of it. 'Now, I need to crack on here. Thanks for calling and checking in. I'll talk to you later, all right?'

'All ri—' she began, but then Logan thumbed the button that ended the call, and slipped the phone back into his pocket.

He turned to the window. His reflection stared back at him from the darkening glass, warped and twisted by the rainwater on the pane.

'Smoothly done, Jack,' he mumbled. 'Really smoothly done.'

–

'Hold on! Wait! Listen!' Marcus Doyle stumbled to a stop halfway down a corridor and leaned a hand on the wall to stop himself falling over. His voice was a whisper. His eyes seemed to swell in their sockets as they scanned the shadows around him. 'Can you feel that, Yvonne?'

At Marcus's side, Yvonne wrung her hands together, the blood draining from her face.

'What is it, Marcus? What's happening? What are you feeling?'

'C-cold,' Marcus hissed, his body shaking. 'It's s-so c-cold, Yvonne. Can't you f-feel it? It's suddenly gone so c-c-cold!'

Yvonne hugged herself and rubbed her arms, very much suggesting she was experiencing the same phenomenon, even as she shook her head in complete denial.

'No, Marcus. I don't feel cold. I feel fine. The temperature's normal.' She let out a gasp. 'Wait! Could it be…'

'Oh! Yes! Oh. It's from the other side, Yvonne,' Marcus croaked. He raised a trembling hand, then recoiled like the air itself had electrocuted him. 'Oh! Oh, yes. Yes. That's what it is. It's definitely from the other side.'

'The other side?' Yvonne whispered. She appeared gobsmacked by the concept, as if she hadn't had dozens of conversations not a million miles away from this one over the years. 'Do you mean the spirit world?'

'They're from the spirit realm, yes! From beyond the veil,' Marcus confirmed, the mysterious onset of cold now apparently forgotten. 'But they're stuck, Yvonne. They're stuck here on this plane with us!'

Yvonne raised her voice as if she was talking to someone hard of hearing. 'Can you hear them, Marcus? *What are they saying?*'

Marcus's eyes had closed now. He screwed his face up, his head jerking forward and back like he was some semi-aquatic bird struggling to swallow a whole live fish.

'Oh. No. No, no. Oh, no, no, Yvonne. No. You mustn't. You mustn't ask that! You mustn't!'

'What's happening, Marcus? What are they saying?' Yvonne whispered. She put a steadying hand on his arm, then craned her neck to address the ceiling above her. 'What do you want, spirits? Why are you here? Can you hear me? What do you want of us?'

'They can hear you, Yvonne. They can hear you,' Marcus said, his voice a dry scrape at the back of his throat. He shook his head violently, his eyes still shut. 'No. Don't. You can't. Please, don't.'

'What are they saying, Marcus? What's happening?'

'They're saying...'

'What are they saying, Marcus? Tell us what they're saying. What do they say?'

'They're saying...' Marcus's eyes jerked open. His mouth twisted into a sneer. 'Slut!' he squealed. 'That's what you are! Dirty little slut! Dirty, *dirty* little slut!'

Yvonne stepped back, a hand flying to her mouth. 'Marcus? Marcus, is that you?! What's happening, Marcus? Marcus, what's happening?'

'Slut! Whore! Filthy, dirty whore!' her co-presenter cried in a voice that wasn't quite his own.

And yet, still mostly his own.

'Slut, bitch, *show us your tits, show us your tits*!' he shrieked, jerking towards her with a look of demented glee etching itself into the lines of his face.

'Bloody hell, steady on!'

At the sound of the voice from behind them, Marcus and Yvonne both turned back along the corridor to look in the direction it had come from. Gavin lowered the camera, pointing it towards the floor.

Tyler stood at the end of the passageway, a hand raised in front of his face to shield his eyes from the beams of the portable lighting rig.

'What the hell do you think you're doing?' Marcus demanded. 'We were filming. That was good stuff we were getting there! That was gold!'

Yvonne tilted her head from side to side, somewhat less convinced. 'You just got possessed and called me a slut again. For, like, the twentieth time.'

'Yes, because that's what people want to fucking see, isn't it, sweetheart? Getting taken over by a ghost and calling you a slut's a classic, and it's a classic for a reason, because people can't get enough of it. Why? Because, deep down, man and woman alike, whether they want to admit it or not, they think it's true.'

'Jesus!' Yvonne protested. 'No, they don't!'

Marcus put a hand on her shoulder in a reassuring, father-like gesture. 'They do. And that's fine. That's why you're on the show.'

Yvonne spluttered with outrage. 'I bring a lot to this show!'

'You do. Course you do!' Marcus agreed. 'All them dads who used to crack one off after watching you jumping about in your wee T-shirt on that awful fucking kids' show. Them. You bring them.'

'It does feel a bit tired,' Gavin ventured, which earned him a scowl and a pointed finger from Marcus.

'You, shut the fuck up. No one asked you. You'—he turned his extended finger in Tyler's direction—'what do you want? We're trying to salvage this shoot here, and you're getting in the way.'

Tyler looked between them all with a sense of trepidation. 'I, uh, I'm pretty sure you shouldn't be filming right now.'

'I beg your pardon?' Marcus asked. He advanced a few steps along the corridor. The glow of the lighting rigs cast him in a deep, brooding silhouette.

'I don't think you should be filming,' Tyler said, hardening his stance on the matter, albeit only ever so slightly. 'I don't think DCI Logan would approve.'

'Well, DCI Logan doesn't have an entire TV show resting on his shoulders, does he?' Marcus shot back. 'He doesn't have a station controller breathing down his neck, or the pay cheques of a full cast and crew to worry about.'

Tyler stole another glance at Yvonne and Gavin. They didn't really feel like much of a 'full cast and crew'.

'I still don't think it's really appropriate for you to be filming when—'

'Do you know about this castle, pal?' Marcus asked, cutting the DC's protest short. 'Do you know the stories about it?'

The skin prickled on the back of Tyler's neck as a cool breeze blew along the corridor.

He didn't want to ask. He didn't want to know.

And yet, he had to.

'What stories?'

'About the ghosts that haunt this place?' Marcus said. He advanced again, and Tyler found himself taking a half-step back. 'They say they stalk the halls. They say they can be heard shuffling around in the dead of night. Crying out. Screaming in anguish. The tormented spirits of three murderers, two rapists, and a big scary dog.'

He took a sudden big step, closing the gap between him and Tyler. Earlier, he hadn't seemed like a particularly imposing man, but here, standing face to face, he was almost giving Logan a run for his money.

'Now, obviously you and I know that's a lot of old bollocks,' he intoned. 'But the people who watch my show? Those cretins? That's manna from fucking heaven, as far as they're concerned. To them, that's the good shit. So, how about you clear off for half an hour, let us get this in the can, then you can ask us anything you want to ask us? All right?'

'I, eh, I wasn't actually looking for you,' Tyler replied. 'I was looking for Monty. Junior, I mean.'

Marcus held his arms out to his sides, gesturing at the corridor around them.

'Do you see him here, anywhere?'

Tyler was forced to admit that no, he didn't.

'Well, then.' The *Ghost Spotters* presenter motioned back the way that Tyler had come. 'If you could clear the set, that'd be very much—'

From behind them, there came a sound like thunder tearing through an industrial kitchen. Everyone—Tyler most of all—jumped in fright and spun around in time to see the helmet of a suit of armour come rolling along the passageway towards them.

The rest of the armour lay in an unceremonious heap, one metal boot sticking up into the air, a chest plate rocking from side to side like the shell of an upturned turtle.

After a moment, the head of a little girl swung briefly into view from around the corner, her eyes wide with panic.

'*Claire!*'

Marcus's shout was like the roar of some raging beast. It made the girl shrink back in fright.

And, to be fair, it had a similar effect on Tyler.

'What *the hell* did I tell you about touching anything?! What did I say about doing something so bloody stupid?!'

The beam of one of the spotlights caught the way her face collapsed and picked out the silvery trails of her tears.

Sobbing, she turned on her heels and went racing off, her clattering footsteps fading as she raced away into the maze-like castle corridors.

'Oh, smoothly done, Marcus,' Yvonne snapped. 'For God's sake.'

'Bit much, mate,' Gavin said, sucking air in through his teeth.

'I'm not your mate,' Marcus replied.

He stared at the fallen suit of armour for a few moments, then tutted, shook his head, and turned back to the producer.

'Right, get that camera rolling. I want to get this in the can so we can move on.'

Tyler cleared his throat, drawing Marcus's attention again.

'So, you're going to let her run off like that, are you? Upset and on her own?'

'Yes. She's not an infant. She's six.'

'Seven,' Yvonne corrected.

Marcus didn't skip a beat. 'She's *seven*. She can't exactly go anywhere. What's the worst that can happen to her?'

'Well, there's a murderer on the loose,' Tyler reminded him. 'So, you know, that's potentially pretty bad.'

Marcus rolled his eyes. 'Jesus Christ, don't be so melodramatic. She's going to be fine. She does this all the time, fucks something up, then runs off like I'm the bad one. She'll come back like she always does, but if you're that worried about her, you feel free to go find her.'

He sniffed, turned back to Gavin, then motioned for him to start the camera rolling again.

'Some of us have got work to be getting on with.'

# *Chapter 25*

Logan stood aside, making way for Monty Jr to enter the damp-smelling interview room.

'Take a seat at the table there, Mr McQuarrie. Be right with you,' he said, then he pulled the door closed and turned to Tammi-Jo. 'Where was he?'

'In his room, sir. I had to ask around a bit. It's crazy, the size of this place. I nearly got lost twice. And then I did get lost once, but I found myself again after a few minutes, so it was fine.'

'Right—'

'Found myself in a literal sense, I mean. Not a spiritual way, or anything.'

'I see. Have—'

'Although, I did have a bit of a moment when I thought I might be wandering the halls forever. I wouldn't say I found God or anything, but I definitely had a moment when I felt sort of—it sounds funny—sort of in harmony with everything. Sort of one with the whole universe.'

'OK, but—'

'But then I found the stairs, and it was fine.' She smiled brightly. 'Sorry, sir. What were you going to say?'

'Did you see Tyler?' Logan asked, taking a big swerve around the vast majority of everything the DC had just said.

Tammi-Jo looked back along the corridor. 'No, sir. Isn't he with you?'

'He's supposed to be helping you find Monty Junior.'

'I already found him, sir.'

'No. I know. But Tyler was…' Logan sighed. 'Forget it. You're here. You can help me with the interview.'

'No problem, sir. Happy to help.'

'Good. Aye.' Logan rubbed his chin for a moment, deep in thought, then turned back towards the door. 'But maybe don't mention the whole becoming one with the universe thing, eh? I can't help but feel that might just complicate matters.'

–

'Hello? Claire? You there?'

Tyler's voice echoed down the length of a long, narrow passageway, most of which lay shrouded in darkness. He had no urge to go that way, and several different urges all telling him to head in the opposite direction entirely.

But the girl had to have gone down there.

The only other option involved her climbing out of a window, and given that most of those didn't open, either by design or through generations of overly generous paintwork, this seemed unlikely.

Besides, even if she'd been able to climb out, doing so would be insanity. The storm was still building, the rain hammering against the glass, the wind groaning and creaking through the trees outside, so their spindly branches clawed hungrily at the walls.

Not for the first time in its history, Tyler assumed, the castle was under attack. And, as attackers went, Mother Nature was about as brutal as they came.

Taking his phone from his pocket, Tyler activated the flashlight function. The light from it was weak, and only illuminated half a dozen or so metres into the passageway, before fading into a dim, insipid glow further along.

He wished he had the proper torch with him—the big, long-handled one they'd taken from Logan's car. The light it gave off was far more powerful, and it had the added benefit of being solid enough to use as a pretty effective weapon.

Unfortunately, that had been left locked up in the library, along with all their notes on the investigation so far. The thin beam of light emitted by his phone was just going to have to do.

The passage felt like it had been hewn from a single piece of solid stone. The walls were bumpy and uneven, and the raised ridges cast shadows that scurried and scampered across the craggy rock face as Tyler shuffled his way along.

'Claire? It's me. It's, eh, DC Neish. With the police. Are you all right?'

The only reply was his own echo. It bounced around inside the narrow space until it seemed to be coming from all directions at once.

The curved roof of the passage scraped across the top of Tyler's head, forcing him to duck and eject a hissed, 'Ow!'

There was no way DCI Logan would fit through this space. It was just wide enough that he might be able to ease himself through it sideways, but the gradual slope of the roof meant that his height would make the passage impassable.

It was even becoming tight for Tyler, in fact, and he had just about decided to turn back when the narrow confines opened up again, and he stepped into a corridor he'd never seen before.

The walls, floor and ceiling were all made of, or perhaps just covered with, aged and knackered-looking old wood. It had all been lovingly and carefully varnished at some point, by the looks of it, but time had worn away at it, and the elements had blackened and stained it in places.

Water dripped from a sagging bulge in the ceiling. Mould had bloomed all around the leak, so it looked like the building had developed a cancerous growth.

The floor directly beneath it was sagging, and looked in danger of collapsing completely. There was more solid footing to the right of the damage, and Tyler held his breath as he tiptoed past, one hand pressed against the wall like he might be able to cling to it, Spider-Man style, should the floor give way beneath him.

Moisture oozed from the wood beneath his touch, like the building was sweating. Although, he had to admit, it wasn't sweating nearly as badly as he was.

The rotting boards grumbled and groaned as he crept across them, and then he was past the area of damage, and the floor felt reassuringly solid again.

There were no lights here, just the pale grey glow through the dusty windows, and the beam from his phone's torch. It had been several hours since he'd taken the phone off its charger, and the constant searching for a signal had taken its toll on the battery.

He had just over twenty per cent left. Not a problem normally, but the torch would burn through that in no time. If he was going to find the girl, he'd better do it fast.

The route branched a little further along, leading to another darkened stone passageway on the right, and another wood-lined corridor on the left.

At the end of this second corridor, a set of heavy-looking double doors was swinging gently back and forth. Tyler watched as it settled back into place, then waited to see if it would start moving again.

It didn't. So, it wasn't the wind, then. Someone had either gone through it, or nudged it from the other side.

Claire. It had to be.

Didn't it?

As the battery ticked down to nineteen, Tyler raised his phone in front of him like it was a crucifix with which to ward off all evil, and ventured onwards in search of the girl.

# *Chapter 26*

Maybe it was because he was tired. Maybe it was because he was stressed. Whatever the reason, Monty Jr's enlarged right eye seemed particularly exaggerated when Logan and Tammi-Jo sat down across the table from him.

He sat bolt upright in the chair, his hands clasped on the table in front of him, his tongue rubbing back and forth against the front of his teeth so that his top lip moved like it was alive.

'Thanks for talking to us, Mr McQuarrie,' Logan began. 'I should stress at this point that this is just an informal chat. You're not under arrest. You're free to leave at any time. You're not being treated as a suspect at this time, and while my colleague, DC Swanney, will be making some notes, we won't be recording the interview. Does that all work for you?'

'At this time,' Monty Jr said.

Logan raised an eyebrow. 'I'm sorry?'

'I'm not being treated as a suspect "at this time".'

Logan smiled grimly. 'Correct.' He checked that Tammi-Jo had her notebook open and was ready to write, then clasped his hands together, mirroring Monty's pose. 'I'd like you to tell me about this morning. Walk me through it, if you would.'

'From when?'

'From whenever you feel is appropriate.'

Monty tapped his thumbs together a few times, pursed his lips tightly together, then gave a nod.

'I woke up at half-six. I'd had a sleepless night. The storm. As you've no doubt gathered, the castle isn't great at keeping the noise out. Certainly, my bedroom isn't. The sound isn't as bad down here.'

He gestured around the room, and Logan noted a suggestion of confusion on his face.

'But up on the top floor, it sounds considerably worse.'

'What's this room for?' Logan enquired.

'I have no idea,' Monty admitted. 'I was just wondering that same thing. I've never been in here before.'

'Haven't you lived here most of your life?' Logan asked.

'On and off. Papa has a number of houses around the world. But, as with many of those, much of this place was off-limits to my sister and I.'

'And why's that?'

Monty blew out his cheeks. 'Because Papa liked rules, I think? Often just for the sake of them. He liked to establish who was in charge at home, as well as in business. He'd set arbitrary boundaries just so everyone understood that he could.'

He glanced around the room again.

'Although, to be fair to the old goat, it doesn't look like we were missing much.'

'I'm starting to get the impression that he was quite a difficult man,' Logan said. The bluntness of it took Monty Jr aback.

'That's quite a statement, considering you never met him!'

'I'm right, though.'

Monty unclasped his hands and drummed his fingers on the tabletop. 'You're not wrong, let's say that much. Papa had quite… exacting standards.'

Logan unclasped his hands and leaned back in his chair a little. 'Even that I find interesting.'

Monty's brow creased. 'Even what?'

'You call him "Papa". Your sister calls him "Daddy". Seems quite unusual.'

'That was Papa's decision. He decided what we'd each call him. He instilled it into us from an early age.'

'That must've stung,' Tammi-Jo said.

Both men turned to look at her.

'I beg your pardon?' Monty asked.

'Well, Daddy seems more affectionate than Papa. To me, I mean. Daddy feels loving. Papa feels a bit sort of stand-offish.'

Monty snorted dismissively. 'Nothing of the kind. That's not the case. It couldn't be further from the truth, actually. You don't know what you're talking about. It's the opposite, if anything.'

Logan picked up the baton and ran with it. 'I see. So, you'd say you were closer to your father than your sister was, then?'

'Yes! We were very close. We had a strong father-son relationship. Was he strict? Yes. Did he expect me to meet the standards he'd set for me? Of course. And those expectations made me the man I am today, so I'm nothing but grateful for them.'

Tammi-Jo's pen scratched away at her pad. Logan waited for her to catch up, then continued.

'Going back to this morning. Half-six?'

'Right. Yes. Half-six. I woke up, toileted, showered—I have an en suite.'

'Congratulations,' Logan said. 'Go on.'

'Then I headed for Papa's study. This was about… seven-ish?'

'Why so early?'

'It was the usual routine. He expected me there at seven fifteen every morning. I was permitted into his study then for an hour. That's when we'd discuss the day's business.'

'Just what sort of business was your father in?' Logan asked.

'Every sort of business. He had shares in everything from arms manufacture to green energy, though his early fortune was made mostly through property.'

'Pays to diversify, clearly.'

'If you know what you're doing, yes. Which he did,' Monty said. 'Anyway, I got to the study and knocked, as usual. He normally instructs me to enter, I go in, make him coffee, and then he talks and I make notes.'

A frown troubled him, temporarily shrinking his one big eye. 'But he didn't answer when I knocked. I tried the door, but it was locked. So, although highly irregular, I assumed he was somewhere else. I went searching, but couldn't find him, so I returned to the study and looked through the keyhole. When I realised it was blocked, and that the key was in the other side, I fetched Helen. We both knocked for a while. I tried kicking the door down, but it's frightfully heavy, and so Helen fetched one of the battleaxes from her bedroom and we hacked away until we got it open.'

Tammi-Jo looked up from her notes. 'Your sister has battle-axes in her bedroom?'

'Yes. Several. My sister has always had a keen interest in… dangerous things. That's why her art is so'—he waved a hand around, searching for the word—'visceral.'

'Cool!' the DC remarked, then she went back to writing.

'You broke down the door. Then what?' Logan asked.

'Well, then we found him.' There was a flat, matter-of-factness to the response, but despite Monty's best efforts, Logan could sense a suggestion of rawness belying it. 'We found him in his chair. Dead. He'd been stabbed. I mean, obviously. You saw that. It was quite hard to miss.'

Tammi-Jo glanced up from her notes again. 'His forehead?'

Monty blinked. 'Seeing the knife, I meant,' he said after a pause. 'It was quite hard to miss seeing the knife.'

'Right. Yes. Sorry.'

Logan waited for her pen to return to the paper again, then urged Monty to continue.

'There's not much more to tell,' said the dead man's son. 'Helen screamed. Always the bloody drama queen. Next thing I knew, she was trying to yank the knife out of Papa's head. She was practically standing in his lap at one point. I thought she might rip his head right off his shoulders. I was trying to wrestle her off him when the others arrived.'

'Others?' Logan pressed.

'The TV people. Krystal. Francois.' His lips drew back over his teeth in distaste. 'That frightful creature Helen's got herself in tow with. They were all there.'

'Who arrived first?' Logan asked.

'God, I don't know! How do you expect me to know that?' Monty asked. 'I wasn't standing at the door taking their bloody coats! One minute, it was just Helen and I, the next moment, the room was full of them. Everyone was shouting and screaming. I don't even know who called the police. I know it wasn't me, but in all the chaos, I can't say who actually picked up the phone and placed the call.'

He ran a hand through his hair. It was thinning, and the movement revealed a patch of pale, unsightly scalp.

'The television producer got us out in the end. Told us we were compromising the evidence. Of course, by that point, Krystal had tried yanking the knife out, and had almost scratched my eyes out when I tried to pull her away from him. That woman's a bloody menace. And a charlatan.'

'A charlatan? What makes you say that?'

'Well, come on!' Monty cried. 'She's half his age, and while my father was many, *many* wonderful things, physically attractive wasn't exactly one of them!'

'You think she married him for his money?'

'I know she married him for his money! They always do. That's all they're ever after!' Monty laughed, like the very suggestion Krystal may have married his father for love was comically absurd.

'Usually, his pre-nuptial agreements put the gold-diggers off, but a few of them—Krystal included—just cross their fingers and hope that he'll die before he gets fed up and divorces them. Then, they'll have all that wealth without the obligation to be occasionally rogered by a cantankerous old man who, with the best will in the world, looks remarkably like Mr Toad.'

'Yes! I knew he reminded me of someone!' Tammi-Jo announced. 'Thank you! That's been bugging me all day. It's the neck, isn't it? It's the neck and the eyes.'

'Uh...' Monty Jr stared at her, clearly unsure of how to respond.

Logan gently cleared his throat and tapped on the detective constable's pad, directing her attention back to the task at hand.

'Sorry, sir,' she said, then went back to writing down the last few things that Monty had said.

'Can you think of any reason why anyone would want to kill your father?' Logan asked.

'Dozens. Hundreds, probably. He wasn't a well-liked man. I'm sure there are countless business associates and rivals who would love to see the back of him. Not to mention ex-wives, former lovers, several politicians and a fair few members of the Royal household.'

He tapped the tips of all his fingers together, then interlocked them again.

'Oh, and everyone on Twitter. He was particularly unpopular there.'

'He had a Twitter account?'

'No. Gosh, no. But whenever a news piece would mention him, he'd be torn to shreds on there.'

'Did that bother him?'

'Bother him? Quite the opposite. He loved it. It fuelled him. You must understand, Papa took great pleasure in antagonising people. It was one of his few genuine joys in life.'

'And what about you, Mr McQuarrie?' the DCI asked.

'Me? No. I can't say I enjoy making people suffer. Certainly not simply for the sake of it.'

'I meant, did you have reason to kill him?'

Monty was so quick to spit out his response that he almost choked on it. 'I beg your pardon? No! No, of course not! That man was my inspiration. He was my idol. I worshipped the ground he walked on! I'd never hurt him. I've never so much as said a bad word about him!'

'You said he looked like Mr Toad,' Logan reminded him.

'Well, he did look like Mr Toad! He'd be the first to admit that!' Monty cried. 'But that's all just a bit of fun. I'd never truly speak out against him. I simply wouldn't.'

'Because you had nothing bad to say, or because you were too scared to say it?' Logan pressed.

'Because I respected him too much,' Monty countered. 'Did I always agree with his decisions? No. But I respected them.'

'Is that why you two got into a fight recently?' Logan asked. 'Did you disagree with one of his decisions?'

Monty's hesitation stretched on a moment or two too long. His answer, when it came, sounded so thin the detectives could see right through it.

'Disagreement? I don't recall a disagreement.'

'Well, you had one,' Logan insisted. 'Three or four nights ago. You were heard. Raised voices in the study. A physical altercation. Ringing any bells?'

'Oh, that? That was nothing. We were just discussing business matters.'

'You said you did that in the mornings,' Logan reminded him.

'Pardon?'

'You said…' Logan gave Tammi-Jo a nod, and she took up the thread.

'"He expected me there at seven fifteen every morning",' she said, reading from her notes. '"I was permitted into his study then for an hour. That's when we'd discuss the day's business."'

Monty's mouth opened and closed a few times, searching for a response. The one it eventually settled on hardly seemed worth the wait.

'So?'

'So, you said you discuss business matters in the morning. That's when you're allowed into the study. That was your "usual routine", you said.' Logan shrugged. 'So, what changed? Why were you in there talking shop so late in the day?'

'I don't recall.'

'That's strange. If it was out of the ordinary, and then you had a fight, you'd think that'd stick in your mind.'

'Look, I didn't do anything, if that's what you're getting at. I didn't do anything to my father!' Monty almost shrieked the words, his hands splayed on the tabletop. 'If you should be quizzing anyone, it's my sister! She's the one he was threatening to cut off if she didn't get rid of that ridiculous… bee-headed…'

He tried desperately to find a clever word befitting of his education and station, but one eluded him.

'*Fuck!*' he concluded. He held his hands up. 'I apologise. That's too far. I shouldn't have said that. But he is. He really is. He's a ridiculous, bee-headed, tattooed *fuck*, and Papa was right to be making Helen choose. Us or him. The family, and all the trappings that go with it, or that ludicrous, talentless… thing.'

Logan ran his tongue against the back of his teeth, studying the other man's facial expressions and body language.

'What actually is he?' Tammi-Jo asked. 'The bee-head man?'

'Yes! Precisely! What even is he?' Monty Jr cried.

This didn't really help Tammi-Jo, who'd been asking a genuine question, but she went back to writing, regardless.

'Let me get this straight, Mr McQuarrie,' Logan intoned. 'Your father was making your sister choose between her partner and her family?'

'And all the money,' Tammi-Jo added.

'Yes! And quite bloody right, too! He'd given her a lot of leeway in the past, but it was time to grow up. It was time to make a choice. Frankly, if I'd been in his shoes, and had to watch Helen parade freak after freak around in front of the cameras all these years, I'd have taken a stand long ago.'

'He didn't approve of her lifestyle, then?'

'He didn't care about her lifestyle. Not really. He was perfectly happy for her to swan around pretending to be an artist. She was free to do what she wanted.'

There was a heavy emphasis on that first 'she' that spoke volumes about Monty Jr's own level of freedom.

'But the men. God, the men. Each one worse than the one before. I'd been saying to Papa for years that he needed to put a stop to it, and when he finally agrees, when he finally listens, when he finally delivers his ultimatum, what happens?' He brought up his hands and made air quotes with his fingers. '"Someone" murders him. Ha! Do you believe in coincidences, Detective Chief Inspector?'

'Not really, no.'

'No,' Monty said. 'Nor do I.' He slouched back in his chair. 'You want to find out what happened to my father? You're talking to the wrong sibling.'

## *Chapter 27*

Tyler had barely set foot in the room when he saw the ghost. It hovered just at the edge of his torch's light—a full-sized floating figure that made his heart leap into his throat and his blood run cold, even as the logical part of his brain hurried to point out that what he was looking at was, in fact, a dust sheet covering a standing lamp.

Fortunately, on this occasion, he was able to retain just enough composure to be able to listen to the reassuring inner voice without first screaming and running away.

It was a lamp. That was all. Just a lamp.

Wood groaned behind him.

'Hi,' whispered a voice.

Tyler made a noise that defied all description, leaped into the air, and then scrambled for his phone as it flew out of his hands. The torchlight lurched across the walls and ceiling as the phone flipped in the air, and Tyler caught just the briefest glimpse of a pale face with wide eyes before the mobile thudded to the floor.

The torch landed pointing down, trapping the light against a single square inch of floor, and plunging the rest of the room into darkness.

Frantically, Tyler dropped to his knees and snatched the phone up again. As he raised it, the face of a seven-year-old girl was illuminated less than a foot from his own.

'Claire?' he whispered, his voice a heady mix of relief and bone-chilling terror.

The girl slowly put a finger to her lips. 'Stay quiet,' she said, and the white bloom of her breath rolled out as she spoke. 'Or you'll make the man angry.'

Tyler's buttocks squeezed together in fright. They were followed by all the other muscles below his waist until the whole lower half of his body felt like it was puckering up.

He tried to speak, but barely a squeak emerged on the first attempt. The second try was a little more successful. 'What man?'

Her eyes shimmered just beyond the edge of his torchlight as she looked past him.

'That man. The bad man.'

Despite the warning, Tyler ejected a wobbly, 'Fuuuck!' and sprang to his feet, spinning around and sweeping the torchlight around, frantically searching for any and all bad men who might be standing and/or floating in mid-air behind him.

He saw nothing.

No one.

'There's nobody there,' he said, though his eyes continued to dart up, down, left, right, hunting for any sign of movement.

'You can't see him. But I can,' Claire said. 'He's angry. He doesn't like you.'

'What do you mean? Why, what the hell have I done to him?' Tyler heard himself say, before he remembered that he was not only the adult in this situation, but a member of the constabulary.

He drew in a breath through his nose, let it out as a cloud of white mist through his mouth, then attempted a smile for the benefit of the girl beside him.

'There's nobody there, Claire. You're all right.'

'The man doesn't like that you said that,' the girl warned.

Tyler felt panic rising again. 'Well, the man can fu—' He stopped. Swallowed. Smiled again. 'There is no man, Claire. It's just your imagination. There's no such thing as ghosts.'

'No such thing as ghosts?'

Claire's eyebrows danced around for a moment like they were animated, then bunched together above the bridge of her nose. She looked around the room, into all the shadows, nooks and crannies.

'Then who are all those people?'

Tyler didn't look. He didn't dare. His heart was a hummingbird in his chest now. Blood pulsed through veins in his head that he had previously been unaware even existed. Sweat was pooling at the base of his spine, then chilling him as it made contact with the cold, damp air.

'There's no one there,' he insisted. The shake in his voice didn't really help to sell the statement, but it was the best he could do in the circumstances. 'It's just us, Claire. There's nobody else here.'

Claire slowly shook her head. Her gaze was fixed on him now. She looked incredibly intense for a seven-year-old.

'Not just here,' she whispered. 'They're everywhere. I see them all round the castle. Everywhere I go, I see them.'

She touched his hand. He hadn't seen her move, so he recoiled in fright, whipping his arm away and letting out a noise that was completely different to the one he'd made earlier, yet equally as indescribable.

'I see dead people,' Claire rasped.

Tyler's entire central nervous system would've shut itself down then, had it not been for the slightest suggestion of a smirk that tugged at one corner of the girl's mouth. The detective constable brought the beam of the torch up higher, so the glow illuminated her face, almost blinding her.

'Here! Are you winding me up?'

Claire bit down on her lip, but the giggle was too far along to be halted now. It exploded out of her with such force that a little bubble of snot inflated, then popped in one of her nostrils.

'You little bitc— You little cow!' Tyler cried. 'I almost had a bloody heart attack there! Bloody *dead people*! I nearly joined them.'

His outburst only made Claire laugh harder. Despite his recent terror, or perhaps because of it, Tyler couldn't help but find it infectious. He chuckled along, and all his tension burst like a bubble.

'You properly had me going for a minute there. I genuinely thought there was a ghost behind me.'

'Don't worry, there's not,' Claire assured him. She pointed to one of the room's many pools of shadow. 'He's over there.'

'Aye, very good. I'm not falling for that again,' Tyler told her. He held a hand out. 'Come on, you shouldn't be down here. It's dangerous.'

Claire glanced at his offered hand, but didn't reach for it.

'I always come down here,' she said, with a note of defiance that suggested she wouldn't be leaving anytime soon.

'Since when?' Tyler asked.

'Since we got here a few days ago. I found it while playing, but I come here when my dad's angry at me. Or angry at anyone. I don't like it when he shouts.'

She'd lowered her head and was fiddling with her hands, suddenly a different girl to the one he'd been speaking to just moments before.

'Does he shout a lot?'

Claire hesitated for a moment, but then nodded.

'At you?'

She nodded again.

'I do stupid stuff sometimes. Break things. Knock them over. Not on purpose, but. By accident. I'm just… I'm stupid.'

'Does he tell you that? That you're stupid?'

Claire shrugged. It wasn't a denial.

'Well, here, listen. I'm telling you now, you're not stupid, all right? Get that idea right out of your head.'

'I do stupid stuff,' Claire insisted.

'Here, so what? I do stupid stuff! And they let me join the police!'

Claire smiled, but it didn't last. 'You're just saying that.'

'No, I'm not! I crashed my car, got run over, nearly got hit by a train, then fell off a bridge.'

Claire's eyes widened. 'What, all at the same time?'

'Well, no,' Tyler admitted. 'Thankfully not. That would've been a pretty bad day. But I do stupid stuff all the time.' He glanced around, then leaned closer, as if sharing a big secret. 'Have you ever been chased by a big dog while you were dressed as a squirrel?'

The unexpectedness of it made Claire snort out a laugh. 'No!'

'I have! And I got locked in a cupboard for hours. Oh, *and* I ran away from my own wedding.'

Of everything he'd said, this seemed to shock the girl the most. 'What? You're married?'

'Yes! Try and not sound so bloody surprised! I'm a catch, I'll have you know!'

'Did you wear the squirrel suit to the wedding?'

'Very funny,' Tyler said.

Her smile crumbled, and she lowered her head again. 'It wasn't an accident.'

'What wasn't?'

The girl squirmed. 'The armour falling over. I did it on purpose.'

'Oh. Why?'

She shrugged. 'Don't know. The internet's not working, and I got bored.'

This was the first Tyler had heard about the internet. He checked his phone screen, and sure enough, the little WiFi signal had a line through it.

Beside him, Claire's voice gave a wobble. 'And I'm just bad. And stupid.'

'Here, listen to me. No, you're not,' he said. 'You're not bad, and you're not stupid. People make mistakes sometimes. Even grown-ups make mistakes. Especially grown-ups!'

Claire didn't look like she was buying it. Tyler sighed. There was only one thing for it.

'Can you keep a secret?' he asked.

She raised her head enough to nod, her interest clearly piqued.

Tyler glanced around again to make sure that no one was listening. And this time, he meant it.

'I thought about stealing something today.'

Claire's whole face seemed to swell in surprise. 'What? But you're the police.'

'I know! How mad is that?' Tyler let out a sigh, and felt a weight lifting from him. 'I mean, I didn't. I wouldn't. But for a second, I thought about it. I really did.'

'You shouldn't steal. Stealing's wrong,' Claire told him.

Tyler grinned. 'Aye, well, pushing over an antique suit of armour's not exactly ideal behaviour either, is it?'

It was a risky move. Fortunately, the girl took it as it was intended, and smiled back at him, albeit sheepishly. 'Not really,' she admitted.

'Tell you what,' Tyler said. 'You keep my secret, and I'll keep yours. You've told me what you did, and I'm the police, so you've confessed. You're in the clear. I won't tell anyone if you don't want me to.'

She nodded, hesitantly at first, then with growing enthusiasm.

'I wanted them to throw us out,' she explained. 'I don't like it here. I want to go home to my mum, but Dad says we're here until he's finished filming, even though the man said we had to go.'

Something tingled at the nape of Tyler's neck. Not fear this time.

'What man?'

The girl's gaze swept left and right, like she was suddenly searching for an exit.

'What man said you had to go, Claire?'

She shrugged. 'Him and Dad were shouting at each other. They were both angry. I came down here to hide, but I heard the man say we had to leave. He didn't want us here.'

'What man said that?'

Claire stretched out a toe and scuffed it across the floor, like she was drawing an imaginary line between them.

When she didn't reply, Tyler kneeled on one knee before her. The cold floor chilled him through his trousers.

'Who was your dad shouting at, Claire?'

Her head remained lowered, but her eyes raised to meet his.

'The dead man.'

'Oi!' Tyler tutted, but it was good-natured. 'You're not winding me up about ghosts again, are you?'

Claire's expression didn't change. She shook her head. It was only when a tear dripped from the end of her nose that Tyler realised she was crying.

'The real dead man. The man that was killed last night,' she whispered. 'That's the man that Dad was shouting at.'

# *Chapter 28*

'Where the hell have you been?' Logan demanded. He and Tammi-Jo arrived in the main hall just as Tyler was crossing it, leading Claire by the hand. 'You were meant to be in on that interview.'

'Search and rescue mission, boss,' Tyler said. He marched on with a determination in his stride that forced Logan to do a double take. 'Be right back. Claire's dad's been a bit out of order. He and I are going to have a word.'

'Right, well…' the DCI began, but Tyler had already pulled open one of the doors leading away from the foyer, and was gesturing for Claire to go first. 'Fair enough, then,' Logan found himself concluding to a rapidly closing door.

'Someone seems in a hurry,' Tammi-Jo remarked.

Logan nodded. 'Aye.'

'Tyler, I mean.'

The DCI glanced back over his shoulder at her. 'Aye, I worked that out.'

'Wonder what her dad's done?'

'Christ knows,' Logan muttered. He scraped at the stubble on his chin, deep in thought. 'What's the situation with your old man? He still being an arsehole?'

Tammi-Jo crinkled up her nose. 'Eh, on and off. He's better than he was. I think you having that word with him on the phone that time helped.'

'That's good.'

'And I told him if he didn't stop being such a dick, I'd burn his house down with him inside it.'

Logan's face contorted in shock. 'Jesus Christ!'

'I wasn't being serious!' the DC laughed. 'Of course I'm not going to *actually* burn his house down.' Her eyes sparkled mischievously. 'He doesn't know that, though.'

'Eh, good,' Logan replied, because he wasn't quite sure what else to say on the matter. 'I'm glad he's easing off on you a bit.'

'Yeah. He's still hard work, but then they quite often are, aren't they? Dads?'

Logan picked at a flap of loose skin by his thumbnail. 'Aye. They can be.'

Tammi-Jo let out a little gasp. 'I mean, I'm sure you're brilliant. As a dad, I mean. And in general, obviously. I'm sure you're brilliant at everything. I mean, boss, friend'—the next word was out of her mouth before she could stop it—'lover.'

Her eyes almost burst out of their sockets. 'Oh, God! Not that. Not… lover. I didn't mean… Although, I'm sure you're… That's none of my business. What you get up to in your own…'

She shook her head, stoated the heel of one hand against her temple a couple of times, then took a steadying breath and plastered on a smile.

'I'm sure you're a great dad!' she concluded, before throwing in a double thumbs up to help sweeten the deal.

Logan turned away. Outside, Storm Agatha continued to hammer at the castle's walls. Inside, the eyes of countless stuffed dead things fixed him with cold, accusing stares.

'Fatherhood was never actually my strong suit,' he admitted.

'Oh!' DC Swanney considered this for a moment, then shrugged. 'Well, everyone deserves a second chance. Especially your parents. Even mine, and he's, well, you know what he's like, you've spoken to him. Maybe you should give yourself a second chance. Try again. Take two, sort of thing.' She winced, like she may have once again put her foot in it. 'Unless… Are you too old now?'

'No, I am bloody not!'

'Well, then!' She gave him an encouraging slap on the upper arm. 'Good for you! Your little swimmers all still swimming away!' Her smile took on a desperate edge. 'Not that. I didn't mean to say that. About your little… Forget I said that.'

Logan stared at her for a while, then considered his arm where she'd hit him. He wasn't quite sure what had just happened, but felt it best not to delve too deeply.

'Happy to. Consider it forgotten,' he intoned. 'Now, let's not hang around waiting for Tyler to show his face again.' He picked an apparently random direction and started walking. 'I think it's time we had another chat with Helen Bach.'

-

Marcus Doyle had just delivered the performance of his career when the detective constable stepped into shot, ruining it completely.

'What the hell do you think you're doing?!' the *Ghost Spotters* presenter roared. Beside him, Yvonne crossed her arms, visibly bracing herself for the oncoming tantrum. 'I was absolutely nailing the delivery of that. That was TV fucking gold, that was! And you just waltzed into shot and screwed it all up!'

Tyler felt Claire's hand tightening in his. He turned to Gavin, the DC's usual cheerful demeanour notable by its absence.

'Can you stop filming, please?'

'No, he bloody well cannot!' Marcus fired back.

Tyler held the producer's eye. 'It wasn't a request. Camera off. Now.'

After the briefest glance at Marcus, Gavin turned off the camera and pointed it at the floor.

'What the hell do you think you're doing?' Marcus demanded. 'You can't just walk onto our set and start issuing orders!'

'Aye, I can,' Tyler corrected. 'Because this isn't your set, Mr Doyle. It's our crime scene. So, from now on, there'll be no more filming without our—without *my*—express permission. Is that clear?'

'We were given permission to film here!' Marcus protested.

'Were you, though?' Tyler asked.

He arranged his features into what he hoped was a threatening glare. He was aiming to deliver an eyeballing similar to those that Logan did so well, but instead landed somewhere close enough to a Bob Hoon-style squint that Marcus backed off a step.

'Did you really have permission?'

Marcus swallowed. 'Yes. I… I mean, of course. Why wouldn't—?'

Gavin sighed. 'Marcus. Just leave it. We'll leave it. We can carry on later, once everything's sorted.'

Marcus seized on the chance to direct his anger somewhere other than the detective constable. 'Oh, we just stop, do we, Gavin? We just hang around, do we? And what are we supposed to do while we wait?'

'You could try spending time with your daughter,' Tyler suggested. 'Quality time, I mean. Not just shouting at her, or telling her she's stupid.'

'What? No. Listen, I didn't mean that she's stupid, I was just saying that she—'

'No point telling me that, Mr Doyle,' Tyler said. 'Try telling it to her.'

He looked down at the girl still holding his hand, and winked.

'You all right?' he asked her.

After a moment, she nodded. 'You?'

'I reckon I'll be OK,' Tyler told her. 'As long as them ghosts aren't still knocking about.'

Claire made a show of looking around them, then shook her head. 'All clear. I think you're good.'

'Great. Thanks. And if you need me, you come find me, all right?'

She nodded again, gave his hand a big squeeze, then let her fingers peel away from his.

'I think they've got some ice cream in the kitchen,' Tyler told Marcus. 'Maybe take her there and get some of that.'

He started to turn away, but quickly spun back.

'But, eh, maybe keep her away from the big fridge. Probably not ideal for her to be in there.'

The big burst of confidence that had carried him through the whole exchange was fading now. He smiled a little shyly at Gavin and Yvonne, gave Claire a little wave, then put his hands in his pockets and nodded.

'Right, then. I'll just…'

He walked off, suddenly very conscious of his gait.

Once he'd disappeared around the corner, Yvonne sidled up to Marcus. 'Wow. He told you.'

'Shut up.'

'He's actually pretty hot, isn't he?'

'Christ. You know what, Yvonne?' Marcus spun to face her, his anger reddening his face. It was only when, from the corner of his eye, he saw his daughter flinch that he swallowed back his planned outburst. 'He's not really my cup of tea.'

He looked down at Claire. Her eyes flitted up to him, then darted away, like she was too afraid to hold his gaze for long.

'So,' he said, holding a calloused hand out to her. 'Are we getting this ice cream, then, or what?'

## *Chapter 29*

They found Helen and her bee-headed beau in a grand dining hall that a sign on the door had laughably identified as 'The Snug'.

There was nothing snug about it. The dining table alone was the size of a small boat, and had seats and placements for eighteen people—eight along each side, and one at either end.

Three different plates, and a whole drawer's worth of cutlery, had been laid out at each placing, like the table was being readied for some sort of banquet.

Silver salt and pepper cellars were positioned at equal intervals along the table, each within reach of at least two guests. There was also, to Logan's surprise, a family-sized bottle of Heinz Tomato Ketchup up near the far end, a few blobs of sauce coagulating on the inside of the open cap.

Something that looked like a deconstructed chandelier hung from the ceiling, wires crisscrossing the beams like the web of some giant spider. It was dotted in a thousand different places by bulbs that looked tiny from where Logan was standing, but which were probably the size of tennis balls up close.

The light they gave off was faint and twinkled in a pattern that undulated from one end of the hall to the other, so the shadows in the room were always shifting and changing.

Three large windows looked out over the darkened castle grounds. Evening was drawing in, and the only movement visible outside was the rain running down the panes, and the occasional swaying of a spindly fingered branch.

'Helen,' Logan said, still point-blank refusing to do the *Mx* thing. 'We've been looking for you. We'd like a word.'

Helen was seated at the head of the table, with Donatello sitting just to her left in the first chair on that side. There was a dusty bottle of red wine open in front of her, and as Logan spoke, she necked the last few dregs from her glass, then gave herself a top-up.

Donatello slid his glass towards her, but either she didn't notice, or she completely ignored his request for more booze.

The artist, or musician, or whatever the hell he was had got tarted up a little since they'd last seen him. Mostly, he was still dressed in the same frilly shirt, parachute pants, and high-heel combo, but having clearly decided that wasn't ridiculous enough, he'd added a spotty black and white fur coat with a wide, fluffy, smokey grey collar.

'Detective Chief Inspector. I suspected you would show up sooner or later.' She raised the now almost-full glass in a toast, then drank down a generous glug. 'Have you found out who killed Daddy yet?'

'We're still working on it,' Logan assured her. He gestured to two of the seats on her right. 'Do you mind?'

'Not at all. You'll have to eat.' She leaned in towards him as he sat, and Logan got the impression that she was on a slippery slope that led steeply away from sobriety. 'You do eat, don't you? Policemen? And women, of course!'

She winked at Tammi-Jo, made a vague sign of the cross in front of herself, then smiled gummily.

'I'm sorry. Sisterhood, and all that. Viva feminism! Down with men and that sort of thing!'

Her Mr Whippy hair was losing some of its structural integrity, Logan couldn't help but notice. It was possible that the rest of her wasn't all that far behind.

'Totally agree, babes!' Donatello said. He laughed. It was an oily, snivelling sort of thing. 'Feminism. Totally!'

He reached a hand across the table to lay it on top of hers. She tolerated it for a few scant seconds, then pulled hers away.

'What can I help you with? Oh! Francois will be bringing food soon. If you're hungry.' She frowned cartoonishly and propped up her head on a clenched fist. 'Did I say that already? Déjà vu!'

She hummed the theme to *The Twilight Zone*, laughed drily, then took another swig of her wine.

'Help yourself, by the way. It's a 1975 Bordeaux, apparently.'

Logan picked up the bottle and studied the label. In the chair beside him, Tammi-Jo tensed. She'd been informed about Logan's battles with alcoholism, and although she'd been assured that was all in the past, she'd also been given strict instructions to keep an eye on him, and never to let him fall off the wagon.

These instructions had come from Logan himself, so she felt like she should probably take them seriously.

'Uh, sir,' she said, when he raised the bottle to his nose and took a sniff. 'Should you…?'

'Hm? Oh. No. Don't worry. I'm not really a wine guy.' He set the bottle back down on the table. 'All tastes like vinegar to me.'

Donatello took offence on his partner's behalf. 'It's three thousand pounds a bottle.'

'Expensive vinegar, then,' Logan said. 'Where did you get that fur coat, by the way? Was Cruella de Vil having a fire sale?'

Helen snorted out a laugh, which seemed to put her boyfriend's back up.

'It's one of Stella McCartney's, actually,' he said, throwing in a haughty sniff for good measure.

'Aye, well, if she's got any sense, she'll no' be asking for it back,' Logan said. 'Although, actually, while we're on the subject of fashion, Helen, it looks like your father usually wore a ring on his right hand.'

'Mm. Yeah. The slut's ring.'

'I'm sorry?'

Helen grimaced, like this wasn't a conversation she particularly wanted to get into. 'The slut's ring. A woman gave it to him. The woman who broke up his marriage with my—with my and Monty's—mother, leading directly to her suicide.'

'I'm sorry to hear that,' Logan told her. The suicide was news to him. 'You're saying your father had an affair?'

Helen laughed at that. 'No doubt he had hundreds of affairs. I even caught him with one of my friends on my eighteenth birthday, for God's sake. Right next to the cake, would you believe? No, affairs were my father's stock in trade. But the slut? The slut was different.'

'How so?'

'They knew each other before. Before I was born. Possibly before he was with Mummy, I'm not sure. I think she worked for him in some capacity. Honestly? I got the impression that they were very much in love, once upon a time.'

Tammi-Jo was sitting with her mouth half-open, transfixed by the tale.

'What happened?' she asked.

'I have no idea. They drifted apart, perhaps. He met Mummy, life went on, then she came here one day on some job or other. Something to do with the hotel business.'

She patted at her pile of hair, like she was concerned it might be getting upset.

'Mummy caught them in one of the ground floor bedrooms. It wasn't the first time she'd stumbled upon such a thing—we all had—but this one was different. Because of the ring.'

Logan shook his head, not understanding. 'How do you mean?'

'He'd worn it the whole time. All through their marriage. It was a cheap thing, and whenever she asked him about it, he just said it had been a gift and had sentimental value. Considering my father didn't have a sentimental bone in his body, that probably should've been a bit of a red flag.'

'And this woman had given it to him?' Logan said, clicking the pieces together. 'When they were together the first time.'

'Spot on, Miss Marple!' Helen crowed. 'It all came out in the subsequent catfight, after Mummy caught them in flagrante delicto. The slut had given it to him before he and Mummy had got together. Said it was proof that Daddy had been hers first.

'Mummy stood up to him that day, for the first time ever. She told him he had to choose—her, or the slut. He chose the slut. Mummy left. Three weeks later, she took an overdose in a hotel in Paris. A two-star, would you believe?'

'That must've been awful,' Logan asked.

Helen nodded vaguely. 'According to the Tripadvisor reviews, yes.'

'No, I meant her passing. Not the…' Logan began, then he decided it wasn't worth the effort. 'How old were you?'

Helen wrinkled her nose. Judging by the way her features moved, the wine was starting to have an effect.

'Twenty-eight? Twenty-six? It was ten years ago or so. Twelve, maybe. I forget.'

'You forget when your mother took her own life?' Logan asked.

Helen's lips pursed tightly together. 'I try my best to, yes.'

'Is Krystal the slut?' Tammi-Jo asked. The look on her face made it clear she immediately regretted the question. 'That's not what… I didn't mean…'

'No. Well, I mean, she's *a* slut, obviously, but she's not *the* slut,' Helen said. 'Ironically, she turned Daddy down. I think she'd had a kid by that point, and felt that he wasn't perhaps the most stable of father figures.' She knocked back some more wine. 'Can't for the life of me think why.'

'Can you think why anyone would want to take the ring?' Logan asked.

'No. It was worthless. Just some old tat. He'd probably taken it off while going for a shower or something, I don't know. It'll turn up.'

Donatello had been sitting through Helen's whole story with his hands clasped together in front of his mouth like he was in prayer. He drew in a deep, shaky breath, then fixed her with a look as solemn as the grave.

'Babes, I am *so* sorry. I had no idea about any of that stuff.'

'Well, no. Because I didn't tell you,' Helen replied. 'Why would I?'

'Yeah, but shagging your mate? On your eighteenth birthday? That's just so *wrong*, babes.'

Helen peered back at him like he was some strange alien specimen. 'That's what you took from that story, is it? That's what jumped out?'

Logan didn't give the bee-headed idiot a chance to respond.

'Would you mind giving Helen and me a few minutes?' he asked. 'I have more questions that I hope she can help me with.'

'Yes, I do mind, actually. I actually do mind, quite a lot, actually. Anything you want to say to Helen, you can say to me. Right, babes?'

Helen drained the wine from her glass and shrugged as she reached for the bottle. 'Sure. Fuck it. At this point, why not?'

'Some of it might be quite personal,' Logan pointed out.

'What, more personal than "a slut made my mother kill herself"?' Helen asked.

Donatello's hand clamped down on top of Helen's, and this time he wasn't letting her go.

'Listen, after the things we've done to each other? We've been about as *personal* as any two people can get.' He picked up the wine bottle and drained the last dribble into his glass. 'Sometimes even three people.'

'Ew,' Tammi-Jo murmured, her gaze flitting between them both.

Logan blew out his cheeks, then shrugged. 'Fine. If that's how you want to do it, I don't really care either way.'

He shot Tammi-Jo a meaningful sideways look, and she hurriedly took out her notebook and pen.

'Ooh, it's all getting very official!' Helen said. 'Should I be calling my lawyer?'

'That's up to you, but you're not under arrest, or being treated as a suspect at this time.'

She peered at him over the rim of her now-empty glass. The alcohol was not helping with her squint, and the smaller of her eyes was now close to being closed.

'Really? Nah! We're bound to be suspects, aren't we? All of us. Someone has to have murdered the old bastard.'

'If you'd like to contact your solicitor…' Logan began. He deliberately didn't finish the sentence. If she wanted legal representation with her, she was well within her rights to ask for it. It would, however, grind his investigation to a complete halt.

'It's fine. He's in New York. And he's a twat.' Helen laughed at that until tears rolled down her cheeks. 'Sorry, Simon, but you are!' she called out to the world at large. 'You're an absolute twat!'

Tammi-Jo caught Logan's eye, twirled her pen around near the side of her head for a moment to let him know her professional opinion on Helen's current mental state, then returned to writing.

'We spoke to your brother earlier,' Logan said.

'Oh, I bet you did. I bet he came running.'

'Actually, no. He didn't come to us, we tracked him down. He seemed to be under the impression that you and your father weren't on the best of terms lately.'

'Lately? Is that what he said? Lately? We've never been on the best of terms. *Nobody* has ever been on the best of terms with that crinkly old shit. If you were lucky—if you were somehow blessed—then he tolerated you. That was it. That was as good as it got with Daddy. It was contempt or…' She frowned, her eyebrows working independently, but eventually falling into sync. 'Toleration? Is that a word?'

'Toleratedness?' Donatello suggested, which drew him a look of contempt from Logan, and absolutely no response whatsoever from Helen.

Tammi-Jo looked up from her pad. 'I don't have to write "toleratedness", do I?'

'Please don't,' Logan urged, keeping his focus on the now gently swaying Helen. 'Your brother mentioned some kind of ultimatum?'

'Oh. That! Yes. That was Daddy all over. Do *this* or X. Do *that* or Y. He loved to set his little rules. He loved to feel like he was in control of our lives.'

She tipped the very last of her drink down her throat, then set the glass down with a heavy *thunk*.

'He wanted me to "come back to the fold", as he put it. Ditch Donatello, give up the art, return home, and work by his side.'

'Can you believe that?' the man with the bees-for-hair cried. 'Cheeky fucker, eh?'

'You knew about this?' Logan asked.

'Course I did! We tell each other everything.' Donatello grinned along the table at his ice cream-haired other half. 'But you told him where to ram it, didn't you, babes?'

Silence.

Helen continued to stare at Logan, but the smaller of her eyes scrunched up completely, and the detective realised this was what she looked like when she winced.

'Didn't you, babes?' Donatello said again. All the tattoos on his face made it difficult to get an accurate bead on his emotions, but Logan definitely detected a drop-off in confidence. 'You told him exactly where to stick it. Didn't you, babes?'

Logan clasped his hands and tapped his thumbs together, quite enjoying the moment.

'I take it, from your lack of response, that you agreed to his offer?'

Bees-for-hair almost choked. 'What? Haha! Nah! Of course she didn't! She wouldn't. We're rock solid. We're *star-crossed*. Ain't we, babes? Tell him, babes.'

Helen's eyes swapped roles, one opening wider, while the other took its turn at shutting up shop. She flashed Donatello a smile that could only be read as an apology.

'I said I'd think about it.'

Donatello's emotions came across loud and clear then. Even the tattooed eyes on his cheeks seemed to be working hard to convey his upset.

'What? No, babes. Nah, babes. We talked about it. We said you'd tell him to shove it. We agreed, babes.'

'For God's sake!' Helen slammed a hand on the table, and eighteen sets of cutlery all rattled at once. 'Will you stop calling me "babes"? I mean, Jesus Christ, "babe" would be bad enough, but at least it's fucking singular!'

All four of Donatello's eyes stared at her in disbelief, then a patronising smile crept through the debris of tattoos and piercings on his face.

'I get it, babes. You're stressed. I would be, too, if someone had knifed my old man in the face. You're not thinking straight, that's all.'

'And you seem quite drunk,' Tammi-Jo added.

'I'm not. Not really,' Helen said. She sat up straighter, and the blurred lines of her body redrew themselves more sharply. 'I like to lean into it sometimes. You know, if I don't want to drink too much, or I'm not enjoying the company.'

Her gaze flitted to Donatello for a moment, then returned to the detectives.

'Appearing inebriated helps deflect attention sometimes.'

Logan grunted. 'Funny. I generally always found the opposite to be the case.'

'I mean, some of the more predatory menfolk might suddenly express an interest, so there's that, of course,' Helen said. She really did seem starkly sober now. The transformation was impressive. 'But it also frees you up to say things you might otherwise feel the need to keep bottled up. Tell someone your true feelings on a matter, for example. Or end a suffocating relationship.'

She didn't look at Donatello this time. She didn't have to. Her meaning was clear.

He, however, didn't seem to register it.

'I see. Well, it's good that you're sober,' Logan said. 'I was starting to get a bit conflicted about interviewing you in that state.'

'I'm in no "state", Detective Chief Inspector, I assure you,' Helen said, and she seemed a little annoyed by the accusation. 'You may proceed.'

'Fine. The ultimatum your father gave you, then. When was this?'

'Ooh, every day for the past sixteen years or so,' Helen said. 'He's been trying to get me to ditch lovers, or quit careers, or change cities since I first stepped out of his shadow and discovered how exciting the world is.

'He was desperate for me to return home, even though he barely spoke to me for the first eighteen years of my life, and rarely said much when I was here. He never approved of my lifestyle. Hated that I was an artist. Hated even more seeing me in the papers.'

'What sort of art is it that you do?' Logan asked. It might not be entirely relevant to the investigation, but for his own curiosity, he needed to know.

Helen waved a frail hand. 'Mostly existential pieces with a nihilist bent. The futility of self. In simple terms, mourning the loss of the things we never had, viewed through a patriarchal lens. That sort of thing.'

Logan and Tammi-Jo both sat in silence, staring blankly back at her.

It was the detective constable who finally spoke.

'So, watercolours, or…?'

Donatello threw back his head and laughed like a supervillain from an old black and white movie. 'Watercolours! Pah! The bloody nerve! Eh, babes?'

He reached for Helen's hand again, but it scuttled out of his reach like a spider tiptoeing across the tabletop.

'Why now?' Logan asked.

Helen frowned, not quite understanding the question.

'I don't follow.'

'If he's been trying to make you do all this—give up the life you've built—for over fifteen years, why did you agree now?'

'I didn't agree. I told him I'd think about it.'

'OK. Had you thought about it any of the other times?'

'No. Not for a moment.'

Logan nodded. 'So, again, why now?'

'Is it the bees on his head?' Tammi-Jo asked. She waved a hand below her throat, while staring in horror at the padlocks stretching the skin of Donatello's neck. 'And all this business he's got going on?'

'What?' Helen followed the detective's gaze, then blinked in surprise, like she'd only just remembered her boyfriend was there. 'Oh. No. That doesn't bother me at all. That? That's nothing.'

Donatello gently ran his fingers across his scalp of plastic bees, almost as if he was worried they might've taken offence and was rushing to soothe them.

'My last partner's looks were far more extreme,' Helen announced, with a note of real pride. 'Tonto Razors.'

The name drew further blank looks from both detectives.

Helen recoiled, visibly taken aback by their complete lack of response.

'The self-sculptor? Cut off both his ears? Gave himself a pig nose, and swapped his lips around? No?' She looked between the DCI and the DC. Both their expressions had changed, but not into anything that suggested they had any idea who she was talking about. 'You're not honestly telling me you haven't heard of Tonto Razors!'

'Thankfully not, no,' Logan replied.

'He's one of the most exciting artists of his generation!' Helen exclaimed.

'He's mentally ill,' Logan countered. 'I mean, I'm no expert, and I've only just this minute heard of the man, but I'd stake my bloody career on it. He needs ongoing psychiatric help, not access to sharp objects.'

Helen rolled her eyes in a way that suggested she'd heard this same argument countless times before from Luddites who knew nothing whatsoever about art.

'Anyway, no. It wasn't Donatello. He's… you know… perfectly fine.'

'Thanks, babes!' her partner said, and he genuinely seemed touched by what Logan had taken to be a rather cutting insult.

'Daddy offered me the business.'

Logan's chair creaked as he leaned forward a little. 'He offered you the business?'

'Yes. A week ago. The whole thing. I'd be CEO of all his companies. Of the whole empire. He'd anoint me as his successor, and transfer all his shares into a holding company that I would have sole control of.'

'Wouldn't that cut your brother out?'

'Completely. Oh, completely, yes. That's the whole point, I suspect. It's fine to have your quirky artist daughter running your business, but your'—Logan could practically hear the distaste nestled between the air quotes she made around the next part—'"faggot son"? No. Heavens, no, that wouldn't go down well in Daddy's circles. That would not do at all!'

Logan sat back again and crossed his arms, considering this new information.

'Did he know? Your brother? Did he know this was happening?'

'That Daddy hated him for his sexuality? Oh, yes. There was no secret made of that, even though Monty never officially outed himself to the old fucker.' She ran a finger around the rim of her wineglass. It hummed a low, ominous note. 'Did he know that I was being offered everything he'd dreamed of and worked for? I'm not sure. But I hope not.'

'Why's that?' Logan asked.

Helen dipped her finger into the little well of wine at the bottom of the glass, then licked it off.

‘Because, if he did know what Daddy was planning, I’d say that would be more than enough motivation to kill him. And, while my brother and I aren’t exactly close, it would sadden me greatly if he was revealed to be a murderer.’

A gong chimed. Logan turned in his chair, looking around until he eventually spotted a big brass-coloured disc hanging from a mount above the dining room door. A mechanically operated striker jerked back, then struck again with a slow, steady rhythm.

*BONG.*

*BONG.*

*BONG.*

‘Aha. I fear our discussion is going to have to be concluded at another time, Detective Chief Inspector,’ Helen said. She picked up her napkin, unfolded it with a flick, then laid it across her lap. ‘Dinner is about to be served.’

## *Chapter 30*

'I hope you folks are hungry!'

Hamza and Sinead smiled and nodded gratefully as they took their seats at the B&B's dining table. Four places had been set out, and since there were no other guests that the detectives were aware of, it looked like their hosts would be joining them.

'Christian's made his famous vegetable curry!' Chrissie declared, clapping her hands with excitement. 'You're in for a treat!'

The old woman was positively buzzing with excitement. This was going to have to be some curry to live up to the expectations she was setting.

The smell was promising as Christian came waddling in with a big pot of the stuff clutched in two oven-gloved hands.

'Now, it's not my usual method,' he warned, slowly making his way over to the table. Chrissie patted a placemat she'd set down, indicating the target landing zone for the pot. 'I usually don't put this stuff in it.'

'What stuff's that?' Sinead asked, leaning back to make room for him to set the food down.

Christian let out a sigh of relief when the pot was successfully lowered into place.

'Vegetables,' he said as he carefully straightened himself up.

'You don't usually put vegetables in your famous vegetable curry?' Hamza asked.

'No. I usually put chicken,' Christian said.

He shot his wife a worried sideways look. Chrissie was fiddling with the hem of her apron, running it back and forth through her withered fingers, her head lowered a little as if in embarrassment or shame.

'We, uh, we weren't sure if you could… If you were allowed to eat…'

'We didn't want you to feel…' Christian said.

Neither of them could quite find the words, but their good intentions were clear for all to see.

'Wow. Thank you. That's very thoughtful of you,' Hamza told them. 'But it's fine, honestly. I can eat chicken.'

'Oh!' Christian put a hand on his wife's shoulder and they both sagged together in relief. 'Thank the Lord for that.' He winced, but it soon morphed into a smile. 'I *may* have accidentally used a chicken stock cube by mistake. I don't need to feel guilty about it now.'

They all took their places and chatted while Chrissie dished up the food. For a first attempt at a vegetable curry, it seemed like Christian had done an admirable job. It smelled amazing, it looked great, and as it was ladled into their bowls, both detectives felt their stomachs rumble hungrily.

They were just one forkful into the meal when the spices kicked in.

It was Sinead who noticed first. A prickling at the back of her throat that lit a fire on her tongue, and quickly spread. She covered her mouth and coughed, then poured herself a big glass of water from the jug that had been set in the middle of the table.

Beside her, Hamza's mouth formed a little circle as he sucked in some air. He wasn't a stranger to spicy food—he was a big fan of it, generally—but he raised a thumb in thanks when Sinead placed a glass in front of him, and quickly poured himself some water while the DC necked her own.

'It's spicy,' Sinead croaked, her eyes watering.

'Rubbish!' Christian laughed. He shoved a big chunk of what might have been a carrot into his mouth and gummed away at it. 'I went canny with it this time.'

'Although, our taste buds aren't as sharp as they used to be. Is it OK? Can you eat it?' Chrissie asked, and the worry on the old woman's face meant there was only one answer the detectives could give.

'Absolutely,' Hamza said between gulps of water.

Sinead waved a hand in front of her mouth, trying to cool her tongue and lips, then did her best to arrange the whole burning mess into a smile. 'No, it's delicious, really. It's just… surprisingly hot. I wasn't quite prepared for it.'

All four of them went back to eating, some more cautiously than others. Conversation moved on from the amount of spice in the food to the weather, and when it was expected to let up.

Christian spoke for a while about his old career in the building trade, while Chrissie told the detectives at great length about the couple's three children and five grandchildren, who used to be frequent visitors to the house when they were younger, but were now more interested in boys and 'Poke-a-mans', to have much time for their out-of-touch old grandparents.

'Well, their loss,' Sinead wheezed, before helping herself to more water.

'And what about you two?' Chrissie asked. 'What brings you out here on a day like this?'

'We were called out on… an emergency,' Hamza explained, while keeping things vague.

'Oh? In Ullapool?' Christian chewed thoughtfully. 'I hadn't heard anything.'

'No. At the big house. McQuarrie Hall,' the DS said.

A fork scraped across a plate. The horrible screech of it sent a shiver along the length of Sinead's spine.

Across the table, Chrissie and Christian had both stopped chewing, though their mouths were still half-full.

'Is everything all right?' Sinead asked, noticing the expression on the old couple's faces. She reached for the jug. 'Do you need some water?'

'The castle?' Christian said. There was a tremble to his voice that immediately made Sinead uneasy.

The detectives watched as Chrissie and Christian fumbled for one another's hands, and clutched them tightly.

'You were going to the castle?'

Hamza swallowed another mouthful of water. 'Uh, yeah,' he said, returning his glass to its coaster. 'We were.'

This seemed like the worst possible news. Chrissie crossed herself with her free hand, while Christian clutched his knife so tightly his arthritic knuckles turned white.

Then again, the couple had mostly turned white in general.

'Well, thank the Lord you didn't get there,' Chrissie said. She shot a look towards the man upstairs that seemed to be saying she owed him one. 'It's a terrible place. Cursed, so it is.'

'Cursed?' Hamza laughed, and Sinead joined in, assuming the remark was some sort of joke.

When the couple failed to so much as smile, however, their laughter died in their throats.

'It's a terrible place. An awful place, full of demons and monsters,' Chrissie said, her words coming out as a low, sinister whisper.

Her husband was continuing to stare, his eyes wide, the knife in his hand now trembling.

'It's a blessing you didn't make it there. Not today, of all days.'

Sinead almost asked what was special about today, before remembering it was Halloween. That made her reconsider if this whole thing was just a wind-up by the old couple, but their terror seemed genuine, and they didn't exactly seem the type for practical jokes.

'Our, eh, colleagues are there,' Hamza said. 'They made it across.'

'My husband,' Sinead added. She wasn't sure why she felt the need to throw that out there. It was out before she'd had time to think it through.

A clatter made her jump. Christian's knife had fallen and landed on his plate. The hand he'd been gripping it with flew to his mouth, shaking so uncontrollably that it took him three attempts to find the target.

His wide eyes shone with tears. His voice, when it came, was a croak of desperation.

'Then God help them,' he whispered. 'God help them all!'

With that, the old couple got up from the table, bundled up their dishes, and headed for the kitchen. Christian was moving more quickly than they'd seen him move before, like the urge to get away from the conversation was fuelling his aged muscles and driving him on.

'What the hell was that about?' Hamza wondered, once the door to the kitchen had slammed shut.

Sinead didn't know.

But she didn't like it one little bit.

Somewhere, far off in the distance, thunder rumbled.

-

Ben sat in the canteen at Burnett Road Police Station, getting stuck into a Scotch pie and chips. He'd added a big ladle of beans on top of the chips, and was focusing on the pie for now, giving the bean juice a chance to really soak into the already soggy sticks of salty, oily potato.

The place was busier than usual, which was no real surprise. It was dinnertime, after all, and everyone was trying to hide out from the weather for as long as possible. Breaks that should've ended five minutes ago were dragging on a little longer, and crews who should've still been out and about had returned to base slightly earlier than planned.

Ben had taken a seat at the far end of a table meant for ten, spent a couple of minutes chatting with the Uniforms sitting further along, then taken out his mobile.

There was a notification on the screen alerting him that he had a message. He took his reading glasses from the pocket of his shirt, popped them on the end of his nose, then spent a good forty seconds trying to remember how to get into the messages.

He smiled when he saw the message was from Moira Carson, and then brightened further at the picture that greeted him. It was the latest front cover of *Love It!* magazine. He read one of the headlines with a chuckle.

'My teenage daughter was drained dry by vampire death cult.'

He broke off a chunk of crispy pie crust and crunched on it.

'Poor cow,' he remarked to nobody in particular, then he went back to reading the rest of the cover.

The issue was, as usual, a smorgasbord of misery and suffering. As well as the vampire lassie, there was a story about a man burning to death in a hotel lift, and a grandmother being smothered by a big dog. Whose dog, and what its motivation was, the headline didn't say.

Sometimes, it was best not to know.

'Sir! There you are.'

Ben looked up from his phone to find a slightly breathless uniformed sergeant approaching his table.

'Aye, here I am, Sergeant. Enjoying my dinner,' Ben said.

'Sorry, sir. Didn't mean to interrupt,' the Uniform said. 'Oh! Have they still got pies?'

'Last one,' Ben told him.

The sergeant attempted to hide his disappointment, but didn't do a particularly good job of it.

'What can I do for you, son?' Ben asked.

'Oh. Yes. Sorry. You know those phone calls you had us helping with? Digging around on those people in the house?' He held out a folder he'd been carrying under his arm. 'We found something you might want to take a look at.'

Ben set down his phone, dusted the pie crust crumbs from his hands, then took the thin cardboard file.

Pushing his plate aside, he opened the folder, readjusted his glasses, and began to read.

It took a few seconds, but then he was on his feet, his eyes zigzagging frantically down a page of typed text.

'Bloody hell,' he said.

'Aye, that's what we thought, sir.'

Ben snapped the folder closed, tucked it under his arm, then picked up his plate.

'Here you go, son. Knock yourself out,' the DI declared, handing his dinner over to the sergeant. 'Looks like my dinner's going to have to wait!'

He started off for the door, slowed, then turned back.

'Actually…'

The sergeant looked down at his hand as the plate was gently prised back out of it again.

'On second thoughts, I could just eat it upstairs.'

# *Chapter 31*

'*Et voilà!* Sumac-roasted breast of pheasant with a parsnip silk, dukkah-dusted broccoli, and peach gastrique. Bon appétit!'

DC Neish regarded the plate that had been set before him with all the enthusiasm of a death row prisoner facing down his final meal. He'd never really been one for overly fancy or fussy food, and the pile of unfamiliar ingredients on the plate fit both those descriptors.

It had all been stacked together and layered up, with a smear of something greyish-brown around one side of the plate, and a dribble of something orangey-red dotting the opposite edge.

There were also very clearly things in the pile that the chef had failed to mention. He could see some little tomatoes, for one, and something that looked like lentils, or barley, or something along those lines.

Chickpeas, maybe? Or were they bigger?

Of course, the fanciness of the meal wasn't the only problem Tyler had with it. He was more concerned with the fact that at least some of the ingredients almost certainly came from the big walk-in fridge.

'Eh, sorry—'

He caught the chef's eye just before the Frenchman turned from the table.

'*Oui, monsieur?*'

'Don't suppose you've got any chips?'

'Chips?!' Francois sneered, his accent and his outrage turning the *i* into an elongated double-*e*. 'Non. I do not 'ave any *chips*! Nor do I have any chicken nuggets, or… or Turkey Twizzlers.'

He looked the detective constable up and down, his face puckering in contempt. In that moment, he looked just about as French as it was possible for a man to look. Stick him on a bicycle and throw in a string of onions, and he'd be nailing it.

'Chips!' he exclaimed, throwing his hands up in the air. Then, muttering below his breath in French, he about-turned and marched out of the room in disgust.

'I think that's a "no", to you getting any chips,' Tammi-Jo said.

She wanted to say it quietly, but because they were sitting directly across the wide table from one another, she had to put a bit of volume behind it. The acoustics of the room carried the remark all along the table, from Helen at the top, to Monty, who sat all the way down at the far end, facing his sister.

He had kicked off a bit about the seating arrangements when he'd first entered the room. Helen was sitting in his seat, he'd insisted. Now that Papa was gone, he was the man of the house. He deserved to sit at the head of the table.

When he'd seen the way Logan was watching the discussion, though, he'd backed off. By the time everyone else had started to file into the room, he'd grabbed another bottle of wine from a rack in the corner, and plonked himself down at the far end with it.

He hadn't said a word since, and there had been no acknowledgement, much less a 'thank you', when the chef had unloaded his meal from the serving trolley.

As the table had filled up, everyone had gravitated away from the younger—and now only—Montgomery McQuarrie, possibly sensing his seething resentment. This didn't require a lot of intuition. For a man who'd been brought up never to show emotion, he wasn't exactly hiding his current feelings towards his sister.

Tyler had arrived to find Yvonne sitting beside Tammi-Jo, and Logan had directed him to take the seat across from DC Swanney, instead. To his dismay, this placed him side by side with Donatello. Fortunately, the man with the bees-for-hair was too busy staring glumly into his empty glass to even notice Tyler's arrival.

The rest of the house's current residents had turned up moments later. Claire had made a beeline to sit beside Tyler, but Krystal had swooped in first, tracing a manicured hand across the detective constable's shoulders as she squeezed in beside him.

'Room for a small one, sugar?' she'd purred, shuffling her chair a little closer to his.

Claire, unsure what to do, had taken the closest available seat—the one on Krystal's left—then looked simultaneously relieved and disappointed when her dad came to sit beside her.

*Ghost Spotters* producer, Gavin Hall, had wandered in a few seconds behind the rest of his group, and had taken the seat across from Claire, after checking with Yvonne whether or not she minded him sitting there.

She didn't. Of course she didn't. Why would she?

They'd laughed, and Logan had immediately concluded that they were sleeping together and that nobody was supposed to know—especially Marcus, given the way that they both avoided his eye.

There were four empty seats on Gavin's right, and three to the left of Marcus. Neither man made any attempt to engage with Monty Jr at the foot of the table, which appeared to suit him just fine.

The only person missing was Rab, the uniformed constable who continued to stand guard over the dead man's study. Tammi-Jo had gone to fetch him, but he'd insisted he was fine where he was—partly because he wanted to do his job properly, but mostly because he couldn't bear the thought of having dinner with the victim's family.

At the mention of food, Taggart had abandoned his post and followed the DC back down the stairs. Now, he sat below the table, scanning the floor for any carelessly dropped scraps.

For the most part, everyone ate in awkward silence, with occasional requests to pass the salt, or comments on how delicious the food and wine was. Those remarks largely came from Logan's side of the table. Tyler's side didn't seem overly enamoured with the meal they'd been served.

Donatello prodded glumly at the meat, pronging bits onto his fork, then sliding them off again. No doubt he was still coming to terms with the fact that he was almost certainly about to be dumped, if he hadn't been already.

Tyler was having a bash at the food, though his knife and fork kept hovering around the plate, searching for things he recognised. There was something almost gladiatorial about it, Logan thought—a combatant circling his opponent, bracing himself for a battle he knew he was sure to lose.

Beside him, Krystal hadn't even picked up her cutlery. Instead, she was tanning her way through a bottle of red wine, one leg crossed over the other, an elbow perched possessively on the back of Tyler's chair.

She had ditched the exercise gear and Barbour jacket from earlier, and was now dressed in something that Logan wasn't entirely convinced wasn't some sort of negligee. It was a sheer, silken green dress that stopped mid-thigh and left very little to the imagination on the cleavage front.

At every opportunity, she contorted herself so the cleavage was aimed squarely in Tyler's direction, but if he had noticed, then he'd done an admirable job of not letting on.

On Krystal's left, Claire was eyeing her plate with similar levels of suspicion as Tyler. She'd picked up the long-stemmed broccoli with her fingers and eaten the heads off some of that. To the casual observer, it would seem like she was making good progress on the pheasant, but the hungry chewing noises from below the table suggested an alternative explanation.

Only Marcus on that side of the table seemed to be enjoying his meal. He had bundled stacks of the meal up on his fork and wrestled them into his mouth, before quaffing back a mouthful of wine to help force it all down.

There was an intensity to the way he was eating that made him fascinating to watch. Something had upset the man, Logan thought. Filling his mouth was the only thing keeping him quiet.

And he'd just swallowed his last bite.

Logan took a drink of his water, a bite of his broccoli, then counted down in his head from ten.

He had just reached 'four' when Marcus spoke.

'So, do we have your permission to carry on yet, *Constable*?' the presenter asked, really emphasising the first syllable of that final word.

He had half-turned himself in his chair, and glared along the table at Tyler, swirling what was left of his wine around in his glass.

'What's this?' Logan asked.

'Hm?' Tyler looked up from his plate. 'Oh. Yeah. I, uh, I asked them not to film while the investigation is ongoing, boss.'

Marcus snorted. 'You didn't *ask*. You *ordered* us. You came in throwing your weight around, demanding that we stop filming.' He redirected his attention from Tyler to Logan. 'Completely out of line, he was. Storming in like the big man. You want to keep the lad in line.'

Logan chewed thoughtfully, then pointed across the table with his fork. 'Good call, Detective Constable. Well done. I'd have done the same, except I assumed nobody would be bloody callous enough to be making a ghost programme on a murder scene.'

Tyler smiled. 'Cheers, boss. That's pretty much what I said.'

'We weren't on the murder scene!' Marcus protested. 'The whole place isn't the murder scene. He wasn't killed *everywhere*.'

'Marcus,' Gavin warned. He frowned and shook his head. 'Leave it.'

'No, I won't bloody leave it, Gavin. Time's money, and we're burning through both sitting on our arses here!'

Tyler took a chance on a cherry tomato, stabbed it with his fork, then popped it in his mouth.

'You're quite an argumentative man, Mr Doyle,' he said, moving the warm tomato around without yet daring to bite into it. He was fine with tomatoes, but this one had *stuff* on it, and he had absolutely no idea what it was. 'You were arguing with Monty senior, I'm told. Before he died.'

Along the table, Claire kept her gaze fixed on her plate, saying nothing.

'Is that right?' Tyler asked.

Marcus fell silent for a moment, then snorted. 'No.'

'Yeah, he was,' Krystal said in her southern drawl. 'My Monty told me all about it. Said he'd had cross words with both you gentlemen.'

She looked from Marcus to Gavin, then leaned in even closer to Tyler.

'Some very cross words, he told me. Said he'd instructed both these gentlemen to pack up and leave.'

Gavin forced down a swallow, set down his cutlery, then held his hands up in a calming gesture. 'No. That's not exactly what happened.'

'What did happen?' Logan asked.

'Yes,' Helen said. She, too, had set down her knife and fork, and now leaned forward with her elbows on the table and her hands clasped. 'This is news to me. Do tell.'

'It was mostly him,' Marcus spat, stabbing an accusing finger across the table. 'He was the one who had the fight with him.'

'Fight?' Monty Jr's voice took them all by surprise. 'What do you mean?'

'Not "fight". He doesn't mean *fight* fight. We just…' Gavin rubbed his forehead and sighed. 'An issue came up. Mr McQuarrie wasn't happy about something, and things got a little heated.'

'And what wasn't Daddy happy about?' Helen pressed. 'Specifically, I mean, beyond just being miserable in general?'

Gavin's mouth flapped open and closed a few times. 'I shouldn't… It's not my place to…'

'Go ahead, Mr Hall,' Logan urged. 'We're all ears.'

The producer's gaze flitted to Claire, then to Marcus. 'Maybe she shouldn't be here for this?'

'She's fine. Anything you want to say, you just say it, Gavin. Just you go ahead. Claire's fine, aren't you?'

Claire didn't look up from her plate, but shrugged.

'See? Nothing to worry about.'

Gavin took a small sip of wine, a big breath, then came out with it.

'He caught Marcus doing coke in one of the bathrooms.'

'Jesus *Christ*, Gavin!' Marcus cried. He clamped his hands over his daughter's ears and shook his head reproachfully. 'Seriously? With Claire here? Well done. Well bloody done.'

'I said she should leave!' Gavin protested. 'You told me to say it.'

'Not *that*! I didn't know you were going to say *that*,' Marcus shot back.

'You knew what the argument was about! You were there the whole time.'

'Bollocks I was! I was there at the start, then you told me to leave.'

Gavin's eyes almost bulged out of their sockets. 'Because you were making it worse! You kept shouting at him to get a grip of himself and "chill the fuck out".'

Helen let out a little giggle. 'Oh, I'd have loved to have seen Daddy's face when you said that. I'll bet he turned quite the colour.'

'I don't see the big deal!' Marcus said, still covering his daughter's ears. 'So, I did a bit of charlie. Is that a crime?'

'Yes,' all three detectives replied at the same time.

This took the wind from the presenter's sails. 'Is it? What, not dealing it, just having it? Seriously? In this day and age?' He shook his head in disbelief. 'This fucking country.'

He removed his hands from Claire's ears, then reached for the nearest bottle and topped up his wine.

'Montgomery wanted us to leave,' Gavin explained. 'I managed to calm him down and convinced him to let us stay until filming was done.'

At the far end of the table, the victim's son let out a snort of disbelief. 'You managed to get him to change his mind on something? You? I find that quite impossible to believe.'

'As do I,' Krystal said, eyeing Gavin over the rim of her glass. 'When he and I spoke, I didn't get the impression he had rowed back on his decision to evict y'all one little bit.'

'Well, I, uh, I don't know what to tell you. That's what he said to me,' Gavin insisted, then he went back to his food.

'What brought you here in the first place?' Logan asked.

Yvonne shrugged. 'Spooky castle, innit? We're always at places like this.'

'But why this one? Why now?' Logan pressed.

Yvonne frowned like she didn't quite understand the question. 'Gavin picked it,' she said. 'He always picks them.'

'Actually, no. Not this one,' Gavin corrected. 'I mean, I usually pick them, but this one was Marcus. He found it. Didn't you?'

'Did I?' Marcus shifted in his seat, suddenly aware of the DCI's gaze. 'I don't think I did.'

'Yes, you did!' Gavin insisted. 'You told me it was perfect. You kept going on about it.'

'He's right,' Yvonne said. 'I remember now. You'd seen adverts for it on Facebook.'

'Oh, yeah. So I did,' Marcus said. 'Fine. Yeah. I found it.'

'We don't run any adverts on Facebook,' Monty Jr chipped in.

Marcus tutted. 'Yes, you do. I saw them.'

'It's a private house. What would we be advertising?'

'Well, I don't bloody know, do I?' Marcus shot back. 'They were ads. Like… "Most haunted house in Scotland", sort of thing.'

Monty sneered. 'Well, we most certainly wouldn't run advertising like *that*!'

'Well some bugger did!'

Marcus stole another quick look at the detectives, then turned his attention to his empty plate and began mopping up the parsnip silk with the tip of a finger.

Another awkward hush descended. This one, however, didn't get time to bed in.

'So, Monty,' Donatello began, his eyes focusing like he was coming out of a trance.

Beside him, Helen whispered something urgently, but he took pleasure in ignoring her.

'Helen says she's the head of the company now.'

The silence from Monty Jr was a dark and ominous thing. 'I beg your pardon?' he eventually said.

'Yeah, he said if she dumped me, she could have it all. Be in charge. Have all his shares, or whatever.' Donatello grinned and bit the head off a piece of broccoli. 'What do you think about that?'

Monty didn't answer right away. He took a glug of wine, then wiped his mouth on the back of his hand.

'So, he told you, did he? I wasn't sure if he'd said anything.'

'He did. Weeks ago.'

'*Weeks?!*'

Monty slammed his knife and fork down on the table. The bang they made reverberated around the room, startling Claire and making her let out a little gasp.

'After how hard I worked? All these years? After everything I did for that… that… twisted, selfish, ungrateful bastard!'

'It was nothing to do with how hard you worked, brother dearest,' Helen said. Logan thought it was a genuine attempt at brokering peace, but clearly Monty didn't see it that way.

'Oh, then what was it to do with, *sis*? Why was he rewarding you for all my hard work? Do tell. If it wasn't because of what I'd done, what was it? Was it because of who I am?'

He was on his feet now, his chair toppling backwards and clattering to the floor.

'Because I'm a *homo*? A *faggot*? A *queer*? Or one of the many, many more creative names he used for me after he found out?'

'I don't know. You'd have to ask him,' Helen said.

'Well, that's very convenient,' Monty spat.

He looked along both sides of the table, suddenly aware that everyone in the dining room was staring at him, waiting to see what he'd do next.

'So, you knew?' Logan asked. 'He'd told you what he was planning?'

'To cut me out of my inheritance in favour of her? Oh, yes. He told me. Last night, in fact. Told me that it was all going to his precious *first-born*. That I was getting nothing. That he was changing his will.'

Krystal sat forward. 'Say what, now?'

'Oh, don't worry, he didn't mention you. But then, I'm sure you were never in it in the first place. His trophy wife of the month never is,' Monty continued, picking his chair up and settling himself back down on it. 'But Helen and I were. At least, we both used to be. He told me last night that, "It's all going to the first-born, boy. Get over it."'

Marcus grinned. He'd pinched a bit of fatty meat from Claire's plate and was chewing away on it. 'Bloody hell, this is better than watching a soap.'

'I didn't ask for it, Monty,' Helen told him. 'I didn't ask for any of it.'

'But you were happy to take it, weren't you?' her brother seethed.

Helen smiled, not unkindly. 'It must've come as quite a shock, after all those promises he'd made you.'

'Shut up, Helen.'

'I'd imagine you must've been furious.'

'That's enough!' Monty barked.

'Murderous, even!'

Her brother leaped to his feet again. 'I said that is enough!'

Silence fell. Only the rasping of Monty's breathing was audible above the howling of Storm Agatha, and the rumbling of thunder from somewhere close by.

It was only as his rage started to fade that Monty realised he was clutching the handle of the serrated knife he'd been using to cut up his pheasant. The tip of the blade was embedded into the tabletop, and when he released his grip, it remained there, wobbling gently back and forth.

The tension was broken when the door to the snug was opened, and Francois came marching in. He made a beeline straight for Tyler, then dumped a large metal mixing bowl in front of him with an air of disgust.

'*Voici!*' he spat. 'Chips!'

Tyler's eyes lit up when he saw the big mound of homemade chips filling the bowl. They shone slightly with a fine film of oil and were dotted with specks of sea salt.

'Aw, nice one! Cheers!' he said to the already exiting chef's back. 'But, eh, I don't suppose you've got any vinegar?'

Thunder rumbled around the room, and Tyler winced, as if his request had angered the gods.

Francois spun around, but before he could say anything, the room's windows were all illuminated by a crackle of lightning.

Somewhere in the castle, something went *bang*.

When the lightning faded, it took all the other light with it, plunging the room and its occupants into a darkness so deep and suffocating that nobody could see the person sitting next to them.

'Oh,' whispered Tyler. 'Bollocks.'

From somewhere in the darkened castle came the shrill ringing of an old, long-forgotten telephone.

# *Chapter 32*

It took them a few minutes to fumble their way towards the ringing phone, using only the torches on their mobiles to light the way.

Monty Jr and Helen both picked up speed when they entered what had once been the hotel's reception and it became clear that the sound was coming from somewhere beneath the dust sheets.

They practically got into fisticuffs as they hurried to trace the ringing to its source, shouldering and slapping at each other, both desperate to be the one to answer.

The siblings were so preoccupied with stopping one another's progress, though, that they completely missed Krystal striding straight past them and pulling aside a sheet to reveal an old-fashioned desk phone with a manual dial on the front and a receiver hanging by a hook on the side.

She picked up the receiver, and the ringing stopped. Monty and Helen froze, mid-wrestle, their wonky eyes shooting daggers at the latest in their long line of stepmothers.

'This is McQuarrie Hall. How can I help y'all?' Krystal said, with a brightness that clearly conveyed the friendly smile she'd willed into existence a split second before answering the call.

Customer service background. Logan would put money on it.

The other occupants of the room—Logan, Monty Jr, Helen and Tyler—all waited, straining to listen to the faint, tinny voice on the other end of the line that was just a fraction too quiet for them to make out.

'I see. I see. Yes. I see,' Krystal said, her smile concreted in place. She removed the handset from her ear and held it out to the DCI. 'It's for you.'

Logan frowned. 'Me? Who the hell's calling me here?'

'Who even has this number?' Helen wondered aloud.

Tyler eyed the phone warily as it was handed over. 'Careful, boss.'

Logan tutted. 'Of what? It's no' going to suck me in.'

The detective constable pulled a face that implied Logan shouldn't come running to him if it did, then stepped in a little closer to try and hear what was being said.

'DCI Logan. Who's this?'

'All right, sir? It's Hamza,' came the reply. The line was crackly, and the detective sergeant sounded like he was calling from deep underwater. 'Been trying to get you on *FaceTime*, but it looks like your internet's down.'

'Oh, aye, boss,' Tyler whispered. 'Forgot to say. Internet's down.'

Logan shot him a look, then went back to his conversation.

'So I've just been told. Lights are out now, too. Everything all right there?'

'Ask them how they got this number,' Helen urged, but Logan waved her away with the back of his hand and switched the receiver from one ear to the other.

Hamza had heard the question, however, and got the answer out of the way.

'The guy at the B&B here. Christian. The company he worked for helped build the castle. Or, you know, move it and rebuild it,' the detective sergeant explained. 'Your victim, he bought the company over and put all the guys out of work. Let's just say that, as a result, Christian and his wife aren't exactly big fans of the man, or of the place itself. He's got loads of info on the building, though, including a list of phone numbers.'

'Right,' Logan said, but he chose not to relay any of that.

'He's got a list of other things, too, sir. Things that might be useful to you,' Hamza continued. 'And, eh, it might be worth getting a bit of privacy, sir. Because DI Forde's been trying to get hold of you, too. Something's come to light about one of the people in the house.'

Logan pressed the phone more firmly to his ear, and stole a look around at the victim's assembled family members.

'Something that might just change *everything*.'

## *Chapter 33*

The library had been spooky enough with the electricity on. Now, with the light from half a dozen candles flickering across the antique books and stone walls, it had taken on real Gothic horror vibes.

Tyler had moved his chair in closer to Tammi-Jo's, and they both now watched, nursing a mug of tea and a glass of milk respectively, while Logan did his best to update the upturned-table-come-Big-Board.

Though they'd locked the door when they left, they'd returned to find their scattering of Post-its strewn on the floor at the foot of the table, like all the little sticky strips had just given up trying to cling on.

It was the breeze that blew through the whole building that had knocked them off, Logan had said. The same breeze that was making the candles flutter and dance, wobbling the shadows back and forth.

Tyler wasn't so sure, though. If it had been the breeze, wouldn't they have blown around the room, rather than just dropping to the floor?

'It's more like they just lost the will to stick, boss,' he'd said, and after a prolonged blank stare at the detective constable, Logan had moved on.

He decided to save the revelations from Hamza's call for last, and instead focus on recapping what they'd all learned in the past few hours.

One thing they'd discovered was that a lot of people had reason to wish harm upon the late Monty senior.

Even if the victim's son *hadn't* just been made aware that he was being cut out of the business, he'd been forced to endure his old man's homophobia, along with a lifetime of what could be generously described as 'bad parenting', and more accurately described as 'abuse'.

Could he be the killer? Absolutely. And Logan almost wouldn't blame him if he was.

The sister was a little more complicated. Yes, she'd endured the same upbringing, and her father was forcing her to choose between him and her love life.

But she didn't seem all that invested in her love life, and the offer had been sweetened with access to literally billions of pounds.

'If someone was offering to make me a billionaire, I'd bite their hand off, boss, not stab them in the face,' Tyler reasoned.

'Maybe she was worried he'd change his mind again,' Tammi-Jo suggested. 'Maybe she thought he might take it all away.'

'There is that,' Tyler agreed. 'I might stab him in the face then, right enough.'

The inheritance could well be the key to the case. One of them had been cut out completely. One of them had been promised it all, provided she gave up the life she'd built for herself.

As motives went, money was a classic. Sure, Monty might have been able to contest the will after the old bastard snuffed it, but why go to all that trouble and pay all those legal fees when you could stop the change before it even happened?

Or, if the will had already been altered in favour of Monty's 'first-born', then it would make sense for Helen to do away with him there and then, ensuring it couldn't be changed again.

'You're right, boss. It's got to be one of them. Has to be.'

'Unless the ring's important,' Tammi-Jo said.

'Aye. True.' Tyler nodded, then he turned to the other DC in the half-light. 'Wait, what's this about the ring?'

Tammi-Jo explained, at unnecessary length, what Helen had told them about the missing ring, who had given it to him, and how the McQuarrie siblings believed it had contributed to their mother's death.

'It might just be in that bowl in his study,' Tyler reasoned. 'There's loads of jewellery in there. Nothing that really fits that description, though, I don't think.'

'Worth a check,' Logan said.

Lightning flashed outside, casting the DCI's shadow onto a wall that was suddenly and briefly a blinding shade of white.

Thunder rumbled just a second or two later. The storm was practically overhead now, and the candles flickered like they were afraid.

'What about the *Ghost Spotters* lot?' Tyler asked. 'I don't trust that Marcus guy. Think there's anything there?'

'Bit weird him being the one to choose the place, if he's never done that before,' Tammi-Jo replied. 'Especially if he's lying about seeing adverts for it.'

Logan agreed the advert thing was odd. Monty Jr had been insistent that they didn't advertise on social media. If that was true, then Marcus couldn't possibly have seen ads popping up on Facebook for the castle.

At least, that was Logan's first assumption. A quick chat on the technicalities of the matter while on the phone with Hamza had proved to be quite enlightening.

'The drug thing could be a motive,' Tyler said. 'If it got out that he was doing coke, it could've messed up his career.'

Logan shook his head. 'He works in TV. If people thought he *wasn't* bunging half his wages up his nose, then they might have something to say. It wouldn't do him or the show any real harm.'

'Might have an impact on his custody situation, though,' Tammi-Jo remarked. 'Yvonne told me he's got shared custody of his daughter. Don't think his relationship with her mother's great, so maybe she'd be able to use a drugs charge against him.'

'I don't think he'd give a shit,' Tyler said, sitting back in disgust. 'Don't think he gives a damn about Claire, so I can't see that losing custody would bother him.'

'Aw. That's sad,' Tammi-Jo said. She tutted. 'Dads are such dicks sometimes.'

'Here, steady on!' Tyler objected.

'Not all of you! I didn't mean *all* dads. Just some dads. Most? No. I don't know. Some. We'll say *some dads are dicks* and leave it at that. OK? OK.'

She dipped her head towards both of them in what might have been a nod, but could equally have been a bow, then urged the DCI to continue.

After reattaching the old notes to the table, Logan picked up the pad and, by the light of the candles, scribbled down a list of what they knew, and some questions regarding what they didn't.

They had motives for a few different suspects. Monty Jr and Helen had already been discussed at length, but though he'd seemed confident that Helen was choosing him over her family, Donatello also wasn't out of the frame.

Despite his outlandish appearance, and the self-confidence required to replace all the hair on your head with a swarm of densely packed plastic bees, the man struck Logan as desperate and needy. If he had even an inkling that his gravy train was about to be catastrophically derailed, would that be motivation enough to murder his lover's father?

No doubt.

'And Krystal, too, boss,' Tyler said. 'She seemed shocked to hear she wasn't going to be in his will, so until then she must've assumed she was.'

'What was it that Monty Junior said in the interview, sir?' Tammi-Jo asked. 'Something about gold-diggers who cross their fingers and hope he dies before he gets bored of them? Maybe she thought he was going to give her the elbow, and so couldn't wait for natural causes to do her dirty work.'

'Not very subtle, though, is it?' Tyler said. 'Big knife through the head.'

'She doesn't strike me as a very subtle sort of person,' Tammi-Jo countered. 'I mean, you've seen and heard her, yeah?'

Logan set down the stack of blank Post-its.

'Aye, about that,' he began, but then the room was lit up again by a jagged bolt of lightning.

For a moment, illuminated by the electrical crackle, a wild-eyed face appeared at one of the windows, long grey hair slicked across its forehead by the rain, its nose and one cheek pressed flat against the glass like it was trying to force its way inside.

'Jesus Christ!' Logan hissed.

Thunder rumbled, and the darkness returned.

'What is it, boss? What's wrong? What's happened?' Tyler yelped, leaping to his feet. Logan's reaction had been one of genuine alarm, and the DC's imagination was already racing into overdrive. 'Did you see something? What did you see?'

He followed the bigger man's gaze until he spotted the window. Lightning flashed again, and for a moment, he could just make out a silhouette moving across the garden.

'Jesus Christ!' They were the precise same words that Logan had used, but Tyler spat them out in a significantly higher register. 'Who the hell is that?'

'No idea,' Logan said.

He picked up the long-handled torch he'd taken from his car, clicked it on, and directed the high-powered beam at each of the library's windows in turn.

When the light failed to pick out any more faces pressed against the glass, he turned it towards the door.

'But I'm sure as hell going to find out.'

–

Logan ran, head down and hunched against the wind, hand raised to shield his eyes from the rain that seemed to batter him from all directions at once. Including, somehow, below.

His coat was still hanging up in the castle, and the torrential downpour had made short work of his shirt, turning the material almost totally transparent.

The grass beneath his boots had been churned into mud. Water ran down the slope away from McQuarrie Hall, rushing past his feet, threatening to whip his legs out from beneath him.

The beam of his torch cleaved a line through the darkness, picking out the grasping branches of trees that clawed at him, like the forest itself was trying to drag him in and swallow him whole.

'Hello? Who's out here?' he bellowed, but the wind stole the words away and smashed them into pieces.

It had taken him over a minute to find a fire exit that led out to where he'd seen the figure at the window. By the time he'd arrived outside the library, whoever had been out here was gone.

Logan pressed on regardless. The interloper couldn't have got far in this weather, not unless he'd literally been blown away. Which, considering that even the heavier-than-most Logan was struggling to stay on his feet, was not entirely impossible.

He'd ordered Tyler and Tammi-Jo to stay inside. It was one thing to risk his own life out here, but he was damned if he was putting theirs in jeopardy, too.

Besides, if Tyler's hair got messed up, Logan would never hear the bloody end of it.

A gust of wind hit him like a charging rhino, staggering him just as another clap of thunder pushed down on him from above.

He felt the air sizzle around him, then ducked as the clouds were filled with an explosive burst of lightning.

As the darkness was briefly driven back, he swept his gaze across the grass, the trees, the building beside him, searching for any sign of the man he'd seen through the glass.

He stumbled and slid to what he thought was one of the library windows, cupped one hand around his eyes, and peered inside. Sure enough, the flickering candles picked out the makeshift Big Board.

Directing his torch at the ground, Logan saw a few muddy footprints that were even larger than his own. The window was six feet off the ground, so for someone to have been looking in, they had to be at least his height. Logan was sure the face had been near the centre of the glass, which would have put the man close to seven feet tall.

Another face appeared at the window, though on the inside this time. Tammi-Jo was shouting to him, asking him to come back inside, her face all knotted up with worry.

Rain lashed at his back, a torrent of icy cold through his shirt.

Whoever had been out here, giant or not, they were gone. Continuing the search in this weather was reckless at best, suicidal at worst.

With a nod to the detective constable on the other side of the glass, Logan wiped the water from his face, swept the hair from his forehead, and headed back the way he'd come.

# *Chapter 34*

Logan had barely stepped back inside when he heard the scream. It was a shrill, piercing thing that cut through the rain and the rumbling of thunder, and echoed throughout the castle.

He barrelled through a door on his right and found himself back in the main entrance hall, where all the stuffed and mounted creatures watched to see what he would do next.

A dozen candles had been lit and placed around the room, but the light barely made a dent in the darkness, and only served to make the glassy eyes of the dead things shimmer and dance.

'Boss!'

Tyler's shout came breathlessly down the stairs. Logan looked up in time to see the detective constable tearing up the final few steps to the mezzanine level, then disappearing around the bend.

He set off after him, water dripping from his hair and his clothes, his boots leaving prints on the stone floor behind him which faded as he ran. His torchlight bounced from step to step, so the shadows of the paintings and tapestries expanded and contracted across the walls.

The run outside in the rain had already taken most of the wind from his sails, and by the time Logan found Tyler outside Montgomery's study, his breath was rasping in and out.

The detective constable was looking deeply uncomfortable as a sobbing Krystal clung to him, her arms wrapped around his back, tears painting streaky lines of mascara down her cheeks.

Aside from the light from Logan's torch, the corridor was in darkness. A quick glance around revealed a candle lying on its side on the floor, the wick glowing faintly, a thin line of smoke rising into the air.

The same quick glance found no sign of Rab, the uniformed constable who was supposed to be standing guard over the place.

'Oh, it was horrible! It was horrible!' Krystal wailed. 'My heart! My blessed heart!'

'What's happened?' Logan demanded, leaning on a wall while he fought to get his breath back. 'What was the scream?'

Tyler looked the soaking wet Logan up and down, Krystal's arms still hugging him like her life depended on it.

'Rain still on, then, boss?' he said.

'The scream, Tyler!' Logan barked. 'What the hell was the scream?'

Tyler raised a hand and pointed to Krystal, then shrugged. 'Dunno. She's not said yet. I just got here.'

'I saw him! He's in there!' Krystal cried, raising a shaky hand and indicating the closed door of the study. 'I saw him with my own two eyes!'

'Saw who?' Logan asked.

'Monty! I saw Monty!'

Logan looked across to the door. 'Your stepson?'

'My *husband*!' Krystal wailed. 'I saw my husband, standing by his desk, large as life!'

Tyler's face paled. 'Oh, great. That's all we need.'

'I can assure you, Mrs McQuarrie, whoever you think you saw in there, it wasn't your husband.'

'Well, see for yourself!' Krystal said, finally releasing her bear-like grip on Tyler. She pointed to the door again, but took a few faltering backwards steps. 'He's still in there. I shut him in, and he ain't come out.'

Tyler held his hands up in a calming gesture. 'Maybe we shouldn't rush into this, boss,' he suggested, but Logan had already crossed the corridor, and with a twist of the handle and the application of a shoulder, he went stumbling into the study.

The empty study.

'Is he there, boss?' Tyler called from the darkness, as Logan directed his torchlight around the room.

'Of course he's not here. It wasn't him, Tyler. Nobody's here.'

There was a clattering of footsteps out in the passageway. A moment later, Helen Bach appeared in the room behind the DCI, a candelabra clutched in one hand. Three candles flickered in their holders, picking out some of the details of the room around them.

'What's happened? What's going on?' she asked. 'I heard a scream.'

'That was me,' Krystal said, sidling into the room, but staying close to the door.

Helen rolled her eyes. 'I guessed that, yes. Why? What happened?'

'I saw my darling Montgomery, right here. Right on that spot!'

She pointed to the other side of the desk. Logan leaned over and saw that all three of the desk's drawers were open, the contents scattered like someone had been rummaging around inside them.

Helen fixed her stepmother with a scathing look. 'And what about now, Krystal? Can you see him now? Is my father here with us now?'

'Well, of course not! But I know what I saw!'

'Shift!' Logan barked, all but elbowing Helen aside. He thrust his torch into her hands. 'Hold that.'

Bending, he gave the coffee table a shove. It slid sideways with little effort, and as it moved, it pushed aside the study's large antique rug. Metal and wood scraped. As the rug moved, a hatch beneath it slid open, revealing a rectangular hole in the floor.

Metal rungs embedded into the stone blocks ran down a few feet, then a crawlspace led off at a slightly downward angle.

Logan snatched back his torch, swept it down into the secret passageway, then looked up at Helen and Krystal in turn.

'Where does this lead? Where does it come out?'

'I… I have no idea,' Helen said, still staring into the hole. 'I had no idea this was here.'

'Don't look at me, sugar. I ain't seen nothing like this before.'

'You must know where it goes!' Logan spat. 'Come on, think!'

'I don't!' Helen protested. 'I mean it, I had no idea. Monty and I always thought there were hidden passages in the castle, but I don't remember us finding any.'

'Well, someone did,' Logan said.

He barged past the women and almost crashed straight into Tammi-Jo who was just arriving on the scene.

'Everything all right?' she asked. 'There was a scream.'

'You,' Logan said, pointing to Tyler. 'Get them two out of that room, then stand guard. Nobody in, nobody out.'

'Will do, boss.'

'DC Swanney, go find that constable. He should've been standing guard here. Where the hell is he?'

'On it, sir! I'll go look in the toilets! Well, I'll knock, I won't just go in and—'

She was still talking, but Logan was already on the move, squelching as he ran for the stairs and set off down them two at a time.

He'd asked Helen and Krystal where the secret passageway led because he wanted to see their reactions. They'd seemed genuinely surprised, and when they'd said they hadn't been aware of it, he'd believed them.

Fortunately, Hamza and Sinead were currently staying with a man who did know about the passageway. He'd helped to build it.

And he knew exactly where it came out.

–

Francois was boiling a large pan of water on a gas stove when Logan came thundering into the kitchen. He turned, startled, and the DCI was stopped in his tracks by the knife in the chef's hand.

'Oh. It is you,' Francois said, returning the knife to the worktop. '*Pardonnez-moi, monsieur.* I think, with the power out and a killer still on the loose, I am more on edge than I thought. Rushing in, looking like that… You startled me.'

There were ten or so candles placed strategically around the kitchen to maximise the spread of their light. They revealed the stacked-high dishes from the earlier dinner service, all scraped and waiting to be washed.

'The hot water is powered by electricity. No power means no hot water, so no dishes. Hence…' He indicated the pot on the stove. 'I improvise.'

'Aye, very good.' Logan pointed to a door at the back of the kitchen with the beam of torch. 'That the pantry?'

'Uh, *oui*. Why?'

Logan didn't bother to explain. He made a beeline for the door, pulled it open, then directed his light inside. The pantry was about as large as the bathroom in his house, and was lined on three sides by deep racks of metal shelving.

Kneeling by the rack directly across from the door, he tugged on the bottommost shelf, then fell backwards onto the floor when it moved far more easily than he'd expected.

The whole lower half of the wall swung outwards, revealing the mouth of a narrow tunnel that angled upwards into darkness.

'Oh my God!' Helen's voice came sharply from the pantry doorway. 'Is this the same tunnel? How the hell did you know about this?'

Logan shone the light inside the crawl space. There was no way he could possibly squeeze himself through there, even if he wanted to.

Launching himself to his feet, he barged back through into the main kitchen, forcing Helen to stagger out of his path.

Krystal had followed her stepdaughter, and was now standing by the door of the big walk-in fridge, the candlelight dancing across her tear-stained face. She had one hand on Francois's arm, like she was using him for support.

When Logan appeared from inside the pantry, though, the chef jumped back and crossed his hands behind his back.

'Is everything all right, Inspector?'

'It's *Detective Chief Inspector*,' Logan corrected. 'And no. Not really.'

He brought the torch up so the light hit the chef in the face. Francois grimaced and looked away, blinking away the circle of blinding white light.

'Did anyone come and go through this kitchen?' Logan demanded.

'What, apart from all of you?' Francois asked. '*Non*.'

'Nobody? Nobody came or went in the last ten minutes?'

Francois shrugged. He thumbed at his eyes, clearly still feeling the effects of the torchlight. 'Nobody. I 'ave been here the whole time.'

Logan searched the Frenchman's face, searching it, hoping to find some sign that he was lying. The DCI was usually pretty good at that sort of thing. He had a knack for it.

Unfortunately, his instincts were all telling him that the chef was telling the truth.

Which meant…

'Shite!' Logan spat, breaking into a run in the direction of the kitchen door.

Before he could get there, another scream from Krystal screeched around the room, rattling the stack of crockery by the sink.

'Jesus Christ,' Logan grimaced. He'd been passing the woman at the time, and had taken the full force of the scream to the side of the head. 'What now?'

Krystal couldn't speak. Instead, she stabbed a finger against the small circular window in the door of the fridge, one hand clamped over her mouth, tears trailing down her face once again.

Logan steered her aside, pulled open the door, then stopped when his torchlight fell on the empty space where Montgomery McQuarrie's body should have been.

'I told you!' wailed Krystal, finding her voice again. She fell against Francois, who put an arm around her, holding her up. 'I told you, I saw him! I saw my Monty, risen from the grave!'

Logan grimaced and ran a hand down his face. Before he could dwell too much on the missing body, though, he remembered where he'd been rushing off to before Krystal had stopped him.

If Francois was telling the truth—if nobody had come out of the hidden doorway in the pantry—then that could mean only one thing.

'He's still in the tunnel,' Logan muttered.

And that meant…

'*Tyler!*'

# *Chapter 35*

Tyler didn't see what all the fuss was about, or why Logan was looking at him with quite such an expression of concern.

'You all right, boss?' he asked.

'Am I all right? Aye. Are you all right?'

'Why wouldn't I be, boss?' Tyler asked. He frowned, and became dimly aware of a throbbing at the base of his skull.

'Because you're lying on the floor, son,' Logan told him.

'Eh?' The DC slid his hands around beside him and confirmed that, yes, he was indeed sprawled on the cold stone floor. 'Oh! Shit, aye. So I am. How did—?'

The pain kicked in then—a sharp, stabbing sensation on the back of his head, near the crown. It made his teeth grind together and his neck retract into his chest.

'Oof. Ow. Fuck.'

He gingerly rubbed the affected area, and felt the beginnings of what could well turn out to be a sizeable lump.

'The door,' he said, craning his neck towards the study. The unsteady glow of Montgomery's gas lamp shone through the gap. 'I heard the door opening, and then…'

He looked at his hand and found a smear of blood on his fingertips.

'Someone must've cracked me one. Sorry, boss. I let them get away.'

'Don't worry about it, son.' Logan took the detective constable's hand and hoisted him onto his feet with a single tug. 'We've got bigger problems right now.'

Tyler prodded carefully around the site of his injury, wincing whenever he pressed too hard, or too close to the epicentre.

'What now, boss?'

'Monty's body's missing.'

Tyler stopped prodding. His lips moved as he silently repeated what the DCI had just said.

'Missing? How's it missing, boss?' he asked. He shot a wary look back at the study. 'So does that mean… Was it him, right enough? In there?'

'Of course it wasn't bloody him! He's dead.'

'But you said he was up and about!'

'No, I didn't. I said his body's gone. The trolley, too. So, unless he's woken up and wheeled himself away, I'd say chances are that someone has taken him.'

'Surely not, boss? Someone would've seen him being rolled through the castle, wouldn't they?'

A cool breeze stuck Logan's damp shirt to his back. He peeled it away, remembering the grass that had been churned into mud outside the house.

'Maybe he wasn't taken through the castle,' he muttered. 'Maybe he was taken around it…'

–

'You. Wig of Bees. Where the hell do you think you're going!'

Donatello had been dragging an impractical, old-fashioned trunk-style suitcase across the hallway, headed for the main doors. The luggage was clearly meant for two people to carry, and the noise it made as the back end was scraped along the floor did Tyler's headache no favours whatsoever.

He stopped and looked around at the sound of Logan's voice, then let the trunk fall the rest of the way to the floor when he spotted the detectives approaching from the bottom of the stairs.

'I'm leaving,' Donatello said. 'I know where I'm not wanted.'

'Aye, I'd imagine that's pretty much everywhere,' Logan said. 'But no, you're not. Nobody's leaving. Not until I bloody well say so.'

Donatello puffed out his cheeks. This made all the little padlocks hanging from the hoops in his neck swing back and forth.

'Fine.'

'That was easy,' Tyler said.

The artist shrugged. 'Can't exactly go anywhere, can I? I just thought, if it looked like I was leaving, then Helen might decide that she couldn't—'

'I don't care,' Logan barked, cutting the sob-story short. 'Where is she?'

'Don't know. Think she's avoiding me,' Donatello replied. 'Monty's in the reading room, though, if—'

Logan didn't wait to hear the rest of the sentence. He set off on the most direct route towards the reading room, forcing Donatello to hastily side-step out of his path.

'Do you want me to come? Do you need me for anything?'

'Absolutely not,' Logan called back over his shoulder.

Tyler caught up with Logan just as he threw open the door of the reading room. Sure enough, Monty sat there, leaning back in one of the big leather chairs, swigging from a big glass of what was undoubtedly very expensive whisky.

His hair was tousled. His shirt was creased and unbuttoned to halfway down his chest, revealing a triangle of smooth, hairless skin. A thin film of perspiration on his forehead suggested he was either in the early throes of illness or had recently worked up a sweat.

Logan noted his appearance, filed it away for later, then spoke so sharply Monty almost choked on his drink.

'Big bastard, long white hair, creeping about outside. Who is he?' the DCI demanded.

Monty's response was an empty stare. 'Sorry?'

Logan closed the gap between the door and the younger man's chair in a few big strides. He plucked the glass of Scotch from his fingers, tipped it onto the floor, then slammed the empty glass down on the table beside him.

'Big bastard. Long white hair. Creeping about outside,' he said again, and the look on his face made clear how intently Monty should be paying attention. 'Who is he?'

Monty's eyes darted left and right, searching the detective's face. He was sinking back into the folds of his chair, like he might be able to retreat straight through it and out the other side.

After a moment of breathless, panicky staring, some spark of recollection ignited deep in the archives of Monty's memory banks.

'Wait. Mungo?'

'Who the hell's Mungo?' Logan asked.

'*Mungo*,' Monty said.

Logan gritted his teeth. 'Putting a different emphasis on it isn't clarifying matters, son. Who is he?'

'He's, uh, I mean… I'm not even sure he's around anymore. I suppose he must be. Papa never mentioned him leaving. I just… I haven't thought about him in years.'

'Still not helping,' Logan warned. His patience was atom-thin now, and the younger McQuarrie sibling had enough sense to recognise that fact.

'He was Papa's sort of… assistant, I suppose. Handyman. I think he's a relative. A cousin of my father's, maybe, or an uncle. I was never really clear on that. Utterly terrified me as a child. Helen, too. Completely mute, poor fellow. And a bit simple. Thick as pig shit, if I'm honest. Lovely chap, though, I'm told. Dedicated to Papa in a way I'm not sure anyone else ever has been.'

He picked up his empty glass with one hand and the whisky bottle with another, then motioned towards the door as he poured.

'He stuffed all the animals you see out there. Killed most of them, too. With his bare hands, would you believe? Throttled the life right out of them. Only way he could truly minimise damage.'

'Jesus,' Tyler muttered.

'So Papa always told us, anyway. There's no saying it's true. I mean, who chokes out a wild boar?'

Logan remembered the face at the window, and the height the man beyond the glass must have been.

He didn't know if him strangling stags to death was true or not, but he wasn't dismissing it out of hand.

'So, what are you saying? There's been someone else in the castle this whole time...? Wait. No. Let me rephrase that. There's been *a giant man with murderous tendencies* in the castle this whole time, and nobody thought that might be worth a wee bloody mention?'

'I wouldn't call him "murderous",' Monty said, but his voice was a mumble, haemorrhaging confidence. 'And I didn't know he was here. I haven't seen him in years!'

'Do you know where we might be able to find him?'

Monty set down the now almost empty bottle of Scotch, then started to raise the glass carefully towards his mouth. He'd filled it almost to the brim and didn't want to risk spilling a drop of the precious amber liquid.

'He'd be in his workshop, I'd imagine. If it even exists anymore. But he must be eighty by now. I'd be surprised if he's not dead.'

'Well, he's looking bloody good for it, if he is,' Logan said. Once again, he snatched the glass away from Monty. Once again, he tipped it onto the floor. 'How about we go find out?'

–

It took a few wrong turns and some hasty backtracking, but five minutes after they'd left the reading room, Logan and Tyler found themselves in an area of the castle they'd never been in before.

It was an area that Tyler would've been happy to never have set foot in at all. Water ingress had slicked the stone walls with green, and turned the air so thick and musty he could taste it every time he inhaled.

Spiders scurried along the walls, their webs somehow snagging at him as he walked, even though Logan and Monty Jr were both in front. He couldn't understand that. The DCI was larger than him in every possible direction and dimension. He should've cleared the path of cobwebs, and yet Tyler was constantly being snared at head height by the bloody things, forcing him to wipe his face every few seconds to clear them away.

A gust of wind had whistled along the corridor a couple of left turns ago, snuffing out the candles that Tyler and Monty Jr had been carrying. Tyler's phone battery was too low to risk using the flashlight function, so he'd stuck close to Logan and the reassuring light from his police-issue torch.

At last, they turned onto another damp corridor, and Monty slowed to a stop. At the far end, a set of heavy double doors blocked the passage. There were small frosted glass windows in each door, but dust, grime and a few clumps of moss had accumulated on them over time, making them impossible to see through.

Not that Tyler wanted to see through them. Seeing through them was way down his list of *things to do*. He was actively against the idea, in fact.

The old paint was peeling from the doors' woodwork, and mould had started to colour outside the edges, spreading up the frame and onto the decaying plasterboard wall above.

The fact that the wall wasn't made of solid stone suggested it was a more recent addition than the rest of the place. Someone, at some point, had felt the need to separate this part of the castle from the part on the other side of the doors. Someone had felt that the world was better off if whatever was beyond those doors were to remain there.

Maybe it was the general atmosphere of the castle, maybe it was the way the circle of torchlight trembled across the rotting wood, or maybe it was because he'd recently taken quite a hard blow to the head—whatever the reason, Tyler reckoned these were, by quite some margin, the most foreboding doors he'd ever seen.

Exactly what it was they forbade, he didn't know. But whatever it was, they were being pretty damned emphatic about it.

'Workshop's through there,' Monty whispered.

Tyler swallowed. Of course it was through there. Where else would it have been but on the other side of the scary doorway?

Logan directed his torchlight downwards until the beam lit up the floor. Two shiny trails of water and mud led all the way along the corridor, then disappeared below the doors.

Trolley wheels. It had to be.

'Lead the way,' Logan instructed, but Monty was quick to shake his head.

'No. This is as far as I go. Like I said, Mungo scared me then, and if he's still around, I'd rather not come face to face with him.' He drew himself up to his full, unimpressive height. 'This is my house. My home. You may be the police, but you can't just come in here and force me to do things I don't want to do. So'—he turned his back on the doors, looked Tyler up and down, then smiled falsely—'good luck. But you're on your own from here.'

## *Chapter 36*

Tammi-Jo wasn't having much luck tracking down the missing constable. He wasn't in any of the nearby bathrooms, hadn't popped to the kitchen for a snack, and wasn't milling around anywhere else obvious, either.

She'd returned to the study a few times, hoping that he might reappear there, but as of her third trip up there, he was yet to rematerialise.

Nobody she asked had seen him, either. She wished she'd taken a note of his mobile number so she could call him, but then remembered that her phone had no signal.

She could've used the landline in the old reception, she thought.

Until she realised that he'd have no signal, either.

Now, she had resorted to wandering aimlessly through some of the corridors, shouting, 'Rab!' and 'Yoo-hoo!' and 'Constable!' because she'd completely forgotten his surname.

She was half a dozen twists and turns, plus a couple of long straight passageways away from the main hallway, when she heard breathing coming from somewhere up ahead. Fast. Urgent. The panting of something not human.

Recognising it, Tammi-Jo whistled, clapped her hands on her thighs, and then bent down to pat the tangle of tail, tongue and legs that came barrelling around the corner towards her.

'Hey, Tag!' the DC said, squatting beside him and setting her candle on the ground as he ran in joyous circles, every part of him wagging from the tip of his tail to the end of his nose.

Very quickly, his excitement proved too much for him, and he flopped over onto his back, legs raised, tongue lolling down onto the stone floor.

'What are you doing here, eh?' Tammi-Jo asked, *scritching* at his belly with all her fingers at once. 'What are you doing all the way down here?'

The candle flickered in a sudden breeze.

'We were playing.'

Tammi-Jo was jolted by the closeness of the voice. She shot to her feet, startling the girl who had appeared around the same corner Taggart had come from.

'Is that OK?' Claire asked. 'I was looking after him.'

'Uh, yeah.' Tammi-Jo bent and retrieved her candle. As far as she could tell, Claire didn't have one. 'How are you seeing down here, though? It's dark. I mean, obviously it's dark, you can see it's dark. But how are you seeing anything?'

There was an odd *voom-voom-voom* sound from over by the girl. She raised an arm, and in the light of the candle, Tammi-Jo could just make out that Claire was holding a small, hand-cranked torch.

With a flip of a switch, a weak beam of yellow light painted a spot on the floor between them.

'I've got this. It's not very good, though.'

'Aren't you scared? Down here on your own?'

'I'm not on my own,' Claire replied. Her voice was solemn, and the way she was staring made Tammi-Jo uneasy.

The detective constable raised her candle, trying to see into the shadows behind the girl.

'Oh, you mean because you've got Taggart here?' she asked.

Claire shook her head. 'No. There's someone else, too.' She held out a hand. 'Come with me. I'll show you,' she said in a whisper. 'But you have to stay very, *very* quiet…'

–

'Do we knock, boss?' Tyler whispered.

They were standing by the rotten double doors at the end of the corridor that Monty had led them to. This close, the light from Logan's torch revealed all the scabs and blisters in the paintwork, and the patterns of mould across the wood.

There was a smell that Tyler couldn't quite place. Not dirty, exactly. Perhaps even the opposite. Something chemical and abrasive.

'I think we should knock,' Tyler said. 'If he's a big bastard like you say, then we don't want to surprise him. He might, you know'—Tyler looked the door up and down, then gulped—'squash us.'

'He's no' an actual giant, Tyler. We're no' in Jack and the fucking Beanstalk here.' Logan placed the flat of a hand on one of the doors. 'Just follow my lead, all right? And whatever happens, try not to scream.'

'Can't make any promises there, boss,' Tyler muttered, then he braced himself and stuck close as Logan nudged open the doors and stepped into the room beyond.

The place was lit by six candles, positioned strategically around the place. They were well-burned down—barely stumps—and Logan got the impression that they'd been in use long before the power had gone out.

'Christ. That smell,' Tyler coughed, burying his nose and mouth in the crook of an elbow. 'What is that?'

There was definitely something chemical about it, like a bleach, or an antiseptic, or something along those lines. It was so strong that, were it to come in contact with germs, it would not only kill them, it would be an extinction-level event.

Eyes shone back at them from the shadows, at floor level, on high, and tucked away in the corners. Logan directed his torch at them, and Tyler recoiled at the faces of stags, stoats, foxes and badgers.

Unlike the skilfully restored creatures out in the castle's main hallway, however, these all looked twisted and broken and wrong. The eyes weren't in the right places, or the noses were stunted and pig-like, or the mouths were pulled into grotesque grins.

Those weren't the worst ones, either. At least you could tell what was wrong with them. Some of the dead things staring back at the detectives were close enough to their original form that it was impossible to identify a fault, but far enough away for them to unsettle something deep within the subconscious.

'I don't like this, boss,' Tyler whispered.

Logan turned slowly on the spot, his torchlight moving from one uncanny face to the other.

'It's no' exactly the highlight of my week, either,' he admitted below his breath.

He directed the torch downwards until he found the wet, muddy trails on the floor. He followed them with the light, tracking them to the same metal trolley they'd loaded into the fridge just a few hours earlier.

'The body's gone,' Logan remarked, finding the top of the trolley bare.

'Shit!' Tyler pulled in closer to the DCI and grabbed onto the sleeve of his shirt. 'What do we do, boss?'

Logan slapped the junior officer's hand away. 'You can quit that for a bloody start!' he said, then even he drew in a breath when the beam of his flashlight stuttered and died.

'Boss?!' Tyler yelped, as the darkness seemed to rush in around them.

Logan gave the end of the torch a smack against the heel of his hand. The light returned, but there was something untrustworthy about it now, like it might choose to flick itself off again at any moment.

'The body's not here, boss. It was worth a try. We did our best, but we should probably go now.'

Logan sighed. 'Take a breath and calm yourself down, for God's sake. It's just a room, Tyler. There's nothing to worry about, see?'

He swept the torchlight around again. It passed across a big pile of sawdust, and a large wooden workbench, then stopped and crept slowly backwards.

There was a large leather bag open on the bench. Beside it, someone had carefully set out a range of tools. Quite surgical-looking tools.

The sort of tools that one of Shona Maguire's predecessors might have been familiar with.

Albeit, one of the very early ones.

'Still quite worried, boss,' Tyler whispered. 'More so, if anything.' He swallowed, completely transfixed by the saws, and hooks, and sharp, pointy implements carefully set out on the workbench. 'Who the hell lives back here? Frankenstein's interior designer?'

Just beyond the corner of the detective constable's eye, mostly hidden in the dark void between two pools of candle-light, an impossible shape shambled through the shadows.

–

'See?' Claire whispered, pointing to the floor. 'There were more of them, but they've gone now.'

'Can I…?' Tammi-Jo asked, holding a hand out for the girl's torch.

Claire *voom-voomed* the lever that charged up the dynamo, then passed it over. Tammi-Jo thanked her and promised to give it back, before directing the beam down at the floor.

The faint outline of a footprint was only just visible and fading fast. Just the one. Just on its own, halfway along a corridor with no doors on either side.

'Huh,' she said.

There was no point taking out her phone to snap a picture. At the rate the print was fading, it would be gone before she had opened the camera app.

She directed the torchlight back the way they'd come. Taggart sat a few feet away, his head raised and his back straight, like he was waiting for the 'Good boy!' to which he clearly felt entitled.

Tammi-Jo obliged, and the little dog's stubby tail thumped happily against the floor.

When she looked back at the floor beside her, the footprint was nowhere to be seen.

She clicked her tongue against the roof of her mouth, nodded, then stood up.

'You said there were more?'

Claire nodded, then pointed off along the corridor in the direction the print had been heading away from.

The detective constable pursed her lips until her mouth formed a tight little circle, then shifted it from side to side as she considered her options.

Finally, she reached a decision.

'OK, then.' She held a hand out to the girl and gave the torch a *voom-voom-voom*. 'You up for some more exploring?'

–

For the third or fourth time that day—possibly fifth, he'd lost count—Tyler made a noise he'd never heard before. It rose from somewhere deep inside him, a random string of strangled sounds and syllables that culminated in a bellowed, '*A-cha-fuck?!*' and a whole-body convulsion that threatened to turn him inside out.

'Jesus Christ, boss! What the hell is that?!'

He brought up his fists, but that was pointless, he knew. No way he was fighting the monster that had come lurching from the darkness. He'd be like a gnat getting in the ring with King Kong. Aye, he might be able to get on his nerves for a bit, but there was only one way the bout was ending.

He was a full head taller than Logan. Bulkier, too, despite his age. His face was a topographical map of wrinkles and scars. His long white hair was still wet, and hung down like a pair of recently steam-cleaned curtains.

He'd clearly changed his clothing, though, as the dark denim dungarees he was wearing were as dry as a bone. He wore nothing underneath—on his top half, at least—and a forest of white hair covered the sinews of his ape-like chest.

Incredibly, none of this was the most remarkable thing about the man.

The most remarkable thing about him was the corpse he carried over one shoulder like it weighed next to nothing.

The detectives assumed it was the corpse, at least. It was about the right size and shape, and was still secured within the black bags Logan had wrapped and taped it up in.

The giant stared down at them, his mouth hanging open slightly. He didn't move, didn't even blink when Logan shone the torch in his face.

'Eh… all right?' Logan asked.

Tyler had never heard the DCI sound so unsure before, which didn't help his ever-increasing anxiety levels.

'I'm guessing that you must be Mungo?'

## *Chapter 37*

At first, because of the bigger man's lack of response, Logan had assumed he couldn't understand him. Certainly, he wasn't saying much, though Monty had told them that Mungo was mute, so it would've been a surprise if he'd started chatting away.

He drew back a pace when Logan indicated the body draped across his shoulder, his dark eyes boring deep into the DCI's soul.

'You need to put that down,' Logan instructed. 'Down. You can't… You shouldn't have taken that. You've committed a crime.'

'I don't think we've got handcuffs his size, boss,' Tyler whispered, but Logan ignored him.

The DCI took a step closer to Mungo, and the giant shuffled back to maintain the distance between them.

'Nobody's going to hurt you. You're not in any trouble,' Logan said. 'Not yet. But if you don't listen, and don't put the body back on that trolley, then you will be. You understand? If you don't put the body down, you'll go to prison. You'll go to jail.'

The DCI sighed.

'Is any of this getting through to him, do you think?'

'Don't know, boss. I'm terrified beyond the ability to think straight,' Tyler admitted. 'What the hell's he going to do with the body, anyway?'

Tyler's gaze flitted to the workbench full of tools, then down to the big pile of sawdust on the floor beside it.

From the shadows, all the deformed dead things watched on with interest.

'Oh, Jesus!' Tyler's face paled. 'Surely not? Surely he isn't…?' He shook his head, trying to rid himself of the thought. 'I think he's going to stuff him, boss!'

'You've finally got there, have you?' Logan asked. 'Wondered how long it would take you to figure that one out.'

He hadn't taken his eyes off Mungo, and Mungo had continued to stare right back.

Tyler took a shuffled sideways step. If a scrap kicked off between Logan and the other man, he didn't want to get caught in the middle of it. Intervening in one of Logan's fights hadn't exactly stood him in good stead the last time, and that one hadn't involved battling a man with the stature and dimensions of a Norse god.

'We're going to need you to put the body down, Mungo,' Logan said, speaking a little more slowly this time. 'This… what you're planning… It's not allowed. You can't.'

Slowly, like an ancient oak tree starting to fall, Mungo's head dipped forward into a nod.

'You do understand. Good. Good, that's…' Logan smiled. It was a grim, tight-lipped thing, but it was the best he could manage, given the circumstances. He used the torch to indicate the bagged-up body, then to point at the empty trolley. 'Put it down there, Mungo. Put it down there, and let's talk.'

Mungo didn't react for several seconds, then his wide brow furrowed, like the words were just filtering through. He reached into the front pocket of his dungarees and pulled out an envelope that was bent at the edges and yellowed with age.

Without a word, he held it out to Logan.

'Careful, boss,' Tyler whispered, but Logan took the envelope, opened it, and read the handwritten letter inside.

'Jesus Christ,' he mumbled when he reached the signature at the bottom.

He'd never seen Montgomery McQuarrie senior's legal signature before, but he imagined this was the real deal.

'What is it?' Tyler asked, still staring at the giant man with the corpse on his shoulder.

'It's a letter from Monty seniorr requesting that he be stuffed and displayed out front, in the main hallway.'

'What? No. No, no, no, boss. He can't do that, can he?'

'Of course he bloody can't,' Logan said. He raised his voice and slowed his diction, turning back to Mungo. 'He might have said this, but it's not allowed. It's illegal. Against the law. If you do this, if you... you know, stuff him, you'll be breaking the law, Mungo. You'll be arrested. Is that what you want?'

Mungo's gaze shifted to the note in Logan's hand. He nodded solemnly and pointed at it, but the detective just shook his head.

'It doesn't matter what he asked you to do. Even if he gave permission, it's not allowed. We can't let you do it. Do you understand? We can't allow this to happen.'

Again, it took a while for Mungo to register what had been said. This time, the message got through. With a few cautious paces, he reached the trolley, then carefully laid the makeshift body bag and its contents on top.

A hand that could've enveloped Tyler's entire head was laid gently on the corpse for a moment. Mungo closed his eyes, and the detectives watched as, for the first time, someone displayed a moment of genuine emotion over the passing of Montgomery McQuarrie senior.

'I'm sorry for your loss,' Logan said.

Mungo's eyes opened. His gaze flitted gratefully towards the DCI, then he turned on his heel so suddenly that Tyler jumped back and brought his fists up again.

'Easy, son,' Logan urged. 'You'll only hurt yourself.'

The giant vanished into the darkness again. Tyler searched the shadows for him, then almost screamed when Mungo reappeared on his left, stalking towards him with a determination and purpose that potentially spelled death.

Instead of snapping the detective constable like a twig, however, Mungo stopped and thrust a padded envelope into his hands. He nodded down at it, urging Tyler to open it.

The envelope was almost as yellowed as the one that had held Monty's macabre last wish. One end had already been torn open, and when Tyler tipped it, a DVD case slid out and almost landed on the floor.

He managed to catch it, and, in the glow of Logan's torchlight, he read the title on the front of the case. The text was superimposed on a photograph of the very castle they were standing in now.

'McQuarrie Hall In Room Guest Welcome', he read.

Before he could pass any more comment on it, Mungo took the DVD from him, turned it over, then tapped the back of the case.

'An introduction to the history of this Scottish country house, plus information on amenities available to guests. Not to be removed from guest bedrooms or communal areas.'

Mungo shook his head, like he was annoyed. He tapped the back of the case again, closer to the bottom this time, right on the logo for the production company.

'A McQuarrie Hall production.'

Mungo nodded keenly. He tapped the case again.

'What? I don't… I don't get it,' Tyler admitted. 'It was produced in-house?'

Mungo pointed to the body, then prodded the back of the case again.

Logan took the DVD case from Tyler, squinted at the text in the half-light, then turned it over to check the front.

As well as the picture of the castle, there was an image of what was presumably the person presenting the DVD. She was a blonde-haired woman in her fifties, and was smiling right down the barrel of the camera.

Her outfit didn't look particularly dated, and another check of the back revealed a production date of 2009.

'Must've been made just a few years before the place stopped being run as a hotel,' Logan reckoned.

Mungo nodded again. Tyler was still visibly uncomfortable being this close to the man, but no longer appeared to be at risk of cardiac arrest.

'Any idea what he's trying to tell us, boss?'

Logan scanned the back of the DVD case, lingering for a moment on the production company logo.

'Maybe,' he said. 'And if I'm right, it might give us a pretty good idea of who the killer is.'

Tyler leaned in closer to Logan. He spoke quietly, trying not to move his mouth. 'Is it him?'

'What? No. Of course it's not him,' Logan said.

Tyler relaxed, though not by much. 'How do you know?'

'I'm going to leave you to figure that out for yourself, Detective Constable,' Logan said. 'Shouldn't be too difficult.'

Tyler wasted five seconds trying to work it out, then hastily changed the subject. 'So, if it's not him, boss, who do you reckon did it?'

Logan opened his mouth like he was about to respond, then thought better of it.

'Let me get back to you on that, son,' he said. 'There's something I want to check first.'

# *Chapter 38*

There was an awed hush when Logan and Tyler returned to the main hall with Mungo pushing the body of Monty McQuarrie along behind them. The wheels gave the same piercing *squeak, squeak, squeak*, and the rustling of the giant's movements made Tyler realise that he'd been the one to drop the trolley off outside the library in the first place.

For a guy his size, Mungo was clearly pretty skilled at sneaking around the castle.

Exactly, Tyler reckoned, like a killer would do. Logan seemed certain that Mungo wasn't the murderer, though. Tyler just wished he could figure out why.

On her return from her search, Tammi-Jo had rounded up all the others and asked them to meet her in the hall.

The family members were all pretty easy to find. Monty had been back in the reading room drinking, while Helen and Donatello had been arguing in the snug. Krystal had been descending the stairs just as Tammi-Jo was headed up them, which left her with only the *Ghost Spotters* team to find.

Monty thought they were all in their rooms, and after he'd rattled off the numbers from memory, the detective constable hunted them out.

Marcus had been very quick to answer his bedroom door, and had repeatedly sniffed and thumbed at his nose while listening to what the detective constable had to say.

Gavin had taken a little longer to answer, as he'd been in the shower, and came to the door dripping wet and wrapped in a towel. Yvonne hadn't been in her room, but had arrived downstairs with the other two a few minutes later.

Tammi-Jo had informed the assembled group about the missing constable and had been in the process of quizzing them on what they knew of his possible whereabouts when Logan had entered.

Now, Monty and Helen both lowered their heads like they couldn't bring themselves to look at the grey-haired giant, while the others—Krystal, Donatello, the *Ghost Spotters* team and Tammi-Jo herself—could do nothing but stare.

'What the fuck is that?' Marcus muttered, watching the big man duck his way in through the door.

'This is Mungo,' Logan announced. 'He's a… staff member?'

He looked across at Helen and Monty Jr seeking confirmation on this, but neither met his eye.

'Tyler, go with him and put the trolley back in the fridge, will you? And ask Francois to come join us.'

'Eh, aye,' Tyler said. He had become less intimidated by Mungo during their walk back from his workshop, but was still quite a distance away from being comfortable in the man's presence. 'Sure thing, boss,' he said, since he was unable to think of a reasonable excuse.

He jerked his head in the direction of the kitchen and smiled nervously up at the giant.

'If, eh, if you'll just follow me, Mr, um, sir…?'

Mungo *screeched* the trolley along after Tyler. Once they'd left the room, Logan turned to find Tammi-Jo standing close behind him.

'Sir! Couple of things. The disappearing footprints, we can get to in a minute. I can't find Constable…'

'Rowan.'

'Rowan! Yes! Wow, that's been bugging me. Constable Rowan, no sign of him. Like, anywhere. Not upstairs, not downstairs. Not through the back, not out front—'

'I get the point, DC Swanney,' Logan said.

'Ah, but wait, sir. There is *something*. Look.'

She beckoned Gavin over and shuffled from foot to foot while the *Ghost Spotters* producer took out his phone.

'Wait and you'll see this, sir. It's from the van. His van. The camera. Wait and you'll see.'

'When she mentioned the constable was missing, I checked the footage,' Gavin said. He angled his phone to give Logan a view of the screen, then tapped the little 'play' icon in the middle of the image.

It showed the same view of the castle Gavin had called up on his mobile earlier. The picture shuddered as the wind rocked the van, and part of the view was obscured by a blur of raindrops on the lens, but Logan could make out a man in a police uniform walking away from the house like he was headed along the driveway.

He had his head lowered against the storm, and was clutching his cap to stop it being whipped away by the wind.

Logan kept watching the footage until the constable had vanished out of sight, then shifted his gaze to the man holding the phone.

'When was this taken?'

'About forty minutes ago,' Gavin said. 'Looks like he just walked away.'

'In this weather? With the bridge out?' Tammi-Jo chirped. 'Can you believe that, sir? I mean, where would he be going? It doesn't make any sense. He's getting blown around in that video. No saying where he's ended up. Maybe we should be out looking for him.'

'No. Too dangerous,' Logan said. He looked around at the hall's other occupants, let his gaze linger on Monty Jr for a moment, then lowered his voice as he addressed Gavin again.

'Don't react, but I need a wee word in private. I need a favour.'

The producer blinked. 'A favour?'

Logan turned to Helen, who sat on the bottom step of the grand staircase, her now ex-partner, Donatello, reclining a few steps further up.

'Is there a TV we can connect this to somewhere?' he asked her. 'I want to see it on the bigger screen.'

'Uh, yes.' She pointed to one of the doors leading away from the hall. 'There's a guest lounge through there. It's got a TV in it. Old, though.'

'Fine,' Logan said, setting off in the direction she'd pointed.

'Uh, if it's old, I might not be able to—' Gavin began, but Logan summoned him with a glare and a click of his fingers.

'We'll figure it out, Mr Hall. You're a smart man.'

He opened the door, stood aside to let Gavin through, then closed it behind them. The passageway they found themselves in was as dark as the rest of the castle, and far more so than the candlelit hall.

As soon as they were out of sight and earshot of the others, Logan stopped and turned to the producer. The light from his torch faltered, but steadied again when he dunted it against his leg.

'Right. That footage gave me an idea,' the DCI said. 'Hidden cameras.'

Gavin blinked. 'Sorry?'

'Dotted around the castle. Hidden cameras,' Logan said again.

'We, uh… Are you asking if we have any? Because we don't.'

'OK, but let's pretend you do,' Logan told him.

'Um, all right,' Gavin said. 'But… why?'

'I want the killer to think he's been caught on camera,' Logan said. 'Not in the act, necessarily, but near the scene around the time of the murder.' He nodded to the door at Gavin's back. 'Do you have footage of any of that lot? Monty Junior, in particular?'

'Uh, yes. Yes, we got some B-Roll stuff of the family on the first day here. Just walking about, though. Nothing exciting.'

'Can you add a timestamp to that, or something? Make it look like it was recorded around the time of Monty's death?'

Gavin stared back at him, the light reflecting off his eyes. Outside, Storm Agatha raged against the castle walls.

'Isn't that…? Wouldn't that be fraud or entrapment, or something?'

'We're not going to use it in evidence,' Logan said. He glanced at the door again. 'It's just going to help me get a confession.'

The producer considered the request. 'Footage? Of… of Monty? Just walking about?'

'With the time of death on it. That's the important bit,' Logan insisted. 'That's how we'll nab the bastard.'

'I mean…' Gavin blew out his cheeks and shrugged. 'My laptop's still got battery, so I can try. But there's no saying he'll fall for it.'

Logan put a hand on the producer's shoulder and smiled. 'Well, nobody, including him, thought to question how the hell we were going to watch TV in the middle of a power cut, so let's not go giving the bastard too much credit, eh?'

## *Chapter 39*

Once Monty senior's body had been safely put back into cold storage, Tyler led Mungo and Francois back to the main hall, as Logan had instructed. Everyone was still gathered there, with the exception of the DCI himself.

Tyler assured the Frenchman and the giant that whatever was going to happen would be happening shortly, then headed over to where Tammi-Jo stood examining a stuffed golden eagle. It was positioned as if in flight and was carrying a fish in one of its talons.

Unlike the failed attempts back in his workshop, Mungo had absolutely nailed this one. He'd captured not just the shape of the bird, but the movement. The outstretched wings were curving inwards, while the claws were stabbing forward, like it was plucking the fish right out of the water.

It looked less like a stuffed animal than it did a moment frozen in time.

'All right?' Tyler asked.

Tammi-Jo turned away from the eagle. Her candlelight reflected off her pristine teeth as she smiled.

'Hey! How you doing? Everything good with you?'

'Uh, yeah. Cheers,' Tyler said. 'You?'

'Great! Perfect!' Tammi-Jo chirped, then her face fell. 'I'm a bit worried.'

'About what?'

'I'm not meant to be here. Now, I mean. I mean, I am—DCI Logan asked me to come, we all heard him—but I'm not. I'm meant to be in Glasgow. First day on the new job tomorrow, and tomorrow technically starts in'—she checked her watch—'two and a bit hours. I'm not going to make it, am I?'

'Unlikely,' Tyler agreed. 'But I wouldn't worry about it. It's hardly your fault.'

'No. No, you're right. You're right, it's not my fault,' Tammi-Jo said, but she was clearly still worried. 'And, I mean, I'm sure this DI Filson's pretty reasonable, right? Even though everyone seems a bit terrified of her, I'm sure she's fine. Isn't she?'

Tyler opened his mouth, considered his response, then changed the subject. 'You seen the boss?'

'He's phoning DS Khaled,' Tammi-Jo said. 'Got some stuff he wants him to check out.'

'What stuff?'

'Dunno. Just stuff, he said. Something about a DVD, maybe?' She pointed across to Mungo. 'That's a big man.'

'Eh, aye. He is,' Tyler confirmed.

'I'd imagine you shat yourself a bit when you saw him?'

Tyler pulled an 'as if', sort of face, then shook his head. 'Nah. You've got to be prepared for all sorts in this game, haven't you?'

'Right. Yeah. I mean, you do. You're not wrong,' Tammi-Jo said. Tyler didn't like the smirk that played across her face. 'It's just that DCI Logan mentioned you screamed...'

Tyler snorted. 'Nah. What? No. I didn't scream. I wasn't screaming. I was just'—his mind raced, searching for a plausible explanation for the noise he'd made—'whistling.'

Tammi-Jo fought hard to keep her smile from growing any further. 'Whistling?'

'Aye.' Tyler nodded. 'I was whistling. You know, like to draw his attention.'

'Right. You were whistling, "Jesus Christ, boss, what the fuck is that?"'

Tyler quietly cleared his throat. 'He told you that, did he?'

'He may have mentioned it.'

Tyler blushed and looked down at his feet for a moment.

'How's the head? I hear someone knocked you out?'

'Aye. Apparently. Don't remember much,' Tyler admitted, carefully rubbing the lump on the back of his skull. 'Not my finest moment. Although, to be fair, probably not my worst, either.'

A few months ago, when Tammi-Jo had first joined them, she'd been thrilled to find herself on the same team as Tyler.

He was a bit of a hero, she'd said. All the new recruits thought so. That had been a nice thing to hear, even if he'd never quite believed it.

And now, she was leaving, and would no doubt go out and tell everyone what he was *really* like.

'I'm guessing I probably turned out to be a bit of a disappointment in the end,' he said. 'After all that stuff you said when we first met. Not quite the legend you thought I was, eh?'

'No. God, no.' Tammi-Jo shook her head and let out a little laugh that drove another stake into the heart of Tyler's ego. 'You're way better. Legends are boring. Not *The Legend of Zelda*, that was great. But in general, I mean. And you are anything but boring, Detective Constable Neish. I'm going to miss you.'

Tyler beamed and stood just a little taller. 'I'm going to miss you, too, Detective Constable Swanney. It's not going to be the same without you.'

'It'll be quieter,' Tammi-Jo said. It was the second time today she'd thrown in that punchline. She'd heard it often enough during her life to always be ready with it.

Tyler wrinkled his nose, like he was unimpressed by the thought. 'Meh. Quiet's overrated.'

'Sorry to interrupt this touching moment.'

Tyler recoiled in fright at the sound of the voice from right beside him.

'Jesus Christ, boss!' he yelped. 'Are you trying to do me in or something?'

Logan shook his head. 'No,' Logan said, in a sombre monotone. 'If that's what I was trying to do, I'd just break your neck.' He mimed the action, bringing up both hands then jerking them sharply. 'Just grab and twist. You wouldn't even know what had happened.'

Tyler stared back at him in horror. 'Jesus, boss! That's quite detailed. Have you thought about that before?'

'No. Well, not often,' Logan said, then he looked back over his shoulder at the assembled residents of McQuarrie Hall. 'Everyone here?'

'The producer guy, Gavin, he left right after you, sir,' Tammi-Jo told him. 'Said he had to go check something, then headed upstairs.'

'That's fine. He's helping me with something.'

'Claire's not here,' Tyler realised. 'The wee girl. She's not here.'

'She's just through there,' Tammi-Jo said, pointing to one of the hallway's many doors. 'I found her wandering with Taggart earlier. We saw some ghost footprints.'

'Shit, seriously?!' Tyler gasped.

Logan tutted. 'No. Not seriously, Tyler. How many times do I have to tell you, there's no such—'

'Actually, sir. It was a bit weird,' Tammi-Jo said, then she explained to the other detectives what she'd seen.

Tyler spent the whole time looking increasingly concerned, his eyes widening as the colour drained from his face.

Even Logan didn't dismiss it straight away. Instead, once she'd finished describing the disappearing footprints, he'd asked her just one question.

'Where?'

Tammi-Jo had described the location of the corridor in as much detail as she could. Too much detail, if anything, and Logan stopped her mid-flow with a nod and a muttered, 'Thanks. I get the picture.'

'Are you just going to keep us sitting here all night?'

Logan and the other detectives turned to see Donatello rising to his feet on the staircase. Helen was forced to quickly shuffle aside to avoid being trampled as he stomped down them.

'Watch it!' she yelped, but a sharp turn of his bee-encrusted head and a four-eyed glare made her shrink back on the step.

'This is bullshit!' Donatello barked. He looked around at all the others, but the remark was clearly for Logan's benefit. 'They can't just keep us here like this. They can't hold us hostage.'

'Nobody's holding you hostage, son. We're keeping you here for your own safety. You wouldn't last five minutes out there in that storm.'

Krystal sidled up to the tattooed artist and stood shoulder-to-shoulder with him. She had a glass of wine in one hand, and the liquid sloshed around in the glass as she gestured with it.

'But you can leave? You police? You can just walk out of here whenever you like?'

'No.'

'Well, the other one did! We all saw the video! He just upped and walked out the front door, happy as you like! Well, I say what's good for the goose is good for the gander!'

'Hear bloody hear!' Marcus agreed, showing his support with three slow claps.

A crack of lightning illuminated the world beyond the castle walls. Thunder rumbled overhead.

Krystal swished her glass around, her gaze flitting to one of the rain-covered windows.

'I mean, obviously *I* ain't leaving. This is my home, after all. But it ain't right to hold the others if'n they're looking to go.'

The muscles in Logan's jaw shifted as he clenched his back teeth. 'Where is that accent from, exactly?' he asked.

Krystal drew back a step, a hand going to her chest. 'I beg your pardon?'

Before Logan could say any more, there was a sharp, shrill bark from the other side of a door, followed by the scratching of claws on wood. Tyler, who was closest to the door, walked over and opened it, revealing Taggart pacing back and forth in the darkened corridor beyond.

'All right, Tag?'

The dog's head was lowered as he ran back and forth in the passageway, his stubby tail curved downwards, his ears pressed flat. Taggart whined and darted back when Tyler reached out to pat him, and for a moment it looked like he might make a run for it.

'What's the matter?' Logan asked.

'Dunno, boss. He's acting weird.'

Logan shone his torch along the corridor behind the dog. The light picked out nothing but woodwork and old stone. Taggart was on his own.

'Wait,' said Tammi-Jo. 'Where's Claire?'

And then, like it had been waiting in the wings for just the right moment, the scream of a terrified child came bursting forth from the darkness.

Taggart was the first to move, but Tyler was close behind. He plunged on into the dark with only the light from Logan's torch and the dying echoes of a little girl's scream to guide him.

Logan and Tammi-Jo followed, racing through the corridor, the torchlight bouncing violently from floor, to wall, to ceiling.

They skidded around a corner, and the light picked out the outline of Tyler as he tripped on something, flew gracelessly through the air, then landed in a heap on the floor.

Taggart's barking roared like gunshots in the narrow passageway. Logan's torch swept across Tyler, checking he was moving, then fell on the thing he had tripped over.

It had tumbled from inside a shadowy alcove, and now lay half on the floor, half-twisted against the opposite wall.

Further along the corridor, beyond Tyler, Claire's hand-cranked torch lit her tear-stained face from below.

'It wasn't me. I didn't do it. It wasn't me,' she babbled, through big, gulping, unsteady breaths.

'You're OK, you're all right,' Tyler assured her, then he turned and looked back at what he'd tripped over.

There, his eyes open, his head jammed against the wall so his neck formed a right angle to his torso, lay the semi-naked body of PC Rab Rowan.

# *Chapter 40*

'What the hell's this?'

Marcus Doyle's voice was a gruff bark that made Claire shrink further back in fright.

The *Ghost Spotters* presenter elbowed past Tammi-Jo, saw the body on the floor, then drew in a sharp intake of breath when he spotted his daughter cowering just a few feet away.

'What the hell were you doing down here?' he demanded. 'You shouldn't have been playing down here, you bloody idiot!'

'Oi!' Tyler snapped, heaving himself to his feet. 'Enough! She's not an idiot. Quit speaking to her like that.'

'She's my daughter. I'll speak to her however the hell I like!'

'Claire, don't listen to him, all right. He's being a…'

Tyler's voice fell away when he turned to find the spot where the girl had been now empty. In the distance, further on through the dark, he heard the fading of her footsteps, and the whispering of her sobs.

'Oh, nice one,' he said, scowling at Marcus.

His gaze drifted down to the body on the floor. Logan was kneeling beside the dead constable, while Tammi-Jo stepped in front of Marcus and directed him back towards the hall.

'You got this, boss?' Tyler asked.

Logan had a hand over his mouth, his fingers and thumb pressing into his cheeks as he contemplated the dead young man lying on the floor.

'Boss?'

'Hm? Oh. Aye. Go find her. Make sure she's all right. We'll…' He ran his hand all the way down his face and sighed. 'We'll look after Rab.'

Taggart had already disappeared after the girl. Tyler had no candle or torch with him, but he followed the sound of the dog, one hand held out in front of him to stop him running smack into a dead end, the other trailing along the wall beside him to help him get his bearings.

'Claire?' he called. 'You there? It's DC Neish. It's Tyler! It's—'

His leading hand brushed against rough stone. Despite his best efforts, Tyler failed to stop before the corridor became a much narrower passageway, and he grunted as the top of his head scraped against the suddenly lowered ceiling.

Up ahead, along the passage, Taggart's barking sounded shriller and more panicked.

Tyler pressed on. Squeezed through. Fingertips pulling him on through the tight, compact darkness. The sound of his own breathing was all around him, bouncing off walls just inches from his face.

Was this the same way he'd come earlier when he'd found Claire the first time? Was this the way to her hidey-hole? It felt familiar, although one narrow, pitch-dark tunnel in a haunted castle on Halloween probably felt much like any other.

He tried shouting again, but the passageway seemed to trap the sound in there with him. Even if she was right beyond the end of this tunnel, standing out there in the corridor, he was convinced she wouldn't hear him.

Nobody would hear him. He was lost, blind and partly pinned between immovable walls, and no one would hear him if he—

The passageway widened, and he fell out of it with a gasp and an, 'Ooh, shit!'

As he fought to stay upright, he saw Taggart running from side to side about fifteen feet ahead. The dog was agitated again—even more than he'd been a few minutes before.

It took Tyler a moment to work out how he was able to see the animal, given that the entire corridor was shrouded by a blanket of black.

It took him a moment to see the pool of yellow light that the dog was splashing around in.

It took him a moment to see the torch lying on its side on the floor.

To see the hole in the rotten floorboards beside it.

It took him a moment.

And then, he ran.

'Claire? Claire!'

The floor groaned a warning at him, the damp, decaying boards bouncing beneath his feet.

He grabbed for the wall, his fingertips digging into the cracks between the old stone blocks where the mortar had crumbled away. Slowly, carefully, he crept over to the gaping wound in the floor. Earlier, the hole had barely covered half the width of the corridor, but now a chasm spread from one side to the other, and the sound of running water rose from below.

'Claire? Claire, can you hear me?'

Tyler tightened his grip on the wall and leaned over the edge of the hole as far as he dared. When he couldn't see anything, he picked up the dropped torch, *voom-voom-voomed* a burst of charge into the bulb, then shone it down into the dark.

The light danced across dark, rippling water. He heard a desperate splashing, and redirected the beam until he found Claire slapping at the surface of the stagnant pool, struggling to keep her head above water.

Tyler turned back towards the narrow tunnel he'd just squeezed through, sucked in a sour-tasting breath, then shouted with everything he had.

'Boss! She's fallen in, boss! She's in the basement!'

And then, kicking off his shoes, Tyler lowered himself onto the sloping floor and slid himself off the edge.

–

'Did you hear something, sir?' Tammi-Jo asked.

Logan looked up from the body of PC Rowan to find the detective constable peering along the corridor in the direction Tyler had gone, her candle raised in front of her like it might light more than a few feet of the path ahead.

'No. You?'

'I don't... Maybe,' Tammi-Jo said.

'Give me the candle. Take the torch. Go check,' Logan urged.

The swap was made, and the detective constable hurried off, leaving Logan alone with the body.

He'd checked for a pulse, because that's just what you did, even when it was blindingly obvious that life had been snuffed out.

He couldn't determine the cause of death, though there was blood on the back of the PC's head. It trickled down his neck and across his bare shoulders. He'd taken a hit to the skull, though there was no way of saying yet if that was the killing blow.

The body was cold, but Logan didn't think he'd been dead for long. A couple of hours at most. Someone had killed him and stuffed him in a darkened alcove, presumably planning to shift him later when nobody was around.

Some bastard had murdered him, then cast him aside in a convenient corner.

Logan realised that he knew next to nothing about the constable. Did he have a family? A wife? Kids? Someone was going to miss him, certainly. Someone always did.

And someone was going to pay for taking the man's life. Logan was going to make damn sure of that.

'Sir?'

Tammi-Jo was breathless and frantic when she came clattering back along the corridor, Taggart close at her heels.

'We've got a problem!'

## *Chapter 41*

The underground level of McQuarrie Hall was, as far as either sibling could remember, even more of a rabbit warren than the upstairs. Neither one of them was overly familiar with the basement level, as it had been far too creepy for them to explore when they were kids, and nowhere near interesting enough for them to bother with as adults.

There was a wine cellar below the kitchen. That much they knew. Francois was able to confirm, and a quick check down a set of curving stone steps revealed that the place was bone dry, meaning only parts of the house's foundations were flooded.

Mungo had proven more useful. Everyone had watched, Marcus pacing impatiently, as the giant had drawn the layout of the sublevel, and marked where he thought Claire and Tyler might be.

Parts of the drawing felt a bit vague, and Logan wasn't sure how much they could rely on the old man's memory, but it was all they had to go on for now.

'Right, what do we do?' Marcus asked. 'How do we get there?'

The others just looked down at the drawing on the table, still trying to make sense of how it all connected.

'Well?!' Marcus cried. 'My Claire's down there! How do we get to her?'

'We can't go in through that corridor,' Tammi-Jo said. 'The floor's giving way. It could collapse right on top of them.'

'Christ! We have to do something!' Marcus wailed.

'We are,' Logan assured him. 'Tyler's with her. They're OK for now.'

Marcus rounded on him. 'Well, maybe he should make himself useful and get her out of there!'

'Well, maybe you shouldn't have lost your rag with her and sent her running off in the bloody first place!' Logan fired back.

He stared the other man down, then prodded a finger onto the X that marked the location of the girl and the detective constable.

'Are there stairs?' he asked. 'Is there another way down?'

Mungo fiddled with a button on his dungarees and gave a regretful shake of his head.

Marcus threw his hands in the air and turned away. 'Oh, great! Then what the hell do we do?'

It was Gavin, the *Ghost Spotters* producer, who stepped forward. 'There,' he said, pointing to a room adjoining the one with the X marking the spot. 'I think I saw that when I was doing the location scout. It's like a… I don't want to say "dungeon", but it's basically a dungeon. It's under the library.'

'Yes! He's right!' Helen said. 'There's a door behind a bookcase. It's the only secret passageway we ever found.'

'Yes, Gavin!' Marcus grabbed the producer by the back of the neck and gave him a shake that felt unnecessarily aggressive. 'Good lad! Good lad, well remembered!'

Logan caught Marcus by the arm and set off with him towards the door. 'Right, we'll go down and get them.'

'We?' Marcus pulled his arm free. 'Hold on. I get claustrophobic. I can't go down there.'

Logan stopped. Turned. Stared in disbelief.

'What are you talking about?' he demanded. 'She's your daughter.'

'And you're the police!'

'And you're her father!'

'You're meant to do this stuff,' Marcus said. He glanced around, saw that all eyes were on him, then awkwardly shifted his weight from one foot to the other. 'It's your job. You and her go.' He pointed to Tammi-Jo.

'No. She's going to be up top, keeping them calm.'

'Fuck's sake. Gavin, then! Gavin, as show creator and executive producer, I order you to go.'

'I can't swim!'

'What the fu—? You're an adult man, Gavin! How can you not swim?'

Logan's eyebrows shot halfway up his forehead. 'Are you winding me up here? Your daughter is down there. Terrified. She doesn't want him. She doesn't want me. She wants her dad. She *needs* her dad.'

He stepped in closer to the other man and pinned him in place with a glare.

'So, you're going to come with me, and you're going to help me get your daughter back.'

Marcus didn't seem like the sort of man to scare easily, but when he spoke, his mouth sounded as dry as a desert floor.

'I told you,' he said. 'I get claustrophobic.'

–

The girl was shivering. No surprise, really—the water was bloody freezing—but her whole body was convulsing as she clung on to Tyler's neck, the floodwater lapping up her back and around her shoulders.

Her teeth were chattering. Properly chattering, like a set of wind-up gnashers in an old cartoon. Then again, another few minutes down there in the cold, and Tyler reckoned he'd be doing the same.

'You're OK. It's all right. I've got you,' he told her, for about the tenth time. He was standing on his tiptoes, keeping them above the surface without having to swim or tread water.

But a moment ago, he'd been standing flat on his feet. How long until the water level was too high for him to stand?

Not long enough.

The water was cascading down the stone walls, seeping through the slimy green moss that had been building there for some time. The wooden beams of the floor above had rotted away, then collapsed completely. Part of a rafter stuck up from below the water like the mast of a sunken ship.

The faint yellow light from the hand-cranked torch was fading away. Tyler depressed the lever a few times, giving it another blast of juice. Being stuck down here was quite terrifying enough without them being plunged completely into darkness.

There were no doors out of the room that he could see, although it was possible they were below the water level. Right now, though, the only way out seemed to be the same way he'd come in, but while sliding down into the basement had been relatively easy, he couldn't see any way to climb back out.

'I'm going to shout again, OK? Don't get scared,' he told Claire.

She covered her ears with her hands and screwed her eyes shut as Tyler called out for all he was worth.

'*Help!*'

The reply came from somewhere overhead.

'It's coming. Help's coming.'

The beam of a torch hit Tyler full in the face. He hissed, shut his eyes, and turned away.

'Sorry, sorry, sorry!' Tammi-Jo babbled. 'Lucky shot. Or unlucky, I suppose. Didn't know you were literally right there.'

'It's fine. We're all right, aren't we, Claire?'

The girl nodded, though she didn't seem entirely convinced.

'Someone's coming though, right?' Tyler asked. Tammi-Jo had angled the torchlight by a few inches so she could see his face without blinding him. Even in the half-dark, his concern was clearly visible. 'Like, soon?'

'Soon,' Tammi-Jo replied. 'We think we've found a way in. We think we can get to you.'

'Hear that? They found a way in. They can get to us,' Tyler said, forcing a smile for the benefit of the girl in his arms, and downplaying the double usage of the phrase 'we think'. 'Everything's going to be just fine.'

–

Logan crouched halfway down a decaying wooden staircase, inches above the dark, scum-coated surface of the water. Old plastic plant pots and bits of tarpaulin bobbed around like old ghost ships. A few shelves had been fixed to the wall above the water level. There were books on them, their antique pages bloated and swollen by the moisture in the air.

Gavin stood on the next step up, pointing into the murky water. Behind him, lurking in the gap left by a sliding bookcase, Marcus watched and listened on.

'It should be down there. It's like a half-sized door that leads through into the next room over.'

Logan didn't like '*should*'. He wasn't all that excited about '*half-sized*' either. Absolutes would've been preferable, and a full-sized door wouldn't go amiss.

Still, Gavin was working from memory, and a hazy, half-remembered one at that. He'd seen this place once, he said, during a one-off recce of the site. The fact that he remembered it at all was something of a miracle.

Unless, of course, he'd misremembered it completely, in which case the bastard would need a miracle to save him from Logan's wrath.

'You're sure?' the DCI asked, seeking even a little bit of reassurance.

'No. Not remotely,' Gavin admitted. 'Seventy per cent. But that big lad in the dungarees seemed to agree, so…' He shrugged. 'I don't know. I think so, but I don't know.'

'Aye, well, that'll have to do, I suppose.'

Logan looked back up the steps. Marcus could only hold his gaze for a fraction of a second before he looked away again.

'Right. Here goes,' the DCI announced.

He descended a couple of steps, grimaced as the icy cold surface rose up to slap him on the groin, then lowered himself in the rest of the way. The sheer size of him displaced enough water that Gavin was forced to back up another step to avoid getting his feet wet.

'This way?' Logan asked, pointing in roughly the same direction the producer had.

'Yes. Should be right down there.'

'Right. Keep that torch shining down here,' Logan ordered.

He took a few deep breaths.

One big final one.

And then he ducked his head beneath the surface, kicked with his feet, and pulled himself on through the cold and silent dark.

-

The water was rising, and it was rising fast. The very tips of Tyler's toes were now barely touching solid ground. He was holding onto Claire with one hand and clutching the torch with the other. In a moment, he'd need to swim, and that would mean sacrificing the flashlight.

Right now, Tammi-Jo's torch was providing light, but if that went out, or if she had to leave, then they'd be treading water in darkness.

'I'm c-c-cold,' Claire whispered.

'I know. I know. You're OK,' Tyler assured her.

He tightened his grip. Teetering on his tiptoes as he was, her weight was making him sway. Any sudden movements from the girl and they'd both be dragged off balance. If they fell in, there was no saying he'd be able to keep her from going under.

And he was damned if he was letting that happen.

'I'm going to pass her up to you,' he said, craning his neck to look up at Tammi-Jo. The water lapped around his ears and soaked the back of his head. 'You need to take her.'

'It's too far,' DC Swanney pointed out. 'I can't reach.'

'You can if you lie down. If you lie down and lean right over, you can grab her arms.'

'I can't, Tyler. The floor's crumbling. It's not safe. It might collapse.'

'Tammi-Jo, listen to me, all right?' Tyler said. Even to his ears, his voice sounded remarkably calm. Much calmer than he currently felt, that was for sure. 'You have to take her. I can't keep holding onto her here. The water's getting too high.'

'Tyler—'

'If you take her, I can swim. I can find a way out. But you have to take her, all right. You have to—'

His sentence collapsed into a cry of panic as something not unlike a sea monster rose from the deep beside him. Logan exhaled sharply, ran his sopping-wet shirtsleeve across his face, then rubbed at his eyes with both hands.

'Jesus Christ, boss!' Tyler yelped. 'I thought you were Godzilla!'

Logan spat out some dirty water. 'The way this day's going, son, maybe best no' to tempt fate.'

He looked from the DC to the girl cooried in his arms, then back again.

'We all right?'

Claire released her grip on Tyler just long enough to raise a thumb. Tyler smiled shakily and held her closer to him.

'Was getting a bit hairy for a second there, boss. But, aye. All good now.'

Something about the look on Logan's face made Tyler realise he may have spoken too soon.

'What is it? What's wrong?'

'We're going to have to swim. Underwater,' Logan said. 'It's a tight gap, and it's dark, but I think I know the way.'

'You *think*, boss?'

'Aye, well, I didn't exactly have a trail of breadcrumbs to leave behind me. But it's fine. I can find it.' He turned to Claire. 'You'll need to hold your breath and swim, though, all right?'

The girl shook her head, though she was shivering so violently that it wasn't immediately obvious.

'I c-can't,' she whimpered.

'Aye, you can,' Tyler assured her. 'You'll be fine. We can do it. I'll be with you.'

Tears rolled down her cheeks. Her head continued to shake, like the movement had become just another part of her ongoing whole-body tremor.

'I can't. I can't d-do it.'

'We have to,' Logan told her. 'It's the only way out.'

'Where's my dad? I want my dad!'

Tyler shot a look at Logan. Clearly, he'd been wondering the same thing.

'He's going to be waiting for us, all right?' the DCI said. 'He's going to be waiting for us right on the other side. You just need to shut your eyes and hold your breath for a wee second, and we'll get you through.'

Claire's grip tightened around Tyler's neck until he feared she might choke him unconscious.

'Claire. Claire, easy. Calm down,' he wheezed. Her wriggling made him stumble. The water pulled at him. His balance went, and he fell.

Hands caught the girl before she could go under, rising from below the surface to save her just in time.

Marcus held her against him, pulling her in close, her face burying itself into the folds of his neck.

'You're all right, princess. You're all right. I've got you,' he wheezed, his chest heaving from the effort of the swim.

He shot Logan a sideways look. The DCI nodded. Not exactly a ringing endorsement, but it was the best he was going to get.

'Dad's got you,' Marcus told his daughter. 'And I'm never letting you go.'

## *Chapter 42*

Logan and Tyler sat shivering beside the fire in the reading room, towels wrapped around their shoulders. They were dressed in borrowed clothes, their own shirts and trousers lightly steaming on a rack in front of the fireplace.

Marcus had taken Claire upstairs to get dried off and changed. They had returned fifteen minutes later, hand in hand, Claire excitedly telling everyone who'd listen about how her dad had saved her life.

'Come on, it was nothing,' Marcus said. 'You're my special girl. God help anyone who tried to keep me from jumping in there to save you!'

He spotted Logan watching him, and quickly turned away, steering the girl over to join Gavin and Yvonne, who both took turns hugging her.

'Nice of him to take all the credit,' Tyler remarked.

'Aye. I practically had to beg the bastard to get in the water,' Logan muttered. 'And even then, I thought he was having none of it.'

Most of the household was gathered in the reading room, except for Monty, Helen and Donatello. Francois, the chef, was talking and laughing with Mungo like they were old friends, although the conversation was notably one-sided, even if the laughter was not.

Krystal sat alone in a wingback armchair, one leg crossed over the other, her raised foot kicking as she sipped on a glass of wine. She looked tense.

But then, it had been a tense sort of day.

Tammi-Jo appeared beside the detectives, clutching two big steaming mugs of tea. She'd filled them almost all the way to the top, and handed them over with all the care of someone handling an unstable fusion reactor.

'There we go,' she said, her face fixed in a mask of concentration. 'I boiled the water using the gas thing. Did I nearly set myself and everything in the kitchen on fire? Yes. Yes, I did. So, I hope it was worth it.'

'Cheers, TJ,' Tyler said, carefully accepting the on-the-brink-of-overflowing mug.

'Much appreciated,' Logan said, taking his mug with the same care and attention as Tyler.

Tammi-Jo sat down heavily on the couch between them, and both men grimaced as the hot tea sloshed out of their mugs, over their hands, and onto their thighs.

'Sorry, sorry! My fault!'

'No bloody argument there,' Logan said, scowling as he adjusted his grip on the now substantially emptier mug. He and Tyler used the towels to mop at their borrowed trousers, then sipped at their tea.

'Bloody hell,' Tyler choked. 'That's sweet.'

'How many sugars are in these?' Logan asked, his face contorting.

'Eight,' Tammi-Jo said.

'Eight?!' Logan choked. 'So, what, four in each?'

The DC winced. 'Sixteen, then,' she said. 'They always say hot sweet drinks are good for shock, don't they?'

'What, for causing it?' Logan asked. 'Because if so, they're not bloody wrong.'

'Do you want me to try again?'

Logan wrapped his hands around his mug. Despite the sweetness overload, he didn't want to be parted with it quite yet.

'It's fine. I'll suffer through it,' he said.

'I quite like it,' Tyler said, taking another slurp. 'It's like drinking a Twix.'

Pleased by this, DC Swanney sat back. 'So, what did I miss?'

'Nothing, really. We were just saying that Marcus is taking all the credit for the rescue,' Tyler said. 'Even though the boss had to practically drag him into the water.' He took another drink of tea. 'Bit unfair.'

'To who?' Tammi-Jo asked.

Tyler and Logan both looked at her, confused. 'Well, to us,' Tyler replied. 'We did most of the actual saving. I was in there for ages.'

'Yeah. Suppose,' the other DC agreed. 'It's just... Claire seems pleased.'

Both men turned to look at her through the steam from their mugs. She was clinging to Marcus's arm now, regaling Gavin and Yvonne with tales of the big rescue.

'I've never really got on with my dad, but if I thought he'd risked his life to rescue me...' Tammi-Jo inhaled like she was breathing in the idea of it. 'I'd feel pretty amazing. Even if he only did a little bit of the actual work.'

Logan watched as Claire rested her damp hair on her dad's shoulder. Marcus craned his neck to kiss the top of her head, and her face lit up with a beamer of a smile.

'Second chances,' the DCI muttered.

Tammi-Jo nodded. 'Maybe this has given them a chance. Who knows? They're complicated things, dads.'

Tyler nodded sagely. 'Aye. We are that, all right.'

Logan filled his mouth with tea, swished it around for a bit, then decided it was just too damn sweet to swallow. He spat it back into the mug as subtly as he could, then confronted the reality he had been avoiding facing up to all day.

'Minc's dying.'

There was silence from the two detective constables. It lasted almost six whole seconds, which had to be something of a record.

'Boss?'

Logan didn't look at them. He didn't dare. Instead, he just watched Claire and her father huddling together, all past transgressions forgiven and forgotten.

'Got a call this morning. Cancer. Only a matter of time, and not a lot, at that.'

'Shite. Sorry, boss,' Tyler said. He blew out his cheeks, his eyebrows dipping. 'Didn't you…? I thought you'd said before that your dad was already… you know?'

'That was my stepdad,' Logan said. 'Though, he was pretty much the only dad I ever knew. This is my real one. He and I haven't really spoken in… Christ. I don't know. Twenty years.'

'I'm so sorry, sir.' Tammi-Jo put a hand on the DCI's arm. 'You should be there. You should go see him. You'll regret it if you don't.'

'She's right, boss. You need to see him,' Tyler said.

Logan raised his mug to his mouth, remembered the whole spitting incident from a few moments before, then lowered it again.

'He had his chance. Second, third, fourth, fifth… I could go on,' the DCI said. 'I don't owe that bastard anything.'

'No. God, no, sir,' Tammi-Jo said. 'I think you owe it to yourself, though. I think that, if you don't go, you'll be stuck with that. You'll wish you'd gone.'

From a couple of rooms over, there came the sound of the old reception phone ringing. Logan set his mug down on the floor, then hurriedly got to his feet.

'Saved by the bell. Eh, boss?'

Logan grunted. 'Aye. Good timing. That'll be Hamza.'

He was about to set off when there was a loud *clunk* from overhead. The lights came on as the electricity returned, and everyone in the room—with the exception of Mungo—gave a cheer.

'Seems like things are looking up,' Logan said, forcing a smile for the sake of the two detective constables.

He met Gavin Hall's eye, and a nod passed between the men.

Logan rubbed his hands together. 'Right, go round up the rest of the family and bring them down here. Keep everyone together until I get back. Nobody leaves.'

From the reception, the old phone continued to ring.

'It's time we wrapped this whole thing up.'

–

Tammi-Jo hummed to herself as she meandered through the corridors towards Helen's room. She'd already met Monty on the stairs and directed him to the reading room, and now just had Helen and her bee-headed partner to find.

The family's bedrooms were in a nicer wing of the castle. Certainly nicer than the part that was collapsing, anyway.

That had been a bit weird, Tammi-Jo thought. A big stately place like this, with a billionaire owner, surely shouldn't be in such a state of disrepair? The storm couldn't have helped, but that damage wasn't recent. The corridor that Claire had fallen through looked to have been neglected for years.

Then again, you did have to squeeze through what felt like the eye of a concrete needle to reach it—she still had the grazes to prove it—so she couldn't blame them for not keeping it in better nick.

This part had been better maintained. This part was lovely.

Bit dusty, maybe—the suits of armour and frames of some of the paintings could do with a clean—but there wasn't water running down the walls, and the floor felt reassuringly solid beneath her feet.

So, you know, yay for that.

Having lights on helped, too. Everywhere looked better with lights on.

OK, maybe not everywhere. Most places. Some places.

It really depended on the place, she supposed.

She thought of poor Rab, still lying there in that corridor. The storm was starting to ease, and there was a chance that a helicopter might be able to get to them soon. DCI Logan had decided it best not to move the constable's body until Scene of Crime and Shona had both had a look at it.

Poor Rab.

And poor DCI Logan, too. It was awful news about his dad.

Some of the pictures here really were *very* dusty.

Had she locked the library door when she'd left? she wondered.

Was she definitely going the right way?

It was at this point that Tammi-Jo realised it had been several hours since she'd taken her ADHD medication.

That explained a few things.

When she reached the door to Helen's bedroom, it stood slightly ajar. The room beyond it was in darkness. When she knocked, the door swung inwards a few inches, then was yanked violently open from the other side.

Helen launched herself from the room, her face twisted in fury, two trails of blood drawing a number eleven on her top lip before spreading out across her mouth and chin. Her mascara had run down her cheeks, and her eyes were ringed with red circles. She was a real mess. Even her Mr Whippy hair looked as if it had melted.

Tammi-Jo saw the axe in the other woman's hands. As it swung, she noticed the way the corridor lights glinted off the polished blade. Noted the ornate pattern in the metal. Heard the *whumming* as it sliced through the air towards her.

Even without medication, it was amazing how some things could *really* help you focus.

She ducked, felt the air be cleaved in two above her head, then grimaced at the rattling *clank* the axe head made when it connected with the stone wall beside her.

That must've hurt.

Moving on instinct, she launched herself at Helen, closing the gap between them so that taking an axe to the side of the head was no longer on the cards. She grabbed the handle of the antique weapon, but Helen was already releasing it, her trembling hands flying to her face, her eyes widening in horror.

'I'm sorry! I'm sorry!' she wailed, her voice muffled behind her hands. When she took them away, Tammi-Jo saw the blood on her teeth. 'I thought you were him!'

'Who?' the detective constable asked. She dropped the axe onto the floor and pinned the handle beneath a foot. 'Who did this? Was it Donatello?'

'Don't fucking listen to her. She'll only lie to you, too.'

Helen shrank back in fright at the sound of Donatello's voice. He had somehow appeared in the corridor behind Tammi-Jo, and the detective constable positioned herself between him and his injured ex.

'Did you do this?' Tammi-Jo asked.

'Course I fucking didn't!'

'He did! He did!' Helen sobbed. 'I told him it was over, that I wanted him gone. I told him he looked'—she raised her voice, momentarily finding some of her usual defiance—'*completely fucking ridiculous* and he punched me. He punched me, then when I fell, he hit me again.'

'You're so full of shit!'

'Sir, please,' Tammi-Jo said, shuffling over to block Donatello when it seemed like he was going to make a grab for his ex. 'Stay where you are.'

'He... he grabbed me by the hair. Dragged me. I thought he was going to kill me.'

'Yeah? Well, maybe I should have, you stupid fucking *bitch*!'

Donatello's hand clamped down on Tammi-Jo's shoulder, pushing her aside. He wasn't a large man, and nor was he in particularly good shape. But he was angry, and anger could lend a man strength, just for a little while. Just long enough.

It could also make him careless.

Tammi-Jo grabbed for the hand on her shoulder, found a pressure point at the base of his thumb, and wrenched. There was an audible click, which was followed almost immediately by a much more audible squeal.

She kept hold of the hand, introduced his thumb to his wrist, then felt his weight shift as he swung at her with his other hand.

The DC stepped in closer, avoiding the punch. Her arm drew back smoothly, like a weapon being slid from its sheath. The tip of her elbow found the centre of his throat with precisely enough force to rattle all his dangling padlocks and make him seriously reconsider a number of his recent life choices.

He stumbled backwards, gasping for air, but Tammi-Jo was still holding his thumb to his wrist, and with a twist and a jerk, she brought him up over her shoulder, then crashing to the floor.

His face was pressed hard against the wood. He sobbed and whimpered as his other arm was dragged out from beneath him, and both hands were cuffed together.

The whole thing, from the moment he'd laid his hand on the detective constable to the application of the handcuffs, had taken seconds.

Helen stood in the doorway, her eyes wide, tears cutting tracks through her mask of mascara and blood.

'How… how did you do that?' she asked.

Tammi-Jo looked up. Her blue eyes seemed to sparkle as she flashed the other woman a dazzling, toothy grin. 'Practice,' she said. 'Now, DCI Logan wants to see us all in the reading room. If you want to get cleaned up and meet us there…'

She grabbed Donatello by the scruff of the neck and dragged him, still wheezing, up onto his knees. A handful of his plastic bees slid off his head and *pinged* in all directions across the floor.

'I'll take care of Muggins here!'

# Chapter 43

Twenty minutes later, everyonewas assembled in the reading room, the chairs pulled into a wide semi-circle around the roaring fire.

Monty and Helen sat close together on one side of the grand fireplace, united in their hatred for Donatello, who sat in the opposite corner, cuffed to an old wooden chair that had been pulled in from elsewhere in the castle specifically to make the bastard less comfortable.

Helen had done an admirable job of cleaning herself up. Tammi-Jo had expected her to return caked in makeup, but her face was nude, and a band of bruising was already visible across the bridge of her nose and around her eyes.

It must've hurt, but if it did, she wasn't letting anyone see it.

The semi-circle progressed like a rainbow from there, graduating from the family at one end, through both members of the castle's staff, to the group of relative strangers that was the *Ghost Spotters* crew. Marcus sat second from the end, having given up his space next to the fire to Claire, who snuggled in the two-seater couch beside him, yawning contentedly.

Maybe there was hope for the man yet.

Tyler and Tammi-Jo stood back from the group, waiting for Logan to finish up his call with Hamza. It was really dragging on. Clearly, the detectives had a lot to discuss.

'I can't believe that guy,' Tyler said, glaring across at Donatello. 'I should've went and got them. You shouldn't have had to deal with that.'

'Ach, it's fine. I quite enjoyed it, actually. Why should you get all the excitement?' She bit her lip. 'Is that wrong? That I quite enjoyed elbowing a man in the throat and wrestling him to the ground?'

Tyler smiled. 'Not when it's that man. I felt like doing the same from the moment I set eyes on him. Sorry again, though. I should've done it. But sounds like you were all over it, anyway.'

Tammi-Jo shrugged. 'Dad had me doing martial arts since I was seven. He said I needed to know how to protect myself so I wouldn't get raped. At seven. He told me that *at seven*.'

'Jesus,' Tyler muttered. 'But seriously? You're, like, a karate expert?'

'Tae Kwon Do,' Tammi-Jo corrected. 'And a few years of Krav Maga. And yes, some karate, but not much. Only, like, brown belt.'

'Oh, is that all? Just brown? Slacker,' Tyler replied. 'I didn't know that! How didn't I know that?'

DC Swanney fixed him with a deadly serious look. 'The first rule of Fight Club? You don't talk about Fight Club.'

Tyler laughed. 'You know, TJ, I reckon you and DI Filson might actually get along just fine. I don't know what I was worried about.'

Tammi-Jo's fine features folded into a smile of relief. 'I hope you're right. Because everyone's made her sound terrifying!'

Before Tyler could confirm that, yes, she absolutely was, the door to the reading room opened. All eyes went to the detective standing in the doorway in a pair of borrowed, three sizes too large dungarees, and an expensive designer shirt that barely fastened across the chest.

'Sorry to keep you, ladies and gentlemen,' Logan said.

Storm Agatha was fading fast, leaving the castle behind as she pressed onwards towards the Western Isles and the Atlantic Ocean beyond. She still had enough left in her for one final faraway rumble of thunder, though, as Logan closed the door behind him.

'If you're all sitting comfortably, we can begin.'

# *Chapter 44*

'I wouldn't normally do this sort of thing,' Logan began, as he took up a spot in front of the roaring fire. 'Big dramatic reveals aren't really my cup of tea, but… old castle, stormy Halloween night, the suspects all assembled…' He shrugged. 'Felt a bit rude not to.'

He was distracted by the sight of Donatello sitting cuffed to the chair in the corner.

'What's the story with him?' he asked.

'He's a horrible piece of shit,' Helen spat.

Logan couldn't let that one pass without comment.

'I mean, aye. That goes without saying,' he replied. 'But why specifically is he cuffed right now?'

'Mr Liberace was acting aggressively towards Miss Bach,' Tammi-Jo said, and Helen didn't bother correcting her on her choice of prefix. She didn't even seem to notice. 'He attempted to attack her, so I intervened and placed him under arrest, sir.'

Logan nodded slowly, considering this new information.

'Right. Well done. We can deal with him later,' he said. He stood closer to the fire, letting the flames warm his back. 'Right now, we've got bigger fish to fry. Namely, the murderer of Montgomery McQuarrie and Constable Robert Rowan.'

Krystal, sitting on Helen's right, let out a gasp. 'You think they were both killed by the same man?'

'Or woman, Mrs McQuarrie,' Logan said. 'The same man or woman. And aye, I do.'

He turned as if to talk to the *Ghost Spotters* team, then turned back like he'd just remembered something.

'Oh. And you can drop the accent, by the way.'

Krystal paused for a little too long, looked a smidgeon too confused. 'I beg your pardon?'

'The accent, Krystal. Well, Carol. Can I call you Carol? That is your actual name, isn't it? The accent. The whole homely southern American bollocks you've been doing? You can quit it now.'

'What are you talking about?' Monty Jr asked, sitting forward in his chair. 'What are you saying?'

'Your stepmother's not who she says she is, son,' Logan said. 'One of my colleagues back in Inverness, he did a bit of digging. On all of you, in fact.'

There was some awkward, uncomfortable shuffling from a few of the people sitting in the semi-circle.

'And it came to light that Krystal McQuarrie doesn't actually exist.' Logan shrugged. 'Well, I mean, she does now. You went through the process, but until you met your late husband, you were Carol Smith, born in Coventry, not Tennessee, or wherever that accent was meant to be from.'

'I don't believe I'm hearing this!' Krystal cried. The accent was still there, but now that the DCI had called it out, it was possible to hear all the bum notes contained within it. 'This is slanderous!'

'You did two years in prison for fraud, Carol. Diddled a few old folk out of their life savings. I suppose that's what the goal was here, too, just in a different way.'

'Why I—! I mean—!'

The accent faltered, then fell away completely. When she spoke again, the change in the way she spoke was so jarring, it was like someone else had taken control of her body.

'I didn't kill him. I didn't kill anyone. I swear to God, I didn't!'

'What the hell?!' Helen tried to shuffle her chair away from her stepmother, but it was far too heavy for her to shift, so she just sort of bounced up and down on the cushion instead. 'You've been lying this whole time?'

From the corner, Donatello let out a snort. 'Must run in the family,' he said in a deep, croaky-sounding voice.

'You, shut your mouth,' Logan said, stabbing a finger at him.

'So… what? They weren't even really married?' Monty Jr asked, his gaze shifting between Krystal and Logan so quickly it was like he was watching some imaginary tennis match. 'It was all just a scam?'

'Of course we were married! What would the point be if we weren't actually married?' She glared daggers at the DCI standing over her. 'And my name is Krystal, not Carol. I changed it. Legally.'

'So, you did just marry him for his money, then?' Helen asked, and she sounded almost disappointed.

'Of course! Why the hell else would I have married him? What possible attractive qualities did he have except money?' Krystal asked, her voice becoming sharper and more shrill. Clearly, she'd been holding all this in for quite some time. 'He was a cruel, spiteful little man, who looked like… like…'

'Mr Toad?' Monty Jr suggested.

'Yes! Exactly. Like Mr Toad! I was all about the money, princess. That's the only reason I was here!'

She sat back in her chair and let out a big sigh. As she exhaled, a weight seemed to lift from her, and a smile spread across her face.

'Wow. Wow, that actually feels good to get that off my chest!' she said, then she shot a look around the room before settling back on Logan. 'But, again, I didn't kill him. That wasn't me.'

'You went to his study earlier to look for his will. Didn't you?' Logan said. 'You got worried when you heard that Monty senior never left anything to his wives. You wanted to check for yourself. But someone beat you to it. Someone who had their own reason to go looking for the will.'

He turned his gaze on Monty Jr, and left it there just long enough for the victim's son to start squirming in his seat.

'Did you know about all this, Francois?' Logan asked. 'Since you and Krystal were having an affair?'

There was a gasp from the *Ghost Spotters* side of the room.

'Fucking hell, the wife was shagging the chef,' Marcus mumbled. 'This is better than telly.' He gave Gavin a nudge. 'You should be filming this.'

'He is,' Logan said. 'There are cameras all over the castle. Isn't that right, Mr Hall?'

'Yes. That's right,' Gavin said. He nodded. It was slightly overplayed, but clearly convincing enough, as the family, Donatello, and even Marcus and Yvonne all erupted angrily.

'What? How dare you?' Helen cried.

'You didn't have permission for that!' Monty Jr added. 'We'd never have allowed that.'

'First I've heard of it,' Marcus said. 'Since when did we start doing that?'

'Gavin?' asked Yvonne. 'You never said you had cameras.' Her eyes widened. 'Wait, not in the bedrooms?'

'Uh, no. What? No.'

Gavin was clearly struggling under the weight of all the attention. Logan stepped in before he buckled.

'You can shout at him later. I'd like to hear what Francois has to say.' He turned to the chef. 'During your affair—well, I call it an affair, but I don't think either of you actually cared for the other. Quite the opposite, in fact. So, let's just say during your *sexual encounters* did Krystal let slip her real identity?'

Francois clenched his jaw. He was sitting straight in his chair, his hands on the knees of his white chef's trousers.

For a moment, it looked like he was going to remain silent, but then he gave a single shake of his head, and mumbled a curt, '*Non*.'

'Not even on the night her husband died?' Logan asked. He looked from Francois to Krystal and back again. 'You were together that night, aye? That's why the stories of your whereabouts didn't quite match up. You were with Krystal in her room all night.'

'*Non*,' Francois said, after a pause.

'Oh, come on, Francois! That's why you tried pointing me towards her. You knew that, if she cracked, you'd be in the clear,' Logan said. 'So, think very carefully. Because if you were together all night, that would've meant that neither of you could have killed Monty. And, considering that one of your knives was used, you had access to the keys, *and* there's a tunnel that literally leads directly from your kitchen to the murder scene, an alibi would really help your case right now.'

Francois swallowed. His eyes crept across to Krystal, who shrugged and nodded. It wasn't like she had a whole lot left to lose at this point, least of all her reputation.

'She was in my room,' the chef said.

'There we are!' Logan crowed. 'All night, aye?'

'*Oui*.'

'Good stuff. And here's the thing—I think the killer knew about your affair. Or, at least, they knew when the kitchen was going to be empty. And, of course, they knew about the secret passageway, because they've been exploring this place for a very long time. That's how they were able to come and go and get whatever keys they might have needed.'

He crossed his arms behind his back, letting that bed in for a moment.

It was Monty Jr who seized on a solution.

'Mungo!' he cried.

Everyone's gaze shifted to the grey-haired giant. He blinked, like he hadn't been fully paying attention, then fiddled with his fingers under the weight of all their stares.

'Yes!' Helen said. 'Mungo's been here forever. He knows this place better than anyone.'

'And he's always listening!' her brother hissed, despite the fact that Mungo's demeanour suggested he was barely even listening now.

Logan looked across to Tyler and beckoned him forward. 'DC Neish?'

This time, everyone turned to look at Tyler as he shuffled into the semi-circle. He cleared his throat and rubbed at the lump on the back of his head before speaking.

'It, uh, it couldn't have been him. No way he could've fit in that secret passage. It's a tight space, and he's'—he glanced over at the wide-eyed Mungo—'you know, that size. So, um, that's why it couldn't have been him, boss.'

Logan nodded encouragingly. 'Anything else?'

Tyler fought to keep the grimace off his face. He'd been pleased with himself for working that part out. Now the DCI wanted more?!

'Uh, no, I think that's it, boss,' he said before a thought struck him. 'Oh! Except…'

Logan raised his eyebrows. 'Except?'

'I think he's the only one who cared. About the victim. I think he's the only one who's actually sad to see him go.'

One corner of Logan's mouth tugged upwards just a fraction. It was there one moment, gone the next, but Tyler could've sworn he saw something not a million miles away from pride in it.

'Thank you, Detective Constable. That'll be all,' he said.

He waited until Tyler had gone back to join Tammi-Jo, then folded his arms across his chest. With the storm now mostly over, the room was almost completely silent, aside from the occasional hiss and pop from the fireplace.

'What else do we know about this case?' Logan asked. 'Who had a motive to kill Montgomery McQuarrie?'

'Everyone who'd ever met him?' Marcus guessed.

Leaning against him, half-asleep, Claire giggled softly.

'You, Mr Doyle,' Logan said, rounding on the *Ghost Spotters* host. 'You had reason to want him dead. If he went public with your'—he glanced at the girl—'extracurricular activities, there was every chance you'd lose shared custody of your daughter. Maybe it would even impact the show you're so proud of, even though it's basically just *Most Haunted*, isn't it?'

'Fuck off!' Marcus barked. 'It's nothing like *Most Haunted*.'

'It's exactly like *Most Haunted*,' Yvonne argued.

'No, Derek Acorah's dead, and I'm not, so...' Marcus scowled, but there was a real sense of triumph to it, like it was the closing remark to an airtight argument. 'And my *extracurricular activities* are nothing major. It was a pick-me-up, that's all.'

'Still, if it got back to your wife, how would she have reacted, do you think?' Logan pressed. 'From what my colleagues back at base tell me, she's just itching for an excuse to cut your access.'

'I didn't murder the old bastard!' Marcus protested. 'Anyway, if fucking... *Gigantor* couldn't fit up that tunnel, then neither could I.' He patted his stomach. There was something triumphant about that, too. 'Can you see me squeezing this through a secret passageway? With my back? Anyway, you said the killer knew his way around the castle. I could barely find the bathroom. And it's an en suite.'

'And yet, for the first time ever, you picked the filming location. This place. Out of all the stately homes and creepy old castles in the country, the one and only time you decided where to film, it turned out to be the site of a double murder. What are the chances of that, Mr Doyle?'

'Well, the chances are a hundred per cent, because that's what happened,' Marcus objected. 'I told you, I saw ads for the place on Facebook.'

'And I told you, we don't run ads on Facebook,' Monty Jr shot back.

'Well, I don't fucking know, then, do I?' he barked. Then, when Claire stirred in her half-slumber, he lowered his voice to a whisper. 'Anyway, we've only got your word on that, haven't we?'

'He's right,' Logan said, turning his attention to Monty. 'For all we know, you've got a full marketing campaign running round the clock.'

'Why? Why would we do that?' Monty asked.

'I have no idea,' Logan admitted. 'I can't think of a reason why you'd do that.'

'Thank you!'

'But I can think of several reasons why you'd want to murder your father,' the DCI continued, which wiped the smile clean off the younger man's face. 'I mean, where do we even start? An abusive childhood. Months, if not years, of homophobia. And that betrayal.'

Logan winced, drawing a sharp intake of breath in through his teeth.

'After all your hard work? Everything you put up with? For him to then leave his entire fortune and his business to your sister? Jesus. I mean, I'd have been half-tempted to kill him myself on your behalf, and I don't even like you.'

'I didn't kill him. How dare you? I wouldn't.'

'But you wanted to?'

'No!'

'Why were you outside your father's study around the time he was killed?'

'What?!' Monty spluttered. 'I wasn't!'

'Monty?' Helen whispered. She stared at her brother like she didn't recognise him. 'Is that true?'

'No! No, it's nonsense! It's not true in the slightest!'

Logan didn't take his eyes off the dead man's son. 'Mr Hall?'

Behind the detective, on the other side of the semi-circle, Gavin got to his feet. 'Yes?'

'Would you do the honours?'

The producer retrieved a laptop from under his seat, then scurried over with it. He turned the screen towards Monty and Helen, and a tap of the spacebar started the clip playing.

It had been made to look like it was a lower resolution than the original footage, and a wash of green had been applied to suggest a night vision camera.

Down at the bottom, a timestamp counted steadily upwards, the time rolling by in twenty-four-frames-per-second intervals.

'That's you, outside your father's study. Correct?' Logan said, examining the screen.

Monty squinted at the laptop. 'I mean… I don't know. It's not very clear.'

'It is,' Helen confirmed. 'That's him. Look at the walk.'

'It's a walk! It's just a normal person's walk!' her brother protested.

'That's definitely him,' Krystal confirmed, still in her original Coventry accent. 'He lurches.'

'I don't *lurch*! Anyway, even if it is me, there's no saying that's outside Papa's study. It could be anywhere!'

'It came from a camera right outside the door,' Logan said. He moved on quickly before anyone could question it. 'Can you tell me the time on the footage?'

Monty's eyes darted around the screen, either not seeing or deliberately avoiding the very obvious timer.

'Ten thirty-three,' Helen said.

Logan nodded. 'Ten thirty-three. Thank you. I want everyone to keep that in mind. That's important.' He nodded to Gavin, who folded his laptop closed and retreated to his seat.

Judging by the look on Yvonne's face, she clearly had questions for the producer, but she wisely elected to save them for another time.

'You had the motive, Monty. Several of them,' Logan intoned. 'You had the means, and you had the opportunity. You'd know the kitchen schedule. You've lived here most of your life, so you'd know about all the secret passages.'

'I had no idea!'

'You'd just found out you were being robbed of everything you thought was rightfully yours. You were angry. You could've grabbed a knife, headed up that tunnel, and killed your father right there in his study!'

'I didn't! That's not true! I didn't kill him!'

'No,' Logan said.

Monty stumbled halfway through another denial, then stopped. 'What?'

'You didn't kill him,' Logan said. 'He was sitting down when he was murdered. If you'd come climbing through his floor with a knife in your hand, I suspect he might've at least stood up.' He shook his head. 'No, the killer was already waiting in the study when your old man came in. Your father just finished breaking the news to you down here that you were out of the will. No way you could've got up there in time.'

'Then… what about the video?' Krystal asked.

'The video's nothing. That's fake. There are no hidden cameras.' He looked back over his shoulder. 'Sorry, Gavin. That turned out to be a waste of your time.' He looked around the room again. 'But ten thirty-three. Remember that. That's still important.'

'So, wait,' Helen said, working something out. 'If you know it wasn't Monty, you know it wasn't me. I'd been with Daddy down here, too.'

'But you left five minutes before your father did,' Logan reminded her.

'Ten! More like ten!' Monty corrected. His face puckered into a sneer. 'You made damn sure to get out of there before he broke the news that he was leaving everything to you. You had plenty of time to sneak up there and lie in wait.'

'Yes!' Donatello cried. 'Of course she did it!'

Monty didn't respond, but became emboldened by the show of support.

'Might as well hurry the inheritance along, right, sister dearest? Get rid of the old man before he changed his mind again! We both know how fickle he could be!'

Helen twisted in her chair, and for a moment it looked like she was about to start slapping at her brother. Monty was ready for her, and brought his hands up, ready to fight back.

A single sentence from Logan stopped them both in their tracks.

'He wasn't talking about you.'

The siblings both looked up at the detective.

'I beg your pardon?' Helen said.

'He didn't leave you anything,' Logan told her. 'Either of you.'

'What? No,' Helen snorted out an incredulous half-laugh. 'But… he said. He told me he would give me the business. His shares. Everything. He promised!'

'He promised me, too,' Monty muttered. 'Just throwing that out there.'

'But… but he told you, too! He told you the night he died that he was leaving it all to me! He told you!'

'No. He didn't,' Logan insisted. 'He told your brother he was leaving everything to his "first-born".'

'Yes! Which is—'

The penny dropped with a clang that was practically audible.

'Wait. What are you…? What are you saying?'

'You weren't your father's first child, Helen. Sorry to have to break it to you,' Logan said. 'He had another one. To his first love.'

He reached into the pocket of the dungarees he'd borrowed from Mungo, pulled out the DVD that the giant had given him, and tapped the picture of the woman on the front.

'This woman. The woman who gave him that ring.'

Monty and Helen both gasped and leaned closer.

'That's her?' Monty asked.

'That's the slut?'

'That's the mother of your father's first-born child,' Logan said. He turned the DVD over and held it out again so the siblings could see the back. 'Can you tell me what that logo says?'

'"A McQuarrie Hall Production",' Helen replied.

Logan shook his head. 'Try again.'

Brother and sister both leaned closer still.

'It does. It says "A McQuarrie Hall Production",' Monty insisted.

'No. It doesn't.'

Tyler chimed in from across the room. 'Um, I'm pretty sure it does, boss.'

Logan tutted and shook his head. 'Details, son,' he said, walking over to where the detective constables were both standing. 'You need to start paying attention to the little details.'

He handed the DVD case to Tammi-Jo, then returned to his spot by the fire.

'DC Swanney, can you tell us what that logo says?'

Tammi-Jo stared blankly at the text for a moment, then her head snapped up, her eyes widening. '"A McQuarrie-slash-Hall Production".'

Logan rocked back on his heels. '"A McQuarrie-slash-Hall Production". Not one production company. Two. One owned by the late Mr McQuarrie.' Logan turned on the spot until he was facing Gavin. 'And one owned by the late Madeline Hall. Your mother and father, Gavin.'

The *Ghost Spotters* producer flattened himself against his seat, his eyes darting frantically around the room.

Beside him, Yvonne smiled questioningly. 'Gavin?'

'What the fuck's he on about?' Marcus demanded.

'I don't know! I don't know!' Gavin said, his voice snagging in his throat. 'He's... That's not...'

'Your mother died recently. She'd spent the last few years of her life struggling financially, which is why you had to ask friends to chip in for the funeral. And... what, Gavin? Did you find something when dealing with the estate that told you who your father was? Or had you known before? You were here when they filmed that promo for the hotel, weren't you? Your name's listed as a runner on the credits inside. Did you know back then?'

'I don't know what you're talking about,' Gavin cried. 'All of this is nonsense!'

'You arranged to come here to film your ghost show. You couldn't be seen to have chosen it yourself—that might look suspicious if people dug around in your past—but, hang on, you handle all the social media for the show! You're a dab hand at it, you said so yourself. All the social media, and all the Facebook advertising.'

'Wait! *You* ran those bloody adverts?!' Marcus asked. 'I'd better not have been paying for those! I'm not paying good money to advertise a castle to myself just so you can come here and kill your fucking dad!'

He looked up at Logan.

'That is what you're saying, yes?'

'That's exactly what I'm saying,' Logan confirmed.

He returned his attention to Gavin. The castle was far from warm, but his face glistened with a sheen of sweat now, and his breathing was a series of staccato gasps.

'When you heard about the will earlier—that Monty was going to leave everything to his first-born—you panicked,' Logan continued. 'You'd heard about the secret passageways from your mum. Or maybe you'd found them yourself while filming the hotel promo. Either way, you know your way around them. You proved that when you told us how to find Claire.

'Francois was in the kitchen this time, though, so you couldn't sneak up the secret passageway. That's why you killed the constable on guard duty. You killed Rab, hid his body, then walked outside wearing his uniform, because you knew the camera in your van would make it look like he'd left.

'You also knew the field of view it covered, so knew when you could safely turn around and head back in through a side door.'

'The disappearing footsteps!' Tammi-Jo realised.

'Aye,' Logan confirmed. 'Not a ghost, just a man in wet shoes.'

'His hair was wet, too!' the DC cried. 'When I went to get him, his hair was wet. He said he'd been in the shower!'

'Considering there's been no hot water for the past few hours, I'm guessing that's another lie.'

'So, it was him that brained me, boss?' Tyler asked.

Logan nodded. 'He didn't expect Krystal to come looking for the will, too. He's about the same height and build as his father was, so in the dark, she thought it was Monty back from the dead.'

'OK, in hindsight, I panicked, all right?' Krystal said. 'And I was in character. It felt right in the moment.'

'I don't care,' Logan told her. 'When she shut Gavin in the room, all he could do was hide. Francois was in the kitchen, so he stayed in the tunnel, out of sight, and came back up when he thought the coast was clear. Only, it wasn't, so he clouted you on the noggin and legged it.'

Tyler rubbed at the back of his head and glared at the producer, who was now practically a puddle on the seat of his chair.

'Wait? What are you saying?' Monty Jr demanded. He stabbed a finger across the semi-circle. '*He's* our brother?'

'Good God, Monty, keep up.' Krystal sighed. 'Yes. That's what he's saying. That's what he's been saying for the past few minutes. And that he killed the old man.'

'I didn't! I didn't do anything!' Gavin's head jerked around the group. Everyone was staring at him now. Even Claire had roused from her sleep, and was peering at him from behind her dad's arm. 'None of this is true. It's all nonsense!'

'Ten thirty-three,' Logan said.

Gavin's expression went from one of confusion to one of stifled horror.

He'd worked it out. He realised, in that moment, that he'd doomed himself.

'What about it, boss?' Tyler asked.

Logan wandered back to the fire, addressing the group as he went.

'Earlier tonight, I asked Mr Hall to mock-up that footage of Monty Junior, so it looked like he was outside the study,' the

DCI explained. 'I told him to stick on a timestamp for around the time that Monty senior was killed.'

He stared into the flickering flames for a moment, then turned back to the producer.

'But we haven't told anyone here what time he was killed,' Logan said. 'Only the killer would know. And, I have to say, Gavin, you were bang on.'

Gavin's protests got as far as a strangled, 'No, I…' before he lost the will to continue. The game was up. Everyone in the room knew it.

'Murderer!' Helen hissed, her bruised, bloodshot eyes narrowing in contempt. 'Attacking a vulnerable old man. You're sick. You're disgusting!'

Something about the outburst made Gavin sit up straighter. He laughed—a spiteful, joyless hiss of a thing that rose from somewhere deep in his gut.

'Oh, come on. You all wanted him dead. But none of you had the balls to do it yourself!' he spat. He eyed Monty, Helen and Krystal accusingly. 'Despite everything he'd done, despite how he'd treated every single one of you, all the years of abuse, you just accepted it. You allowed it. You gave him permission to keep being the sadistic, miserable old bastard that he'd always been.'

No one from the family had a response to that. Certainly not a denial.

'There's one thing I don't understand,' Logan said. 'Were you always going to kill him? Was that why you came? Was that your plan from the start?'

Gavin jumped to his feet. Tyler and Tammi-Jo tensed, ready to jump in, but Logan held up a hand to stop them.

'Yes! God, yes!' the producer cried. His eyes blazed, and the words flew from his mouth on flecks of foam. 'But first, I wanted him to know. I wanted to look him in the eye and tell him who I was. Tell him how the woman he claimed to have loved had suffered in her last few years. How much she'd struggled. How he'd failed her. I wanted him to know it all.'

'The argument,' Logan said. 'He was reacting to what you'd told him. You weren't arguing about Marcus's drug use at all.'

'He didn't give a shit about that. After the things he's done, you really think he'd care about some washed-up fucking has-been doing a few lines of coke in his bathroom?'

'Here!' Marcus spat, when all that had filtered through. 'Who's a fucking has-been?'

'Sorry, Marcus, you're right. You're absolutely right,' Gavin said. 'You're not a has-been, you're a *never-was*.'

'Wait? Daddy didn't know about you?' Helen asked.

'Of course he knew! He knew I existed all along. He just didn't care.' The producer snorted. There was something pitying about the way he looked at his half-sister and brother. 'But then, why should that come as any surprise? He was never exactly father material, was he?'

Monty got to his feet. Neither Tyler nor Tammi-Jo made any move to intervene this time, both quietly confident that Logan could handle any threat from the youngest of the McQuarrie siblings.

'What are you saying? That after *one meeting* with you, he was going to change his will? He was going to cut us out for some bastard he'd never had any sort of relationship with?'

Logan raised an index finger. The preciseness of the movement suggested he'd been waiting for just this moment to arrive.

'Aye, about that,' he said. 'One of my colleagues tracked down Mr McQuarrie's solicitor. Turns out, he'd already given instructions to change the will. He did it right after his conversation with Gavin.' He smiled grimly. 'Congratulations, Mr Hall. You're named as the sole recipient of your father's shares.'

'No!' Helen screeched.

'*Fuck!*' Monty Jr echoed.

'And all his debts,' Logan concluded.

There was silence for a moment.

'Excuse me?' Monty said.

'Your father's businesses, they're all on the brink of bankruptcy,' Logan said. 'They owe millions. Even this place, the castle, it's mortgaged to the hilt, and in default several times over. It'll all be gone within a month.'

Monty and Helen were both staring at the DCI, their brows furrowed. Logan could almost hear the whirring of the cogs as they both tried to work out what this meant for them.

'You're both broke, but it could be worse,' Logan told them. 'Your father wasn't punishing you by changing his will. He was doing the opposite. He was setting you free. He was freeing you from carrying all that baggage he'd left you with, financial and emotional.' He looked into the fire for a moment. 'And maybe that's about the best we can hope for from them, in the end.'

'Maybe he wasn't such a monster, after all,' Yvonne suggested.

There was a moment of silence while everyone considered this, then some general murmurings of disagreement.

*No*, seemed to be the general consensus. He was definitely a monster, all right.

'Anything you'd like to say, Mr Hall?' Logan asked. 'Anything you'd like to add before I arrest you for the murder of Montgomery McQuarrie and Constable Robert Rowan?'

Gavin considered his options, then sneered around at the group.

'Marcus, your show is a pile of shit. Everyone here's an arsehole, even you, Yvonne—in fact, especially you, Yvonne.'

Yvonne gasped. 'Wait, what?'

Gavin thrust his wrists out to Logan, inviting him to slap on the handcuffs.

'That bastard's dead, so I regret nothing,' he said, and the sneer became a manic, wide-eyed grin. 'Happy fucking Halloween!'

## *Chapter 45*

Logan's clothes were still damp, but he was damned if he was meeting the choppers in his mismatched dungarees-and-designer-shirt combo, especially as Shona, Ben and Geoff Palmer were all aboard one of them.

He could just about cope with the ribbing Ben and Shona would give him about the outfit, but there was no way he was letting Palmer see him like that. The bastard would never stop making jokes about it, and not a single one of them would be so much as remotely amusing.

He'd half-expected Shona to turn up wearing a scary costume, but as it was now past midnight, and Halloween was officially over, he'd held out hope that she wouldn't.

And, to his relief, she hadn't. She'd arrived decked out in waterproofs and welly boots, but even before she opened her mouth to speak, Logan had realised she was wearing a set of plastic vampire teeth.

He let her get a single, 'I vant to suck your blood!' out of her system, then ran through everything that had happened over the past few hours for the benefit of Ben, Shona, Palmer and the half-dozen Uniforms who'd arrived in the other helicopter.

And then, to everyone's surprise, he'd informed them that DI Forde was now in charge and that he had somewhere he needed to be.

Shona spat her saliva-drenched plastic fangs into her hands, then hung back with Logan long enough for him to explain his reason for leaving. She held his hand while he explained, then hugged him when he reached the end.

'Oh, God, Jack. I'm sorry. Are you OK? Do you need me to come?' she asked.

Logan shook his head. 'No. I'll be fine,' he said. He scratched his head and puffed out his cheeks. 'But, eh, tomorrow. When I get back. If you want to talk to social services about Olivia, then…' He took a big breath, put his hands on his hips, and nodded. 'Aye. We'll do that.'

Shona stared up at him, eyes wide. 'Are you sure?'

'Absolutely not,' Logan said. He shrugged. 'But maybe I'll make a better job of the whole parenting thing the second time around.'

An irritated shout from Palmer cut the conversation short. Shona hugged Logan again and planted a kiss on his cheek. She made him promise to keep her updated, then picked up her bag and set off into the castle.

Somewhere in the distance, another helicopter was approaching. Soon, McQuarrie Hall would be swarming with officers.

The killer had been caught. The machinations of justice would soon rumble into action. Logan's work here was done.

And not just his.

'You fit then, Detective Constable?' he asked, tapping Tammi-Jo on the shoulder.

She had been talking at DI Forde, and Ben's relief at the interruption was written all over his face.

'Sir?'

Logan tilted his head in the direction of the helicopters. 'I've arranged us a ride. You can still make it down to Glasgow for your shift in the morning.'

She considered the waiting choppers, then shook her head. 'I think I'd rather stay here tonight, sir. Help finish up. I can be a day late.'

'Heather's not going to like that,' Logan told her. 'Might not be the best idea to start off on the wrong foot with her.'

The detective constable smiled. 'Meh. I'm sure I'll win her round.'

Logan chuckled. 'Aye,' he said. 'I'm sure you will.' He held a hand out for her to shake. 'Thank you, DC Swanney. For everything you've done. It's been a pleasure to work with you. Mostly.'

Tammi-Jo laughed. 'I'll take "mostly".' She shook his hand. 'Thank you, sir. It has also been a pleasure to work with you. By and large.'

'I'll take that, too,' he told her, then he blinked in surprise as she threw her arms around him in a hug.

He was too broad for her hands to reach around his back, but she gave it her best shot.

'Good luck, sir,' she whispered. 'Look after yourself.'

Logan hesitated, then patted her on the back. 'Aye,' he said, and the hoarse note to his voice surprised him even more than the hug had. 'You, too.'

–

'We really can't thank you enough,' Sinead said, as she and Tyler each loaded one of the twins into the back of the car. 'We're so sorry you got stuck with them overnight.'

Berta Hoon stood on the driveway of her brother's house, her arms crossed like a bouncer escorting an unwelcome guest off the premises.

'Well, it was an absolute fucking liberty, and it wasn't just "overnight", it's almost bloody lunchtime,' Berta said. She sniffed and shifted her weight from one sturdy, sensible shoe to the other. 'But we quite enjoyed it, didn't we, Bobby?'

'Oh, aye, there's nothing I fucking love more than being woken up every forty minutes by a greeting-faced wee bastard,' replied Hoon. He handed Sinead a bag of empty milk bottles and a half-pack of nappies. 'Fuck knows how you cope with three of them.'

Tyler frowned. 'We haven't got…' He tutted as the penny dropped. 'Oh. Right. Aye, very funny.'

Sinead smiled at him. There had been no room in the helicopters for Tyler, so he'd been taken across the river by dinghy and Hamza had picked him up.

Because the detective sergeant had been driving, she and Tyler hadn't been able to talk about their argument the day before, or the root cause of it. That was a conversation still to come.

But she already knew what the outcome would be. As they'd all swapped stories of the day before and laughed together, she knew she'd forgive him. She knew they'd get there, somehow.

Of course, she wasn't going to tell him that yet. She'd make him sweat a bit first. She deserved that much, surely?

'You. Ninety-nine pence shop Ken Doll. A word,' Hoon said. He headed for the side of the house, and snapped his fingers for Tyler to follow.

'Eh, we need to be getting off,' Tyler ventured. 'Tammi-Jo's leaving soon, so—'

Hoon stopped abruptly and pointed to his face. 'Look at my fucking coupon, son. Does it look like I was making a polite fucking request?'

Tyler looked to Sinead for backup, but she just shrugged and went back to loading the babies' overnight bags into the boot of the car.

'I wouldn't piss him about, boy,' Berta warned. 'He's been like a bear with an itchy arse since yesterday. Something's shat in his porridge.'

Tyler swallowed. A weak, desperate smile stretched across his face. 'Wasn't me. I didn't do it.'

Berta peered down her long, humped nose at him. 'I didn't mean literally.' She shook her head in disgust. 'Dirty, dirty bastard.'

He thought about protesting, but reckoned that might be taking his life in his hands, and so set off after Berta's brother, instead.

Tyler had just rounded the corner when Hoon caught him by the front of his jacket with both hands and slammed him against the wall.

'You, ya wee prick!'

Tyler let out a panicky croak. 'What? What about me? What have I done?'

'You had visitors yesterday. At your house. Couple of burly bastards looking for money. A *lot* of fucking money.'

Tyler swallowed. 'Shit. Aye. I'm dealing with it. I'm sorting it.'

Hoon brought his face closer, his teeth gnashing just inches from the younger man's face.

'Funny, that's no' what they were saying. They were saying I'd been ignoring all their fucking correspondence for months.'

The detective constable frowned. 'You?'

'They thought I was you.'

Tyler blinked. 'Why did they think you were me?'

'Because I was in your fucking house,' Hoon told him. 'And because I told them I was you. They wanted to come in and mark up all your stuff to take away. No' that any of it's worth a tuppenny fuck, but they'd have been well within their fucking rights to take it. You know that, aye?'

'Aye,' Tyler said. 'I know. Did… did you let them in?'

Hoon eyeballed the detective constable for a few dangerous seconds, then released his grip. Tyler slid down the wall, dropping several inches to the ground.

'Did I fuck.'

Tyler rubbed at his throat, then smoothed down the front of his jacket. 'Thanks.'

'I set up a payment plan,' Hoon said. He was watching the DC closely, studying his reaction. 'Three hundred quid a month.'

'Three hundred?!' Tyler cried, then he dropped his voice into a whisper. 'That's… I can't afford that. We're already paying off other stuff. We can't do another three hundred.'

‘Aye, well, good fucking thing it’s no’ coming out of your account, then,’ Hoon said. ‘It’s coming out of mine.’

Tyler stared back at him, saying nothing, like some sort of mental block was preventing him from processing this information.

When it did all filter through, his response wasn’t particularly noteworthy.

‘You what?’

‘You fucking heard me,’ Hoon said.

‘You’re paying it?’ Tyler asked.

Hoon snorted. ‘Am I arse! What the fuck do you think I am, son, your fucking guardian angel? It’s coming out of your wages.’

There was another lengthy delay in replying.

‘My wages?’

Hoon nodded. ‘This whole polis consultant thing’s no’ really working out for me. So, I thought, fuck it—man of my skills and experience? I should be fucking killing it. I should be raking it in. So, I’m setting out on my own.’

‘What? Like… a private detective?’

Hoon sniffed and crossed his arms. ‘Among other things, aye. And you’re going to be working with me.’

Tyler smiled uncertainly and pointed a thumb back over his shoulder. ‘But, uh, I’ve already got a job.’

‘Aye, well, now you’ve got two,’ Hoon said. He saw the worried look on the detective constable’s face and tutted. ‘I’m no’ going to be getting you to do anything fucking dodgy, if that’s what you’re worried about. Everything that you do’ll be all legal and above board.’

‘Right,’ Tyler scratched the back of his head, and winced when he hit the lump he’d been given the day before. ‘But you mean “we”, right? Everything *we* do will be legal and above board?’

‘Aye, Boyband,’ Hoon said. He grinned, then gave the DC a friendly, if not particularly gentle, slap on the face. ‘If that helps, just you keep fucking telling yourself that.’

–

The room felt stiflingly warm. Uncomfortably so.

The man in the bed was too far gone to care.

He lay partly propped up on a large hospital pillow, a clear plastic tube taped to his face, feeding oxygen up through his nostrils. That was the intention, at least, but they'd come loose at some point during the past few hours and slipped out of place, so he was no longer getting the benefit.

Logan groaned as he adjusted himself in the uncomfortable chair that he'd spent half the night in, and looked over at the closed door, hoping there might be a nurse hovering there.

When he saw that there wasn't, he reluctantly rose from the chair and, with uncharacteristic uncertainty, repositioned the oxygen tube in the half-light of the room's single wall-mounted lamp.

On the bed, the old man's paper-thin eyelids fluttered. His skin was so dry that Logan would've sworn he heard it rustling as the lids opened halfway. It was the first movement he'd made since Logan had arrived during the night—the first sign that there was more life to him than the one the machines were providing.

His father had always been a large, imposing figure—Logan had got his height from that side of the family—but he was shrivelled and shrunken now. A dried-out raisin of the man that Logan remembered.

When Logan had arrived, a nurse had directed him towards the uncomfortable-looking chair by the bed. It was intended for visitors, but had largely gone unused, the nurse had said, aside from when the hospital chaplain had swung by for a chat.

Logan had enjoyed the thought of that encounter. His old man had never had much truck with religion of any flavour. Had he been in any fit shape to do so, he'd have very vocally told the padre exactly which orifice he should feel free to ram his God up.

Or maybe he wouldn't. Maybe, when the end was so close, he'd have accepted any and all help he could get. Maybe Logan would, too, when the day came.

Maybe everyone would.

By the sounds of it, though, the old man had been too out of it to have any opinion on the matter. The chaplain had hung around for a couple of minutes, said a few words, and then moved on.

And that had been that.

Logan stretched his aching limbs, creaked his neck around in a couple of rolling circles, then lowered himself back into the chair. It felt even less comfortable than it had last night, when exhaustion had rounded some of the edges and softened the ancient springs.

His father's eyelids fluttered for a second time. Dilated pupils swam, rolled, then found some sort of semi-focus.

A voice Logan hadn't heard in years, and which had aged several lifetimes since then, rasped softly through the half-dark of the windowless room.

'Jack?'

Logan's jaw clenched. Prickles of heat burned at the back of his eyeballs. He didn't reply.

Something like panic tightened his chest.

He shouldn't be here. This wasn't right. He owed this bastard nothing.

The chair groaned as he gripped the arms and started to rise.

'Jack?' The eyes of the man in the bed had closed again. His hand rolled over so it lay there, palm-upwards, frail, crooked fingers curved like the legs of a long-dead insect. 'Is… that you, Jack?'

Logan stared down at the hand. Had he ever held it? he wondered. If he had, he couldn't remember. They'd never had that sort of relationship. They'd never really been father and son, and nothing could possibly change that now.

But maybe that wasn't what this was. Maybe this was no longer about a neglectful old man and his bitter, disillusioned offspring.

Maybe this was just two men saying their goodbyes.

After everything, though, did he even deserve that much?

How many chances had the old man had? Logan had told Tammi-Jo it was five or six, but it was more than that. Way more. Fifty. A hundred, maybe.

Aye. And then some.

The chair creaked again as Logan let his weight sink back down into it.

Just one, he thought.

Just one more.

One more wouldn't hurt.

'Aye,' he whispered. For perhaps the first time, his fingers interlocked with those of the man on the bed. 'Aye, Dad, it's me.'